WOMEN of the NIGHT

WOMEN *of the* NIGHT

EDITED BY

Martin H. Greenberg

**BARNES
& NOBLE**

NEW YORK

Book designed by Judy Gilats

ISBN-13: 978-0-7607-9198-1
ISBN-10: 0-7607-9198-8

Printed and bound in the United States of America

10 9 8 7 6 5 4 3 2 1

Contents

john
helfers

Introduction

At first glance, it would seem that the rise of the vampire in 18th, 19th, and 20th century fiction to the forefront of the public eye was propagated solely by poetry and prose about male vampires. The short German poem "The Vampire," by Heinrich August Ossenfelder, published in 1748, first used the myth of the vampire gaining dominance over the opposite sex, when a rejected suitor plans to drink his intended's blood, giving her "the kiss of the vampire," and proving his desires and intent are stronger than her mother's Christian convictions.

Lord Byron used the myth of the vampire in his poem "The Giaour," which was published in 1813. His physician, John Polidori, wrote what many consider to be the first actual vampire story—based on a fragment of a story written and abandoned by Byron himself—that was published in *New Monthly Magazine* in 1819. The story's main character, Lord Ruthven, was a satire of Byron himself, and was the first portrayal of a vampire not as a bestial, repulsive creature, but as a suave, refined being that moved among and preyed upon the aristocratic class. In 1845–47, the "penny dreadful" serial *Varney the Vampire, or The Feast of Blood* was published. Written by James Malcolm Rymer, the 868-page serial recounted the trials and tribulations of Varney during the reign of King George the II.

Then came was the novel that has done more to elevate the undead creature's status in myth and legend than anything else, *Dracula*, by Bram Stoker, published in 1897. His story, while technically a treatise against foreigners coming to England, fixed the idea of the vampire as carnal predator in the mind of an all-too-eager public with a firmness that had not been seen before, and which still holds a fascination for audiences today.

With the advent of film in the 20th century, the male vampire solidified into the role that he is best known for—the bloodsucking creature of darkness, existing only to sate his eternal thirst on the blood of his victims—preferably attractive young women. Films like *Nosferatu* (1922) and the first adaptation of *Dracula* (1931), followed by many other vampire films in the next seventy-five years, brought the myth and legend of the vampire to an entire new audience. Even in the latter half of the century, some of the most popular vampire tales feature men as their protagonists, such as the Count St. Germain novels by Chelsea Quinn Yarbro and the books by Anne Rice, including the seminal *Interview with the Vampire*, that recount the stories of Lestat de Lioncourt and his vampiric progeny and cohorts.

Where, then, does that leave female vampires?

Far from being the weak, helpless victims of the vampire as portrayed in fiction, the concept of the woman as vampire stretches back farther than her male counterpart to ancient civilizations and religions. Babylonian mythology told of the *Lilu*, and there are even older Sumerian legends about the *Akhkharu*, female demons that prowled the night searching for their favorite meals—pregnant women and newborn babies. One of the Sumerian demons, Lilitu, was even adapted into later Jewish mythology as the demon Lilith. There is also a heroic interpretation of the female vampire in one of the stories about the Indian god of time and/or death Kali, often depicted with fangs and a garland of skulls. When she and the goddess Durga battled the demon Raktabija, who could reproduce himself every time a drop of his blood hit the ground, Kali drank all every drop that was spilled in combat so that he couldn't reproduce, and thus defeated him.

In poetry and prose, the female vampire begins to appear closely after the introduction of the male version; again, first in poetry, as in "Lenore" by Gottfried August Bürger in 1773, and the 1797 poem "The Bride of Corinth" by Johann Wolfgang Goethe, and then in the short novel *Carmilla* by Joseph Sheridan Le Fanu, in which not only is the vampire female, but the object of her desire is also female. In the 20th century, the female vampire occasionally kept appearing in short fiction, as in F. G. Loring's "The Tomb of Sarah," Hume Nisbit's "The Vampire Maid," and E. F. Benson's classic tale "Mrs. Amworth."

There has also been many attempts to portray the female vampire in film, in such efforts as the French film *Female Vampire* (1973); the cult film *The Hunger* (1983), starring Catherine Deneuve, Susan Sarandon, and David Bowie; the sex comedy *Once Bitten* (1985), starring Lauren Hutton and a young Jim Carrey; and the hybrid comedy/horror film *Vamp* (1986) featuring rock star Grace Jones. Once of the more relatively recent female vampire films, *Innocent Blood* (1992), starred Anne Parilland as a female vampire who survives by her own strict rules until she accidentally creates another vampire, and must hunt him down and slay him.

Indeed, only in the last thirty years or so have female vampires truly risen to take their place in the world of fiction alongside their male counterparts, exploring many of the same themes of power, sex, and mortality. The 1970s saw publication of *The Vampire Tapes* by Arabella Randolphe and *The Virgin and The Vampire* by Robert J. Myers. These were followed in the 1980s by Chelsea Quinn Yarbro's historical trilogy about Atta Olivia Clemens, a lover of her fictional creation Count St. Germain, *Sabella* by Tanith Lee, the celebrative vampirism of Whitley Strieber's *The Hunger*; *Live Girls* by Ray Garton, and *Black Ambrosia* by Elizabeth Engstrom. The decade culminated with Nancy Collins' *Sunglasses After Dark*, the first of her Sonja Blue novels featuring an unrepentant female vampire living amidst the squalor and decay of the contemporary urban environment who takes what she needs when she needs it. The last decade of the 20th century saw the publication of Traci Briery's two substantial novels, *The Vampire Memoirs* and *The Vampire Journals*. Kathyrn Meyer Griffith's *The Last Vampire* combined the vampire novel with a future disaster theme. And *The Gilda Stories*, by Jewelle Gomez, updated the *Carmilla* trope with her modern spin on the lesbian vampire plot.

As shown by these novels, there is certainly no reason to think that female vampires cannot be every bit as seductive, as cunning, as attractive as their male counterparts, and perhaps even more so. As women are often characterized as both more cerebral, intuitive, and emotional than men, joining them with the powers of the vampire would create a creature as deadly as she is intelligent, as predatory as she is seductive.

In fact, a long-running theme of the vampire, whether they be male or female, has been the creature's enhanced sensuality. The very essence of drinking another person's blood has been transformed over the centuries from what should be a horrifying act to one of pleasure and eroticism. And for most men, the idea of a beautiful woman with the capacity to bestow eternal life with a biting kiss from those perfect lips should speak to the male of the species as strongly as the idealized male versions seem to speak to the women.

Fortunately, for as many authors that write about male vampires, there are plenty of women—and more than a few men as well—who have explored the idea and mores of the female vampire. *Women of the Night* has collected sixteen of the best tales featuring these denizens of the darkness. From the master himself, Stephen King, comes an old-school tale of terror that could easily be told at any New England bar on a cold winter's night. Kristine Kathryn Rusch weaves a tale of politics and the undead in a world where vampires walk freely among the living. Neil Gaiman retells a classic fairy story and adds a chilling twist as only he can. Esther Friesner imagines what might happen when a vampire is let loose to roam among the *nouveau riche* in the 1920s. Tanya Huff's fictional female vampire,

Vicki Nelson, must track down another of her undead kind that threatens her very existence. And Norman Partridge tells a story of what might have happened after Stoker's *Dracula*, and of a love that goes beyond life—and death.

While the male vampire may hold sway over the masses, there comes a time when the female of the species must receive her due. These women of the night are revealed in their full, wondrous, and terrifying glory in these sixteen chilling tales.

stephen king

One for the Road

It was quarter past ten and Herb Tooklander was thinking of closing for the night when the man in the fancy overcoat and the white, staring face burst into Tookey's Bar, which lies in the northern part of Falmouth. It was the tenth of January, just about the time most folks are learning to live comfortably with all the New Year's resolutions they broke, and there was one hell of a northeaster blowing outside. Six inches had come down before dark and it had been going hard and heavy since then. Twice we had seen Billy Larribee go by high in the cab of the town plow, and the second time Tookey ran him out a beer—an act of pure charity my mother would have called it, and my God knows she put down enough of Tookey's beer in her time. Billy told him they were keeping ahead of it on the main road, but the side ones were closed and apt to stay that way until next morning. The radio in Portland was forecasting another foot and a forty-mile-an-hour wind to pile up the drifts.

There was just Tookey and me in the bar, listening to the wind howl around the eaves and watching it dance the fire around on the hearth. "Have one for the road, Booth," Tookey says, "I'm gonna shut her down."

He poured me one and himself one and that's when the door cracked open and this stranger staggered in, snow up to his shoulders and in his hair, like he had rolled around in confectioner's sugar. The wind billowed a sand-fine sheet of snow in after him.

"Close the door!" Tookey roars at him. "Was you born in a barn?"

I've never seen a man who looked that scared. He was like a horse that's spent an afternoon eating fire nettles. His eyes rolled toward Tookey and he said, "My wife—my daughter—" and he collapsed on the floor in a dead faint.

"Holy Joe," Tookey says. "Close the door, Booth, would you?"

I went and shut it, and pushing it against the wind was something of a chore. Tookey was down on one knee holding the fellow's head up and patting his cheeks. I got over to him and saw right off that it was nasty. His face was fiery red, but there were gray blotches here and there, and when you've lived through winters in Maine since the time Woodrow Wilson was President, as I have, you know those gray blotches mean frostbite.

"Fainted," Tookey said. "Get the brandy off the back bar, will you?"

I got it and came back. Tookey had opened the fellow's coat. He had come around a little; his eyes were half open and he was muttering something too low to catch.

"Pour a capful," Tookey says.

"Just a cap?" I asks him.

"That stuff's dynamite," Tookey says. "No sense overloading his carb."

I poured out a capful and looked at Tookey. He nodded. "Straight down the hatch."

I poured it down. It was a remarkable thing to watch. The man trembled all over and began to cough. His face got redder. His eyelids, which had been at half-mast, flew up like window shades. I was a bit alarmed, but Tookey only sat him up like a big baby and clapped him on the back.

The man started to retch, and Tookey clapped him again.

"Hold on to it," he says, "that brandy comes dear."

The man coughed some more, but it was diminishing now. I got my first good look at him. City fellow, all right, and from somewhere south of Boston, at a guess. He was wearing kid gloves, expensive but thin. There were probably some more of those grayish-white patches on his hands, and he would be lucky not to lose a finger or two. His coat was fancy, all right; a three-hundred-dollar job if ever I'd seen one. He was wearing tiny little boots that hardly came up over his ankles, and I began to wonder about his toes.

"Better," he said.

"All right," Tookey said. "Can you come over to the fire?"

"Mywifeandmydaughter," he said. "They'reoutthere . . . in the storm."

"From the way you came in, I didn't figure they were at home watching the TV," Tookey said. "You can tell us by the fire as easy as here on the floor. Hook on, Booth."

He got to his feet, but a little groan came out of him and his mouth twisted down in pain. I wondered about his toes again, and I wondered why God felt he had to make fools from New York City who would try driving around in southern Maine at the height of a northeast blizzard. And I wondered if his wife and his little girl were dressed any warmer than him.

We hiked him across to the fireplace and got him sat down in a rocker that used to be Missus Tookey's favorite until she passed on in '74. It was Missus Tookey that was responsible for most of the place, which had been written up in *Down East* and the *Sunday Telegram* and even once in the Sunday supplement of the Boston *Globe*. It's really more of a public house than a bar, with its big wooden floor, pegged together rather than nailed, the maple bar, the old barn-raftered ceiling, and the monstrous big fieldstone hearth. Missus Tookey started to get some ideas in her head after the *Down East* article came out, wanted to start calling the place Tookey's Inn or Tookey's Rest, and I admit it has sort of a Colonial ring to it, but I prefer plain old Tookey's Bar. It's one thing to get uppish in the summer, when the state's full of tourists, another thing altogether in the winter, when you and your neighbors have to trade together. And there had been plenty of winter nights, like this one, that Tookey and I had spent all alone together, drinking scotch and water or just a few beers. My own Victoria passed on in '73, and Tookey's was a place to go where there were enough voices to mute the steady ticking of the death-watch beetle—even if there was just Tookey and me, it was enough. I wouldn't have felt the same about it if the place had been Tookey's Rest. It's crazy but it's true.

We got this fellow in front of the fire and he got the shakes harder than ever. He hugged onto his knees and his teeth clattered together and a few drops of clear mucus spilled off the end of his nose. I think he was starting to realize that another fifteen minutes out there might have been enough to kill him. It's not the snow, it's the wind-chill factor. It steals your heat.

"Where did you go off the road?" Tookey asked him.

"S-six miles s-s-south of h-here," he said.

Tookey and I stared at each other, and all of a sudden I felt cold. Cold all over.

"You sure?" Tookey demanded. "You came six miles through the snow?"

He nodded. "I checked the odometer when we came through t-town. I was following directions . . . going to see my wife's s-sis-ter . . . in Cumberland . . . never been there before . . . we're from New Jersey . . ."

New Jersey. If there's anyone more purely foolish than a New Yorker it's a fellow from New Jersey.

"Six miles, you're sure?" Tookey demanded.

"Pretty sure, yeah. I found the turnoff but it was drifted in . . . it was . . ."

Tookey grabbed him. In the shifting glow of the fire his face looked pale and strained, older than his sixty-six years by ten. "You made a right turn?"

"Right turn, yeah. My wife—"

"Did you see a sign?"

"Sign?" He looked up at Tookey blankly and wiped the end of his nose. "Of course I did. It was on my instructions. Take Jointer

Avenue through Jerusalem's Lot to the 295 entrance ramp." He
looked from Tookey to me and back to Tookey again. Outside, the
wind whistled and howled and moaned through the eaves. "Wasn't
that right, mister?"

"The Lot," Tookey said, almost too soft to hear. "Oh my God."

"What's wrong?" the man said. His voice was rising. "Wasn't that
right? I mean, the road looked drifted in, but I thought . . . if there's a
town there, the plows will be out and . . . and then I . . ."

He just sort of trailed off.

"Booth," Tookey said to me, low. "Get on the phone. Call the
sheriff."

"Sure," this fool from New Jersey says, "that's right. What's
wrong with you guys, anyway? You look like you saw a ghost."

Tookey said, "No ghosts in the Lot, mister. Did you tell them to
stay in the car?"

"Sure I did," he said, sounding injured. "I'm not crazy."

Well, you couldn't have proved it by me.

"What's your name?" I asked him. "For the sheriff."

"Lumley," he says. "Gerard Lumley."

He started in with Tookey again, and I went across to the telephone. I picked it up and heard nothing but dead silence. I hit the
cutoff buttons a couple of times. Still nothing.

I came back. Tookey had poured Gerard Lumley another tot of
brandy, and this one was going down him a lot smoother.

"Was he out?" Tookey asked.

"Phone's dead."

"Hot damn," Tookey says, and we look at each other. Outside the
wind gusted up, throwing snow against the windows.

Lumley looked from Tookey to me and back again.

"Well, haven't either of you got a car?" he asked. The anxiety was
back in his voice. "They've got to run the engine to run the heater.
I only had about a quarter of a tank of gas, and it took me an hour
and a half to . . . Look, will you *answer* me?" He stood up and
grabbed Tookey's shirt.

"Mister," Tookey says, "I think your hand just ran away from your brains, there."

Lumley looked at his hand, at Tookey, then dropped it. "Maine," he hissed. He made it sound like a dirty word about somebody's mother. "All right," he said. "Where's the nearest gas station? They must have a tow truck—"

"Nearest gas station is in Falmouth Center," I said. "That's three miles down the road from here."

"Thanks," he said, a bit sarcastic, and headed for the door, buttoning his coat.

"Won't be open, though," I added.

He turned back slowly and looked at us.

"What are you talking about, old man?"

"He's trying to tell you that the station in the Center belongs to Billy Larribee and Billy's out driving the plow, you damn fool," Tookey says patiently. "Now why don't you come back here and sit down, before you bust a gut?"

He came back, looking dazed and frightened. "Are you telling me you can't . . . that there isn't . . . ?"

"I ain't telling you nothing," Tookey says. "You're doing all the telling, and if you stopped for a minute, we could think this over."

"What's this town, Jerusalem's Lot?" he asked. "Why was the road drifted in? And no lights on anywhere?"

I said, "Jerusalem's Lot burned out two years back."

"And they never rebuilt?" He looked like he didn't believe it.

"It appears that way," I said, and looked at Tookey. "What are we going to do about this?"

"Can't leave them out there," he said.

I got closer to him. Lumley had wandered away to look out the window into the snowy night.

"What if they've been got at?" I asked.

"That may be," he said. "But we don't know it for sure. I've got my Bible on the shelf. You still wear your Pope's medal?"

I pulled the crucifix out of my shirt and showed him. I was born and raised Congregational, but most folks who live around the Lot wear something—crucifix, St. Christopher's medal, rosary, something. Because two years ago, in the span of one dark October month, the Lot went bad. Sometimes, late at night, when there were just a few regulars drawn up around Tookey's fire, people would talk it over. Talk around it is more like the truth. You see, people in the Lot started to disappear. First a few, then a few more, then a whole slew. The schools closed. The town stood empty for most of a year. Oh, a few people moved in—mostly damn fools from out of state like this fine specimen here—drawn by the low property values, I suppose. But they didn't last. A lot of them moved out a month or two after they'd moved in. The others . . . well, they disappeared. Then the town burned flat. It was at the end of a long dry fall. They figure it started up by the Marsten House on the hill that overlooked Jointner Avenue, but no one knows how it started, not to this day. It burned out of control for three days. After that, for a time, things were better. And then they started again.

I only heard the word "vampires" mentioned once. A crazy pulp truck driver named Richie Messina from over Freeport way was in Tookey's that night, pretty well liquored up. "Jesus Christ," this stampeder roars, standing up about nine feet tall in his wool pants and his plaid shirt and his leather-topped boots. "Are you all so damn afraid to say it out? Vampires! That's what you're all thinking, ain't it? Jesus-jumped-up-Christ in a chariot-driven sidecar! Just like a bunch of kids scared of the movies! You know what there is down there in 'Salem's Lot? Want me to tell you? Want me to tell you?"

"Do tell, Richie," Tookey says. It had got real quiet in the bar. You could hear the fire popping, and outside the soft drift of November rain coming down in the dark. "You got the floor."

"What you got over there is your basic wild dog pack," Richie Messina tells us. "That's what you got. That and a lot of old women who love a good spook story. Why, for eighty bucks I'd go up there and spend the night in what's left of that haunted house you're all so worried about. Well, what about it? Anyone want to put it up?"

But nobody would. Richie was a loudmouth and a mean drunk and no one was going to shed any tears at his wake, but none of us were willing to see him go into 'Salem's Lot after dark.

"Be screwed to the bunch of you," Richie says. "I got my four-ten in the trunk of my Chevy, and that'll stop anything in Falmouth, Cumberland, *or* Jerusalem's Lot. And that's where I'm goin'."

He slammed out of the bar and no one said a word for a while. Then Lamont Henry says, real quiet, "That's the last time anyone's gonna see Richie Messina. Holy God." And Lamont, raised to be a Methodist from his mother's knee, crossed himself.

"He'll sober off and change his mind," Tookey said, but he sounded uneasy. "He'll be back by closin' time, makin' out it was all a joke."

But Lamont had the right of that one, because no one ever saw Richie again. His wife told the state cops she thought he'd gone to Florida to beat a collection agency, but you could see the truth of the thing in her eyes—sick, scared eyes. Not long after, she moved away to Rhode Island. Maybe she thought Richie was going to come after her some dark night. And I'm not the man to say he might not have done.

Now Tookey was looking at me and I was looking at Tookey as I stuffed my crucifix back into my shirt. I never felt so old or so scared in my life.

Tookey said again, "We can't just leave them out there, Booth."

"Yeah. I know."

We looked at each other for a moment longer, and then he reached out and gripped my shoulder. "You're a good man, Booth." That was enough to buck me up some. It seems like when you pass seventy, people start forgetting that you are a man, or that you ever were.

Tookey walked over to Lumley and said, "I've got a four-wheel-drive Scout. I'll get it out."

"For God's sake, man, why didn't you say so before?" He had whirled around from the window and was staring angrily at Tookey. "Why'd you have to spend ten minutes beating around the bush?"

Tookey said, very softly, "Mister, you shut your jaw. And if you get the urge to open it, you remember who made that turn onto an unplowed road in the middle of a goddamned blizzard."

He started to say something, and then shut his mouth. Thick color had risen up in his cheeks. Tookey went out to get his Scout out of the garage. I felt around under the bar for his chrome flask and filled it full of brandy. Figured we might need it before this night was over.

Maine blizzard—ever been out in one?

The snow comes flying so thick and fine that it looks like sand and sounds like that, beating on the sides of your car or pickup. You don't want to use your high beams because they reflect off the snow and you can't see ten feet in front of you. With the low beams on, you can see maybe fifteen feet. But I can live with the snow. It's the wind I don't like, when it picks up and begins to howl, driving the snow into a hundred weird flying shapes and sounding like all the hate and pain and fear in the world. There's death in the throat of a snowstorm wind, white death—and maybe something beyond death. That's no sound to hear when you're tucked up all cozy in your own bed with the shutters bolted and the doors locked. It's that much worse if you're driving. And we were driving smack into 'Salem's Lot.

"Hurry up a little, can't you?" Lumley asked.

I said, "For a man who came in half frozen, you're in one hell of a hurry to end up walking again."

He gave me a resentful, baffled look and didn't say anything else. We were moving up the highway at a steady twenty-five miles an hour. It was hard to believe that Billy Larribee had just plowed this stretch an hour ago; another two inches had covered it, and it was drifting in. The strongest gusts of wind rocked the Scout on her springs. The headlights showed a swirling white nothing up ahead of us. We hadn't met a single car.

About ten minutes later Lumley gasps: "Hey! What's that?"

He was pointing out my side of the car; I'd been looking dead ahead. I turned, but was a shade too late. I thought I could see some sort of slumped form fading back from the car, back into the snow, but that could have been imagination.

"What was it? A deer?" I asked.

"I guess so," he says, sounding shaky. "But its eyes—they looked red." He looked at me. "Is that how a deer's eyes look at night?" He sounded almost as if he were pleading.

"They can look like anything," I says, thinking that might be true, but I've seen a lot of deer at night from a lot of cars, and never saw any set of eyes reflect back red.

Tookey didn't say anything.

About fifteen minutes later, we came to a place where the snow-bank on the right of the road wasn't so high because the plows are supposed to raise their blades a little when they go through an intersection.

"This looks like where we turned," Lumley said, not sounding too sure about it. "I don't see the sign—"

"This is it," Tookey answered. He didn't sound like himself at all. "You can just see the top of the signpost."

"Oh. Sure." Lumley sounded relieved. "Listen, Mr. Tooklander, I'm sorry about being so short back there. I was cold and worried and calling myself two hundred kinds of fool. And I want to thank you both—"

"Don't thank Booth and me until we've got them in this car," Tookey said. He put the Scout in four-wheel drive and slammed his way through the snowbank and onto Jointner Avenue, which goes through the Lot and out to 295. Snow flew up from the mudguards. The rear end tried to break a little bit, but Tookey's been driving through snow since Hector was a pup. He jockeyed it a bit, talked to it, and on we went. The headlights picked out the bare indication of other tire tracks from time to time, the ones made by Lumley's car, and then they would disappear again. Lumley was leaning forward, looking for his car. And all at once Tookey said, "Mr. Lumley."

"What?" He looked around at Tookey.

"People around these parts are kind of superstitious about 'Salem's Lot," Tookey says, sounding easy enough—but I could see the deep lines of strain around his mouth, and the way his eyes kept moving from side to side. "If your people are in the car, why, that's fine. We'll pack them up, go back to my place, and tomorrow, when the storm's over, Billy will be glad to yank your car out of the snowbank. But if they're not in the car—"

"Not in the car?" Lumley broke in sharply. "Why wouldn't they be in the car?"

"If they're not in the car," Tookey goes on, not answering, "we're going to turn around and drive back to Falmouth Center and whistle for the sheriff. Makes no sense to go wallowing around at night in a snowstorm anyway, does it?"

"They'll be in the car. Where else would they be?"

I said, "One other thing, Mr. Lumley. If we should see anybody, we're not going to talk to them. Not even if they talk to us. You understand that?"

Very slow, Lumley says, "Just what are these superstitions?"

Before I could say anything—God alone knows what I would have said—Tookey broke in. "We're there."

We were coming up on the back end of a big Mercedes. The whole hood of the thing was buried in a snowdrift, and another drift had socked in the whole left side of the car. But the taillights were on and we could see exhaust drifting out of the tailpipe.

"They didn't run out of gas, anyway," Lumley said.

Tookey pulled up and pulled on the Scout's emergency brake. "You remember what Booth told you, Lumley."

"Sure, sure." But he wasn't thinking of anything but his wife and daughter. I don't see how anybody could blame him, either.

"Ready, Booth?" Tookey asked me. His eyes held on mine, grim and gray in the dashboard lights.

"I guess I am," I said.

We all got out and the wind grabbed us, throwing snow in our faces. Lumley was first, bending into the wind, his fancy topcoat billowing out behind him like a sail. He cast two shadows, one from Tookey's headlights, the other from his own taillights. I was behind him, and Tookey was a step behind me. When I got to the trunk of the Mercedes, Tookey grabbed me.

"Let him go," he said.

"Janey! Francie!" Lumley yelled. "Everything okay?" He pulled open the driver's-side door and leaned in. "Everything—"

He froze to a dead stop. The wind ripped the heavy door right out of his hand and pushed it all the way open.

"Holy God, Booth," Tookey said, just below the scream of the wind. "I think it's happened again."

Lumley turned back toward us. His face was scared and bewildered, his eyes wide. All of a sudden he lunged toward us through the snow, slipping and almost falling. He brushed me away like I was nothing and grabbed Tookey.

"How did you know?" he roared. "Where are they? What the hell is going on here?"

Tookey broke his grip and shoved past him. He and I looked into the Mercedes together. Warm as toast it was, but it wasn't going to be for much longer. The little amber low-fuel light was glowing. The big car was empty. There was a child's Barbie doll on the passenger's floormat. And a child's ski parka was crumpled over the seatback.

Tookey put his hands over his face . . . and then he was gone. Lumley had grabbed him and shoved him right back into the snowbank. His face was pale and wild. His mouth was working as if he had chewed down on some bitter stuff he couldn't yet unpucker enough to spit out. He reached in and grabbed the parka.

"Francie's coat?" he kind of whispered. And then loud, bellowing: *"Francie's coat!"* He turned around, holding it in front of him by the little fur-trimmed hood. He looked at me, blank and unbelieving. "She can't be out without her coat on, Mr. Booth. Why . . . why . . . she'll freeze to death."

"Mr. Lumley—"

He blundered past me, still holding the parka, shouting: *"Francie! Janey! Where are you? Where are youuu?"*

I gave Tookey my hand and pulled him onto his feet. "Are you all—"

"Never mind me," he says. "We've got to get hold of him, Booth."

We went after him as fast as we could, which wasn't very fast with the snow hip-deep in some places. But then he stopped and we caught up to him.

"Mr. Lumley—" Tookey started, laying a hand on his shoulder.

"This way," Lumley said. "This is the way they went. Look!"

We looked down. We were in a kind of dip here, and most of the wind went right over our heads. And you could see two sets of tracks, one large and one small, just filling up with snow. If we had been five minutes later, they would have been gone.

He started to walk away, his head down, and Tookey grabbed him back. "No! No, Lumley!"

Lumley turned his wild face up to Tookey's and made a fist. He drew it back . . . but something in Tookey's face made him falter. He looked from Tookey to me and then back again.

"She'll freeze," he said, as if we were a couple of stupid kids. "Don't you get it? She doesn't have her jacket on and she's only seven years old—"

"They could be anywhere," Tookey said. "You can't follow those tracks. They'll be gone in the next drift."

"What do you suggest?" Lumley yells, his voice high and hysterical. "If we go back to get the police, she'll freeze to death! Francie *and* my wife!"

"They may be frozen already," Tookey said. His eyes caught Lumley's. "Frozen, or something worse."

"What do you mean?" Lumley whispered. "Get it straight, goddamn it! Tell me!"

"Mr. Lumley," Tookey says, "there's something in the Lot—"

But I was the one who came out with it finally, said the word I never expected to say. "Vampires, Mr. Lumley. Jerusalem's Lot is full of vampires. I expect that's hard for you to swallow—"

He was staring at me as if I'd gone green. "Loonies," he whispers. "You're a couple of loonies." Then he turned away, cupped his hands around his mouth, and bellowed, *"FRANCIE! JANEY!"* He started floundering off again. The snow was up to the hem of his fancy coat.

I looked at Tookey. "What do we do now?"

"Follow him," Tookey says. His hair was plastered with snow, and he *did* look a little bit loony. "I can't just leave him out here, Booth. Can you?"

"No," I says. "Guess not."

So we started to wade through the snow after Lumley as best we could. But he kept getting further and further ahead. He had his youth to spend, you see. He was breaking the trail, going through that snow like a bull. My arthritis began to bother me something terrible, and I started to look down at my legs, telling myself: A little further, just a little further, keep goin', damn it, keep goin' . . .

I piled right into Tookey, who was standing spread-legged in a drift. His head was hanging and both of his hands were pressed to his chest.

"Tookey," I says, "you okay?"

"I'm all right," he said, taking his hands away. "We'll stick with him, Booth, and when he fags out he'll see reason."

We topped a rise and there was Lumley at the bottom, looking desperately for more tracks. Poor man, there wasn't a chance he was going to find them. The wind blew straight across down there where he was, and any tracks would have been rubbed out three minutes after they was made, let alone a couple of hours.

He raised his head and screamed into the night: *"FRANCIE! JANEY! FOR GOD'S SAKE!"* And you could hear the desperation in his voice, the terror, and pity him for it. The only answer he got was the freight-train wail of the wind. It almost seemed to be laughin' at him, saying: *I took them Mister New Jersey with your fancy car and camels-hair topcoat. I took them and I rubbed out their tracks and by morning I'll have them just as neat and frozen as two strawberries in a deepfreeze . . .*

"Lumley!" Tookey bawled over the wind. "Listen, you never mind vampires or boogies or nothing like that, but you mind this! You're just making it worse for them! We got to get the—"

And then there *was* an answer, a voice coming out of the dark like little tinkling silver bells, and my heart turned cold as ice in a cistern.

"Jerry . . . Jerry, is that you?"

Lumley wheeled at the sound. And then *she* came, drifting out of the dark shadows of a little copse of trees like a ghost. She was a city woman, all right, and right then she seemed like the most beautiful woman I had ever seen. I felt like I wanted to go to her and tell her how glad I was she was safe after all. She was wearing a heavy green pullover sort of thing, a poncho, I believe they're called. It floated all around her, and her dark hair streamed out in the wild wind like water in a December creek, just before the winter freeze stills it and locks it in.

Maybe I did take a step toward her, because I felt Tookey's hand on my shoulder, rough and warm. And still—how can I say it?—I *yearned* after her, so dark and beautiful with that green poncho floating around her neck and shoulders, so exotic and strange as to make you think of some beautiful woman from a Walter de la Mare poem.

"Janey!" Lumley cried. *"Janey!"* He began to struggle through the snow toward her, his arms outstretched.

"No!" Tookey cried. *"No, Lumley!"*

He never even looked . . . but she did. She looked up at us and grinned. And when she did, I felt my longing, my yearning turn to horror as cold as the grave, as white and silent as bones in a shroud. Even from the rise we could see the sullen red glare in those eyes. They were less human than a wolf's eyes. And when she grinned you could see how long her teeth had become. She wasn't human anymore. She was a dead thing somehow come back to life in this black howling storm.

Tookey made the sign of the cross at her. She flinched back . . .

and then grinned at us again. We were too far away, and maybe too scared.

"Stop it!" I whispered. "Can't we stop it?"

"Too late, Booth!" Tookey says grimly.

Lumley had reached her. He looked like a ghost himself, coated in snow like he was. He reached for her . . . and then he began to scream. I'll hear that sound in my dreams, that man screaming like a child in a nightmare. He tried to back away from her, but her arms, long and bare and as white as the snow, snaked out and pulled him to her. I could see her cock her head and then thrust it forward—

"Booth!" Tookey said hoarsely. "We've got to get out of here!"

And so we ran. Ran like rats, I suppose some would say, but those who would weren't there that night. We fled back down along our own backtrail, falling down, getting up again, slipping and sliding. I kept looking back over my shoulder to see if that woman was coming after us, grinning that grin and watching us with those red eyes.

We got back to the Scout and Tookey doubled over, holding his chest. "Tookey!" I said, badly scared. "What—"

"Ticker," he said. "Been bad for five years or more. Get me around in the shotgun seat, Booth, and then get us the hell out of here."

I hooked an arm under his coat and dragged him around and somehow boosted him up and in. He leaned his head back and shut his eyes. His skin was waxy-looking and yellow.

I went back around the hood of the truck at a trot, and I damned near ran into the little girl. She was just standing there beside the driver's-side door, her hair in pigtails, wearing nothing but a little bit of a yellow dress.

"Mister," she said in a high, clear voice, as sweet as morning mist, "won't you help me find my mother? She's gone and I'm so cold—"

"Honey," I said, "honey, you better get in the truck. Your mother's—"

I broke off, and if there was ever a time in my life I was close to swooning, that was the moment. She was standing there, you see, but she was standing *on top* of the snow and there were no tracks, not in any direction.

She looked up at me then, Lumley's daughter Francie. She was no more than seven years old, and she was going to be seven for an eternity of nights. Her little face was a ghastly corpse white, her eyes a red and silver that you could fall into. And below her jaw I could see two small punctures like pinpricks, their edges horribly mangled.

She held out her arms at me and smiled. "Pick me up, mister," she said softly. "I want to give you a kiss. Then you can take me to my mommy."

I didn't want to, but there was nothing I could do. I was leaning forward, my arms outstretched. I could see her mouth opening, I could see the little fangs inside the pink ring of her lips. Something slipped down her chin, bright and silvery, and with a dim, distant, far-away horror, I realized she was drooling.

Her small hands clasped themselves around my neck and I was thinking: Well, maybe it won't be so bad, not so bad, maybe it won't be so awful after a while—when something black flew out of the Scout and struck her on the chest. There was a puff of strange-smelling smoke, a flashing glow that was gone an instant later, and then she was backing away, hissing. Her face was twisted into a vulpine mask of rage, hate, and pain. She turned sideways and then . . . and then she was gone. One moment she was there and the next there was a twisting knot of snow that looked a little bit like a human shape. Then the wind tattered it away across the fields.

"Booth!" Tookey whispered. "Be quick, now!"

And I was. But not so quick that I didn't have time to pick up what he had thrown at that little girl from hell. His mother's Douay Bible.

That was some time ago. I'm a sight older now, and I was no chicken then. Herb Tooklander passed on two years ago. He went peaceful, in the night. The bar is still there, some man and his wife from Waterville bought it, nice people, and they've kept it pretty much the same. But I don't go by much. It's different somehow with Tookey gone.

Things in the Lot go on pretty much as they always have. The sheriff found that fellow Lumley's car the next day, out of gas, the battery dead. Neither Tookey nor I said anything about it. What would have been the point? And every now and then a hitchhiker or a camper will disappear around there someplace, up on Schoolyard Hill or out near the Harmony Hill cemetery. They'll turn up the fellow's packsack or a paperback book all swollen and bleached out by the rain or snow, or some such. But never the people.

I still have bad dreams about that stormy night we went out there. Not about the woman so much as the little girl, and the way she smiled when she held her arms up so I could pick her up. So she could give me a kiss. But I'm an old man and the time comes soon when dreams are done.

You may have an occasion to be traveling in southern Maine yourself one of these days. Pretty part of the countryside. You may even stop by Tookey's Bar for a drink. Nice place. They kept the name just the same. So have your drink, and then my advice to you is to keep right on moving north. Whatever you do, don't go up that road to Jerusalem's Lot.

Especially not after dark.

There's a little girl somewhere out there. And I think she's still waiting for her good-night kiss.

neil gaiman

Snow, Glass, Apples

I do not know what manner of thing she is. None of us do. She killed her mother in the birthing, but that's never enough to account for it.

They call me wise, but I am far from wise, for all that I foresaw fragments of it, frozen moments caught in pools of water or in the cold glass of my mirror. If I were wise I would not have tried to change what I saw. If I were wise I would have killed myself before ever I encountered her, before ever I caught him.

Wise, and a witch, or so they said, and I'd see his face in my dreams and in reflections for all my life: sixteen years of dreaming of him before he reined his horse by the bridge that day, and asked my name. He helped me onto his high horse and we rode together to my little cottage, my face buried in the gold of his hair. He asked for the best of what I had; a king's right, it was.

His beard was red-bronze in the morning light, and I knew him, not as a king, for I knew nothing of kings then, but as my love. He took all he wanted from me, the right of kings, but he returned to me on the following day, and on the night after that: his beard so red, his hair so gold, his eyes the blue of a summer sky, his skin tanned the gentle brown of ripe wheat.

His daughter was only a child: no more than five years of age when I came to the palace. A portrait of her dead mother hung in the princess's tower room; a tall woman, hair the colour of dark wood, eyes nut-brown. She was of a different blood to her pale daughter.

The girl would not eat with us.

I do not know where in the palace she ate.

I had my own chambers. My husband the king, he had his own rooms also. When he wanted me he would send for me, and I would go to him, and pleasure him, and take my pleasure with him.

One night, several months after I was brought to the palace, she came to my rooms. She was six. I was embroidering by lamplight, squinting my eyes against the lamp's smoke and fitful illumination. When I looked up, she was there.

"Princess?"

She said nothing. Her eyes were black as coal, black as her hair; her lips were redder than blood. She looked up at me and smiled. Her teeth seemed sharp, even then, in the lamplight.

"What are you doing away from your room?"

"I'm hungry," she said, like any child.

It was winter, when fresh food is a dream of warmth and sunlight; but I had strings of whole apples, cored and dried, hanging from the beams of my chamber, and I pulled an apple down for her.

"Here."

Autumn is the time of drying, of preserving, a time of picking apples, of rendering the goose-fat. Winter is the time of hunger, of snow, and of death; and it is the time of the midwinter feast, when we rub the goose-fat into the skin of a whole pig, stuffed with that autumn's apples; then we roast it or spit it, and we prepare to feast upon the crackling.

She took the dried apple from me and began to chew it with her sharp yellow teeth.

"Is it good?"

She nodded. I had always been scared of the little princess, but at that moment I warmed to her and, with my fingers, gently, I stroked her cheek. She looked at me and smiled—she smiled but rarely—then she sank her teeth into the base of my thumb, the Mound of Venus, and she drew blood.

I began to shriek, from pain and from surprise; but she looked at me and I fell silent.

The little princess fastened her mouth to my hand and licked and sucked and drank. When she was finished, she left my chamber. Beneath my gaze the cut that she had made began to close, to scab, and to heal. The next day it was an old scar: I might have cut my hand with a pocketknife in my childhood.

I had been frozen by her, owned and dominated. That scared me, more than the blood she had fed on. After that night I locked my chamber door at dusk, barring it with an oaken pole, and I had the smith forge iron bars, which he placed across my windows.

My husband, my love, my king, sent for me less and less, and when I came to him he was dizzy, listless, confused. He could no longer make love as a man makes love; and he would not permit me to pleasure him with my mouth: the one time I tried, he started, violently, and began to weep. I pulled my mouth away and held him tightly, until the sobbing had stopped, and he slept, like a child.

I ran my fingers across his skin as he slept. It was covered in a multitude of ancient scars. But I could recall no scars from the days of our courtship, save one, on his side, where a boar had gored him when he was a youth.

Soon he was a shadow of the man I had met and loved by the bridge. His bones showed, blue and white, beneath his skin. I was with him at the last: his hands were cold as stone, his eyes milky-blue, his hair and beard faded and lustreless and limp. He died unshriven, his skin nipped and pocked from head to toe with tiny, old scars.

He weighed near to nothing. The ground was frozen hard, and we could dig no grave for him, so we made a cairn of rocks and stones above his body, as a memorial only, for there was little enough of him left to protect from the hunger of the beasts and the birds.

So I was queen.

And I was foolish, and young—eighteen summers had come and gone since first I saw daylight—and I did not do what I would do, now.

If it were today, I would have her heart cut out, true. But then I would have her head and arms and legs cut off. I would have them disembowel her. And then I would watch, in the town square, as the hangman heated the fire to white-heat with bellows, watch unblinking as he consigned each part of her to the fire. I would have archers around the square, who would shoot any bird or animal who came close to the flames, any raven or dog or hawk or rat. And I would not close my eyes until the princess was ash, and a gentle wind could scatter her like snow.

I did not do this thing, and we pay for our mistakes.

They say I was fooled; that it was not her heart. That it was the heart of an animal—a stag, perhaps, or a boar. They say that, and they are wrong.

And some say (but it is *her* lie, not mine) that I was given the heart, and that I ate it. Lies and half-truths fall like snow, covering the things that I remember, the things I saw. A landscape, unrecognisable after a snowfall: that is what she has made of my life.

There were scars on my love, her father's thighs, and on his bal-lock-pouch, and on his male member, when he died.

I did not go with them. They took her in the day, while she slept, and was at her weakest. They took her to the heart of the forest, and there they opened her blouse, and they cut out her heart, and they left her dead, in a gully, for the forest to swallow.

The forest is a dark place, the border to many kingdoms; no one would be foolish enough to claim jurisdiction over it. Outlaws live in the forest. Robbers live in the forest, and so do wolves. You can ride through the forest for a dozen days and never see a soul; but there are eyes upon you the entire time.

They brought me her heart. I know it was hers—no sow's heart or doe's would have continued to beat and pulse after it had been cut out, as that one did.

I took it to my chamber.

I did not eat it: I hung it from the beams above my bed, placed it on a length of twine that I strung with rowan berries, orange-red as a robin's breast, and with bulbs of garlic.

Outside, the snow fell, covering the footprints of my huntsmen, covering her tiny body in the forest where it lay.

I had the smith remove the iron bars from my windows, and I would spend some time in my room each afternoon through the short winter days, gazing out over the forest, until darkness fell.

There were, as I have already stated, people in the forest. They would come out, some of them, for the Spring Fair: a greedy, feral, dangerous people; some were stunted—dwarfs and midgets and hunchbacks; others had the huge teeth and vacant gazes of idiots; some had fingers like flippers or crab-claws. They would creep out of the forest each year for the Spring Fair, held when the snows had melted.

As a young lass I had worked at the fair, and they had scared me then, the forest folk. I told fortunes for the fairgoers, scrying in a pool of still water; and, later, when I was older, in a disk of polished glass, its back all silvered—a gift from a merchant whose straying horse I had seen in a pool of ink.

The stallholders at the fair were afraid of the forest folk; they would nail their wares to the bare boards of their stalls—slabs of gingerbread or leather belts were nailed with great iron nails to the wood. If their wares were not nailed, they said, the forest folk would take them, and run away, chewing on the stolen gingerbread, flailing about them with the belts.

The forest folk had money, though: a coin here, another there, sometimes stained green by time or the earth, the face on the coin unknown to even the oldest of us. Also they had things to trade, and thus the fair continued, serving the outcasts and the dwarfs, serving the robbers (if they were circumspect) who preyed on the rare travellers from lands beyond the forest, or on gypsies, or on the deer. (This was robbery in the eyes of the law. The deer were the queen's.)

The years passed by slowly, and my people claimed that I ruled them with wisdom. The heart still hung above my bed, pulsing gently in the night. If there were any who mourned the child, I saw no evidence: she was a thing of terror, back then, and they believed themselves well rid of her.

Spring Fair followed Spring Fair: five of them, each sadder, poorer, shoddier than the one before. Fewer of the forest folk came out of the forest to buy. Those who did seemed subdued and listless. The stallholders stopped nailing their wares to the boards of their stalls. And by the fifth year but a handful of folk came from the forest—a fearful huddle of little hairy men, and no one else.

The Lord of the Fair, and his page, came to me when the fair was done. I had known him slightly, before I was queen.

"I do not come to you as my queen," he said.

I said nothing. I listened.

"I come to you because you are wise," he continued. "When you were a child you found a strayed foal by staring into a pool of ink; when you were a maiden you found a lost infant who had wandered far from her mother, by staring into that mirror of yours. You know secrets and you can seek out things hidden. My queen," he asked, "what is taking the forest folk? Next year there will be no Spring Fair. The travellers from other kingdoms have grown scarce and few, the folk of the forest are almost gone. Another year like the last, and we shall all starve."

I commanded my maidservant to bring me my looking glass. It was a simple thing, a silver-backed glass disk, which I kept wrapped in a doeskin, in a chest, in my chamber.

They brought it to me, then, and I gazed into it:

She was twelve and she was no longer a little child. Her skin was still pale, her eyes and hair coal-black, her lips blood-red. She wore the clothes she had worn when she left the castle for the last time—the blouse, the skirt—although they were much let-out, much mended. Over them she wore a leather cloak, and instead of boots she had leather bags, tied with thongs, over her tiny feet.

She was standing in the forest, beside a tree.

As I watched, in the eye of my mind, I saw her edge and step and flitter and pad from tree to tree, like an animal: a bat or a wolf. She was following someone.

He was a monk. He wore sackcloth, and his feet were bare, and scabbed and hard. His beard and tonsure were of a length, overgrown, unshaven.

She watched him from behind the trees. Eventually he paused for the night, and began to make a fire, laying twigs down, breaking up a robin's nest as kindling. He had a tinderbox in his robe, and he knocked the flint against the steel until the sparks caught the tinder and the fire flamed. There had been two eggs in the nest he had found, and these he ate, raw. They cannot have been much of a meal for so big a man.

He sat there in the firelight, and she came out from her hiding place. She crouched down on the other side of the fire, and stared at him. He grinned, as if it were a long time since he had seen another human, and beckoned her over to him.

She stood up and walked around the fire, and waited, an arm's length away. He pulled in his robe until he found a coin—a tiny, copper penny—and tossed it to her. She caught it, and nodded, and went to him. He pulled at the robe around his waist, and his robe swung open. His body was as hairy as a bear's. She pushed him back onto the moss. One hand crept, spiderlike, through the tangle of hair, until it closed on his manhood; the other hand traced a circle on his left nipple. He closed his eyes, and fumbled one huge hand under her skirt. She lowered her mouth to the nipple she had been teasing, her smooth skin white on the furry brown body of him.

She sank her teeth deep into his breast. His eyes opened, then they closed again, and she drank.

She straddled him, and she fed. As she did so a thin blackish liquid began to dribble from between her legs. . . .

"Do you know what is keeping the travellers from our town? What is happening to the forest people?" asked the Head of the Fair.

I covered the mirror in doeskin, and told him that I would personally take it upon myself to make the forest safe once more.

I had to, although she terrified me. I was the queen.

A foolish woman would have gone then into the forest and tried to capture the creature; but I had been foolish once and had no wish to be so a second time.

I spent time with old books. I spent time with the gypsy women (who passed through our country across the mountains to the south, rather than cross the forest to the north and the west).

I prepared myself, and obtained those things I would need, and when the first snows began to fall, I was ready.

Naked, I was, and alone in the highest tower of the palace, a place open to the sky. The winds chilled my body; goose pimples crept across my arms and thighs and breasts. I carried a silver basin, and a basket in which I had placed a silver knife, a silver pin, some tongs, a grey robe, and three green apples.

I put them down and stood there, unclothed, on the tower, humble before the night sky and the wind. Had any man seen me standing there, I would have had his eyes; but there was no one to spy. Clouds scudded across the sky, hiding and uncovering the waning moon.

I took the silver knife and slashed my left arm—once, twice, three times. The blood dripped into the basin, scarlet seeming black in the moonlight.

I added the powder from the vial that hung around my neck. It was a brown dust, made of dried herbs and the skin of a particular toad, and from certain other things. It thickened the blood, while preventing it from clotting.

I took the three apples, one by one, and pricked their skins gently with my silver pin. Then I placed the apples in the silver bowl, and let them sit there while the first tiny flakes of snow of the year fell slowly onto my skin, and onto the apples, and onto the blood.

When dawn began to brighten the sky I covered myself with the grey cloak, and took the red apples from the silver bowl, one by one, lifting each into my basket with silver tongs, taking care not to touch it. There was nothing left of my blood or of the brown powder in the silver bowl, nothing save a black residue, like a verdigris, on the inside.

I buried the bowl in the earth. Then I cast a glamour on the apples (as once, years before, by a bridge, I had cast a glamour on myself), that they were, beyond any doubt, the most wonderful apples in the world, and the crimson blush of their skins was the warm colour of fresh blood.

I pulled the hood of my cloak low over my face, and I took ribbons and pretty hair ornaments with me, placed them above the apples in the reed basket, and I walked alone into the forest, until I came to her dwelling: a high, sandstone cliff, laced with deep caves going back a way into the rock wall.

There were trees and boulders around the cliffface, and I walked quietly and gently from tree to tree, without disturbing a twig or a fallen leaf. Eventually I found my place to hide, and I waited, and I watched.

After some hours a clutch of dwarfs crawled out of the hole in the cave-front—ugly, misshapen, hairy little men, the old inhabitants of this country. You saw them seldom now.

They vanished into the wood, and none of them espied me, though one of them stopped to piss against the rock I hid behind.

I waited. No more came out.

I went to the cave entrance and hallooed into it, in a cracked old voice.

The scar on my Mound of Venus throbbed and pulsed as she came toward me, out of the darkness, naked and alone.

She was thirteen years of age, my stepdaughter, and nothing marred the perfect whiteness of her skin save for the livid scar on her left breast, where her heart had been cut from her long since.

The insides of her thighs were stained with wet black filth.

She peered at me, hidden, as I was, in my cloak. She looked at me hungrily. "Ribbons, goodwife," I croaked. "Pretty ribbons for your hair . . ."

She smiled and beckoned to me. A tug; the scar on my hand was pulling me toward her. I did what I had planned to do, but I did it more readily than I planned: I dropped my basket, and screeched like the bloodless old peddler woman I was pretending to be, and I ran.

My grey cloak was the colour of the forest, and I was fast; she did not catch me.

I made my way back to the palace.

I did not see it. Let us imagine though, the girl returning, frustrated and hungry, to her cave, and finding my fallen basket on the ground.

What did she do?

I like to think she played first with the ribbons, twined them into her raven hair, looped them around her pale neck or her tiny waist.

And then, curious, she moved the cloth to see what else was in the basket; and she saw the red, red apples.

They smelled like fresh apples, of course; and they also smelled of blood. And she was hungry. I imagine her picking up an apple, pressing it against her cheek, feeling the cold smoothness of it against her skin.

And she opened her mouth and bit deep into it . . . .

By the time I reached my chambers, the heart that hung from the roof-beam, with the apples and hams and the dried sausages, had ceased to beat. It hung there, quietly, without motion or life, and I felt safe once more.

That winter the snows were high and deep, and were late melting. We were all hungry come the spring.

The Spring Fair was slightly improved that year. The forest folk were few, but they were there, and there were travellers from the lands beyond the forest.

I saw the little hairy men of the forest-cave buying and bargaining for pieces of glass, and lumps of crystal and of quartz-rock. They paid for the glass with silver coins—the spoils of my stepdaughter's depredations, I had no doubt. When it got about what they were buying, townsfolk rushed back to their homes, came back with their lucky crystals, and, in a few cases, with whole sheets of glass.

I thought, briefly, about having the little men killed, but I did not. As long as the heart hung, silent and immobile and cold, from the beam of my chamber, I was safe, and so were the folk of the forest, and, thus, eventually, the folk of the town.

My twenty-fifth year came, and my stepdaughter had eaten the poisoned fruit two winters back, when the prince came to my palace. He was tall, very tall, with cold green eyes and the swarthy skin of those from beyond the mountains.

He rode with a small retinue: large enough to defend him, small enough that another monarch—myself, for instance—would not view him as a potential threat.

I was practical: I thought of the alliance of our lands, thought of the kingdom running from the forests all the way south to the sea; I thought of my golden-haired bearded love, dead these eight years; and, in the night, I went to the prince's room.

I am no innocent, although my late husband, who was once my king, was truly my first lover, no matter what they say.

At first the prince seemed excited. He bade me remove my shift, and made me stand in front of the opened window, far from the fire, until my skin was chilled stone-cold. Then he asked me to lie upon my back, with my hands folded across my breasts, my eyes wide open—but staring only at the beams above. He told me not to move, and to breathe as little as possible. He implored me to say nothing. He spread my legs apart.

It was then that he entered me.

As he began to thrust inside me, I felt my hips raise, felt myself begin to match him, grind for grind, push for push. I moaned. I could not help myself.

His manhood slid out of me. I reached out and touched it, a tiny, slippery thing.

"Please," he said, softly. "You must neither move nor speak. Just lie there on the stones, so cold and so fair."

I tried, but he had lost whatever force it was that had made him virile; and, some short while later, I left the prince's room, his curses and tears still resounding in my ears.

He left early the next morning, with all his men, and they rode off into the forest.

I imagine his loins, now, as he rode, a knot of frustration at the base of his manhood. I imagine his pale lips pressed so tightly together. Then I imagine his little troupe riding through the forest, finally coming upon the glass-and-crystal cairn of my stepdaughter. So pale. So cold. Naked, beneath the glass, and little more than a girl, and dead.

In my fancy, I can almost feel the sudden hardness of his manhood inside his britches, envision the lust that took him then, the prayers he muttered beneath his breath in thanks for his good fortune. I imagine him negotiating with the little hairy men—offering them gold and spices for the lovely corpse under the crystal mound.

Did they take his gold willingly? Or did they look up to see his men on their horses, with their sharp swords and their spears, and realize they had no alternative?

I do not know. I was not there; I was not scrying. I can only imagine . . . .

Hands, pulling off the lumps of glass and quartz from her cold body. Hands, gently caressing her cold cheek, moving her cold arm, rejoicing to find the corpse still fresh and pliable.

Did he take her there, in front of them all? Or did he have her carried to a secluded nook before he mounted her?

I cannot say.

Did he shake the apple from her throat? Or did her eyes slowly open as he pounded into her cold body; did her mouth open, those red lips part, those sharp yellow teeth close on his swarthy neck, as the blood, which is the life, trickled down her throat, washing down and away the lump of apple, my own, my poison?

I imagine; I do not know.

This I do know: I was woken in the night by her heart pulsing and beating once more. Salt blood dripped onto my face from above. I sat up. My hand burned and pounded as if I had hit the base of my thumb with a rock.

There was a hammering on the door. I felt afraid, but I am a queen, and I would not show fear. I opened the door.

First his men walked into my chamber and stood around me, with their sharp swords, and their long spears.

Then he came in; and he spat in my face.

Finally, she walked into my chamber, as she had when I was first a queen, and she was a child of six. She had not changed. Not really.

She pulled down the twine on which her heart was hanging. She pulled off the rowan berries, one by one; pulled off the garlic bulb—now a dried thing, after all these years; then she took up her own, her pumping heart—a small thing, no larger than that of a nanny goat or a she-bear—as it brimmed and pumped its blood into her hand.

Her fingernails must have been as sharp as glass: she opened her breast with them, running them over the purple scar. Her chest gaped, suddenly, open and bloodless. She licked her heart, once, as the blood ran over her hands, and she pushed the heart deep into her breast.

I saw her do it. I saw her close the flesh of her breast once more. I saw the purple scar begin to fade.

Her prince looked briefly concerned, but he put his arm around her nonetheless, and they stood, side by side, and they waited.

And she stayed cold, and the bloom of death remained on her lips, and his lust was not diminished in any way.

They told me they would marry, and the kingdoms would indeed be joined. They told me that I would be with them on their wedding day.

It is starting to get hot in here.

They have told the people bad things about me; a little truth to add savour to the dish, but mixed with many lies.

I was bound and kept in a tiny stone cell beneath the palace, and I remained there through the autumn. Today they fetched me out of the cell; they stripped the rags from me, and washed the filth from me, and then they shaved my head and my loins, and they rubbed my skin with goose-grease.

The snow was falling as they carried me—two men at each hand, two men at each leg—utterly exposed, and spread-eagled and cold, through the midwinter crowds, and brought me to this kiln.

My stepdaughter stood there with her prince. She watched me, in my indignity, but she said nothing.

As they thrust me inside, jeering and chaffing as they did so, I saw one snowflake land upon her white cheek, and remain there without melting.

They closed the kiln door behind me. It is getting hotter in here, and outside they are singing and cheering and banging on the sides of the kiln.

She was not laughing, or jeering, or talking. She did not sneer at me or turn away. She looked at me, though; and for a moment I saw myself reflected in her eyes.

I will not scream. I will not give them that satisfaction. They will have my body, but my soul and my story are my own, and will die with me.

The goose-grease begins to melt and glisten upon my skin. I shall make no sound at all. I shall think no more on this.

I shall think instead of the snowflake on her cheek.

I think of her hair as black as coal, her lips, redder than blood, her skin, snow-white.

eric
van lustbader

In Darkness, Angels

If I had known then what I know now.

How those words echo on and on inside my mind, like a rubber ball bouncing down an endless staircase. As if they had a life of their own. Which, I suppose, they do now.

I cannot sleep but is it any wonder? Outside, blue white lightning forks like a giant's jagged claw and the thunder is so loud at times that I feel I must be trapped inside an immense bell, reverberations like memory unspooling in a reckless helix, making a mess at my feet.

If I had known then what I know now. And yet. . . .

*   *   *

And yet I return again and again to that windswept evening when the ferry deposited me at the east end of the island. It had once been, so I had been told by the rather garrulous captain, a swansneck peninsula. But over time, the water had gradually eaten away at the rocky soil until at last the land had succumbed to the ocean's cool tidal embrace, severing itself from the mainland a mile away.

Of course the captain had an entirely different version of what had transpired. "It's them folks up there," he had said, jerking his sharp unshaven chin toward the castle high atop the island's central mount. "Didn't want no more interference from the other folks

39

hereabouts." He gave a short barking laugh and spat over the boat's side. "Just as well, I say," he observed as he squinted heavily into the last of the sun's watery light. "Them rocks were awfully sharp." He shook his head as if weighed down by the memory. "Kids were always darin one another t'do their balancin act goin across, down that long spit o land." He turned the wheel hard over and spuming water rushed up the bow of the ferry. "Many's the night we'd come out with the searchlights, tryin to rescue some fool boy'd gone over."

For just a moment he swung us away from the island looming up on our starboard side, getting the most out of the crosswinds. "Never found em, though. Not a one." He spat again. "You go over the side around here, you're never seen again."

"The undertow," I offered.

He whipped his ruddy windburned face around, impaling me with one pale gray eye. "Undertow, you say?" His laugh was harsh now and unpleasant. "You gotta lot t'learn up there at Fuego del Aire, boyo. Oh, yes indeed!"

He left me on the quayside with no one around to mark my arrival. As the wide-beamed ferry tacked away, pushed by the strong sunset wind, I thought I saw the captain raise an arm in my direction.

I turned away from the sea. Great stands of pine, bristly and dark in the failing light, matched upward in majestic array toward the castle high above me. Their tops whipsawed, sending off an odd melancholy drone.

I felt utterly, irretrievably alone and for the first time since I had sent the letter I began to feel the queasy fluttering of reservations. An odd kind of inner darkness had settled about my shoulders like a vulture descending upon the flesh of the dead.

I took a deep breath and shook my head to clear it. The captain's stories were only words strung one after the other—all the legends just words and nothing more. Now I would see for myself. After all, that was what I wanted.

The last of the sunset torched the upper spires so that for a moment they looked like bloody spears. Imagination, that's all it was.

A writer's imagination. I clutched at my battered weekender and continued onward, puffing, for the way was steep. But I had arrived at just the right time of the day when the scorching sun was gone from the sky and night's deep chill had not yet settled over the land.

The air was rich with the scents of the sea, an agglomeration so fecund it took my breath away. Far off over the water, great gulls twisted and turned in lazy circles, skimming over the shining face of the ocean only to whirl high aloft, disappearing for long moments into the fleecy pink and yellow clouds.

From the outside, the castle seemed stupendous. It was immense, thrusting upward into the sky as if it were about to take off in flight. It was constructed—obviously many years ago—from massive blocks of granite laced with iridescent chips of mica that shone like diamonds, rubies and sapphires in the evening's light.

A fairy tale castle it surely looked with its shooting turrets and sharply angled spires, horned and horrific. However, on closer inspection, I saw that it had been put together with nothing more fantastic than mortar.

Below me, a mist was beginning to form, swiftly climbing the route I had taken moments before as if following me. Already the sight of the quay had been snuffed out and the cries of the gulls, filtered through the stuff, were eerie and vaguely disquieting.

I climbed the basalt steps to the front door of the castle. The span was fully large enough to drive a semi through. It was composed of a black substance that seemed to be neither stone nor metal. Cautiously, I ran my hand over its textured surface. It was petrified wood. In its center was a circular scrollwork knocker of black iron and this I used.

There was surprisingly little noise but almost immediately the door swung inward. At first I could see nothing. The creeping mist had curled itself around the twilight, plunging me into a dank and uncomfortable night.

"Yes?" It was a melodious voice, light and airy. A woman's voice.

I told her my name.

"I am so sorry," she said. "We tend to lose track of time at Fuego del Aire. I am Marissa. Of course you were expected. My brother will be extremely angry that you were not met at the quay."

"It's all right," I said. "I thoroughly enjoyed the walk."

"Won't you come in."

I picked up my suitcase and crossed the threshold, felt her slim hand slip into mine. The hallway was as dark as the night outside. I did not hear the door swing shut but when I looked back the sky and the rolling mist were gone.

I heard the rustling of her just in front of me and I could smell a scent like a hillside of flowers at dusk. Her skin was as soft as velvet but the flesh beneath was firm and supple and I found myself suddenly curious to find out what she looked like. Did she resemble the image in my thoughts? A thin, pale waif-like creature, faint blue traceries of veins visible beneath her thin delicate skin, her long hair as black as a raven's wings.

After what seemed an interminable time, we emerged into a dimly lighted chamber from which all other rooms on this floor seemed to branch. Directly ahead of us, an enormous staircase wound upward. It was certainly wide enough for twenty people to ascend abreast.

Torches flickered and the smoky, perfumed air was thick with the scent of burning tallow and whale oil. Uncomfortable looking furniture lined the walls: bare, wooden stiff-backed benches and chairs one might find in a Methodist church. Huge, heavy banners hung limply but they were so high above my head and the light so poor I could not make out their designs.

Marissa turned to face me and I saw that she was not at all as I had imagined her.

True, she was beautiful enough. But her cheeks were ruddy, her eyes cornflower blue and her hair was the color of sun-dazzled honey, falling in thick, gentle waves from a thin tortoise-shell band that held it from her face, back over her head, across her shoulders, cascading all the way down to the small of her back.

Her coral lips pursed as if she could not help the smile that now brightened her face. "Yes," she said softly, musically, "you are truly surprised."

"I'm sorry," I said. "Am I staring?" I gave an unnatural laugh. Of course I was staring. I could not stop.

"Perhaps you are weary from your climb. Would you like some food now? A cool drink to refresh you?"

"I would like to meet Morodor," I said, breaking my eyes away from her gaze with a concerted effort. She seemed to possess an ability to draw emotion out of me, as if she held the key to channels in myself I did not know existed.

"In time," she said. "You must be patient. There are many pressing matters that need attending to. Only he can see to them. I am certain you understand."

Indeed I did not. To have come this far, to have waited so long . . . all I felt was frustration. Like a hurt little boy, I had wanted Morodor to greet me at the front door by way of apology for the discourtesy of the utter stillness at the quay when I arrived. But no. There were more important matters for him.

"When I wrote to your brother—"

Marissa had lifted her long pale palms. "Please," she said, smiling. "Be assured that my brother wishes to aid you. I suspect that is because he is a writer himself. There is much time here at Fuego del Aire and lately his contemplation has found this somewhat more physical outlet."

I thought of the grisly stories the ferryboat captain had heaped on me—and others, over time, that had come my way from other loquacious mouths—and felt a chill creeping through my bones at the idea of Morodor's physical outlets.

"It must be fascinating to be able to write novels," Marissa said. "I must confess that I was quite selfishly happy when I learned of your coming. Your writing has given me much pleasure." She touched the back of my hand as if I might be a sculpture of great artistry. "This extraordinary talent must make you very desirable in . . . your world."

"You mean literary circles . . . entertainment. . . ."

"Circles, yes. You are quite special. My brother doubtless divined this from your letter." She took her fingertips from me. "But now it is late and I am certain you are tired. May I show you to your room? Food and drink are waiting for you there."

*   *

That night there was no moon. Or rather no moon could be seen. Nor the stars nor even the sky itself. Peering out the window of my turret room, I could see nothing but the whiteness of the mist. It was as if the rest of the world had vanished.

Gripping the edge of the windowsill with my fingers, I leaned out as far as I dared, peering into the night in an attempt to pick up any outline, any shape. But not even the tops of the enormous pines could poke their way through the pall.

I strained to hear the comforting hiss and suck of the ocean spending itself on the rocky shore so far below me. There was nothing of that, only the odd intermittent whistling of the wind through the stiff-fingered turrets of the castle.

At length, I went back to bed, but for the longest time I could not fall asleep. I had waited so long for Morodor's reply to my letter, had traveled for so many days just to be here now, it seemed impossible to relax enough for sleep to overtake me.

I was itchy with anticipation. Oh more. I was burning. . . In the days after I had received his affirmative answer, the thought of coming here, of talking to him, of learning his secrets had, more and more, come to stand for my own salvation.

It is perhaps difficult enough for any author to be blocked in his work. But for me . . . I lived to write. Without it, there seemed no reason at all to live, for I had found during this blocked time that the days and nights passed like months, years, centuries, as ponderous as old elephants. They had become my burden.

I had been like a machine, feverishly turning out one book after another—one a year—for . . . how many years now? Fifteen? Twenty? You see, the enfant terrible has lost count already. Mercifully.

Until this year when there was nothing, a desert of paper, and I grew increasingly desperate, sitting home like a hermit, traveling incessantly, bringing smiling girls home, abstaining, swinging from one extreme to the other like a human pendulum in an attempt to get the insides in working order again.

Nothing.

And then one drunken night I had heard the first of the stories about Fuego del Aire and, even through the vapors of my stupor, *something* had penetrated. An idea, perhaps or, more accurately at that point, the ghost of an idea. Of lost love, betrayal and the ultimate horror. As simple as that. And as complex. But I knew that imagination was no longer enough, that I would have to seek out this place myself. I had to find Morodor and somehow persuade him to see me . . . .

Sleep. I swear to you it finally came, although, oddly, it was like no slumber I had ever had, for I dreamed that I was awake and trying desperately to fall asleep. I knew that I was to see Morodor in the morning, that I had to be sharp and that, sleepless, I would fall far short of that.

In the dream I lay awake, clutching the bedspread up around my chest, staring at the ceiling with such intensity that I suspected at any minute I would be able to see right through it.

I opened my eyes. Or closed them and opened them again to find the dawnlight streaming through the tall narrow window. I had forgotten to close the curtains before going to bed.

For just an instant I had the strangest sensation in my body. It was as if my legs had gone dead, all the strength flowing out of my muscles and into the wooden floor of my room. But the paralysis had somehow freed my upper torso so that I felt an enormous outpouring of energy.

A brief stab of fear rustled through my chest and my heart fluttered. But as soon as I sat up, the sensation went away. I rose, washed, dressed and went down to breakfast.

Food was waiting in steaming array along the length of an

immense wooden table. In fact, now that I had my first good look at Fuego del Aire in the light of day, I saw that everything was of wood: the paneled walls, the floor where you could see it between the series of dark patterned carpets, the cathedral ceilings; door handles, windowsills, even the lighting fixtures. If I had not seen the outside of the castle myself, I would have sworn the place had been built entirely of wood.

Two formal settings were laid out, one at the head of the table and the other by its left side. Assuming the first was for Morodor, I settled into the side chair and began to help myself.

But it was not Morodor who came down the wide staircase; it was Marissa. She was, that morning, a sight to make the heart pound. It was as if the sun had detached itself from its prescribed route across the heavens and had descended to earth. She wore a sky-blue tunic, wrapped criss-cross between her breasts and around her narrow waist with a deep green satin sash. On her feet she wore rope sandals. I saw that one of her toes was girdled by a tiny gold ring.

Her smile as she approached had the warmth of summer itself. And her hair! How can I adequately describe the way her hair shone in the daylight, sparking and glittering as if each strand were itself some mysterious source of light. Those waves of golden honey acted as if they had a life of their own.

"Good morning," she said easily. "Did you sleep well?"

"Yes," I lied. "Perfectly." I lifted a bowl of green figs. "Fruit?"

"Yes, please. Just a bit." But even with that she left more on her plate than she ate.

"I was hoping to find your brother already awake," I said, finishing up my meal.

She smiled sweetly. "Unfortunately, he is not an early riser. Be patient. All will be well." She rose. "If you are finished, I imagine you are quite curious about Fuego del Aire. There is much here to see."

We went out of the main hall, through corridors and chambers one after another, so filled, so disparate that I soon became dizzied with wonder. The place seemed to go on forever.

At length we emerged into a room that, judging by its accouterments, must once have been a scullery. We crossed it quickly and went through a small door I did not see until Marissa pulled it open.

The mist of last night had gone completely and above was only an enormous cerulean sky clear of cloud or bird. I could hear the distant sea hurling itself with ceaseless abandon at the jagged base of the mount. But lowering my gaze I saw only foliage.

"The garden," Marissa breathed, slipping her hand into mine. "Come on." She took me past a field of tiger lilies, rows of flowering woodbine; through a rose garden of such humbling perfection, it took my breath away.

Beyond, we came upon a long sculptured hedge half again as tall as I stand. There was a long narrow opening through which she led me and immediately we were surrounded by high walls of hedges. They were lushly verdant and immaculately groomed so that it was impossible to say where one left off and another began, seamless on and on and—

"What is this place?" I said.

But Marissa did not answer until, after many twistings and turning, we were deep within. Then she faced me and said, "This is the Labyrinth. My brother had it constructed for me when I was just a child. Perhaps he thought it would keep me out of trouble."

"There *is a* way out," I said uneasily, looking around me at the dark-green screens looming up on every side.

"Oh yes." She laughed, a bell-like silvery tone. "It is up here." And tapped the side of her head with a slender forefinger. "This is where I come to think, when I am sad or distraught. It is so peaceful and still and no one can find me here if I choose to remain hidden, not even Morodor. This is my domain."

She began to lead me onward, through switchbacks, past cul-de-sacs, moving as unerringly as if she were a magnet being drawn toward the North Pole. And I followed her silently; I was already lost.

"My brother used to say to me, 'Marissa, this labyrinth is unique in all the world for I have made it from the blueprint of your mind. All these intricate convolutions . . . the pattern corresponds to the eddies and whorls of your own brain.'"

She stared at me with those huge mocking eyes, so blue it seemed as if the noonday sky were reflected there. The hint of a smile played at the corners of her lips. "But of course I was only a child then and always trying to do what he did . . . to be like him." She shrugged. "He was most likely trying to make me feel special . . . don't you think?"

"He wouldn't need this place to do that," I said. "How on earth do you find your way out of here?" Nothing she had said had lessened my uneasiness.

"The years," she said seriously, "have taken care of that."

She pulled at me and we sat, our torsos in the deep shade of the hedges, our stretched-out legs in the buttery warmth of the sunlight. Somewhere, close at hand, a bumblebee buzzed fatly, contentedly.

I put my head back and watched the play of light and shadow on the hedge opposite us. Ten thousand tiny leaves moved minutely in the soft breeze as if I were watching a distant crowd fluttering lifted handkerchiefs at the arrival of some visiting emperor. A kind of dreamy warmth stole over me and at once my uneasiness was gone.

"Yes." I told her. "It *is* peaceful here."

"I am glad," she said. "You feel it too. Perhaps that is because you are a writer. A writer feels things more deeply, is that not so?"

I smiled. "Maybe some, yes. We're always creating characters for our stories so we have to be adept at pulling apart the people we meet. We have to be able to get beyond the world and, like a surgeon, expose their workings."

"And you're never frightened of such things?"

"Frightened? Why?"

"Of what you'll find there."

"I've discovered many things there over the years. How could all of them be pleasant? Why should I want them to be? I sometimes think that many of my colleagues live off the *un*pleasant traits they find beneath the surface." I shrugged. "In any event, nothing seems to work well without the darkness of conflict. In life as well as in writing."

Her eyes opened and she looked at me sideways. "Am I wrong to think that knowledge is very important to you?"

"What could be more important to a writer? I sometimes think there is a finite amount of knowledge—not to be assimilated—but that can be used."

"And that is why you have come here."

"Yes."

She looked away. "You have never married. Why is that?"

I shrugged while I thought about that for a moment. "I imagine it's because I've never fallen in love."

She smiled at that. "Never ever. Not in all the time—"

I laughed. "Now wait a minute! I'm not that old. Thirty-seven is hardly ancient."

"Thirty-seven," she mouthed softly, as if she were repeating words alien to her. "Thirty-seven. Really?"

"Yes." I was puzzled. "How old are you?"

"As old as I look." She tossed her hair. "I told you last night. Time means very little here."

"Oh yes, day to day. But I mean you must—"

"No more talk now," she said, rising and pulling at my hand. "There is too much to see."

We left the labyrinth by a simple enough path, though, left to myself, I undoubtedly would have wandered around in there until someone had the decency to come and get me.

Presently we found ourselves at a stone parapet beyond which the peak dropped off so precipitously that it seemed as if we were standing on the verge of a rift in the world.

This was the western face of the island, one that I had not seen on my journey here. Far below us—certainly more than a thousand feet—the sea creamed and sucked at the jagged rocks, iced at their base by shining pale-gray barnacles. Three or four large lavender and white gulls dipped and wheeled through the foaming spray as they searched for food.

"Beautiful, isn't it?" Marissa said.

But I had already turned from the dark face of the sea to watch the planes and hollows of her own shining face, lit by the soft summer light, all rose and golden, radiating a warmth. . . .

It took me some time to understand the true nature of that heat. It stemmed from the same spot deep inside me from which had leaped that sharp momentary anger.

"Marissa," I breathed, saying her name as if it were a prayer.

And she turned to me, her cornflower blue eyes wide, her full lips slightly parted, shining. I leaned over her, coming closer inch by inch until I had to shut my eyes or cross them. Then I felt the rush of her lips against mine, so incredibly soft, at first cool and fragrant, then quickly warming to blood-heat.

"No," she said, her voice muffled by our flesh. "Oh, don't." But her lips opened under mine and I felt her hot tongue probing into my mouth.

My arms went around her, pulling her to me as gently as I would handle a stalk of wheat. I could feel the hard press of her breasts, the round softness of her stomach, and the heat. The heat rising. . . .

*   *
*

And with the lightning comes the rain. That's from an old poem my mother used to sing to me late at night when the storms woke me up. I cannot remember any more of it. Now it's just a fragment of truth, an artifact unearthed from the silly riverbed of my mind. And I the archeologist of this region as puzzled as everyone else at what I sometimes find. But that, after all, is what has kept me writing, year after year. An engine of creation.

The night is impenetrable with cloud and the hissing downpour. But still I stand at my open window, high up above the city, at the very edge of heaven.

I cannot see the streets below me—the one or two hurrying

people beneath their trembling umbrellas or the lights of the cars, if indeed there are any out at this ungodly hour—just the spectral geometric patterns, charcoal-gray on black, of the buildings' tops closest to mine. But not as high. None of them is as high.

Nothing exists now but this tempest and its fury. The night is alive with it, juddering and crackling. Or am I wrong? Is the night alive with something else? I know. *I know.*

I hear the sound of them now. . . .

*   *
*

The days passed like the most intense of dreams. The kind where you can recall every single detail any time you wish, producing its emotions again and again with a conjurer's facility.

Being with Marissa, I forgot about my obsessive desire to seek out Morodor. I no longer asked her where he was or when I would get to see him. In fact, I hoped I never would, for, if there were any truth to the legends of Fuego del Aire, they most assuredly must stem from his dark soul and not from this creature of air and light who never left my side.

In the afternoons we strolled through the endless gardens—for she was ill at ease indoors—and holding her hand seemed infinitely more joyous than looking upon the castle's illimitable marvels. I fully believe that if we had chanced upon a griffin during one of those walks I would have taken no more notice of it than I would an alley cat.

However, no such fabled creature made its appearance, and as the time passed I became more and more convinced that there was no basis at all to the stories that had been told and re-told over the years. The only magical power Marissa possessed was the one that enabled her to cut to the very core of me with but one word or the merest touch of her flesh against mine.

"I lied to you," I told her one day. It was late afternoon. Thick dark sunlight slanted down on our shoulders and backs, as slow-running as honey. The cicadas wailed like beaten brass and butterflies danced like living jewels in and out of the low bushes and the blossoms as if they were a flock of children playing tag.

"About what?"

"When I said that I had never been in love." I turned over on my back, staring up at a fleecy cloud piled high, a castle in the sky. "I was. Once."

I took her hand, rubbed my thumb over the delicate bones ribbing the back. "It was when I was in college. We met in a child psychology class and fell in love without even knowing it."

For a moment there was a silence between us and I thought perhaps I had made a mistake in bringing it up.

"But you did not marry her."

"No."

"Why not?"

"We were from different . . . backgrounds." I turned to see her face peering at me, seeming as large as the sun in the sky. "I think it would be difficult to explain to you, Marissa. It had something to do with religion."

"Religion." Again she rolled a word off her tongue as if trying to get the taste of a new and exotic food. "I am not certain that I understand."

"We believed in different things—or, more accurately, she believed and I didn't."

"And there was no room for . . . compromise?"

"In this, no. But the ironic part of all of it is that now I have begun to believe, if just a little bit; and she, I think, has begun to disbelieve some of what she had always held sacred."

"How sad," Marissa said. "Will you go back to her?"

"Our lime has long passed."

Something curious had come into her eyes. "Then you believe that love has a beginning and an end, always."

I could no longer bear to have those fantastic eyes riveting me. "I had thought so."

"Why do you look away?"

"I—" I watched the sky. The cloud-castle had metamorphosed into a great humpbacked bird. "I don't know."

Her eyes were very clear, piercing though the natural light was dusky. "We are explorers," she said, "at the very precipice of time." Something in her voice drew me. "Can there really be a love without end?"

Now she began to search my face in detail as if she were committing it to memory, as if she might never see me again. And that wild thought brought me fully out of my peaceful dozing.

"Do you love me?"

"Yes," I whispered with someone else's voice. Like a dry wind through sere reeds. And pulled her down to me.

*   .   *

At night we seemed even closer. It was as if I had taken a bit of the sun to bed with me: she was as radiant at night as she was during the day, light and supple and so eager to be held, to be caressed. To be loved.

"Feel how I feel." she whispered, trembling, "when I am close to you." She stretched herself over me. "The mouth can lie with words but the body cannot. This heat is real. All love flows out through the body, do you know that?"

I was beyond being able to respond verbally.

She moved her fingertips on me, then the petal softness of her palms. "I feel your body. How you respond to me. Its depth. As if I were the moon and you the sea." Her lips were at my ear, her esses sibilant. "It is important. More important than you know."

"Why?" I sighed.

"Because only love can mend my heart."

I wondered at the scar there. I moved against her, opening her legs. "Darling!"

*   .   *

I met Morodor on the first day of my second week at Fuego del Aire. And then it seemed quite by chance.

It was just after breakfast and Marissa had gone back to her room to change. I was strolling along the second floor balustrade when I came across a niche in the wall that I had missed before.

I went through it and found myself on a parapet along the jutting north side of the castle. It was like hanging in mid-air and I would have been utterly stunned by the vista had I not almost immediately run into a dark towering shape.

Hastily I backed up against the stone wall of the castle, thinking I had inadvertently run into another outcropping of this odd structure.

Then, quite literally, it seemed as if a shadow had come to life. It detached itself from the edge of the parapet and now I can see that it was the figure of a man.

He must have been nearly seven feet tall and held about him a great ebon cape, thick and swirling, that rushed down his slender form so that it hissed against the stone floor when he moved.

He turned toward me and I gasped. His face was long and narrow, as bony as a corpse's, his skin fully as pale. His eyes, beneath darkly furred brows, were bits of bituminous matter as if put there to plug a pair of holes into his interior. His nose was long and thin to the point of severity but his lips were full and rubicund, providing the only bit of color to his otherwise deathly pallid face.

His lips opened infinitesimally and he spoke my name. Involuntarily, I shuddered and immediately saw something pass across his eyes: not anger or sorrow but rather a weary kind of resignation.

"How do you do."

The greeting was so formal that it startled me and I was tongue-tied. After all this time, he had faded from my mind and now I longed only to be with Marissa. I found myself annoyed with him for intruding upon us.

"Morodor," I said. I had the oddest impulse to tell him that what he needed most was a good dose of sunshine. That almost made me giggle. Almost.

"Pardon me for saying this but I thought . . . that is, to see you up and around, outside in the daylight—" I stopped, my cheeks burning, unable to go on. I had done it anyway. I cursed myself for the fool that I was.

But Morodor took no offense. He merely smiled—a perfectly ghastly sight—and inclined his head a fraction. "A rather common misconception," he said in his disturbing, rumbling voice. "It is in fact *direct* sunlight that is injurious to my health. I am like a fine old print." His dark hair brushed against his high forehead. "I quite enjoy the daytime, otherwise."

"But surely you must sleep sometime."

He shook his great head. "Sleep is unknown to me. If I slept, I would dream and this is not allowed me." He took a long hissing stride along the parapet. "Come." he said. "Let us walk." I looked back the way I had come and he said, "Marissa knows we are together. Do not fear. She will be waiting for you when we are finished."

Together we walked along the narrow parapet. Apparently, it girdled the entire castle, for I saw no beginning to it and no end.

"You may wonder," Morodor said in his booming, vibratory voice, "why I granted you this interview." His great cape swept around him like the coils of a midnight sea so that it seemed as if he kept the night around him wherever he went. "I sensed in your writing a certain desperation." He turned to me. "And desperation is an emotion with which I can empathize."

"It was kind of you to see me."

"Kind, yes."

"But I must confess that things have . . . changed since I wrote that letter."

"Indeed." Was that a vibratory warning?

"Yes." I plunged onward. "In fact, since I came here, I—" I paused, not knowing how to continue. "The change has come since I arrived at Fuego del Aire."

Morodor said nothing and we continued our perambulation around the perimeter of the castle. Now I could accurately judge just how high up we were. Perhaps that mist I had seen the first night had been a cloud passing us as if across the face of the moon. And why not? All things seemed possible here. It struck me as ridiculous that just fifty miles from here there were supertankers and express trains, Learjets and paved streets lined with shops dispensing sleekly packaged products manufactured by multinational corporations. Surely all those modern artifacts were part of a fading dream I once had.

The sea was clear of sails for as far as the horizon. It was a flat and glittering pool there solely for the pleasure of this man.

"I'm in love with your sister." I had blurted it out and now I stood stunned, waiting, I suppose, for the full brunt of his wrath.

But instead, he stopped and stared at me. Then he threw his head back and laughed, a deep booming sound like thunder. Far off, a gull screeched, perhaps in alarm.

"My dear sir," he said. "You really are the limit!"

"And she's in love with me."

"Oh oh oh. I have no doubt that she is."

"I don't—"

His brows gathered darkly like stormclouds. "You believe your race to be run." He moved away. "But fear, not love, ends it." Through another niche, he slid back inside the castle. It was as if he had passed through the wall.

*   *   *

"If I had known that today was the day," Marissa said, "I would have prepared you."

"For what?"

We were sitting in a bower on a swing-chaise. Above our heads arched brilliant hyacinth and bougainvillea, wrapped around and around a white wooden trellis. It was near dusk and the garden was filled with a deep sapphire light that was almost luminescent. A westerly wind brought us the rich scent of the sea."

"For him. We are not. . . very much alike. At least, superficially."

"Marissa," I said, taking her hand, "are you certain that you *are* Morodor's sister?"

"Of course I am. What do you mean?"

"Well, it's obvious, isn't it?" But when she looked at me blankly, I was forced to go on. "What I mean is, he's precisely . . . what he's supposed to be. At least the way the legends describe . . . what he is."

Her eyes grew dark and she jerked her hand away. She gave me a basilisk stare. "I should have known." Her voice was filled with bitter contempt. "You're just like the rest. And why shouldn't you be?" She stood. "You think he's a monster. Yes, admit it. A monster!"

Her eyes welled up with tears. "And that makes me a monster too, doesn't it. Well, to hell with you!" And she whirled away.

"Marissa!" I cried in anguish. "That's not what I meant at all."

And I ran after her knowing that it was a lie, that it was what I had meant after all. Morodor was all the legends had said he should be. And more. My God but he was hideous. Pallid and cold as the dead. An engine of negative energy, incapable of any real feeling; of crying or true humor. Or love.

Only love can mend my heart.

I *had* meant it. How could this golden girl of air and sunlight bear any family ties to that great looming figure of darkness? Where was the sense in it? The rationality? She had feelings. She laughed and cried, felt pleasure and pain. And she loved. She loved.

"Marissa!" I called again, running. "Marissa, come back!" But she had vanished into the labyrinth and I stood there on the threshold, the scent of roses strong in my nostrils, and peered within. I called out her name over and over again but she did not appear and, unguided, I could not bring myself to venture farther.

Instead, I stormed back to the castle, searching for Morodor. It was already dark and the lights had been lit. As if by magic. In just the same way that the food was prepared, the wine bottles uncorked, my bed turned down in the evening and made in the morning, my soiled clothes washed, pressed and laid out with the professional's precision. And all done without my seeing a soul.

I found Morodor in the library. It was a room as large as a gallery: at least three floors of books, rising upward until the neat rows were lost in the haze of the distance. Narrow wooden walkways circled the library at various levels, connected by a complex network of wide wooden ladders.

He was crouched on one of these, three or four steps off the floor. It seemed an odd position for a man of his size.

He was studying a book as I came in but he quietly closed it when he heard me approach.

"What," I said, rather nastily, "no leather bindings?"

His hard ebon eyes regarded me without obvious emotion. "Leather," he said softly, "would mean the needless killing of animals."

"Oh, I see." My tone had turned acid. "It's only humans who need fear you."

He stood up and I backed away, abruptly fearful as he unfolded upward and upward until he stood over me in all his monstrous height.

"Humans," he said, "fear me only because they choose to fear me."

"You mean you haven't given them any cause to fear you?"

"Don't be absurd." He was as close to being annoyed as I had seen him. "I cannot help being what I am. Just as you cannot. We are both carnivores."

I closed my eyes and shuddered. "But with what a difference!"

"To some I have been a god."

"Such a dark god." My eyes flew open.

"There is a need for that, too." He put the book away. "Yet I am a man for all that."

"A man who can't sleep, who doesn't dream."

"Who cannot die."

"Not even if I drive a stake through your heart?" I did not know whether or not I was serious.

He went across the room to where a strip of wooden paneling intervened between two bookshelves. His hand merged from the folds of his voluminous cape and for the first time I saw the long talon-like nails exposed. I shivered as I saw them dig into the wood with ferocious strength. But not in any hot animal way. The movement was as precise as a surgeon peeling back a patient's peritoneum.

Morodor returned with a shard of wood perhaps eighteen inches in length. It was slightly tapered at one end, not needle sharp but pointed enough to do its work. He thrust it into my hands. "Here," he said harshly. "Do it now."

For an instant, I intended to do just that. But then something inside me cooled. I threw the stake from me. "I'll do no such thing."

He actually seemed disappointed. "No matter. That part of the legend, as others, is incorrect." He went back to his perch on the ladder, his long legs drawn up tightly beneath the cape, the outline of his bony knees like a violent set of punctuation marks on a blank page.

"Legends," he said, "are like funerals. They both serve the same purpose. They give comfort without which the encroachment of terrifying entropy would snuff out man's desire—his absolute hunger—for life."

He looked from his long nails up into my face. "Legends are created to set up their own kind of terror. But it is a terror very carefully bounded by certain limitations: the werewolf can be killed by a silver bullet, the medusa by seeing her own reflection in a mirror.

"You see? Always there is a way out for the intrepid. It is a necessary safety valve venting the terror that lurks within all mankind—atavistic darkness, the unconscious. And death."

He rested his long arms in his lap. "How secure do you imagine mankind would feel if all of them out there knew the reality of it? That there is no escape for me. No stake through the heart."

"But you said direct sunlight—"

"Was injurious to me. Like the flu, nothing more." He smiled wanly. "A week or two in bed and I am fit again." He laughed sardonically.

"Assuming I believe you, why are you telling me this? By your own admission, mankind could not accept the knowledge."

"Then you won't tell them, will you?"

"But *I* know."

He took a deep breath and for the first time his eyes seemed to come to life, sparking and dancing within their deep fleshless sockets. "Why did you wish to come here, my friend?"

"Why, I told you in the letter. I was blocked, out of ideas."

"And now?"

I stared at him quizzically while it slowly began to wash over me. "I can tell them, can't I?"

He smiled sphinx-like. "You are a writer. You can tell them anything you wish."

* . *
     *

"When I told you before that I was a man, I meant it."

I was sitting with Morodor high up in one of the castle's peaks, in what he called the cloud room. Like all the other chambers I had been in here, it was paneled in wood.

"I have a hunger to live just like all the rest of the masses." He leaned back in his chair, shifting about as if he were uncomfortable. To his left and right, enormous windows stood open to the starry field of the night. There were no shutters, no curtains; they could not be closed. A sharp, chill wind blew in, ruffling his dark hair but he seemed oblivious to the caress. "But do not mistake my words. I speak not as some plutocrat bloated on wealth. It is only that I am . . . special."

"What happened?"

His eyes flashed and he shifted again. "In each case, it is different. In mine . . . well, let us say that my hunger for life outweighed my caution." He smiled bleakly. "But then I have never believed that caution was a desirable trait."

"Won't you tell me more."

He looked at me in the most avuncular fashion. "I entered into a wager with . . . someone."

"And you won."

"No. I lost. But it was meant that I should lose. Otherwise, I would not be here now." His eyes had turned inward and in so doing had become almost wistful. "I threw the dice one time, up against a wall of green baize."

"You crapped out."

"No. I entered into life."

"And became *El Amor Brujo*. That's what you're sometimes called: the love sorcerer."

"Because of my . . . hypnotic effect on women." He moved minutely and his cape rustled all about him like a copse of trees stirred by a midnight wind. "A survival trait. Like seeing in the dark or having built-in radar."

"Then there's nothing magical—"

"There is," he said, "magic involved. One learns . . . many arts over the years. I have time for everything."

I shivered, pulled my leather jacket closer about me. He might not mind the chill, but I did. I pointed to the walls. "Tell me something. The outside of Fuego del Aire is pure stone. But here, inside, there is only wood. Why is that?"

"I prefer wood, my friend. I am not a creature of the earth and so stone insults me; its density inhibits me. I feel more secure with the wood." His hand lifted, fluttered, dropped back into his lap. "Trees." He said it almost as if it were a sacred word.

In the ensuing silence, I began to sweat despite the coldness. I knew what I at least was leading up to. I rubbed my palms down the fabric of my trousers. I cleared my throat.

"Morodor. . . ."

"Yes." His eyes were half-shut as if he were close to sleep.

"I really do love Marissa."

"I know that." But there seemed no kindness in his voice.

I took a deep breath. "We had a row. She thinks I see you as a monster."

He did not move, his eyes did not open any wider, for which I was profoundly grateful. "In a world where so many possibilities exist, this is true. Yet I am also a man. And I am Marissa's brother. I am friend . . . foe; master . . . servant. It is all in the perception." Still he did not move. "What do *you* see, my friend?"

I wished he'd stop calling me that. I said nothing.

"If you are not truthful with me, I shall know it." His ruby lips seemed to curve upward at their corners. "Something else you may add to the new legend . . . if you choose to write about it."

"I've no wish to deceive you, Morodor. I'm merely trying to sort through my own feelings." I thought he nodded slightly.

"I confess . . . to finding your appearance . . . startling."

"I appreciate your candor."

"Oh, hell, I thought you were hideous."

"I see."

"You hate me now."

"Why should I hate you? Because you take the world view?"

"But that was at first. Already you've changed before my eyes. God knows I've tried but now I don't even find your appearance odd."

As if divining my thoughts, he said, "And this disturbs you."

"It does."

He nodded his head again. "Quite understandable. It will pass." He looked at me. "But you are afraid of that too."

"Yes," I said softly.

"Soon you shall meet my sister again."

I shook my head. "I don't understand."

"Of course you don't." Now his voice sounded softer. "Have patience, my friend. You are young enough still to rush headlong over the precipice merely to discover what is beyond it."

"That's why I came here."

"I know. But that time has passed. Now life has you by the throat and it will be a struggle to the end." His eyes flew open, seeming as hot as burning coals. "And who shall be the victor, my friend? When you have the answer to that, you shall understand it all."

*   *   *

I ate dinner alone that night. I had spent hours searching the castle for Marissa but it was as if she had vanished. Weary at last, I returned to the dining hall and availed myself of vast quantities of the hot food.

I was terrified and I thought that this would act as an inhibitor on my appetite. But, strangely, just the opposite was happening. I ate and ate as if this alone could assuage my fear.

It was Morodor I was terrified of, I knew that. But was it because I feared him or liked him?

Afterward, it was all I could do to drag myself up the staircase. I stumbled down the hallway and into bed without even removing my clothes.

I slept a deep dreamless sleep but when I opened my eyes it was still dark out. I turned over, about to return to sleep, when I heard a sound. I sat bolt upright, the short hairs at the back of my neck stiff and quivering.

Silence.

And out of the silence a weird, thin cry. I got off the bed about to open the door to the hallway when it came again and I turned. It was coming from outside in the blackness of the night.

I threw open the shutters wide and leaned out just as I had on my first night here. This time there was no mist. Stars shone intermittently through the gauzy cloud cover with a fierce cold light, blinking on and off as if they were silently appealing for help.

At first I saw nothing, hearing only the high soughing of the wind through the pines. Then, off to my left, so high up that I mistook it for another cloud, something moved.

I turned my head in that direction and saw a shape a good deal darker than a cloud. It blossomed with sickening speed, blacker even than the night. Wraith or dream, which was it? The noise of the flapping wings, leathery, horned and, what?, scabbed, conjured up in my mind the image of a giant bat.

Precariously, I leaned farther out, saw that it was heading for the open apertures of the cloud room. I hurled myself across the room and out the door, heading up the stairs in giant bounds.

Consequently, I was somewhat out of breath by the time I launched myself through the open doorway to the aerie and there found only Morodor.

He turned quickly from his apparent contemplation of the sky. "You should be asleep," he said. But something in his tone told me that I had been expected.

"Something woke me."

"Not a nightmare, I trust."

"A sound from the night. It was nothing to do with me."

"It is usually quite still here. What kind of sound?"

"It sounded like a scream . . . a terrible cry."

Morodor only stared at me, unblinking, until I was forced to go on.

"I went to the window and looked out. I . . . saw a shape I could not clearly identify; I heard the awful sound of bat wings."

"Oh." Morodor said, "that's quite impossible. We have none here, I've seen to that. Bats are boring, really. As with octopi, I'm afraid their ferocious reputation has been unjustly thrust upon them."

"Just what the hell did I see then?"

Morodor's hand lifted, fell, the arch of a great avian wing. "Whatever it was, it brought you up here."

"Then there *was* something there!" I said in triumph. "You admit it."

"I admit," said Morodor carefully, "that I wanted to see you. The fact is you are here."

"You and I," I said. "But what of Marissa? I have been looking for her all evening. I must see her."

"Do you think it wise to see her now, to . . . continue what has begun, knowing what you do about me?"

"But she is nothing like you. You two are the shadow and the light."

Morodor's gaze was unwavering. "Two sides of the coin, my friend. The same coin."

I was fed up with his oblique answers. "Perhaps," I said sharply, "it's just that you don't want me to see her. After all, I'm an outsider. I don't belong at Fuego del Aire. But if that's the case, let me warn you, I won't be balked!"

"That's the spirit!" His hand clenched into a fist. "Forget all about that which you saw from your bedroom window. It has nothing to do with you." His tone was mocking.

"A bird," I said uncertainly. "That's all it was."

"My friend," he said calmly, "there is no bird as large as the one you saw tonight."

And he reached out for the first time. I felt his chill touch as his long fingers gripped my shoulder with a power that made me wither inside. "Come," he commanded. "Over here at the windowledge."

I stood there, dazed with shock as he let go of me and leaped out into the night.

I screamed, reaching out to save him, thinking that, after all, his apparent melancholy signaled a wish to die. Then I saw his great ebon cape ballooning out like a sail, drawn upward by the cross-currents and, for the first time, I saw what had been hidden beneath its voluminous folds.

I had thought he wore the thing as an affectation, because it was part of the legend. But now I understood. What care had he for legends? He wore the cape for practical reasons.

For now from under it spread a pair of the most extraordinary wings I had ever seen. They were glossy and pitch black, as far away from bat's wings as you could get. For one thing, they were feathered or at least covered in long silky strips that had the appearance of feathers. For another, they were as supple as a humming-bird's and quite as beautiful. And made even more so by the thick, muscular tendons by which they were attached to his back. It was like seeing the most beautifully developed torso: hard muscle tone combined with sleek line. And yet. And yet there was more, in the most literal sense, because more musculature was required in order for those massive wings to support the weight of the rest of the body.

Those wings! Sharply angled and hard, delicate as brushstrokes, they beat at the air like heroic engines. They were a magnificent creation, nothing less than a crowning achievement, an evolutionary pinnacle of the Creator.

But out of the wonder came terror and I thought: Marissa! My God! My God! He means to turn her into this. *El Amor Brujo.*

Without a word, I turned and bolted from the room. Taking the steps three at a time, I returned to the second floor and there found Marissa asleep in her own bed.

My heart beating like a triphammer, I brought a light close to her face. But no. An exhalation hissed from my mouth. There was no change. But still I feared Morodor and what he could do to her.

"Marissa!" I whispered urgently. "Marissa! Wake up!" I shook her but she would not waken. Hurling the light aside, I bent and scooped her up in my arms. Turning, I kicked the door wide and hurried down the stairs. Where I thought to go at that moment remains a mystery to me still. All I know was that I had to get Marissa away from that place.

The way to the disused scullery I knew and this was the route I took. Outside, the wind ruffled my hair but Marissa remained asleep.

I carried her through the field of tiger lilies and the woodbine, down the center aisle of the vast rose garden, to the verge of the labyrinth. Without thinking, I took her inside.

It was dark there. Darker than the night with the high ebon walls, textured like stucco, looming up on every side. I stumbled down the narrow pathways, turning now left or right at random until I knew that I was truly lost. But at least Morodor could not find us and I had with me this place's only key.

Panting, my muscles aching, I knelt on the grass and set Marissa down beside me. I looked around. All I could hear was the faroff whistle of the wind as if diminished by time. Even the booming surf was beyond hearing now.

I sat back and wiped my brow, staring down at that golden face, so innocent in repose, so shockingly beautiful. I could not allow—

Marissa's eyes opened and I helped her to sit up.

"What has happened?"

"I was awakened by a strange sound," I told her. "I saw your brother outside the castle. I thought at first it was a bird but when I went to find out, I saw him."

She looked at me but said nothing.

I gripped her shoulders. I had begun sweating again. "Marissa," I said hoarsely. "He was flying."

Her eyes brightened and she leaned toward me, kissed me hard on the lips. "Then it's happened! The time is here."

"Time," I echoed her stupidly. "Time for what?"

"For the change," she said as if talking to a slow-witted child.

"Yes," I said. "I suspected as much. That's why I've brought you into the labyrinth. We're safe here."

Her brows furrowed. "Safe? Safe from what?"

"From Morodor," I said desperately. "He can't touch you here. Now he cannot change you. You'll stay like this forever. You'll never have to look like him."

For the first time, I saw fright in her eyes. "I don't understand." She shivered. "Didn't he tell you?"

"Tell me what?" I hung on to her. "I ran out of there as soon as I saw him—"

"Oh no!" she cried. "It's all destroyed now. All destroyed!" She put her face in her hands, weeping bitterly.

"Marissa," I said softly, holding her close. "Please don't cry. I can't bear it. I've saved you. Why are you crying?"

She shook me off and stared wide-eyed at me. Even tear-streaked she was exquisitely beautiful. It did not matter that she was filled with pain. No emotion could alter those features. Not even, it seemed, time itself. Only Morodor, her haunted brother.

"He was supposed to tell you. To prepare you," she said between sobs. "Now it has all gone wrong."

"Marissa," I said, stroking her, "don't you know I love you? I've said it and I meant it. Nothing can change that. As soon as we get out of here, we'll—"

"Tell me, how deep is your love for me?" She was abruptly icily calm.

"How deep can any emotion be? I don't think it can be measured."

"Do not be so certain of that," she whispered, "until you've heard me out." She put her hands up before her body, steepling them as if they were a church's spire. "It is not Morodor who will work the change. It is you."

"Me?"

"And it has already begun."

My head was whirling and I put the flat of my hand against the ground as if to balance myself. "What are you saying?"

"The change comes only when we are in love and that love is returned. When we find a mate. The emotion and its reflection releases some chemical catalyst hidden deep inside our DNA helices which has remained dormant until triggered."

Her fingers twined and untwined anxiously. "This is not a . . . state that can be borne alone; it is far too lonely. So this is how it is handled. An imperative of nature."

"No!" I cried. "No no no! What you're telling me is impossible. It's madness!"

"It is life, and life only."

"Your life! Not mine!"

I stood up, stumbled, but I could not escape the gaze of her lambent eyes. I stared at her in mounting horror. "Liar!" I cried. "Where is Morodor's mate if this is true?"

"Away," she said calmly. "Feeding."

"My God!" I whirled away. "My God!" And slammed into the prickly wall of a hedge.

"Can love hold so much terror for you?" she asked. "You have a responsibility. To yourself as well as to me. Isn't that what love is?"

But I could no longer think clearly. I only knew that I must get away from them both. *The change has already begun*, she had said. I do not think that I wanted to see the fruits of that terrible metamorphosis. Not after having known her and loved her like this, all air and sunlight.

Two sides of the coin. Wasn't that what I had said to Morodor? How he must have laughed at that. Yes. Two sides. But of the same coin.

"Don't you see?" I heard her voice but could no longer see her. "You have nothing to fear. It is your destiny—*our* destiny, together."

Howling, I clawed my way from her, staggering, tripping as I ran through the labyrinth. My only coherent thought was to somehow get to the sea and then to hurl myself into its rocking embrace.

To swim. To swim. And if I were lucky I would at last be thrown up onto the soft sand of some beach far, far away.

But the night had come alive with shadows drenched in my own terror. And, like a mirror, they threw up to me the ugly writhing apparitions from the very bottom of my soul, thrusting them rudely into the light for me to view.

And above me the sound of. . . .

Wings.

Even through the horrendous tattoo of the storm I can make out that sound. It's the same sound that reached down into my heavy slumber that night in Fuego del Aire and wrenched me awake. I did not know it then but I know it now.

But I know many things now that I did not then. I have had time to think. To think and to write. Sometimes they are one and the same. Like tonight.

Coming to terms. I have never been able to do that. I have never *wanted* to do that. My writing kept me fluid, moving in and out as the spirit took me. New York today, Capri the next. The world was my oyster.

But what of *me?*

The sound is louder now: that high keening whistle like the wind through the pines. It buzzes through my brain like a downed bottle of vintage champagne. I feel lightheaded but more than that. Light-bodied. Because I know. *I know.*

There is nothing but excitement inside me now. All the fear and the horror I felt in the labyrinth leached away from me. I have had six months to contemplate my destiny. Morodor was right: For each one, it is different. The doorway metamorphoses to suit the nature of the individual.

For me it is love. I denied that when Marissa confronted me with the process of her transmogrificaiton. Such beauty! How could I lose that? I thought. It took me all of this time to understand that it was not her I feared losing but myself. Marissa will always be Marissa.

But what of me? Change is what we fear above all else and I am no different.

Was no different. I have already forgotten the golden creature of Fuego del Aire: she haunts my dreams still but I remember only her inner self. It is somehow like death, this acceptance of life. Perhaps this is where the legends began.

All around me the city sleeps on, safe and secure, wrapped in the arms of the myths of its own creation. Shhh! Don't bother to disturb it. No one would listen anyway.

The beating of the wings is very loud now, drowning out even the heavy pulsing of the rain. It reverberates in my mind like a heart-beat, dimming sight, taste, touch, smell. It dominates me in a way I thought only my writing could.

My shutters are open wide. I am drenched by the rain, buffeted by the chill wind. I am buoyed up by them both. I tremble at the thought. I love. *I love.* Those words a river of silver turning my bones hollow.

And now I lift my head to the place where last night the full moon rode calm and clear, a ghostly idiogram written upon the air, telling me that it is time for me to let go of all I know, to plunge inward toward the center of my heart. Six months have passed and it is time. *I know.* For now the enormous thrumming emanates from that spot. Beat-beat. Beat-beat. Beat-beat.

The heart-sound.

At last. There in the night, I see her face as she comes for me.

philip k.
dick

The Cookie Lady

"Where you going, Bubber?" Ernie Mill shouted from across the street, fixing papers for his route.

"No place," Bubber Surle said.

"You going to see your lady friend?" Ernie laughed and laughed. "What do you go visit that old lady for? Let us in on it!"

Bubber went on. He turned the corner and went down Elm Street. Already, he could see the house, at the end of the street, set back a little on the lot. The front of the house was overgrown with weeds, old dry weeds that rustled and chattered in the wind. The house itself was a little gray box, shabby and unpainted, the porch steps sagging. There was an old weather-beaten rocking chair on the porch with a torn piece of cloth hanging over it.

Bubber went up the walk. As he started up the rickety steps he took a deep breath. He could smell it, the wonderful warm smell, and his mouth began to water. His heart thudding with anticipation, Bubber turned the handle of the bell. The bell grated rustily on the other side of the door. There was silence for a time, then the sounds of someone stirring.

Mrs. Drew opened the door. She was old, very old, a little dried-up old lady, like the weeds that grew along the front of the house. She smiled down at Bubber, holding the door wide for him to come in.

"You're just in time," she said. "Come on inside, Bernard. You're just in time—they're just now ready."

Bubber went to the kitchen door and looked in. He could see them, resting on a big blue plate on top of the stove. Cookies, a plate of warm, fresh cookies right out of the oven. Cookies with nuts and raisins in them.

"How do they look?" Mrs. Drew said. She rustled past him, into the kitchen. "And maybe some cold milk, too. You like cold milk with them." She got the milk pitcher from the window box on the back porch. Then she poured a glass of milk for him and set some of the cookies on a small plate. "Let's go into the living room," she said.

Bubber nodded. Mrs. Drew carried the milk and the cookies in and set them on the arm of the couch. Then she sat down in her own chair, watching Bubber plop himself down by the plate and begin to help himself.

Bubber ate greedily, as usual, intent on the cookies, silent except for chewing sounds. Mrs. Drew waited patiently, until the boy had finished, and his already ample sides bulged that much more. When Bubber was done with the plate he glanced toward the kitchen again, at the rest of the cookies on the stove.

"Wouldn't you like to wait until later for the rest?" Mrs. Drew said.

"All right," Bubber agreed.

"How were they?"

"Fine."

"That's good." She leaned back in her chair. "Well, what did you do in school today? How did it go?"

"All right."

The little old lady watched the boy look restlessly around the room. "Bernard," she said presently, "won't you stay and talk to me for awhile?" He had some books on his lap, some school books. "Why don't you read to me from your books? You know, I don't see too well any more and it's a comfort to me to be read to."

"Can I have the rest of the cookies after?"

"Of course."

Bubber moved over toward her, to the end of the couch. He opened his books, World Geography, Principles of Arithmetic, Hoyte's Speller. "Which do you want?"

She hesitated. "The geography?"

Bubber opened the big blue book at random. PERU. "Peru is bounded on the north by Ecuador and Colombia, on the south by Chile, and on the east by Brazil and Bolivia. Peru is divided into three main sections. These are, first—"

The little old lady watched him read, his fat cheeks wobbling as he read, holding his finger next to the line. She was silent, watching him, studying the boy intently as he read, drinking in each frown of concentration, every motion of his arms and hands. She relaxed, letting herself sink back in her chair. He was very close to her, only a little way off. There was only the table and lamp between them. How nice it was to have him come; he had been coming for over a month, now, ever since the day she had been sitting on her porch and seen him go by and thought to call to him, pointing to the cookies by her rocker.

Why had she done it? She did not know. She had been alone so long that she found herself saying strange things and doing strange things. She saw so few people, only when she went down to the store, or the mailman came with her pension check. Or the garbage men.

The boy's voice droned on. She was comfortable, peaceful and relaxed. The little old lady closed her eyes and folded her hands in her lap. And as she sat, dozing and listening, something began to happen. The little old lady was beginning to change, her gray wrinkles and lines dimming away. As she sat in the chair she was growing younger, the thin fragile body filling out with youth again. The gray hair thickened and darkened, color coming to the wispy strands. Her arms filled, too, the mottled flesh turning a rich hue as it had been once, many years before.

Mrs. Drew breathed deeply, not opening her eyes. She could feel *something* happening; but she did not know just what. *Something* was going on; she could feel it, and it was good. But what it was she did not exactly know. It had happened before, almost every time the boy came and sat by her. Especially of late, since she had moved her chair nearer to the couch. She took a deep breath. How good it felt, the warm fullness, a breath of warmth inside her cold body for the first time in years!

In her chair the little old lady had become a dark-haired matron of perhaps thirty, a woman with full cheeks and plump arms and legs. Her lips were red again, her neck even a little too fleshy, as it had been once in the long forgotten past.

Suddenly the reading stopped. Bubber put down his book and stood up. "I have to go," he said. "Can I take the rest of the cookies with me?"

She blinked, rousing herself. The boy was in the kitchen, filling his pockets with cookies. She nodded, dazed, still under the spell. The boy took the last cookies. He went across the living room to the door. Mrs. Drew stood up. All at once the warmth left her. She looked down at her hands. Wrinkled, thin.

"Oh!" she murmured. Tears blurred her eyes. It was gone, gone again as soon as he moved away. She tottered to the mirror above the mantel and looked at herself. Old faded eyes stared back, eyes deep-set in a withered face. Gone, all gone, as soon as the boy had left her side.

"I'll see you later," Bubber said.

"Please," she whispered. "Please come back again. Will you come back?"

"Sure," Bubber said listlessly. He pushed the door open. "Goodbye." He went down the steps. In a moment she heard his shoes against the sidewalk. He was gone.

*   *

"Bubber, you come in here!" May Surle stood angrily on the porch. "You get in here and sit down at the table."

"All right." Bubber came slowly up on the porch, pushing inside the house.

"What's the matter with you?" She caught his arm. "Where have you been? Are you sick?"

"I'm tired." Bubber rubbed his forehead.

His father came through the living room with the newspapers, in his undershirt. "What's the matter?" he said.

"Look at him," May Surle said. "All worn out. What you been doing, Bubber?"

"He's been visiting that old lady," Ralf Surle said. "Can't you tell? He's always washed out after he's been visiting her. What do you go there for, Bub? What goes on?"

"She gives him cookies," May said. "You know how he is about things to eat. He'd do anything for a plate of cookies."

"Bub," his father said, "listen to me. I don't wan you hanging around that crazy old lady any more. Do you hear me? I don't care how many cookies she gives you. You come home too tired! No more of that. You hear me?"

Bubber looked down at the floor, leaning against the door. His heart beat heavily, labored. "I told her I'd come back," he muttered.

"You can go once more," May said, going into the dining room, "but only once more. Tell her you won't be able to come back again, though. You make sure you tell her nice. Now go upstairs and get washed up."

"After dinner better have him lie down," Ralf said, looking up the stairs, watching Bubber climb slowly, his hand on the banister. He shook his head. "I don't like it," he murmured. "I don't want him going there any more. There's something strange about that old lady."

"Well, it'll be the last time," May said.

Wednesday was warm and sunny. Bubber strode along, his hands in his pockets. He stopped in front of McVane's drug store for a minute, looking speculatively at the comic books. At the soda fountain a woman was drinking a big chocolate soda. The sight of it made Bubber's mouth water. That settled it. He turned and continued on his way, even increasing his pace a little.

A few minutes later he came up on the gray sagging porch and rang the bell. Below him the weeds blew and rustled with the wind. It was almost four o'clock; he could not stay too long. But then, it was the last time anyhow.

The door opened, Mrs. Drew's wrinkled face broke into smiles. "Come in, Bernard. It's good to see you standing there. It made me feel so young again to have you come visit."

He went inside, looking around.

"I'll start the cookies. I didn't know if you were coming." She padded into the kitchen. "I'll get them started right away. You sit down on the couch."

Bubber went over and sat down. He noticed that the table and lamp were gone; the chair was right up next to the couch. He was looking at the chair in perplexity when Mrs. Drew came rustling back into the room.

"They're in the oven. I had the batter all ready. Now." She sat down in the chair with a sigh. "Well, how did it go today? How was school?"

"Fine."

She nodded. How plump he was, the little boy, sitting just a little distance from her, his cheeks red and full! She could touch him, he was so close. Her aged heart thumped. Ah, to be young again. Youth was so much. It was everything. What did the world mean to the old? *When all the world is old, lad. . . .*

"Do you want to read to me, Bernard?" she asked presently.

"I didn't bring any books."

"Oh." She nodded. "Well. I have some books," she said quickly. "I'll get them."

She got up, crossing to the bookcase. As she opened the doors, Bubber said, "Mrs. Drew, my father says I can't come here any more. He says this is the last time. I thought I'd tell you."

She stopped, standing rigid. Everything seemed to leap around her, the room twisting furiously. She took a harsh, frightened breath. "Bernard, you're—you're not coming back?"

"No, my father says not to."

There was silence. The old lady took a book at random and came slowly back to her chair. After a while she passed the book to him, her hands trembling. The boy took it without expression, looking at its cover.

"Please read, Bernard. Please."

"All right." He opened the book. "Where'll I start?"

"Anywhere. Anywhere, Bernard."

He began to read. It was something by Trollope; she only half heard the words. She put her hand to her forehead, the dry skin, brittle and thin, like old paper. She trembled with anguish. The last time?

Bubber read on, slowly, monotonously. Against the window a fly buzzed. Outside the sun began to set, the air turning cool. A few clouds came up, and the wind in the trees rushed furiously.

The old lady sat, close by the boy, closer than ever, hearing him read, the sound of his voice, sensing him close by. Was this really the last time? Terror rose up in her and she pushed it back. The last time! She gazed at him, the boy sitting so close to her. After a time she reached out her thin, dry hand. She took a deep breath. He would never be back. There would be no more times, no more. This was the last time he would sit there.

She touched his arm.

Bubber looked up. "What is it?" he murmured.

"You don't mind if I touch your arm, do you?"

"No, I guess not." He went on reading. The old lady could feel the youngness of him, flowing between her fingers through her arm. A pulsating, vibrating youngness, so close to her. It had never been that close, where she could actually touch it. The feel of life made her dizzy, unsteady.

And presently it began to happen, as before. She closed her eyes, letting it move over her, filling her up, carried into her by the sound of the voice and the feel of the arm. The change, the glow, was coming over her, the warm, rising feeling. She was blooming again, filling with life, swelling into richness, as she had been, once, long ago.

She looked down at her arms. Rounded, they were, and the nails clear. Her hair. Black again, heavy and black against her neck. She touched her cheek. The wrinkles had gone, the skin pliant and soft.

Joy filled her, a growing, bursting joy. She stared around her, at the room. She smiled, feeling her firm teeth and gums, red lips, strong white teeth. Suddenly she got to her feet, her body secure and confident. She turned a little, lithe, quick circle.

Bubber stopped reading. "Are the cookies ready?" he said.

"I'll see." Her voice was alive, deep with a quality that had dried out many years before. Now it was there again, *her* voice, throaty and sensual. She walked quickly to the kitchen and opened the oven. She took out the cookies and put them on top of the stove.

"All ready," she called gaily. "Come and get them."

Bubber came past her, his gaze fastened on the sight of the cookies. He did not even notice the woman by the door.

Mrs. Drew hurried from the kitchen. She went into the bedroom, closing the door after her. Then she turned, gazing into the full-length mirror on the door. Young—she was young again, filled out with the sap of vigorous youth. She took a deep breath, her steady bosom swelling. Her eyes flashed, and she smiled. She spun, her skirts flying. Young and lovely.

And this time it had not gone away.

She opened the door. Bubber had filled his mouth and his pockets. He was standing in the center of the livingroom, his face fat and dull, a dead white.

"What's the matter?" Mrs. Drew said.

"I'm going."

"All right, Bernard. And thanks for coming to read to me." She laid her hand on his shoulder. "Perhaps I'll see you again some time."

"My father—"

"I know." She laughed gaily, opening the door for him. "Good-bye, Bernard. Good-bye."

She watched him go slowly down the steps, one at a time. Then she closed the door and skipped back into the bedroom. She unfastened her dress and stepped out of it, the worn gray fabric suddenly distasteful to her. For a brief second she gazed at her full, rounded body, her hands on her hips.

She laughed with excitement, turning a little, her eyes bright. What a wonderful body, bursting with life. A swelling breast—she touched herself. The flesh was firm. There was so much, so many things to do! She gazed about her, breathing quickly. So many things! She started the water running in the bathtub and then went to tie her hair up.

*   *

The wind blew around him as he trudged home. It was late, the sun had set and the sky overhead was dark and cloudy. The wind that blew and nudged against him was cold, and it penetrated through his clothing, chilling him. The boy felt tired, his head ached, and he stopped every few minutes, rubbing his forehead and resting, his heart laboring. He left Elm Street and went up Pine Street. The wind screeched around him, pushing him from side to side. He shook his head, trying to clear it. How weary he was, how tired his arms and legs were. He felt the wind hammering at him, pushing and plucking at him.

He took a breath and went on, his head down. At the corner he stopped, holding on to a lamppost. The sky was quite dark, the street lights were beginning to come on. At last he went on, walking as best he could.

"Where is that boy?" May Surle said, going out on the porch for the tenth time. Ralf flicked on the light and they stood together. "What an awful wind."

The wind whistled and lashed at the porch. The two of them looked up and down the dark street, but they could see nothing but a few newspapers and trash being blown along.

"Let's go inside," Ralf said. "He sure is going to get a licking when he gets home."

They sat down at the dinner table. Presently May put down her fork. "Listen! Do you hear something?"

Ralf listened.

Outside, against the front door, there was a faint sound, a tapping sound. He stood up. The wind howled outside, blowing the shades in the room upstairs. "I'll go see what it is," he said.

He went to the door and opened it. Something gray, something gray and dry was blowing up against the porch, carried by the wind. He stared at it, but he could not make it out. A bundle of weeds, weeds and rags blown by the wind, perhaps.

The bundle bounced against his legs. He watched it drift past him, against the wall of the house. Then he closed the door again slowly.

"What is it?" May called.

"Just the wind," Ralf Surle said.

nina
kiriki
hoffman

Food Chain

Cissy told me Saturday night that she needed a new mother, so Sunday morning I started the coffeemaker, then woke the others a little before they normally got up. We gathered in Dark House's roomy kitchen.

"What is it this time, Alice?" Francesca said, sprawling at the big round table, her dark eyes heavy lidded and her thick black hair in snarls. I undimmed the overhead light, making it bright enough to read recipes. The kitchen was at the back of the house and didn't get any sunlight until evening. Francesca winced and covered her eyes. She was a chef at the three-star restaurant around the corner from Dark House, and she worked every night except Saturday, when she prowled in search of adventure. Sunday was the worst morning of her week.

Dora got spinach and bacon out of the refrigerator. She always woke up faster than the rest of us, even in summer when she wasn't teaching grade school. She switched on a burner and set a skillet on it. "C'mon," she said, shaking Micki's shoulder. "Wash." She pointed at the spinach by the sink. Micki sat for a moment with her broad shoulders hunched and her eyes closed, probably hoping the job would go away if she ignored it. Then she stood and ambled over to the sink.

Bettina put a full kettle of water on for tea and brought the assortment of things-hot-water-instantly-created to the table so the rest of us could pick through the packets. "What's up?" she said. Her English accent was crisp. Her voice reminded me of BBC radio news. I liked listening to her. "You should be in bed, Alice. It's your morning after."

I did feel tired. I got myself a big glass of orange juice and two chocolate-glazed doughnuts. "We need another mother," I said.

"That's ridiculous," said Zelda. I sipped orange juice and looked at her over the rim of my glass. She had just gotten a new haircut, one quite popular when I was a girl, but in those days crew cuts were only seen on boys. Her blonde stubble glistened as she tilted her head back, the better to stare down her nose at me.

"Coffee?" Gail asked, smothering a yawn with the back of her hand. She was wearing a short silky green nightgown and nothing else. It had taken me some time to accustom myself to her informality. Things were different when I was young. My parents never pranced around the house in next to nothing; if they left their bedroom, they always wore robes, and so had my husband and I when we became parents.

Zelda, Micki, and Dora said yes to coffee. Gail got down four mugs, filled them, and brought them to the table.

"Cissy told me we need another mother," I said.

"Why?" Zelda said. Her blue eyes narrowed as she stared at me. "There's seven of us. That's enough."

I put down my glass. I studied my hands, touched the fingers of the left with the fingers of my right. Skin that had once been smooth, taut with muscle and life, was papery now, pleated. When I pressed it sideways it did not spring back immediately. I felt a monumental tiredness in me. I was always tired the morning after my night with Cissy; we all were. But it had never felt so sapping before; usually it was a pleasant languor, an excuse to linger in bed and eat special foods.

"Oh, Alice," Gail said, putting down her mug and coming around the table to stoop beside me and hug me. Her warmth and her kindness and energy penetrated me as though I were gauze in the path of sunlight, and I lost my frail hold on control. Tears started down my face.

"Alice," Bettina murmured, her voice gentle.

"I'm sorry," I said. Micki came and stroked her big hand down my back, tracing the leaves of elephant clovers there. For a long while, no one else said anything. The only sounds were the sizzle and pop of bacon on the stove, and my breath catching on itself. The fragrance of brewing coffee and frying bacon reminded me of countless breakfasts stretching backward through time, some just the pleasant beginnings to indifferent days, some interrupted by news— Daddy was not coming back from the war (Mother dropped the frypan when she heard, and grease spatters from the bacon burned her legs); my sister Lucy had delivered a boy (a moment of silence, thanks to God); my own precious little daughter Johanna had not survived the night (but that had been a morning smelling of disinfectant and cigarette smoke, in a dingy hospital waiting room, because the doctors did not trust me in the room with my own child, so that I missed her last moments, missed holding her hand until God could take it from me).

I remembered how time had stretched in those moments, how during the bad ones I had thought the pain would never lessen, that I would live in an eternal Now of hurt that tears would not be able to wash away.

But in this Now, I was with those I loved, and no one was dying. Moments moved inexorably from Now to next, and carried me away from my own sorrow. I got myself back under control, patted Gail's head, blotted my tears on a paper napkin, sipped my quiet sobs away with orange juice.

"How long have you been here, Alice?" asked Franceses, wide awake now.

"Thirty-seven years."

Dora set her spinach salad in the center of the table and handed bowls and forks around.

"How old were you when you got here?" Francesca said.

"Twenty-six."

Zelda put her hand over mine. "What happened," she said, "to the other mothers? The ones we replaced?"

"I don't know." The population of Dark House shifted; sometimes people came for a while and left; sometimes there were ten of us and our nights with Cissy were farther between; I knew that others had grown old here, but I could not remember who they had been or where they had gone. I had the feeling that there was only one Cissy, though; despite what the movies and the books said about people like Cissy, what she had wasn't a disease that turned people who came in contact with her into people like her. But then, movies and books were wrong about all sorts of things.

"I'm so afraid of leaving," I said, and hid my eyes behind my hand.

Zelda's hand was warm on mine. Her thumb stroked along the curve formed by my thumb and forefinger. "Is that what happens?" she murmured. "Do people have to leave?"

"I don't know," I said. "My memory is. . . ."

"Cissified," said Micki. She had been at Dark House for seventeen years, and everyone else for less time.

"What?" asked Bettina. She was our newest mother.

"Remember when you decided to come here?" Micki said.

"Of course—I was standing at the fence outside the preschool where Gareth used to go, watching the children, and—no, I didn't know about you or the house then, I just had that overpowering feeling that there was nothing, nothing on Earth left for me to do, that every day would be gray and stars would never shine again. And then. . . ."

"Then," said Zelda, "I woke up. I was lying on a soft bed in a strange room I had never seen before, and little Benjamin was lying next to me. I hugged him and told him never ever to leave me again. And he said he wouldn't. Or at least that I could see him once a week."

Her gaze was fixed on a copper-bottomed pan hanging on the wall, and her voice sounded light and far away, as if she were describing a dream while she was still asleep. "How could that be? At his funeral I touched his face, I had to, because I kept thinking he wasn't really dead, he couldn't be dead, he was only two years old, such a perfect little being, and I would lie awake listening and listening for him to cry again so I could go comfort him. I touched his face and it was cold and stiff and I knew he was gone and Robert hugged me and took me away but even though I knew Benjamin was gone, I still couldn't let go of him and somehow Robert couldn't take it after awhile, and . . . and then I woke up, and there he was, my baby."

I gripped Zelda's hand. After a moment she blinked and looked at me and smiled.

Bettina looked at Micki.

"It's like that for all of us. Cissy can do something to the memories," Micki said. "I know everything I need to know about nursing, and about everyone on staff at the hospital, and I know my brother's phone number—I talk to him every week. I remember my childhood, my marriage, the birth of my child and her every word or act. I even remember her death. And then . . . there's a fuzzy period. I think I went crazy. I really think I must have. I got stuck. I stayed in the house and didn't wash or eat. I was waiting for little Annie to come back. The life was leaking out of me. My husband tried everything to rouse me out of it, but he couldn't.

"Then I woke up," Micki said. She smiled, looking inward. Her big arms curled into a cradle.

"Yes," said Dora. She had dished out salad for everybody and passed it around, but no one was tasting it. "Micki and I have been comparing memories. Cissy can manipulate them, apparently. I don't feel like a different person. I don't feel controlled. I'm here because I want to be. Still, there are some things in my head I can't seem to get to."

An image of my own hands bleeding and hurt flashed through my mind. I remembered. I remembered hammering fists against the beige hospital walls of that waiting room until I left bloody marks. I remembered my own mother trying to catch my wrists and stop me, telling me my behavior was unladylike and undignified, as if I had dropped a spoon at afternoon tea. I remembered the rage rising in me like a great smothering wave.

I blinked and the memory vanished. I was glad it was gone. "I remember Carol and Debbie," said Micki, and as she said the names, pictures of the women came into my head. Carol had been thin and remote, and it seemed to me she came and stayed just a little while and left. Left! I remembered her packing. I remembered touching her hand in farewell, and thinking it felt cold. Debbie had been large, and friendly on the surface, but I had never found myself telling her anything important, not after I told her about the secret party to celebrate Micki's promotion to head nurse of her floor, and Debbie told Micki.

Zelda was prickly and irritable, and Francesca was lazy. There were things about each of the others that annoyed me in small ways, but I felt I could tell them anything and they would not betray me.

Micki said, "Dora and I have been trying to fish up the names of others. Alice . . . "

"I didn't remember until you said them, Micki," I said. "Now I do, and I don't see how that helps. I'm glad they didn't stay."

"The real question is," said Micki, "how did Cissy find us? I can't remember meeting her before waking up in bed with her. If we're going to find another mother—how?"

*   *

Gail cooked Sunday nights. She was the youngest mother in Dark House and had grown up in an age that no longer demanded that its women know how to cook. Francesca had bought her a basic cookbook, and we all helped on occasion. Gail had been in the house four years and no longer lamented the loss of microwaves; Cissy said they disturbed her sleep.

That night she made some kind of Hungarian stew with a lot of spices and chunks of vegetables in a big pot. She had dropped a piece of potato on the burner and the kitchen had that after-an-accident tang in the air. The stew, besides being burnt, was a little strong for me, and I only ate a little, filling up on crusty bakery French bread instead. I was sipping heavily creamed coffee and watching the others (except for Francesca, who worked from four to nine Sunday evenings) struggle to say something nice about the food, or even to finish it, when Cissy came yawning up from the basement.

I didn't know how the others dealt with Cissy's changes. I made two places for her in my mind: Cissy-in-common, a slight, colorless girl of eleven or so, whom no one would have noticed until she smiled—something of her smile was so sweet and sad it burned like raw sugar on the tongue; and Cissy-in-private, whom I called Johanna, and whom the others called by the names of their own departed children. My relationship with Cissy-in-common was very different from my relationship with Cissy-in-private.

"Hi, kiddo," Gail said, waving a fork with a piece of potato on it.

Cissy flapped a hand in front of her face. "Phew! Paprika city!"

"You don't like paprika?" Gail asked, stricken. There were some spices and condiments we had to be careful with. I remembered, suddenly, taking Micki shopping when she first came to Dark House, nixing the garlic powder: "It gets in the milk. Not good for the baby," I had said, and Micki had accepted that without question.

"It's not my favorite," Cissy said. "It's not so bad, though." She smiled.

"So," said Zelda, laying her spoon across an edge of her bowl, "another mother, Cissy? Alice said another mother."

Cissy sat down beside me. She looked breakable. I gripped my left hand in my right. When had it happened? When had I become too old to give her what she needed?

Her small cold hand closed around my wrist and she looked up into my eyes. For a moment I saw my Johanna, her eyes like wet violets, her cheeks pink as sunrise, downy dark hair lying flat on her head no matter how I tried to tease it into curling. A rush of love, hot and red and all embracing, rose in me. I knew that what I lived for, what satisfied me most of anything on this Earth, was to care for this child, this seed of a plant not yet known, this vessel of all potentials;

that the best thing I could ever do was to nurture my little one and take joy in everything she did. I knew this in my mind and in my heart and in that place deep within me that connected me to every mother who had ever lived. My breasts felt warm and full and ready; my eyelids felt too heavy to keep open.

"Alice," Cissy murmured, her small chill hand tugging at mine, pulling my right hand away from my left. "Alice."

I jerked awake again, looked down at her pale, worried face.

"I didn't—" she said. "I didn't mean—"

An arrow of heat touched my left eye and a tear spilled out of it. Sunday wasn't my night. Sunday was Zelda's night. Anyway, Cissy never spent two nights in a row with anyone. Especially not someone who didn't have anything to give her, I thought, looking down at my sagging breasts. Here in Dark House, age had crept up on me while I wasn't watching. It had shocked me when they suggested at the library that it was time for me to retire. I had always felt fine.

I glanced up at Zelda, who for once didn't look supercilious, only sad. Perhaps she had seen love and desire naked on my face in a way that I had never seen it on any of the others'. Today was the first time I had spoken with the others about what Cissy really did for each of us. I had known, the way I had known as a young woman that every woman must menstruate, but I had not let myself know; I had blanked my mind. One night a week I had with Cissy, bright as the sun, and the other nights I went to sleep alone, that was all there was to it.

"Cissy," said Dora after a moment. "We've been trying to remember how we got here, and we can't. We don't know how you recruit mothers."

Cissy patted my hand and then stopped touching me. "Do you need to know?" she asked.

"Alice told us you want somebody new."

"I will find her," said Cissy.

"What happens to those who are too old?" Bettina asked. My mother's voice rose in my memory, telling me that that was an unladylike question, though said in such a lovely tone of voice. One shouldn't speak of such things.

"Do you need to know?" Cissy said.

There was a brief silence. Micki said, "I would like to know. I'm the eldest after Alice. I imagine I'll grow old here in Dark House, as she has. I think Alice might like to know what comes next. I realize you can tell us and then take this memory away from us as you have with other memories. So why not tell us? And what happened to the people who didn't work out?"

Cissy frowned. She stared at the tabletop with furrowed brows.

"Come on, Cissy. What harm could it do?" Micki sounded like a hearty nurse telling you it was time for your shot, but it wouldn't hurt, no matter how often you'd had a hurting shot before.

"I've never told anyone."

"Aw, c'mon, kiddo," said Gail. "Not anybody? In however long you've been at this? Didn't you ever want to?"

"Is what you do so terrible?" Dora asked.

Cissy looked up, meeting each of our gazes in turn. "Everything I do is terrible," she said in a small frozen voice.

"It is not," said Zelda, in the tone one uses to reassure one's child of how special it is, even though it has just made a mistake.

"You do not know what I do," said Cissy, almost whispering, "or what I have done in the past."

I wanted to gather her into my arms and hug her into silence. I wanted to just think about her as the perfect little child who was not old enough to be responsible for its actions, whose only reason for existing was to be loved, and whom I could love in a way that made me a perfect mother. I put my hand on her shoulder. She felt cold, and her shoulder was very small.

Dora said, "We can't know, unless you tell us, Cissy. You can tell us, and then you can untell us, if you like."

Cissy put her hands over her face.

"I don't want to know," I said, surprising myself. "If it hurts you to tell us, I don't want to know."

For a moment no one said anything. Then Cissy's voice came out from between her hands. "The ones who come, the ones who do not stay, I take their memories away and give them a very strong urge to go far away from here and never to speak about it."

"What's so terrible about that?" asked Gail.

Cissy lowered her hands, wove her fingers through each other and gripped hard.

"Those of you who stay," she said, and stopped.

Bettina sipped tea. The click of her cup on her saucer was the only sound.

Cissy spoke to her hands. "You give me what I need. You give, and I take."

"You give us what we need too," Micki said after a long moment.

Cissy shook her head.

Micki cleared her throat, then said, "I would have died."

"No."

Micki, big, solid, practical Micki, said, "I would have died, Cissy."

Cissy closed her eyes and shook her head. "No," she said. "No. You can't even remember that."

"I can. I do. I would have died without you, Cissy. You gave me what I needed."

"I gave you a lie!"

Bettina gasped. Her arms came up, crossed at the wrists, to cover her breasts, as though she had suddenly realized she was nude.

"Sometimes we need lies to survive," Dora said.

Cissy looked up. Her eyes were dark. "I'm a parasite."

"We all live off life, one way or another," said Zelda. "We kill what we eat right away, and you don't."

Cissy licked her lips. Even her tongue was pale. She must, I thought, be very hungry. "Tonight, after I feed," she said, "I will go out and taste the air, searching for a particular flavor of despair. I will follow it to its source, and I will take that source away from everything she has ever known and bring her here."

And I remembered where I had been when I first saw Cissy. Lying in a bed with bars on it, with straps buckled around my wrists and ankles, and all my hair shaved off. Lying in my own urine because the orderly didn't like me; I reminded him of his mother, he had said, and I had screamed. I had still been screaming, off and on, when Cissy called to me through the bars on the window, asking if she could come in. I had screamed yes. And she came and lay on my breast and I had my Johanna back again; and I could let go of my screams.

"You took me away from my despair and gave me back a life," I said.

*　　*　　*

That night I could not sleep. I went down to the kitchen and fixed warm milk with honey, the same potion my mother had brewed for me when I was a little girl and the night seemed full of monsters. I took my mug back up to my room and sat reading in bed, pillows behind me, my wedding ring quilt lapping at my waist. My gaze wandered across the words in my book without fastening on any of them. I stared and stared, trying to drop down into the story the way I usually did, but it was no use.

I put the book away and sat thinking about being a children's librarian, how I had loved to watch the little ones discover words and pictures, as Johanna might have, if she had lived longer, how there were almost always one or two who read deeply and wanted the new and bright and best, how their ever-fresh excitement made my job new and worthwhile, even though there were others who drew on the pages or tore them or lost books. Johanna would never grow older, but other children did; with Cissy in my arms I could dream, a different dream every week, each better than the last, and all of them equally likely to come true.

I no longer had the library, though I went there and did a weekly story hour. The new librarian didn't care for it when I stayed. The children liked me better and came to me with questions.

The library no longer gave me purpose, and Cissy could no longer give me purpose. I didn't think I could stay in Dark House, seeing her every evening but not being able to spend my special time with her. I could not think of anywhere else on Earth to go. The friends of my marriage had dropped away when I went into the mental hospital, and somehow, with so many friends at home, I had not pursued relationships outside of Dark House. My mother was dead, and I had no idea whether my husband was alive.

I was staring beyond the circle of my lamp, trying without success to see the painting across the room (though I had memorized it during the daylight hours, with only a faint illumination it appeared a different picture altogether, more sinister) when the door eased open and Cissy came in, white as any angel and silent as a cloud.

Her cheeks bloomed with the transient health I had once been able to give her; her eyes sparkled. She looked more alive than most of the children I saw in the street. She came to me and climbed up on the bed, sitting nightgowned and barefoot facing me.

"Alice," she said, holding out her hand. I took it and felt the rosy warmth of her fingers.

"What is it?" I said. My throat felt tight.

"I have something to give you," she said. Her words were pregnant with joy and mystery.

My throat closed tighter still. "Cissy, I don't know what to do," I whispered.

"You don't have to know. You don't have to know anything. Close your eyes."

I closed my eyes and felt the tears gathering in my chest and in my throat. Sadness was a swamp; the mire enclosed me and I did not know how to pull free of it.

And then I felt arms come around me, gathering me close into a warm embrace. A breast pillowed my head. I pulled my knees up close to my chest and knew that somehow, someone held me in her lap.

I opened my eyes just a little and the face I saw above mine was not my mother's, but someone's mother, the mother I had always wished I had had. Her smile was gentle, her eyes tender. "You are my special child," she whispered, "the child of all my dreams, and I love you."

She fed me the milk of contentment. There was no longer anything I wanted or could even think of wanting, and so at last I let go of all my desires.

kristine
kathryn
rusch

Victims

i

Her name had shown up twice before, in '68 when Nichols had run for governor of California, and in '72 when he made his unsuccessful bid for the presidency. No one had investigated her. Women's issues were different in those days, and women were not viewed as the voting bloc they are now. Besides, we couldn't make anything on Nichols stick.

We decided to investigate her before we talked with Senator Lurry. The task of interrogating her came to me.

I used Senator Lurry's outer office because it looked properly intimidating—mahogany trim, marble inlay floors. The desks were wide, oak and handmade. A coffeemaker, constantly in use, sat on top of one of the green metal filing cabinets, but the rich scent of French Roast couldn't overlay the mausoleum stench of an ancient building that has stood in humidity for a generation too long.

I arrived a half hour early, then adjusted my tie and peered at my reflection in the shiny glass on top of the secretary's desk. The cowlick had refused to be tamed again. I licked my hand and patted the spot, wishing for the fifteenth time that I could use boyishness to my advantage. From the neck down I was perfect: broad shoulders tapering into narrow hips, legs firm and muscular. My face was the major problem. Oval-shaped with wide eyes and pouty lips, it made me look like a twelve-year-old in his father's body, which was the reason I worked behind the scenes for Senator Lurry instead of out front as most of the Cattons had in the past.

I didn't dare look naive in front of a woman named Veronique.

Especially a woman with a history like hers.

Downstairs a door slammed shut. I jumped. High heels clicked on the marble floor, the sound echoing in the empty building. I had often worked late, but never alone. Near midnight on those evenings, the place had a hum to it that I always associated with an election or a smear campaign. Never with an interview.

She had insisted on the time. "A woman in my profession," she had said, her voice husky through the phone lines, "looks best after dark."

I tugged on my black suit jacket. I wasn't really alone. Morse sat in the senator's office, watching through the fake mirror in case the lady decided to ply her trade on me.

The footsteps grew closer. I rearranged the papers on the desktop, toyed with sitting down, and then decided to remain standing. I still hadn't learned all the tricks to power and intimidation.

The door opened and she slipped in. She was heartbreakingly thin, with perfect legs that tapered from a model's body. She wore spike heels, fishnets, and a leather miniskirt that revealed each curve around her hips. Her black Irish lace blouse set off her porcelain skin. Her lips were dark red, her cheekbones high and her eyes an amazing shade of brown. No wonder she ran the most exclusive escort service in D.C. No man would be able to say no to her.

I stepped from behind the desk, resisting the urge to wipe my hands on my pants legs. I approached her, palm extended. "Reese Catton."

She placed her fingers lightly in mine. Her skin was cool, not cold as I had expected. "Veronique de la Mer."

Her voice was husky and warm. A tingle ran up my spine. Ever since vampires and vampirism had come out of the closet five years ago, the news and the tabloid press had been full of articles on the sensual effect of the predator-victim relationship. It didn't seem to matter that all but a few psychopathic vampires had long ago given up killing human prey—choosing instead to use a handful of willing people to provide blood, much as a blood bank did for a hospital ("the supermarket approach to bloodsucking," the *New York Times* had called it)—the fear, loathing, and sexual tension caused by the human-vampire relationship filled the popular imagination.

Just as she filled mine.

Dry facts weren't giving me control. I took a deep breath and slid into the leather chair behind the desk.

"I hope you understand why we contacted you," I said.

"Oh, yes." Her voice was soft. "It's about Governor Nichols."

She had an edge when she spoke his name, a frisson of anger just beneath the surface. I swallowed, feeling calmer. "I hope you don't mind if I tape this conversation."

"I expected you to," she said, and folded her hands demurely in her lap. I pressed the button underneath the desk, activating the room's taping system, and wondered for a moment if vampires' voices taped. But I knew they did. We had gotten tape on one just a few weeks ago. They didn't reflect or film—but that was because of the silvering in the mirrors, the play of light and shadow.

"I understand," I said, leaning forward and placing my arms on the desk, "that you've never spoken with anyone about Governor Nichols."

She smiled, revealing straight, white teeth. "Oh, I've spoken with people," she said. "Only no one believed me."

I froze. Her last sentence had thrown me. We were planning, with her cooperation, to smear the former governor by linking him to a vampire as her cow. Our preliminary surveys of 150 voters showed that such a thing would work as effectively as gay bashing had in the eighties. "What do you mean?"

"On July 4, 1966, your friend, the former governor of California, raped me." She never took her gaze off mine. She spoke calmly, but the ends to the words were clipped, as if she had to spit them out.

I let out the air I had been holding. She was lying. We couldn't bring this to the media. They would skin her alive. "Why didn't you press charges?"

A half smile, curving those delicate lips into her firm cheekbones. "I tried. It was 1966. I was told that a woman who ran an escort service shouldn't complain when she got famous business."

"Who told you that?"

"The detective in charge," she said. "An unfortunately deceased man named Petrie. His superior officers backed up his prejudice. I haven't spoken of the incident since. I figure it would be even tougher to convince people now that they know I belong to a completely different race."

"Why didn't you go after him?"

Her eyes seemed to tilt downward with an expression of deep sadness, as if she were disappointed in me for asking the question. "Come now, Mr. Catton. What did you expect me to do? Fly into his house on bat wings and rip out his throat?"

"Something like that," I mumbled. My cheeks grew warm. I guess I had expected that. Old fictional images died hard. Studies had shown that vampires lacked the ability to shape-shift and mesmerize, although they did have centuries-long life spans and the appearance of eternal youth.

"Mr. Catton, I have used my political contacts for the better part of two decades to keep the former governor of California out of the presidency. But times are changing, and the country doesn't seem to care what kind of man he is as long as he presents a positive media image. Grandfatherly always seems to work in this country. Well, as you know, any connection with me would ruin Nichols's grandfatherly image." She stood and smoothed her skirt. "The problem you face is that I am unwilling to be linked to that slime romantically or parasitically. We will denounce him as a man capable of extreme violence or you will not have my cooperation."

"Forgive me," I said from my chair, "but I don't think Middle America would care that you got raped."

She took a step backward as if I had slapped her myself. "I suppose you're right," she said. "Middle America would simply figure that a woman like me deserved it."

ii

I was shaking by the time I got home. Alison had gone to bed, leaving a single light on near the fireplace. Embers glowed, light reflecting across the shiny hardwood floor. This place always filled me with a kind of pride—the way the couches framed the oriental rugs, the fresh flowers on the Duncan Phyfe end tables, the lemon-scented neatness of the condo itself. Even though I had been raised a Catton, my mother kept a messy, "lived-in" house in Connecticut that hid my father's wealth. I preferred an immaculate, House Beautiful style.

Except tonight. Tonight I wanted to kick off my shoes, scrunch the rugs, and huddle near the television set. But I pulled off my shoes and hung them on the shoe rack in the closet beside the door, walked stocking-footed across the slippery floor and sat at the dining room table, staring at the fruit basket, perfectly arranged, with bananas on the side, oranges at the base, and apples on top.

Veronique had gotten to me.

I had never been naive, not even when I had come to Washington as a page for Senator Lurry fifteen years ago. Any pretensions I may have had remaining toward Truth, Justice, and the American Way were then bled out of me in George Washington's Poli Sci Department and at Harvard Law. Politics in this country had become the battle of the image. Whoever controlled the media controlled the campaign.

Veronique and her escort service hadn't been necessary in '68 and 72. Nichols had done a good job of destroying his own campaign. Then he disappeared behind the scenes, became a scion of the Republican party, helped Reagan and Bush achieve office, and maintained his own series of perks. The media had forgotten all about the bumbling "youth" candidate who had challenged Nixon in the '72 primaries and saw only the trim, natty grandfather who had helped the Republicans become a power in the eighties. A viceless, happily married man who spoke of family values and allowed Pat Robertson to fund his campaign.

The kind of man Senator Lurry—whose presidential ambitions had died the night of his daughter's suicide in '80—despised. Lurry had vowed to clear the way for the Democratic challenger, whether that might be Clinton, Gore, or a wild card no one had ever heard of. We had demolished Quayle before he even announced, but Nichols was proving to be as Teflon as Reagan had been.

The rape charge wouldn't stand. I had been right. Middle America wouldn't tolerate it. They would bring down the messenger.

I sighed and placed my forehead on my arms. We had contacted Veronique because the call girls had not so inexplicably shut up, the records had disappeared on the reported spousal abuse in the mid-seventies, and the college plagiarism charge hadn't caused a ripple in the polls. An affair with a vampire, we figured, still had taint, even though it was nearly thirty years old.

Although it would be a gamble. If word of the smear got out, Lurry would lose his position as champion of the nontraditional. Vampires, gays, and minorities formed a large percentage of his constituency.

If Lurry got caught, he would, of course, blame his assistants.

He would blame me.

iii

"What'd he do?" Lurry asked. "Force her to bite him at gunpoint?"

He was a big man who barely fit in the desk chair that had been specially designed for him ten years previously. He had long jowls that spoke of too many meals and the red, bulbous nose of a hardcore alcoholic. His voice boomed, even in the small office. It always amazed me that he could tarnish the image of anyone.

I shot a glance at Stuckey, his press secretary. She had a small, heart-shaped face, almond eyes, and café-au-lait skin Her mixed heritage was as much a part of her job as was her way with words.

"She didn't go into the details of the rape," I said.

Stuckey leaned back in her chair, her long, slender fingers playing with the ruby on her left hand. "We would need proof of some kind. Police report, photographs—"

"Photographs are impossible." I picked the lint off my black pin-striped pants leg. "And she said that the police refused to believe her."

"If they were called to the site, someone had to write it up," Stuckey said. "It's probably buried in some back file in a basement somewhere. I'll bet Nichols didn't think to cover his tracks on this one."

"I don't see any reason why he had to. Reese was right. Middle America isn't going to give a damn that some bloodsucking parasite got slapped around thirty years ago."

Stuckey jutted out her narrow chin. Forty years ago, someone might have said the same about her. I hated it when she got that look. "Be careful, Senator," she said. "The Republicans would love to hear you talking like that."

"For God's sake," he said, leaning forward. His exquisitely tailored suit strained at its buttons. "It's the truth."

"There's another truth," Stuckey said. "She has been an influential member of Washington society since the thirties. She contributes to all sorts of charities, and it could be said that her escort business provides a necessary service for this community. There is no overt evidence of prostitution, and any employee who provides sexual services on a regular basis drops off the payroll of the service and appears on the payroll of the client. Would she make an articulate spokesperson, Catton?"

I nodded. Something about Lurry's reaction was bothering me. "She would, except that we can't film her."

"That doesn't matter," Stuckey said. "Neither can they. I say let's see what we've got and then make a decision. We might be able to use the woman after all."

"No," Lurry said. He folded his hands over his chest.

Stuckey raised one eyebrow. She opened her mouth to speak as I put a finger on her arm.

"What's your connection with her, Senator?" I asked.

His expression didn't change, but his gaze seemed to go flat. It was a look I recognized from his press conferences: the Lurry Method of Avoiding the Truth. "She runs an escort service for the Washington elite, Reese. There's no telling what kind of dirt we might inadvertently dig up."

I suppressed a sigh. Lurry had always been a wild man; the wildness had gotten worse since his daughter's death. During my college years, the staff had worked hard at covering his destructive tracks all over this city. I had worked hard when I came on board the second time to hold on to other staff members, particularly the women, who hated his roving hands and not-so-subtle innuendo. The others trusted me, because they knew I was a family man, a man who would never treat others the way Lurry did.

But this was something that had fallen through the cracks.

Stuckey had come to the same conclusion. She hated working for Lurry, hated that the man behind the excellent politic record was a petty tyrant, sexist, and a bigot. "It might be your last chance to get Nichols," she said.

Lurry spun the swivel on his chair so that he looked out the window instead of staring at us. He was silent for a long time. Finally he said, "I don't care. We can't afford the risk. We'll have to find some other way."

"I doubt there is another way," Stuckey said. She left the room. I followed more slowly. As I closed the door, I saw Lurry reach into his liquor cabinet. It was too early to drink, even for him.

iv

Despite Lurry's refusal to pursue the investigation, Stuckey continued. So did I. I was too intrigued to let it go. Maybe after we had the evidence, Lurry would allow us to run to the media. It had happened before.

Stuckey put one of our best detectives on the case, a secret infil-
trator who had no visible connections to us. The detective would
make it look to the police like an investigation of Veronique de la
Mer instead of an investigation of Nichols.

That would keep the information out of the press until we were
ready to put it there ourselves.

Stuckey and I were supposed to meet with the senator after the
detective's report came in, but I had some questions of my own to
answer.

Veronique's escort service had headquarters near the Hill. I
parked a block away, and waited until no one was looking before I
entered the building. The elevator took me to the sixth-floor offices.
As I stepped through the double glass doors, a level of tension left me.

The offices were tasteful. The colors were out-of-date: the muted
grays and pinks of the rnid-eighties, but the garish purples and neon
greens of the early nineties would have looked out of place here.
Flowers in Waterford crystal vases stood on runners that crossed
antique tables. All of the furniture was antique, mixing periods to
great effect: the tables were Early American, the couches late Victo-
rian, the lighting and the crystal were modern. The decor gave the
feel of a place that had been in business for a long, long time. The
carpet absorbed my footfalls, and I was alone in the waiting room.
I assumed that was on purpose. It made the clients feel as if discre-
tion was part of the service.

A woman entered through a sliding glass door. She wore a white
silk dress that flowed around her voluptuous body. Her long black
hair flowed down her back, as untamed as the dress. "Do you have an
appointment, sir?"

Her voice was as well modulated as the rest of her. A shiver ran
down my spine. "No," I said, a little more harshly than I expected.
"I am from Senator Lurry's office. I would like to see Veronique."

The woman nodded once. "Come with me," she said, and without waiting went back through the glass doors.

The hallway was long and narrow and smelled faintly of lilacs.

Closed doors along each side gave this area a forbidding feeling that the front didn't have. Privacy above all else.

How odd. Veronique mastered privacy in her business, yet she was willing to give it all away to bring down Nichols.

She really had to hate him.

The woman opened the double mahogany doors at the end of the hallway, then stepped aside so that I could enter. I stepped into another waiting room, although this one was more flamboyant than the one I had left. The colors were red, black and deep browns, and all of the furniture was late Edwardian: heavy with thick upholstery. The room had a masculine feel, as if it were designed by a man for a woman.

The door closed behind me. I sat on the edge of the couch, feeling sixteen again, and at the interview for my page position. I tugged on the knees of my trousers. They were tight across the groin.

A door opened, and then Veronique was in the room. She wore her hair piled on top of her head, revealing a slender, well-formed neck. This time she wore a suit. The jacket was open, and the shell was cut low across her breasts, revealing cleavage and a bit of nipple. She sat on the edge of her desk and crossed her legs. "I didn't expect to see you here, Mr. Catton."

I swallowed. I was a happily married man. Alison and I had a good sex life. I didn't need anything else. "I'm here on business."

She smiled. "Most people are."

"No," I said. "For Senator Lurry."

"Ah." She got off the desk and retreated behind it, tugging her coat across her chest. "You want to know details. How can a human male rape a woman of superior strength? It's really quite easy, Mr. Catton. It simply takes planning. He must learn where I sleep, for that's when I am most vulnerable, and learn how to tie me up, how to immobilize my mouth. Determination, Mr. Catton—"

"That's not why I'm here," I said. I couldn't stand the calm tone she was using with me. "I've been thinking about this. We're investigating your claim now, but it doesn't completely make sense to me.

Assume that I believe you, what's in this for you? You have other, more subtle ways to bring down Nichols. Why choose a haphazard method that may not work?"

She smiled and leaned back, letting the coat pull open again. The shell was thin, and it stretched across her chest, outlining her breasts in detail. Her nipples were hard points against the material.

I forced myself to look into her eyes.

"You're very smart, Mr. Catton," she said.

I licked my lips. She made me nervous, here, in her lair. "I try to be."

"Then perhaps you will understand that I am tired of being hidden. My people have been out of the closet, to use your quaint phrase, for five years now, and we are still fighting myths and prejudices. We live long lives, and have experiences that encompass entire generations. We understand policy and its ramifications better than you do. But our limitations, Mr. Catton, became obvious once the camera was invented. We cannot run for office. We could not even try until a few years ago."

I tugged again at my pants legs. It was good they couldn't run, good that television cameras couldn't pick them up. With their charisma, they would win, every time. "People are too afraid of you to elect you."

"Yes," she said. "I know. But things change over time. We have seen that with African Americans and with women. We have decided that it is better to fight in an open forum than behind the scenes."

"To put you up against Nichols's media machine is to sacrifice you to the prejudices of the American people. You'll lose."

"Perhaps," she said. "But I'll damage Nichols, and I'll start the awareness that vampires are not the all-evil, all-powerful beings the movies have made them out to be."

I ran a hand along the crushed velvet upholstery. "I don't understand how choosing to become a victim will help you politically."

She shrugged and smiled, just a little. "Then, Mr. Catton, you're not as smart as I thought."

V

I immediately hurried home. Fortunately Alison was there. Much to her surprise, I dragged her to bed, and we made love like newlyweds in their sexual prime. We had just finished when the doorbell rang.

She brushed the hair from her forehead. "You go on," she said, pushing me a little. "I need to shower. I'm already late for a Women in Business meeting."

I slid on a pair of jeans, walked barefoot to the door, and looked through the peephole. Stuckey was there, her face pale beneath the makeup. She clutched a stack of folders to her chest. Her briefcase rested on the floor beside her.

I pulled the door open.

"We need to talk," she said, and came in without an invitation. Her shoes left little prints on the hardwood floor. She set everything on the dining room table, pushing the basket of fruit aside to make room.

I sat down beside her, opened the files, and barely looked up when Alison kissed me good-bye. The files were dusty, the old police reports more detailed than I had expected, as if someone had been planning a case. A client had found Veronique, naked, blood-covered, and half dead in her waiting room. She had been tied with silver wire, a garlic bulb shoved in her mouth, and slashed from groin to sternum with a knife. The reports were filed by four separate officers and a pathologist. Veronique had been conscious enough to demand her private doctor, and instead of being treated by the hospital staff, she had been treated by a man now known as the vampire's equivalent of doctor to the stars.

The files included photos of the crime scene and Veronique's account, both on tape and in writing, of the rape itself. The investigation ended as soon as the nature of Veronique's profession became known.

Stuckey watched me as I read Veronique's account. Nichols had not been alone. Four other politicians of his generation had been there to take care of Veronique properly. Three of the four were dead—one in a single-engine plane crash over the Appalachians, one in an unsolved murder in Mexico, and one of an undiagnosed variety of pernicious anemia which the doctor associated with leukemia but which was now known to be caused by bad reaction to secretions in vampire saliva.

The fourth was alive: Senator Jason Lurry, then a first-term congressman from the great state of Texas.

I brought my head up. Stuckey was watching me, elbow on the table, chin resting on her palm. "She set us up," I said.

Stuckey rolled her eyes. "Veronique is not the problem," she said. "It's Lurry. He lied to us and to his constituents from the beginning. Did you read why he participated?"

I shook my head. I had stopped when I saw his name.

"Because she was withholding favors from them. *Political* favors. She was refusing to use her sexual influence to aid their careers."

I let my breath out slowly. "Raping her was certainly not the way to get her to help."

"No," Stuckey said, "but it sent a message throughout the community. A lot of people knew what she was. They must have figured these men had a lot of muscle behind them to get her as badly as they did."

I rubbed the bridge of my nose. A headache was building behind my eyes. It all made sense now. Lurry and Nichols had ceased being friends in '67. Something must have come between them then, something to do with Veronique. They managed to succeed without her, but not to the heights they had wanted. And whenever they had come close to achieving those heights, something had successfully damaged their careers—like Lurry's daughter's suicide.

"What I don't understand is why she's doing this now," I said. "I talked to her. I said going public would make her a victim, a why would anyone want to be a victim? She laughed at me and called me naive."

Stuckey blinked at me and then grinned. "You're not naïve," she said. "You're just privileged. Reese Catton, son of politicians, product of private schools and Ivy League law schools. Even your name has the sound of wealth."

I squirmed, suddenly cold without my shirt. "What the hell does that mean?"

"It means you're one of the lucky few who've never been victimized." She leaned forward, a flush rising beneath her dusky skin. "Reese, honey, victims are victims when they remain quiet. They gain power when they speak out."

The headache had moved to my temples. "She had power. It looks like she controlled their careers from the inside."

"But that's a revenge cycle," Stuckey said, "and no more empowering than punching a man who mugged you. You need to read more about ways to help the powerless. Look what empathy did for Bobby Kennedy."

"Yeah," I said, standing. "It got him assassinated."

vi

This time we met in neutral territory, at the Lincoln Memorial. I waited on the steps after dark, in the shadow of Honest Abe himself.

Honest Abe, who had suspended civil rights and freed the slaves as a matter of political expediency. Honest Abe, who really wanted to send all the blacks back to Africa.

I heard her before I saw her. Heels clicking against the sidewalk, a purse clutched to her arm. She wasn't wearing hooker clothes or a business suit. This time she wore jeans and a mohair sweater. The outfit suited her more than the others had.

"You set me up," I said, before I could see her face in the streetlight.

"No." She climbed the stairs and sat beside me on the top. She smelled faintly of lilacs. "I have just learned that it is easier to convince people when they discover the information for themselves, you wouldn't have believed me if I attacked your precious senator. You believe me now."

I did that. If nothing else, I believed Veronique's version of those events back in 1966. "What do you want from me?"

"We need a spokesman. You are our best choice. You are young, moving into that youthful handsomeness that this country associates with its romantic leaders. But the problem is you have no dreams, no ideals. We will give those to you." She ran a hand through her hair. There was nothing seductive about her this night. "You see, what your histories have forgotten is that the symbiosis went beyond the physical. Your people provided the energy, the power, and the drive. Ours the sense of community and continuity. Over the centuries, we failed to keep our end. We stagnated, and you rebelled—a rebellion that culminated with the invention of the camera and became codified with the publication of Stoker's horrible political tract. But we have learned our lesson. We would like to forge a new voice in the political history of the Western world. We would like a new alliance, and we need your help."

I leaned back, resting my elbows on the cool concrete stairs. I should have been used to power games; I had initiated enough myself. But I had been off balance in this one from the beginning. "Why me? Why not someone like Stuckey?"

"Because," she said, "you have no personal axes to grind, no commitment to anything except yourself, your lovely wife, and your home. We don't want someone with other ties that might interfere with our cause."

Words were carved into the walls above me. Great words, spoken by a man considered by many to be one of our best leaders. Who knew why he ran for office. Power madness? A belief he could make a difference? Ego? All three or none of the above?

I shook my head. "I'm sorry," I said. "I don't know anything about you people. For all I know, you could be trying to take over the country."

She smiled, her teeth flashing in the streetlights. "Isn't that what every special interest group hopes to do?"

"Not every special interest group has the power of persuasion that you people have."

She touched my hand. Her fingers were cold. "I should make myself clear. I'm not asking you to run for president. I want you to resign as Lurry's aide, then help me make a public case against them."

Her fingers were long and slender, the nails tapered. "Forgive me," I said, keeping my voice soft. "But I was right that first night. Middle America won't care that you were raped."

"Make them care. That would be your job."

I moved my arm out of her grasp. "There are better people for that. Image brokers, people who make their living changing public opinion."

"But none are as unimpeachable as you." She leaned back beside me. "Think of it. You worked for Senator Lurry. You discovered the information yourself. It so appalled you that you are jeopardizing your own political career to speak out against him."

I tilted my head back so that I couldn't see her. Abe's carved legs, spread sightly apart, towered above me. She would do this, with or without me. And she would fail, but the die would be cast. Conversations would start; people would talk; ideas would get aired as they had at the beginning of each intellectual and perceptual revolution.

The balance of power was shifting beneath me. I could cling to the old or leap to the new. Or I could attempt to straddle the middle, and watch the world as I knew it crumble beneath my feet.

I had planned to resign anyway.

I needed a new job.

"Let me bring Stuckey along and I'll do it," I said.

"You may have anyone you want on your team." Veronique stood and wiped off the back of her jeans. "Come to me after you've publicly announced your resignation. We'll finalize our agreement then."

She walked down the steps, heels clicking until the darkness swallowed her. I didn't know how I ever thought she wanted to be a victim. She had more power than all the rest of us combined—the power of her convictions. I envied that. It was something I had never seen in Washington.

Maybe the world was shifting more than I thought.

nancy
holder

Cafe Endless: Spring Rain

It was spring in Yoyogi Park, and not a rain, exactly. Cool mist floated in the air, drawn to the heat of the thousand milling bodies, clinging to all the things that lived: girl groups dressed in black lace and garters, thirty young boys dressed up as James Dean, pompadours and chains and black leather jackets. The perennial hippies in black velvet hats and tie-dyed dusters. Ointen Rose, the most popular Sunday street band in Harajuku, their pride and joy a black bass player who was actually quite good.

It would have been a perfect day to go to the empress's iris garden in the Meiji Shrine complex. If you stood still long enough and stared across the fish pond in a tranquil state, you could see Her Majesty's spirit shimmering in the mist that was not mist but gentle spring rain. But Satoshi's charge for the day was Buchner-san, the American agent for Nippon Kokusai Sangyo, and she had asked to be shown the famous street-dancing kids of Harajuku. She had made the request boldly, knowing it wasn't the polite Japanese thing to do. That was no problem; no one in Ni-Koku-Sangyo expected Buchner-san to act Japanese, and they would never have hired her if she had. She was their American, their contact with the States, and they wanted her as bold and brassy and utterly unsubtle as she was.

"These are great! This is great!" she kept exclaiming as they traversed the closed-off boulevard. As they did each Sunday, the groups had set up as far apart as possible, which was not very far at all; and the din was so great that you couldn't hear the generators that powered their electric guitars. Satoshi had never heard the generators.

The fan clubs of the more popular groups invented gestures and little dances to accompany the songs of their heroes, and as they shouted and pointed and shoo-whopped, Buchner-san shouted in his ear, "It's like *Rocky Horror!* Do you know about *Rocky Horror?"*

"Oh, yes," he said politely. With the arrogance of her countrymen, which he found so charming, she always assumed his ignorance. That there was a fundamental lack in his country. In fact, he had seen the original stage play in London, and had owned a bootleg laser disc before Americans could even purchase laser disc players. "It is very interesting."

"I love Tim Curry." She flashed a smile at him. He was getting tired, but would never let her know. All the English, all her talking and questions. Her energetic curiosity. Not that he was complaining; he was happy to show her this amazing Tokyo phenomenon, and pleased if she enjoyed their Sunday afternoon together. He was Ni-Koku-Sangyo's representative today, and entertaining her was his responsibility. Satoshi was a Japanese man, and fulfilling responsibilities with good effort gave him a sense of pride and accomplishment.

After a while he steered her to the food booths and bought her some doughy snacks of octopus meat and a beer. When she discovered what she was eating, she laughed and said, "I'm eating octopus balls!" and Satoshi laughed back, although other Americans had made the same joke. He didn't mind. He never found their humor offensive or insulting, as some of his colleagues did. Americans to him were like puppies, eager, alert, bounding and fun. Although not to be dismissed as unintelligent or lacking in shrewdness. They were tough businessmen. Business *people.*

"Do you believe in ghosts, Buchner-san?" he asked her after they finished their snack.

"Hmm. Do I believe in ghosts." She looked at him askance. "Why do you ask?"

"If you look across the iris garden at the Meiji Shrine, you can see a ghost."

"If you're Japanese." She grinned at him. "I'm afraid I'm far too earthbound for that, Nagai-san."

"No. Anyone can see it. Because it's there. No special abilities—or genetic traits—are required."

"Then let's go see it."

He inclined his head. "Unfortunately, it is now closed. But you must come back if you have free time before you go. Tell the taxi *Meiji-jingu.*"

"And the subway stop?"

How he admired these American women! "*Meiji-jingu-mae.*"

"Got it." She was writing it down. Abruptly she frowned and looked up. "God, it's raining harder."

Perhaps that was her way of hinting that she would like to go, and not an indirect rebuke that he had not thought to warn her that it might rain, or to bring umbrellas. Or neither; Americans didn't think like that. It might simply be a comment about the weather.

"Shall I take you to Roppongi? The Hard Rock Cafe is there." She had made mention to Satoshi's boss, Iwasawa-san, that she would like to buy a Tokyo Hard Rock Cafe T-shirt for her nephew. Although she was almost forty, she was not married. Iwasawa privately called her "Big Mama." Satoshi thought that was hilarious.

"Oh, the Hard Rock! That'd be great. I want to buy my nephew a souvenir." Obviously she had forgotten she'd told Iwasawa. A Japanese would not have. He—she—would have taken it for granted that the request had been made, and now was about to be fulfilled. And a small notch on the chart of indebtedness was now made in favor of Ni-Koku-Sangyo, to be paid at the proper time.

They walked back down the boulevard, taking one last look at the bands. The rain was falling not harder, but more like gentle rain now than mist. Perhaps the Harajuku kids would have to shut down; all that electricity could not be safe.

He began to hail a cab, but she asked to take the subway 'if it's not too much trouble.' Then she would know how to come back if she had time to 'visit his ghost.' He acquiesced, content to do as she wished, although he was a little disappointed. While with her he was on his expense account, and he far preferred cabs to crowded subways.

He showed her how to walk to the station, pointing out land-marks, and explained how to buy a ticket. In Japan there was no stigma attached to ignorance, only to not trying one's best. They went to the trains and he explained how she could tell she was board-ing the correct one. With a sense of fearless joy she absorbed all he said. He was very sorry she would not meet Tsukinosuke.

But of course, she would have quite happily informed him that she didn't believe in vampires, either.

*   *   *

The ride was not long but it was crowded. He could remember a time years ago when Japanese people stared at Americans and Japan-ese men groped American women on the trains as everyone stood netted together like fish. Now it was Tokyo, London, New York, the three big cities of the world, and such days of primitive behavior were over.

As they ascended the Roppongi station, the rain was falling like strands of spiderwebs catching dew. Satoshi's chest tightened. He took measured steps as they turned the corner past the big coffee-house, Almond, pretending he was scanning for umbrellas. Resourceful Roppongi merchants kept supplies of cheap umbrellas on hand for sudden thundershowers.

People hurried into Almond, jamming the pink-and-white foyer and cramming into booths for hot coffee and pastries. Hordes of young Japanese girls, giggling and beautifully dressed. No other women on earth dressed with as much fashion and taste as Tokyoites. Although Satoshi was almost thirty, he was not married, either. He imagined his reasons were more compelling than Buchner-san's.

As they passed the windows resplendent with bright pink booths, he had to force himself not to look to the right and up to the leaded-glass windows on the third floor of the building. Still, he saw in his mind their exquisite, ancient beauty and his heart began to pound, much as he imagined Buchner-san's heart would if she saw the empress's ghost. The throbbing traveled through his veins and arteries to his groin, a journey often taken in this vicinity.

Ignoring the growing, biting pleasure, Satoshi began to lead his American charge down the main street. Halfway between here and Tokyo Tower was the Hard Rock Cafe. Beers there currently went for eight hundred yen, about eight dollars. That would give her something to talk about back home.

His back was to the windows, but he felt the sudden heat of the spring rain, and he struggled not to turn around.

Buchner-san touched his arm, and he almost shouted. "Wait, Nagai-san, please. What's that place?"

Of course it had drawn her. How could it not? He replied, as evenly as he could, "Oh, that's Cafe Endless."

"Those windows are beautiful!"

As indeed they were, even in the gray light of spring rain: turquoise and emerald and ruby blood; lapis and onyx. There were no designs, no patterns, but one responded to the intention: enticement, seduction, promise.

She said, "I wish I had my camera."

Immediately Satoshi began to scan for instant cameras as well as umbrellas. Buchner-san had no idea he was doing so. She was staring at the windows, unaware that washes of color were shifting over her face. Hypnosis; Satoshi felt only a fleeting pang of jealousy, for he was secure in his love.

And his need.

"Let's go there." She jabbed her finger toward the windows as if he might not know where she meant. "We could get some coffee."

He smiled. If that was what she wanted to do, that was what they would do. "As you wish."

"Oh. That is, if you have time." Now she looked concerned. She checked her watch. Americans were so unbelievably direct, yet they constantly put others in the most awkward of positions. How could he ever admit that yes, he was in a bit of a rush? For now he was beginning to sweat, so close were they to Cafe Endless. The scars on his neck burned; on his chest, burned; on his penis and testicles. Burned up.

"Of course we have plenty of time." He gestured for her to go first, although it made more sense for him to lead the way. She smiled at him, happy puppy, and with his guidance behind her, led the way to the plain gray elevator that opened onto the street.

They got in and he punched the button for the third floor. The doors opened and he shepherded her out, very politely. There was no sign, although it was not a private club.

"Do you think they'll have cappuccino?" she asked over her shoulder. So far they had not been able to find cappuccino for her. He had a feeling they called it something else in Japanese, although he didn't know what. That could have been a cause for embarrassment, but since she was American, it was simply an amusing puzzle for them to solve.

"Perhaps they will," he said. Before he opened the swirling Art Nouveau doors of carved wood flowers and etched pastel glass, he smelled the blood that was for him the essence of Cafe Endless. He breathed in and dreamed of pain, and of *her*.

Cafe Endless.

He had first seen her in the winter, in a *kabuki* play, which was outrageous: even in ultramodern Japan, women did not perform *kabuki*. It was the province of men, men playing men and men playing women and men believing in the women and men believing themselves to be women, so strong was their commitment and talent.

He had ducked into the *kabuki* theater only to get out of a driving winter rain. It was so odd, the streets icy, the sky liquid. It seemed that as soon as the rain hit the earth, it froze. He was loaded with parcels from his shopping expedition: this was the Ginza, the famous shopping district of Tokyo, and he was buying himself a new suit to celebrate his promotion. But he was loaded down, and it was rush hour; so he thought to buy a standing-room-only ticket for one act of *kabuki* until things calmed down.

Inexplicably (to this day), there had been plenty of seats, and he had been able to settle in and relax. The scrim had lifted; the musicians began to play.

Marvel.

She danced of a snow ghost, traveling sadly through a landscape of white. Shimmering white and blue, a figure of distinct and profound loneliness, a creature of tragedy.

And then a bride: moment of joy! Flashing snowflake instant!

And then a heron, a bird of majesty and delicacy. To him, a winged picture of fidelity and forbearance that flew away,

away,

over the snow.

Silence had blanketed the theater, then applause so overwhelming that Satoshi absorbed it as if for himself, and wept. Backstage he tried to find the actor, billed as *Tsukinosuke*. But no one saw *Tsukinosuke* then, nor ever again.

In that winter rain he had stumbled out of the theater, bereft. He was in love with that dancing creature. His new clothes, his promotion, his being were meaningless beside the beauty of that dance. As never before, he understood the vitality of tradition, the dignity of the worship of what had existed before one's own self had come into being. There was no shame in awe; there was exaltation.

The wonder was that *she* believed that, too.

Now, with Buchner-san, he sat at a wrought iron table of leaves and sexual flowers topped with glass. After some discussion the waiter brought Satoshi some absinthe and—voila!—what they called *cafe au lait* in Japan, but in America was *cappuccino*.

"It's like finding the Holy Grail," Satoshi said as the waiter set the cup down before his charge. "I feel that I can die now." Buchner-san laughed long and hard and told him he was a card.

As they sipped their beverages, he couldn't help but look past her toward the doors on the other side of the cafe. She wasn't there; he would feel it if she were. But there was exquisite pain in the longing that made his body tight and hot and breathless.

And then:

Marvel.

As the weak sun began to sink and the windows washed orange, crimson, blood, blood red, the Chinese scarlet of dying birds. Voluptuous and ostentatious, free of restraint, smears and pools of red that transformed the rooms of Cafe Endless into the chambers of a beating heart.

"Oh," Buchner-san murmured, "look." She pointed at a mirror, and for a moment he panicked. Slowly he swiveled his head, and saw his reflection. And he knew in that moment that he did not fully trust *her,* and he was ashamed. Quickly he recovered himself and said nothing, waiting for a cue to reveal what Buchner-san was talking about.

"I look like I'm bleeding." She made a little face. "I look terrible!"

"Never." Satoshi picked up his absinthe and sipped the bitter liqueur. Discreetly he held it in his mouth so that the taste would linger when she kissed him.

"Oh, you're so gallant." She smiled at him and turned her head this way and that. "It's ghoulish."

"No, very lovely. Very *kabuki.*"

She struck a pose, tilting her head and crossing her eyes. *"Banzai!"*

He liked her so very much. For a moment he considered sharing his situation with her, not in the sense of telling her about it but of inviting her to participate. But as she said, she was far too earthbound for that. And he was too selfish.

Then it was dark. "Jesus, we've been here for over an hour!" she said, glancing at her watch. "It seems like we just got here." She drained her cup. "I've got to get going." Satoshi let the last few drops of absinthe slide down his throat and signaled for the check. "No, no, you stay. I'll grab a cab."

"Your Hard Rock T-shirts. It will only take a minute," he said, and then: Marvel. Waves of pleasure, excitement, desire. The blood in his veins warmed, literally; he began to sweat, his organs to warm. Warm, endlessly warm, heat melting away the last snow, the first endless spring rain. His nipples hardened, his penis stiffened and throbbed, his testicles contracted and pulsated with semen.

"I'll have to get them later," she said breathlessly. "I have a dinner tonight."

"Oh, I'm so sorry." It was natural to apologize. He hadn't asked how long she could stay out. His forehead beaded with perspiration and he put his hands in his lap because they were shaking. If he left Cafe Endless now, he would probably fall to his knees in the street, reeling.

He got to his feet. "I'll take you back to your hotel."

"No, no, I'll grab a taxi." She held out a hand. "Don't worry about it, Nagai-san. It's really no problem."

The waiter silently glided over to their glass and metal table. Satoshi signed for the drinks. Moving cautiously, he got to his feet. His mouth was filled with absinthe and the memory of blood. His scars ached and burned. He daubed his forehead with his handkerchief and put it back in his pocket.

"You really don't have to bother," Buchner-san assured him as they went to the elevator. "I'll just grab a cab on the street."

They got to the ground floor. Satoshi felt as if his penis were being pulled through the ceiling of the elevator and back to Cafe Endless, back to the rooms above Cafe Endless. She was there. She was there, and she was waiting, his blue snow goddess.

Buchner-san cried, "Look, there's one!" and waved her hand. Instantly a cab pulled over. Satoshi had been to New York many times, and realized that he would probably never see that loud, raucous place again.

"Thank you so much," Buchner-san told him as she climbed into the cab. Satoshi smiled and told the driver in Japanese exactly where her hotel was. "It's been so nice to see you. I'm really sorry I have to dash off like this."

"Oh, please excuse me," Satoshi replied. His English was beginning to go. "It was nothing." He would order a number of T-shirts from the Hard Rock and have them sent to her hotel. Different sizes and the two choices, white or black. But not too many to overwhelm her. Just enough to impress her and perhaps—if it were possible to so affect this brassy American lady—to make her feel indebted to him and therefore, to Nippon Kokusai Sangyo.

"*Ciao!*" she cried gaily, and the taxi took off, weaving her into the traffic and fabric of Roppongi.

He stumbled, wiping his forehead, and lurched back to the elevator. No one else was inside; he fell against the wall and closed his eyes, his penis fiery, found the buttons and hit the one not for the third floor and Cafe Endless, but for the fourth floor, where she was waiting.

*   *   *

He saw her as he opened the door, as she often appeared to him: *Tsukinosuke, kabuki* master in a *kimono* of ice blue, snowy white and golden herons whose embroidered wings were the long, floor-length sleeves of the fabulous gown. She twirled slowly in a circle, her face chalk white as if with *kabuki* makeup, her eyes black and liquid. Her hair, a long tail of smoke that reached her hips. Her mouth, tiny red flame. In her hands she held two white fans that she moved like heron's wings. The room was Japanese, spare and beautiful and natural, with paper *shoji* walls and straw *tatami* floors. Two pen and ink drawings of irises flanked her as she stood against the black-night window, the curtains pulled back.

"Good evening," he said, locking the door. She regarded him. She rarely spoke. Slowly she waved the fans, as if teasing the flames in his blood to rise.

He pulled off his shoes and clothes and went to her, facing her.

She moved her fans over him. He opened his mouth and she flicked one of the fans shut and held it sideways. He accepted it into his mouth. She pulled from the folds of her *kimono* sleeve white silk sashes, came behind him, and tied one to the ends of the fan, brought it around, tied the other ends behind his head so that he was gagged with the fan. His eyes watered as if from smoke. His body quivered.

A slice across his buttocks. He almost ejaculated.

A slice over the nether part of his testicles. A pearl of semen blossomed on the tip of his penis as he moaned.

The blood, trickling.

Holding his penis, stroking with her frigid hands and long nails, she sliced his neck.

Drinking, drinking as he became a bonfire, taking more, draining more, and more and more as he began to suspect with mounting ecstasy that this was the night, tonight it was the fulfillment, and he groaned louder, fighting not to come.

Too late, almost too late, they fell to the *futon* that, when he touched it, became a field of snow through which tiny iris buds shot. Her long black hair swirled like waves against the moon. She threw open her legs and Satoshi thrust himself into the iciness. From his penis rose steam that was not steam but spring mist.

Oh, he loved her, he loved her; and he filled her as she gave a hoarse growl deep in her chest. And still coming as she came, he reached under the *futon* for the stake and pressed it between her breasts until droplets of blood burbled hot around the tip. Her eyes were wild with pleasure and fear; she threw back her head and convulsed around him. He pushed harder than he ever had before, piercing the skin. She gasped and reached out her hands to stop him.

He captured one of her arms and slipped the black velvet restraint around her white, cold wrist. Pulled on the rope through the hook in the wooden brace of the wall, taking up all the slack until she was stretched, hard. Restrained her other arm. She sobbed once, and he could see the question in her eyes as well: *Tonight?*

He looked past her eyes and into her hair that swirled and moved and made him see ghosts. Then he rose and went to the phone beside the alcove where he prayed to his ancestors. Chrysanthemums, not irises, stood in a black bowl. A scroll of a heron flapped gently against the wall.

He took the gag out of his mouth and called the Hard Rock Cafe and ordered the T-shirts, giving them the number of his Nippon Kokusai Sangyo Enterprises Visa card. Buchner-san's hotel address.

The joy of being Japanese was that each action existed for itself, and fulfillment was possible in infinite, discrete moments. He had been a good representative of Nippon Kokusai Sangyo. He had been a good host. He had been a good man.

He would be a good vampire.

"Satoshi," she whispered, and his heart seized inside him as if she were boiling the blood into a heart attack. Silently he returned to her. She was still bound, and she writhed. Opening her mouth, she beckoned him toward her. He covered her, closing his eyes, bracing himself.

Fire, fire and pain; he felt the blood stripped from his veins and arteries like gunpowder trails. Her white face beneath his as he hardened again and thrust inside her while she sucked and sucked. He wasn't afraid, and he was terrified.

Then it was happening, not as she had ever said it would, because she had never told him what it would be like. But his soul rose into the sky like a vapor and hovered with the stars above Cafe Endless. He had a sense that she was with him; together they soared through the exquisite night sky of Tokyo, lights and clouds and moon and spring rain dropping on umbrellas and upturned faces, the wings of herons.

On the roof garden of the New Otani Hotel, where Buchner-san lay.

In through her window. She stirred and moaned. Soft from a bath, and fragrant, and searing to his touch. She slept naked. Satoshi glided over her burning breasts and parted her burning legs. She protested mildly, asleep or enthralled; he bent over her. He was very, very cold and she was hot enough to melt metal. Where he touched her, steam rose. And smoke.

Then the vapor that was *she* guided him to Buchner-san's neck. Tears slid down his face and became sparkling icicles. He bent, and drank.

Ecstasy! Lava into his freezing loins, his penis, his heart. Warm candle wax, boiling *miso* soup. A bath among steaming rocks and bubbling hot springs. And pleasure of the most sensuous nature, hard and soft, pliant and conquering. It would be his last gift to Buchner-san, whom he admired greatly.

And *she* with him, taking also, then sharing with him, her hands on his body, inside his body.

Ecstasy! Beyond all imagining; the fulfillment of the dance she had promised short months before, indescribable wonder that set him to weeping.

And then:

On top of her body, on the *futon,* as she pulled her teeth from his neck and swallowed the last pearly drops. His eyes barely able to open. He whispered, "Was it just a dream?"

Her black eyes answered. "Wasn't it all just a dream?" And Satoshi was sorrowful for everything left behind, for this discrete, infinite moment that he would lose and for all the other moments that had been his life.

They regarded one another.

She whispered, in her real voice, "It will be soon. Hold me very tightly."

He did, arms around hers, legs around hers. He fought to keep his eyes open. Hers were drooping as well. He had thought they would be aware together.

Moments passed. As he drowsed, he listened to the rain.

Then he felt the heat on his shoulder first. He gasped and his eyes popped open. Beneath him, she took a sharp breath and tensed, and looked at him.

"I'm not afraid," he whispered. And truly as never before, he understood the vitality of tradition, the dignity of the worship of what had existed before one's own self had come into being. There was no shame in awe, there was exaltation.

"Nor I," she said. "Nor am I afraid."

Then at once he ignited. Flames and smoke; he heard the choked cry in his throat but then had no throat to express it. Hair, skin, bone, but no blood as the weak sun began to rise and the window washed orange, crimson, blood, blood red, the Chinese scarlet of dying birds. Forgiving and enduring, free of restraint, crackles and washes of red that transformed the rooms above Cafe Endless into the chambers of a burning, stilling heart.

And then, as she caught fire as well, a moment of joy! Flashing snowflake instant!

Writhing, they danced of ghosts traveling gloriously through a landscape of white. *Kabuki* masters, transcendent beings shimmering white and blue, figures of distinct and profound companionship, creatures of triumph.

And then, two simple herons, birds of majesty and delicacy. A winged picture of fidelity and forbearance that flew away,

away,

into the spring rain that was not rain exactly, but tears of exquisite emotion,

to the empress's iris garden, where the ghosts of other herons lived.

tanith
lee

Bite-Me-Not,
or Fleur de Fur

i

In the tradition of young girls and windows, the young girl looks out
of this one. It is difficult to see anything. The panes of the window
are heavily leaded, and secured by a lattice of iron. The stained glass
of lizard-green and storm-purple is several inches thick. There is no
red glass in the window. The colour red is forbidden in the castle.
Even the sun, behind the glass, is a storm sun, a green-lizard sun.

The young girl wishes she had a gown of palest pastel rose—the
nearest affinity to red, which is never allowed. Already she has long
dark beautiful eyes, a long white neck. Her long dark hair is however
hidden in a dusty scarf, and she wears rags. She is a scullery maid.
As she scours dishes and mops stone floors, she imagines she is a
princess floating through the upper corridors, gliding to the dais in
the Duke's hall. The Cursed Duke. She is sorry for him. If he had
been her father, she would have sympathised and consoled him. His
own daughter is dead, as his wife is dead, but these things, being to
do with the cursing, are never spoken of. Except, sometimes,
obliquely.

"*Rohise!*" dim voices cry now, full of dim scolding soon to be
actualized.

The scullery maid turns from the window and runs to have her ears boxed and a broom thrust into her hands.

Meanwhile, the Cursed Duke is prowling his chamber, high in the East Turret carved with swans and gargoyles. The room is lined with books, swords, lutes, scrolls, and has two eerie portraits, the larger of which represents his wife, and the smaller his daughter. Both ladies look much the same with their pale egg-shaped faces, polished eyes, clasped hands. They do not really look like his wife or daughter, nor really remind him of them.

There are no windows at all in the turret, they were long ago bricked up and covered with hangings. Candles burn steadily. It is always night in the turret. Save, of course, by night there are particular *sounds* all about it, to which the Duke is accustomed, but which he does not care for. By night, like most of his court, the Cursed Duke closes his ears with softened tallow. However, if he sleeps, he dreams, and hears in the dream the beating of wings. . . . Often, the court holds loud revel all night long.

The Duke does not know Rohise the scullery maid has been thinking of him. Perhaps he does not even know that a scullery maid is capable of thinking at all.

Soon the Duke descends from the turret and goes down, by various stairs and curving passages, into a large, walled garden on the east side of the castle.

It is a very pretty garden, mannered and manicured, which the gardeners keep in perfect order. Over the tops of the high, high walls, where delicate blooms bell the vines, it is just possible to glimpse the tips of sun-baked mountains. But by day the mountains are blue and spiritual to look at, and seem scarcely real. They might only be inked on the sky.

A portion of the Duke's court is wandering about in the garden, playing games or musical instruments, or admiring painted sculptures, or the flora, none of which is red. But the Cursed Duke's court seems vitiated this noon. Nights of revel take their toll.

As the Duke passes down the garden, his courtiers acknowledge him deferentially. He sees them, old and young alike, all doomed as he is, and the weight of his burden increases.

At the farthest, most eastern end of the garden, there is another garden, sunken and rather curious, beyond a wall with an iron door. Only the Duke possesses the key to this door. Now he unlocks it and goes through. His courtiers laugh and play and pretend not to see. He shuts the door behind him.

The sunken garden, which no gardener ever tends, is maintained by other, spontaneous, means. It is small and square, lacking the hedges and the paths of the other, the sundials and statues and little pools. All the sunken garden contains is a broad paved border, and at its centre a small plot of humid earth. Growing in the earth is a slender bush with slender velvet leaves.

The Duke stands and looks at the bush only a short while.

He visits it every day. He has visited it every day for years. He is waiting for the bush to flower. Everyone is waiting for this. Even Rohise, the scullery maid, is waiting, though she does not, being only sixteen, born in the castle and uneducated, properly understand why.

The light in the little garden is dull and strange, for the whole of it is roofed over by a dome of thick smoky glass. It makes the atmosphere somewhat depressing, although the bush itself gives off a pleasant smell, rather resembling vanilla.

Something is cut into the stone rim of the earth-plot where the bush grows. The Duke reads it for perhaps the thousandth time. O, *fleur dc feu*—

When the Duke returns from the little garden into the large garden, locking the door behind him, no one seems truly to notice. But their obeisances now are circumspect.

One day, he will perhaps emerge from the sunken garden leaving the door wide, crying out in a great voice. But not yet. Not today.

The ladies bend to the bright fish in the pools, the knights pluck for them blossoms, challenge each other to combat at chess, or wrestling, discuss the menagerie lions; the minstrels sing of unrequited love. The pleasure garden is full of one long and weary sigh.

"Oh flurda fur

"Pourma souffrance—"

Sings Rohise as she scrubs the flags of the pantry floor.

"Ned ormey par,

"May say day mwar—"

"What are you singing, you slut?" someone shouts, and kicks over her bucket.

Rohise does not weep. She tidies her bucket and soaks up the spilled water with her cloths. She does not know what the song, because of which she seems, apparently, to have been chastised, means. She does not understand the words that somehow, somewhere—perhaps from her own dead mother—she learned by rote.

In the hour before sunset, the Duke's hall is lit by flambeaux. In the high windows, the casements of oil-blue and lavender glass and glass like storms and lizards, are fastened tight. The huge window by the dais was long ago obliterated, shut up, and a tapestry hung of gold and silver tissue with all the rubies pulled out and emeralds substituted. It describes the subjugation of a fearsome unicorn by a maiden, and huntsmen.

The court drifts in with its clothes of rainbow from which only the colour red is missing.

Music for dancing plays. The lean pale dogs pace about, alert for tidbits as dish on dish comes in. Roast birds in all their plumage glitter and die a second time under the eager knives. Pastry castles fall. Pink and amber fruits, and green fruits and black, glow beside the goblets of fine yellow wine.

The Cursed Duke eats with care and attention, not with enjoyment. Only the very young of the castle still eat in that way, and there are not so many of those.

The murky sun slides through the stained glass. The musicians strike up more wildly. The dances become boisterous. Once the day goes out, the hall will ring to *chanson*, to drum and viol and pipe. The dogs will bark, no language will be uttered except in a bellow. The lions will roar from the menagerie. On some nights the cannons are set off from the battlements, which are now all of them roofed in, fired out through narrow mouths just wide enough to accommodate them, the charge crashing away in thunder down the darkness.

By the time the moon comes up and the castle rocks to its own cacophony, exhausted Rohise has fallen fast asleep in her cupboard bed in the attic. For years, from sunset to rise, nothing has woken her. Once, as a child, when she had been especially badly beaten, the pain woke her and she heard a strange silken scratching, somewhere over her head. But she thought it a rat, or a bird. Yes, a bird, for later it seemed to her there were also wings. . . . But she forgot all this half a decade ago. Now she sleeps deeply and dreams of being a princess, forgetting, too, how the Duke's daughter died. Such a terrible death, it is better to forget.

"The sun shall not smite thee by day, neither the moon by night," intones the priest, eyes rolling, his voice like a bell behind the Duke's shoulder.

"Ne moi mords pas," whispers Rohise in her deep sleep. "Ne mwar mor par, ne par mor mwar. . . ."

And under its impenetrable dome, the slender bush has closed its fur leaves also to sleep. O flower of fire, oh fleur de fur. Its blooms, though it has not bloomed yet, bear the ancient name *Nona Mordica*. In light parlance they call it Bite-Me-Not. There is a reason for that.

ii

He is the Prince of a proud and savage people. The pride they acknowledge, perhaps they do not consider themselves to be savages, or at least believe that savagery is the proper order of things.

Feroluce, that is his name. It is one of the customary names his kind give their lords. It has connotations with diabolic royalty and, too, with a royal flower of long petals curved like scimitars. Also the name might be the partial anagram of another name. The bearer of that name was also winged.

For Feroluce and his people are winged beings. They are more like a nest of dark eagles than anything, mounted high among the rocky pilasters and pinnacles of the mountain. Cruel and magnificent, like eagles, the sombre sentries motionless as statuary on the ledge-edges, their sable wings folded about them.

They are very alike in appearance (less a race or tribe, more a flock, an unkindness of ravens). Feroluce also, black-winged, black-haired, aquiline of feature, standing on the brink of star-dashed space, his eyes burning through the night like all the eyes along the rocks, depthless red as claret.

They have their own traditions of art and science. They do not make or read books, fashion garments, discuss God or metaphysics or men. Their cries are mostly wordless and always mysterious, flung out like ribbons over the air as they wheel and swoop and hang in wicked cruciform, between the peaks. But they sing, long hours, for whole nights at a time, music that has a language only they know. All their wisdom and theosophy, and all their grasp of beauty, truth, or love, is in the singing.

They look unloving enough, and so they are. Pitiless fallen angels. A travelling people, they roam after sustenance. Their sustenance is blood. Finding a castle, they accepted it, every bastion and wall, as their prey. They have preyed on it and tried to prey on it for years.

In the beginning, their calls, their songs, could lure victims to the feast. In this way, the tribe or unkindness of Feroluce took the Duke's wife, somnambulist, from a midnight balcony. But the Duke's daughter, the first victim, they found seventeen years ago, benighted on the mountainside. Her escort and herself they left to the sunrise, marble figures, the life drunk away.

*   *
*

Now the castle is shut, bolted and barred. They are even more attracted by its recalcitrance (a woman who says "No"). They do not intend to go away until the castle falls to them.

By night, they fly like huge black moths round and round the carved turrets, the dull-lit leaded windows, their wings invoking a cloudy tindery wind, pushing thunder against thundery glass.

They sense they are attributed to some sin, reckoned a punishing curse, a penance, and this amuses them at the level whereon they understand it.

They also sense something of the flower, the *Nona Mordica*. Vampires have their own legends.

But tonight Feroluce launches himself into the air, speeds down the sky on the black sails of his wings, calling, a call like laughter or derision. This morning, in the 'tween-time before the light began and the sun-to-be drove him away to his shadowed eyrie in the mountain-guts, he saw a chink in the armour of the beloved refusing-woman-prey. A window, high in an old neglected tower, a window with a small eyelet which was cracked.

Feroluce soon reaches the eyelet and breathes on it, as if he would melt it. (His breath is sweet. Vampires do not eat raw flesh, only blood, which is a perfect food and digests perfectly, while their teeth are sound of necessity.) The way the glass mists at breath intrigues Feroluce. But presently he taps at the cranky pane, taps, then claws. A piece breaks away, and now he sees how it should be done.

Over the rims and upthrusts of the castle, which is only really another mountain with caves to Feroluce, the rumble of the Duke's revel drones on.

Feroluce pays no heed. He does not need to reason, he merely knows, *that* noise masks *this*—as he smashes in the window. Its panes were all faulted and the lattice rusty. It is, of course, more than that. The magic of Purpose has protected the castle, and, as in all balances, there must be, or come to be, some balancing contradiction, some flaw. . . .

The people of Feroluce do not notice what he is at. In a way, the dance with their prey has debased to a ritual. They have lived almost two decades on the blood of local mountain beasts, and bird-creatures like themselves brought down on the wing. Patience is not, with them, a virtue. It is a sort of foreplay, and can go on, in pleasure, a long, long while.

Feroluce intrudes himself through the slender window. Muscularly slender himself, and agile, it is no feat. But the wings catch, are a trouble. They follow him because they must, like two separate entities. They have been cut a little on the glass, and bleed.

He stands in a stony small room, shaking bloody feathers from him, snarling, but without sound.

Then he finds the stairway and goes down.

There are dusty landings and neglected chambers. They have no smell of life. But then there comes to be a smell. It is the scent of a nest, a colony of things, wild creatures, in constant proximity. He recognises it. The light of his crimson eyes precedes him, deciphering blackness. And then other eyes, amber, green, and gold, spring out like stars all across his path.

Somewhere an old torch is burning out. To the human eye, only mounds and glows would be visible, but to Feroluce, the Prince of the vampires, all is suddenly revealed. There is a great stone area, barred with bronze and iron, and things stride and growl behind the bars, or chatter and flee, or only stare. And there, without bars, though bound by ropes of brass to rings of brass, three brazen beasts.

Feroluce, on the steps of the menagerie, looks into the gaze of the Duke's lions. Feroluce smiles, and the lions roar. One is the king, its mane like war-plumes. Feroluce recognises the king and the king's right to challenge, for this is the lions' domain, their territory.

Feroluce comes down the stair and meets the lion as it leaps the length of its chain. To Feroluce, the chain means nothing, and since he has come close enough, very little either to the lion.

To the vampire Prince the fight is wonderful, exhilarating and meaningful, intellectual even, for it is coloured by nuance, yet powerful as sex.

He holds fast with his talons, his strong limbs wrapping the beast which is almost stronger than he, just as its limbs wrap him in turn. He sinks his teeth in the lion's shoulder, and in fierce rage and bliss begins to draw out the nourishment. The lion kicks and claws at him in turn. Feroluce feels the gouges like fire along his shoulders, thighs, and hugs the lion more nearly as he throttles and drinks from it, loving it, jealous of it, killing it. Gradually the mighty feline body relaxes, still clinging to him, its cat teeth bedded in one beautiful swanlike wing, forgotten by both.

In a welter of feathers, stripped skin, spilled blood, the lion and the angel lie in embrace on the menagerie floor. The lion lifts its head, kisses the assassin, shudders, lets go.

Feroluce glides out from under the magnificent deadweight of the cat. He stands. And pain assaults him. His lover has severely wounded him.

Across the menagerie floor, the two lionesses are crouched. Beyond them, a man stands gaping in simple terror, behind the guttering torch. He had come to feed the beasts, and seen another feeding, and now is paralysed. He is deaf, the menagerie-keeper, previously an advantage saving him the horror of nocturnal vampire noises.

Feroluce starts towards the human animal swifter than a serpent, and checks. Agony envelops Feroluce and the stone room spins. Involuntarily, confused, he spreads his wings for flight, there in the confined chamber. But only one wing will open. The other, damaged and partly broken, hangs like a snapped fan. Feroluce cries out, a beautiful singing note of despair and anger. He drops fainting at the menagerie-keeper's feet.

The man does not wait for more. He runs away through the castle, screaming invective and prayer, and reaches the Duke's hall and makes the whole hall listen.

All this while, Feroluce lies in the ocean of almost-death that is sleep or swoon, while the smaller beasts in the cages discuss him, or seem to.

And when he is raised, Feroluce does not wake. Only the great drooping bloody wings quiver and are still. Those who carry him are more than ever revolted and frightened, for they have seldom seen blood. Even the food for the menagerie is cooked almost black. Two years ago, a gardener slashed his palm on a thorn. He was banished from the court for a week.

But Feroluce, the centre of so much attention, does not rouse. Not until the dregs of the night are stealing out through the walls. Then some nervous instinct invests him. The sun is coming and this is an open place, he struggles through unconsciousness and hurt, through the deepest most bladed waters, to awareness.

And finds himself in a huge bronze cage, the cage of some animal appropriated for the occasion. Bars, bars all about him, and not to be got rid of, for he reaches to tear them away and cannot. Beyond the bars, the Duke's hall, which is only a pointless cold glitter to him in the maze of pain and dying lights. Not an open place, in fact, but too open for his kind. Through the window-spaces of thick glass, muddy sunglare must come in. To Feroluce it will be like swords, acids, and burning fire—

Far off he hears wings beat and voices soaring. His people search for him, call and wheel and find nothing.

Feroluce cries out, a gravel shriek now, and the persons in the hall rush back from him, calling on God. But Feroluce does not see. He has tried to answer his own. Now he sinks down again under the coverlet of his broken wings, and the wine-red stars of his eyes go out.

iii

And the Angel of Death," the priest intones, "shall surely pass over, but yet like the shadow, not substance—"

The smashed window in the old turret above the menagerie tower has been sealed with mortar and brick. It is a terrible thing that it was for so long overlooked. A miracle that only one of the creatures found and entered by it. God, the Protector, guarded the Cursed Duke and his court. And the magic that surrounds the castle, that too held fast. For from the possibility of a disaster was born a bloom of great value: now one of the monsters is in their possession. A prize beyond price.

Caged and helpless, the fiend is at their mercy. It is also weak from its battle with the noble lion, which gave its life for the castle's safety (and will be buried with honour in an ornamented grave at the foot of the Ducal family tomb). Just before the dawn came, the Duke's advisers advised him, and the bronze cage was wheeled away into the darkest area of the hall, close by the dais where once the huge window was but is no more. A barricade of great screens was brought, and set around the cage, and the top of it covered. No sunlight now can drip into the prison to harm the specimen. Only the Duke's ladies and gentlemen steal in around the screens and see, by the light of a candle-branch, the demon still lying in its trance of pain and bloodless. The Duke's alchemist sits on a stool nearby, dictating many notes to a nervous apprentice. The alchemist, and the apothecary for that matter, are convinced the vampire, having drunk the lion almost dry, will recover from its wounds. Even the wings will mend.

The Duke's court painter also came. He was ashamed presently, and went away. The beauty of the demon affected him, making him wish to paint it, not as something wonderfully disgusting, but as a kind of superlative man, vital and innocent, or as Lucifer himself, stricken in the sorrow of his colossal Fall. And all that has caused the painter to pity the fallen one, mere artisan that the painter is, so he slunk away. He knows, since the alchemist and the apothecary told him, what is to be done.

Of course much of the castle knows. Though scarcely anyone has slept or sought sleep, the whole place rings with excitement and vivacity. The Duke has decreed, too, that everyone who wishes shall be a witness. So he is having a progress through the castle, seeking every nook and cranny, while, let it be said, his architect takes the opportunity to check no other window-pane has cracked.

From room to room the Duke and his entourage pass, through corridors, along stairs, through dusty attics and musty storerooms he has never seen, or if seen has forgotten. Here and there some retainer is come on. Some elderly women are discovered spinning like spiders up under the eaves, half-blind and complacent. They curtsy to the Duke from a vague recollection of old habit. The Duke tells them the good news, or rather, his messenger, walking before, announces it. The ancient women sigh and whisper, are left, probably forget. Then again, in a narrow courtyard, a simple boy, who looks after a dovecote, is magnificently told. He has a fit from alarm, grasping nothing, and the doves who love and understand him (by not trying to) fly down and cover him with their soft wings as the Duke goes away. The boy comes to under the doves as if in a heap of warm snow, comforted.

It is on one of the dark staircases above the kitchen that the gleaming entourage sweeps round a bend and comes on Rohise the scullery maid, scrubbing. In these days, when there are so few children and young servants, labour is scarce, and the scullerers are not confined to the scullery.

Rohise stands up, pale with shock, and for a wild instant thinks that, for some heinous crime she has committed in ignorance, the Duke has come in person to behead her.

"Hear then, by the Duke's will," cries the messenger. "One of Satan's night-demons, which do torment us, has been captured and lies penned in the Duke's hall. At sunrise tomorrow, this thing will be taken to that sacred spot where grows the bush of the Flower of the Fire, and here its foul blood shall be shed. Who then can doubt the bush will blossom, and save us all, by the Grace of God."

"And the Angel of Death," intones the priest, on no account to be omitted, "shall surely—"

"Wait," says the Duke. He is as white as Rohise. "Who is this?" he asks. "Is it a ghost?"

The court stare at Rohise, who nearly sinks in dread, her scrubbing rag in her hand.

Gradually, despite the rag, the rags, the rough hands, the court too begins to see.

"Why, it is a marvel."

The Duke moves forward. He looks down at Rohise and starts to cry. Rohise thinks he weeps in compassion at the awful sentence he is here to visit on her, and drops back on her knees.

"No, no," says the Duke tenderly. "Get up. Rise. You are so like my child, my daughter—"

Then Rohise, who knows few prayers, begins in panic to sing her little song as an orison:

"Oh fleur de feu
"Pour ma souffrance—"

"Ah!" says the Duke. "Where did you learn that song?"

"From my mother," says Rohise. And, all instinct now, she sings again:

"O flurda fur,
"Pourma souffrance
"Ned ormey par
"May say day mwar—"

It is the song of the fire-flower bush, the *Nona Mordica*, called Bite-Me-Not. It begins, and continues: *O flower of fire, For my misery's sake, Do not sleep but aid me; wake!* The Duke's daughter sang it very often. In those days the shrub was not needed, being just a rarity of the castle. Invoked as an amulet, on a mountain road, the rhyme itself had besides proved useless.

The Duke takes the dirty scarf from Rohise's hair. She is very, very like his lost daughter, the same pale smooth oval face, the long white neck and long dark polished eyes, and the long dark hair. (Or is it that she is very, very like the painting?)

The Duke gives instructions, and Rohise is borne away.

In a beautiful chamber, the door of which has for seventeen years been locked, Rohise is bathed and her hair is washed. Oils and scents are rubbed into her skin. She is dressed in a gown of palest most pastel rose, with a girdle sewn with pearls. Her hair is combed, and on it is set a chaplet of stars and little golden leaves. "Oh, your poor hands," say the maids, as they trim her nails. Rohise has realised she is not to be executed. She has realised the Duke has seen her and wants to love her like his dead daughter. Slowly, an uneasy stir of something, not quite happiness, moves through Rohise. Now she will wear her pink gown, now she will sympathise with and console the Duke. Her daze lifts suddenly.

The dream has come true. She dreamed of it so often it seems quite normal. The scullery was the thing which never seemed real.

She glides down through the castle, and the ladies are astonished by her grace. The carriage of her head under the starry coronet is exquisite. Her voice is quiet and clear and musical, and the foreign tone of her mother, long unremembered, is quite gone from it. Only the roughened hands give her away, but smoothed by unguents, soon they will be soft and white.

"Can it be she is truly the princess returned to flesh?"

"Her life was taken so early—yes, as they believe in the Spice-Lands, by some holy dispensation, she might return."

"She would be about the age to have been conceived the very night the Duke's daughter d—That is, the very night the bane began—"

Theosophical discussion ensues. Songs are composed.

Rohise sits for a while with her adoptive father in the East Turret, and he tells her about the books and swords and lutes and scrolls, but not about the two portraits. Then they walk out together, in the lovely garden in the sunlight. They sit under a peach tree, and discuss many things, or the Duke discusses them. That Rohise is ignorant and uneducated does not matter at this point. She can always be trained. She has the basic requirements: docility, sweetness. There are many royal maidens in many places who know as little as she.

The Duke falls asleep under the peach tree. Rohise listens to the love-songs her own (her very own) courtiers bring her.

When the monster in the cage is mentioned, she nods as if she knows what they mean. She supposes it is something hideous, a scaring treat to be shown at dinnertime, when the sun has gone down.

When the sun moves towards the western line of mountains just visible over the high walls, the court streams into the castle and all the doors are bolted and barred. There is an eagerness tonight in the concourse.

As the light dies out behind the coloured windows that have no red in them, covers and screens are dragged away from a bronze cage. It is wheeled out into the centre of the great hall.

Cannons begin almost at once to blast and bang from the roof-holes. The cannoneers have had strict instructions to keep up the barrage all night without a second's pause.

Drums pound in the hall. The dogs start to bark. Rohise is not surprised by the noise, for she has often heard it from far up, in her attic, like a sea-wave breaking over and over through the lower house.

She looks at the cage cautiously, wondering what she will see. But she sees only a heap of blackness like ravens, and then a tawny dazzle, torchlight on something like human skin. "You must not go down to look," says the Duke protectively, as his court pours about the cage. Someone pokes between the bars with a gemmed cane, trying to rouse the nightmare which lies quiescent there. But Rohise must be spared this.

So the Duke calls his actors, and a slight, pretty play is put on throughout dinner, before the dais, shutting off from the sight of Rohise the rest of the hall, where the barbaric gloating and goading of the court, unchecked, increases.

iv

The Prince Feroluce becomes aware between one second and the next. It is the sound—heard beyond all others—of the wings of his people beating at the stones of the castle. It is the wings which speak to him, more than their wild orchestral voices. Besides these sensations, the anguish of healing and the sadism of humankind are not much.

Feroluce opens his eyes. His human audience, pleased, but afraid and squeamish, backs away, and asks each other for the two thousandth time if the cage is quite secure. In the torchlight the eyes of Feroluce are more black than red. He stares about. He is, though captive, imperious. If he were a lion or a bull, they would admire this "nobility." But the fact is, he is too much like a man, which serves to point up his supernatural differences unbearably.

Obviously Feroluce understands the gist of his plight. Enemies have him penned. He is a show for now, but ultimately to be killed, for with the intuition of the raptor he divines everything. He had thought the sunlight would kill him, but that is a distant matter, now. And beyond all, the voices and the voices of the wings of his kindred beat the air outside this room-caved mountain of stone.

And so Feroluce commences to sing, or at least, this is how it seems to the rabid court and all the people gathered in the hall. It seems he sings. It is the great communing call of his kind, the art and science and religion of the winged vampires, his means of telling them, or attempting to tell them, what they must be told before he dies. So the sire of Feroluce sang, and the grandsire, and each of his ancestors. Generally they died in flight, falling angels spun down the gulches and enormous stairs of distant peaks, singing. Feroluce, immured, believes that his cry is somehow audible.

To the crowd in the Duke's hall the song is merely that, a song, but how glorious. The dark silver voice, turning to bronze or gold, whitening in the higher registers. There seem to be words, but in some other tongue. This is how the planets sing, surely, or mysterious creatures of the sea.

Everyone is bemused. They listen, astonished.

No one now remonstrates with Rohise when she rises and steals down from the dais. There is an enchantment which prevents movement and coherent thought. Of all the roomful, only she is drawn forward. So she comes close, unhindered, and between the bars of the cage, she sees the vampire for the first time.

She has no notion what he can be. She imagined it was a monster or a monstrous beast. But it is neither. Rohise, starved for so long of beauty and always dreaming of it, recognises Feroluce inevitably as part of the dream-come-true. She loves him instantly. Because she loves him, she is not afraid of him.

She attends while he goes on and on with his glorious song. He does not see her at all, or any of them. They are only things, like mist, or pain. They have no character or personality or worth; abstracts.

Finally, Feroluce stops singing. Beyond the stone and the thick glass of the siege, the wing-beats, too, eddy into silence.

Finding itself mesmerized, silent by night, the court comes to with a terrible joint start, shrilling and shouting, bursting, exploding into a compensation of sound. Music flares again. And the cannons in the roof, which have also fallen quiet, resume with a tremendous roar.

Feroluce shuts his eyes and seems to sleep. It is his preparation for death.

Hands grasp Rohise. "Lady—step back, come away. So close! It may harm you—"

The Duke clasps her in a father's embrace. Rohise, unused to this sort of physical expression, is unmoved. She pats him absently.

"My lord, what will be done?"

"Hush, child. Best you do not know."

Rohise persists.

The Duke persists in not saying.

But she remembers the words of the herald on the stair, and knows they mean to butcher the winged man. She attends thereafter more carefully to snatches of the bizarre talk about the hall, and learns all she needs. At earliest sunrise, as soon as the enemy retreat from the walls, their captive will be taken to the lovely garden with the peach trees. And so to the sunken garden of the magic bush, the fire-flower. And there they will hang him up in the sun through the dome of smoky glass, which will be slow murder to him, but they will cut him, too, so his blood, the stolen blood of the vampire, runs down to water the roots of the fleur de feu. And who can doubt that, from such nourishment, the bush will bloom? The blooms are salvation. Wherever they grow it is a safe place. Whoever wears them is safe from the draining bite of demons. Bite-Me-Not, they call it; vampire-repellent.

Rohise sits the rest of the night on her cushions, with folded hands, resembling the portrait of the princess, which is not like her.

Eventually the sky outside alters. Silence comes down beyond the wall, and so within the wall, and the court lifts its head, a corporate animal scenting day.

At the intimation of sunrise the black plague has lifted and gone away, and might never have been. The Duke, and almost all his castle full of men, women, children, emerge from the doors. The sky is measureless and bluely grey, with one cherry rift in the east that the court refers to as "mauve," since dawns and sunsets are never any sort of red here.

They move through the dimly lightening garden as the last stars melt. The cage is dragged in their midst.

They are too tired, too concentrated now, the Duke's people, to continue baiting their captive. They have had all the long night to do that, and to drink and opine, and now their stamina is sharpened for the final act.

Reaching the sunken garden, the Duke unlocks the iron door. There is no room for everyone within, so mostly they must stand outside, crammed in the gate, or teetering on erections of benches that have been placed around, and peering in over the walls through the glass of the dome. The places in the doorway are the best, of course; no one else will get so good a view. The servants and lower persons must stand back under the trees and only imagine what goes on. But they are used to that.

Into the sunken garden itself there are allowed to go the alchemist and the apothecary, and the priest, and certain sturdy soldiers attendant on the Duke, and the Duke. And Feroluce in the cage.

The east is all "mauve" now. The alchemist has prepared sorcerous safeguards which are being put into operation, and the priest, never to be left out, intones prayers. The bulge-thewed soldiers open the cage and seize the monster before it can stir. But drugged smoke has already been wafted into the prison, and besides, the monster has prepared itself for hopeless death and makes no demur.

Feroluce hangs in the arms of his loathing guards, dimly aware the sun is near. But death is nearer, and already one may hear the alchemist's apprentice sharpening the knife an ultimate time.

The leaves of the *Nona Mordica* are trembling, too, at the commencement of the light, and beginning to unfurl. Although this happens every dawn, the court points to it with optimistic cries. Rohise, who has claimed a position in the doorway, watches it too, but only for an instant. Though she has sung of the fleur de fur since childhood, she had never known what the song was all about. And in just this way, though she has dreamed of being the Duke's daughter most of her life, such an event was never really comprehended either, and so means very little.

As the guards haul the demon forward to the plot of humid earth where the bush is growing, Rohise darts into the sunken garden, and lightning leaps in her hands. Women scream and well they might. Rohise has stolen one of the swords from the East Turret, and now she flourishes it, and now she has swung it and a soldier falls, bleeding red, red, *red,* before them all.

Chaos enters, as in yesterday's play, shaking its tattered sleeves. The men who hold the demon rear back in horror at the dashing blade and the blasphemous gore, and the mad girl in her princess's gown. The Duke makes a pitiful bleating noise, but no one pays him any attention.

The east glows in and like the liquid on the ground.

Meanwhile, the ironically combined sense of impending day and spilled hot blood have penetrated the stunned brain of the vampire. His eyes open, and he sees the girl wielding her sword in a spray of crimson as the last guard lets go. Then the girl has run to Feroluce. Though, or because, her face is insane, it communicates her purpose, as she thrusts the sword's hilt into his hands.

No one has dared approach either the demon or the girl. Now they look on in horror and in horror grasp what Feroluce has grasped.

In that moment the vampire springs, and the great swanlike

wings are reborn at his back, healed and whole. As the doctors predicted, he has mended perfectly, and prodigiously fast. He takes to the air like an arrow, unhindered, as if gravity does not anymore exist. As he does so, the girl grips him about the waist, and slender and light, she is drawn upward too. He does not glance at her. He veers toward the gateway, and tears through it, the sword, his talons, his wings, his very shadow, beating men and bricks from his path.

And now he is in the sky above them, a black star which has not been put out. They see the wings flare and beat, and the swirling of a girl's dress and unbound hair, and then the image dives and is gone into the shade under the mountains, as the sun rises.

¥

It is fortunate, the mountain shade in the sunrise. Lion's blood and enforced quiescence have worked wonders, but the sun could undo it all. Luckily the shadow, deep and cold as a pool, envelops the vampire, and in it there is a cave, deeper and colder. Here he alights and sinks down, sloughing the girl, whom he has almost forgotten. Certainly he fears no harm from her. She is like a pet animal, maybe, like the hunting dogs or wolves or lammergeyers that occasionally the unkindness of vampires have kept by them for a while. That she helped him is all he needs to know. She will help again. So when, stumbling in the blackness, she brings him in her cupped hands water from a cascade at the pool-cave's back, he is not surprised. He drinks the water, which is the only other substance his kind imbibe. Then he smooths her hair, absently, as he would pat or stroke the pet she seems to have become. He is not grateful, as he is not suspicious. The complexities of his intellect are reserved for other things. Since he is exhausted he falls asleep, and since Rohise is exhausted she falls asleep beside him, pressed to his warmth in the freezing dark. Like those of Feroluce, as it turns out, her thoughts are simple. She is sorry for distressing the Cursed Duke. But she has no regrets, for she could no more have left Feroluce to die than she could have refused to leave the scullery for the court.

The day, which had only just begun, passes swiftly in sleep.

Feroluce wakes as the sun sets, without seeing anything of it. He unfolds himself and goes to the cave's entrance, which now looks out on a whole sky of stars above a landscape of mountains. The castle is far below, and to the eyes of Rohise as she follows him, invisible. She does not even look for it, for there is something else to be seen.

The great dark shapes of angels are wheeling against the peaks, the stars. And their song begins, up in the starlit spaces. It is a lament, their mourning, pitiless and strong, for Feroluce, who has died in the stone heart of the thing they prey upon.

The tribe of Ferolure do not laugh, but, like a bird or wild beast, they have a kind of equivalent to laughter. This Feroluce now utters, and like a flung lance he launches himself into the air.

Rohise at the cave mouth, abandoned, forgotten, unnoted even by the mass of vampires, watches the winged man as he flies towards his people. She supposes for a moment that she may be able to climb down the tortuous ways of the mountain, undetected. Where then should she go? She does not spend much time on these ideas. They do not interest or involve her. She watches Feroluce, and because she learned long ago the uselessness of weeping, she does not shed tears, though her heart begins to break.

As Feroluce glides, body held motionless, wings outspread on a down-draught, into the midst of the storm of black wings, the red stars of eyes ignite all about him. The great lament dies. The air is very still.

Feroluce waits then. He waits, for the aura of his people is not as he has always known it. It is as if he had come among emptiness. From the silence, therefore, and from nothing else, he learns it all. In the stone he lay and he sang of his death, as the Prince must, dying. And the ritual was completed, and now there is the threnody, the grief, and thereafter the choosing of a new Prince. And none of this is alterable. He is dead. Dead. It cannot and will not be changed.

There is a moment of protest, then, from Feroluce. Perhaps his brief sojourn among men has taught him some of their futility. But as the cry leaves him, all about the huge wings are raised like swords. Talons and teeth and eyes burn against the stars. To protest is to be torn in shreds. He is not of their people now. They can attack and slaughter him as they would any other intruding thing. Go, the talons and the teeth and the eyes say to him. Go *far off*.

He is dead. There is nothing left him but to die.

Feroluce retreats. He soars. Bewildered, he feels the power and energy of his strength and the joy of flight, and cannot understand how this is, if he is dead. Yet he *is* dead. He knows it now.

So he closes his eyelids, and his wings. Spear-swift he falls. And something shrieks, interrupting the reverie of nihilism. Disturbed, he opens his wings, shudders, turns like a swimmer, finds a ledge against his side and two hands outstretched, holding him by one shoulder, and by his hair.

"No," says Rohise. (The vampire cloud, wheeling away, have not heard her; she does not think of them.) His eyes stay shut. Holding him, she kisses these eyelids, his forehead, his lips, gently, as she drives her nails into his skin to hold him. The black wings beat, tearing to be free and fall and die. "No," says Rohise. "I love you," she says. "My life is your life." These are the words of the court and of courtly love-songs. No matter, she means them. And though he cannot understand her language or her sentiments, yet her passion, purely that, communicates itself, strong and burning as the passions of his kind, who generally love only one thing, which is scarlet. For a second her intensity fills the void which now contains him. But then he dashes himself away from the ledge, to fall again, to seek death again.

Like a ribbon, clinging to him still, Rohise is drawn from the rock and falls with him.

Afraid, she buries her head against his breast, in the shadow of wings and hair. She no longer asks him to reconsider. This is how it must be. *Love* she thinks again, in the instant before they strike the earth. Then that instant comes, and is gone.

Astonished, she finds herself still alive, still in the air. Touching so close, feathers have been left on the rocks, Feroluce has swerved away and upward. Now, conversely, they are whirling towards the very stars. The world seems miles below. Perhaps they will fly into space itself. Perhaps he means to break their bones instead on the cold face of the moon.

He does not attempt to dislodge her, he does not attempt anymore to fall and die. But as he flies, he suddenly cries out, terrible lost lunatic cries.

They do not hit the moon. They do not pass through the stars like static rain.

But when the air grows thin and pure there is a peak like a dagger standing in their path. Here, he alights. As Rohise lets go of him, he turns away. He stations himself, sentry-fashion, in the manner of his tribe, at the edge of the pinnacle. But watching for nothing. He has not been able to choose death. His strength and the strong will of another, these have hampered him. His brain has become formless darkness. His eyes glare, seeing nothing.

Rohise, gasping a little in the thin atmosphere, sits at his back, watching for him, in case any harm may come near him.

At last, harm does come. There is a lightening in the east. The frozen, choppy sea of the mountains below, and all about, grows visible. It is a marvellous sight, but holds no marvel for Rohise. She averts her eyes from the exquisitely pencilled shapes, looking thin and translucent as paper, the rivers of mist between, the glimmer of nacreous ice. She searches for a blind hold to hide in.

There is a pale yellow wound in the sky when she returns. She grasps Feroluce by the wrist and tugs at him. "Come," she says. He looks at her vaguely, as if seeing her from the shore of another country. "The sun," she says. "Quickly."

The edge of the light runs along his body like a razor. He moves by instinct now, following her down the slippery dagger of the peak, and so eventually into a shallow cave. It is so small it holds him like a coffin. Rohise closes the entrance with her own body. It is the best she can do. She sits facing the sun as it rises, as if prepared to fight. She hates the sun for his sake. Even as the light warms her chilled body, she curses it. Till light and cold and breathlessness fade together.

When she wakes, she looks up into twilight and endless stars, two of which are red. She is lying on the rock by the cave. Feroluce leans over her, and behind Feroluce his quiescent wings fill the sky.

She has never properly understood his nature: Vampire. Yet her own nature, which tells her so much, tells her some vital part of herself is needful to him, and that he is danger, and death. But she loves him, and is not afraid. She would have fallen to die with him. To help him by her death does not seem wrong to her. Thus, she lies still, and smiles at him to reassure him she will not struggle. From lassitude, not fear, she closes her eyes. Presently she feels the soft weight of hair brush by her cheek, and then his cool mouth rests against her throat. But nothing more happens. For some while they continue in this fashion, she yielding, he kneeling over her, his lips on her skin. Then he moves a little away. He sits, regarding her. She, knowing the unknown act has not been completed, sits up in turn. She beckons to him mutely, telling him with her gestures and her expression *I consent. Whatever is necessary*. But he does not stir. His eyes blaze, but even of these she has no fear. In the end he looks away from her, out across the spaces of the darkness.

He himself does not understand. It is permissible to drink from the body of a pet, the wolf, the eagle. Even to kill the pet, if need demands. Can it be, outlawed from his people, he has lost their composite soul? Therefore, is he soulless now? It does not seem to him he is. Weakened and famished though he is, the vampire is aware of a wild tingling of life. When he stares at the creature which is his food, he finds he sees her differently. He has borne her through the sky, he has avoided death, by some intuitive process, for her sake, and she has led him to safety, guarded him from the blade of the sun. In the beginning it was she who rescued him from the human things which had taken him. She cannot be human, then. Not pet, and not prey.

For no, he could not drain her of blood, as he would not seize upon his own kind, even in combat, to drink and feed. He starts to see her as beautiful, not in the way a man beholds a woman, certainly, but as his kind revere the sheen of water in dusk, or flight, or song. There are no words for this. But the life goes on tingling through him. Though he is dead, life.

In the end, the moon does rise, and across the open face of it something wheels by. Feroluce is less swift than was his wont, yet he starts in pursuit, and catches and brings down, killing on the wing, a great night bird. Turning in the air, Feroluce absorbs its liquors. The heat of life now, as well as its assertion, courses through him. He returns to the rock perch, the glorious flaccid bird dangling from his hand. Carefully, he tears the glory of the bird in pieces, plucks the feathers, splits the bones. He wakes the companion (asleep again from weakness) who is not pet or prey, and feeds her morsels of flesh. At first she is unwilling. But her hunger is so enormous and her nature so untamed that quite soon she accepts the slivers of raw fowl.

Strengthened by blood, Feroluce lifts Rohise and bears her gliding down the moon-slit quill-backed land of the mountains, until there is a rocky cistern full of cold, old rains. Here they drink together. Pale white primroses grow in the fissures where the black moss drips. Rohise makes a garland and throws it about the head of her beloved when he does not expect it. Bewildered but disdainful, he touches at the wreath of primroses to see if it is likely to threaten or hamper him. When it does not, he leaves it in place.

Long before dawn this time, they have found a crevice. Because it is so cold, he folds his wings about her. She speaks of her love to him, but he does not hear, only the murmur of her voice, which is musical and does not displease him. And later, she sings him sleepily the little song of the fleur de fur.

vi

There comes a time then, brief, undated, chartless time, when they are together, these two creatures. Not together in any accepted sense, of course, but together in the strange feeling or emotion, instinct or ritual, that can burst to life in an instant or flow to life gradually across half a century, and which men call *Love.*

They are not alike. No, not at all. Their differences are legion and should be unpalatable. He is a supernatural thing and she a human thing, he was a lord and she a scullery sloven. He can fly, she cannot fly. And he is male, she female. What other items are required to make them enemies? Yet they are bound, not merely by love, they are bound by all they are, the very stumbling blocks. Bound, too, because they are doomed. Because the stumbling blocks have doomed them; everything has. Each has been exiled out of their own kind. Together, they cannot even communicate with each other, save by looks, touches, sometimes by sounds, and by songs neither understands, but which each comes to value since the other appears to value them, and since they give expression to that other. Nevertheless, the binding of the doom, the greatest binding, grows, as it holds them fast to each other, mightier and stronger.

Although they do not know it, or not fully, it is the awareness of doom that keeps them there, among the platforms and steps up and down, and the inner cups, of the mountains.

Here it is possible to pursue the airborne hunt, and Feroluce may now and then bring down a bird to sustain them both. But birds are scarce. The richer lower slopes, pastured with goats, wild sheep, and men—they lie far off and far down from this place as a deep of the sea. And Feroluce does not conduct her there, nor does Rohise ask that he should, or try to lead the way, or even dream of such a plan.

But yes, birds are scarce, and the pastures far away, and winter is coming. There are only two seasons in these mountains. High summer, which dies, and the high cold which already treads over the tips of the air and the rock, numbing the sky, making all brittle, as though the whole landscape might snap in pieces, shatter.

How beautiful it is to wake with the dusk, when the silver webs of night begin to form, frost and ice, on everything. Even the ragged dress—once that of a princess—is tinselled and shining with this

magic substance, even the mighty wings—once those of a prince—
each feather is drawn glittering with thin rime. And oh, the sky, thick
as a daisy-field with the white stars. Up there, when they have fed
and have strength, they fly, or, Feroluce flies and Rohise flies in his
arms, carried by his wings. Up there in the biting chill like a pane of
ghostly vitreous, they have become lovers, true blind lovers,
embraced and linked, their bodies a bow, coupling on the wing. By
the hour that his first happened the girl had forgotten all she had
been, and he had forgotten too that she was anything but the essen-
tial mate. Sometimes, borne in this way, by wings and by fire, she
cries out as she hangs in the ether. These sounds, transmitted
through the flawless silence and amplification of the peaks, scatter
over tiny half-buried villages countless miles away, where they are
heard in fright and taken for the shrieks of malign invisible devils,
tiny as bats, and armed with the barbed stings of scorpions. There
are always misunderstandings.

After a while, the icy prologues and the stunning starry fields of
winter nights give way to the main argument of winter.

The liquid of the pool, where the flowers made garlands, has
clouded and closed to stone. Even the volatile waterfalls are stilled,
broken cascades of glass. The wind tears through the skin and hair to
gnaw the bones. To weep with cold earns no compassion of the cold.

There is no means to make fire. Besides, the one who was Rohise
is an animal now, or a bird, and beasts and birds do not make fire,
save for the phoenix in the Duke's bestiary. Also, the sun is fire, and
the sun is a foe. Eschew fire.

There begin the calendar months of hibernation. The demon
lovers too must prepare for just such a measureless winter sleep, that
gives no hunger, asks no action. There is a deep cave they have lined
with feathers and withered grass. But there are no more flying things
to feed them. Long, long ago, the last warm frugal feast, long, long
ago the last flight, joining, ecstasy and song. So, they turn to their
cave, to stasis, to sleep. Which each understands, wordlessly, thought-
lessly, is death.

What else? He might drain her of blood, he could persist some while on that, might even escape the mountains, the doom. Or she herself might leave him, attempt to make her way to the places below, and perhaps she could reach them, even now. Others, lost here, have clone so. But neither considers these alternatives. The moment for all that is past. Even the death-lament does not need to be voiced again

Installed, they curl together in their bloodless icy nest, murmuring a little to each other, but finally still.

Outside, the snow begins to come down. It falls like a curtain. Then the winds take it. Then the night is full of the lashing of whips, and when the sun rises it is white as the snow itself, its flame very distant, giving nothing. The cave mouth is blocked up with snow. In the winter, it seems possible that never again will there be a summer in the world.

Behind the modest door of snow, hidden and secret, sleep is quiet as stars, dense as hardening resin. Feroluce and Rohise turn pure and pale in the amber, in the frigid nest, and the great wings lie like a curious articulated machinery that will not move. And the withered grass and the flowers are crystallised, until the snows shall melt.

At length, the sun deigns to come closer to the earth, and the miracle occurs. The snow shifts, crumbles, crashes off the mountains in rage. The waters hurry after the snow, the air is wrung and racked by splittings and splinterings, by rushes and booms. It is half a year, or it might be a hundred years, later.

Open now, the entry to the cave. Nothing emerges. Then, a flutter, a whisper. Something does emerge. One black feather, and caught in it, the petal of a flower, crumbling like dark charcoal and white, drifting away into the voids below. Gone. Vanished. It might never have been.

But there comes another time (half a year, a hundred years), when an adventurous traveller comes down from the mountains to the pocketed villages the other side of them. He is a swarthy cheerful fellow, you would not take him for herbalist or mystic, but he has in a pot a plant he found high up in the staring crags, which might after all contain anything or nothing. And he shows the plant, which is an unusual one, having slender, dark, and velvety leaves, and giving off a pleasant smell like vanilla. "See, the *Nona Mordica,*" he says. "The Bite-Me-Not. The flower that repels vampires."

Then the villagers tell him an odd story, about a castle in another country, besieged by a huge flock, a menace of winged vampires, and how the Duke waited in vain for the magic bush that was in his garden, the Bite-Me-Not, to flower and save them all. But it seems there was a curse on this Duke, who on the very night his daughter was lost, had raped a serving woman, as he had raped others before. But this woman conceived. And bearing the fruit, or flower, of this rape, damaged her, so she lived only a year or two after it. The child grew up unknowing, and in the end betrayed her own father by running away to the vampires, leaving the Duke demoralised. And soon after he went mad, and himself stole out one night, and let the winged fiends into his castle, so all there perished.

"Now if only the bush had flowered in time, as your bush flowers, all would have been well," the villagers cry.

The traveller smiles. He in turn does not tell them of the heap of peculiar bones, like parts of eagles mingled with those of a woman and a man. Out of the bones, from the heart of them, the bush was rising, but the traveller untangled the roots of it with care; it looks sound enough now in its sturdy pot, all of it twining together. It seems as if two separate plants are growing from a single stem, one with blooms almost black, and one pink-flowered, like a young sunset.

"Flur de fur," says the traveller, beaming at the marvel, and his luck.

Fleur de feu. Oh flower of fire. That fire is not hate or fear, which makes flowers come, nor terror or anger or lust, it is love that is the fire of the Bite-Me-Not, love which cannot abandon, love which cannot harm. Love which never dies.

gene
wolfe

Queen of the Night

"Queen of the Night," the ghouls called her, and, more frequently, "Her Highness."

Because they referred to meat in the state they preferred as "high," the usage had confused the boy when he was smaller. "Her Highness must see you." "Her Highness will never approve you." He had pictured one of them taller than any—although they were all tall—fragrant with decay, as they were.

He could not eat the putrid flesh they relished, as he and they had learned when he was still very small. For him, meat in summer could be not more than two days in the grave, and in the dry harsh heat at the end of August (when fevers raged and many were buried) even two days might be too long. Mostly he lived on food that the pious living offered to their dead: hot breads three times wrapped in clean cloths sewn with crosses and holy verses he could not read, and the boiled turnips and cabbages of the poor, these last wrapped once or twice or even five times in clean rags that were only rarely decorated with crude religious pictures executed in the red blood of beets.

He supplemented these foods with roots and stalks snatched from gardens by night, pears and cherries filched from orchards, and certain herbs and berries that he had discovered himself, though rarely with the fungi the ghouls enjoyed, which ofttimes made him ill.

"If her Highness does not approve, will I die?" he asked Eeesheeea.

"She will approve."

"You may eat of me."

"Not dancing." Eeesheeea bowed her head and seemed a stone.

"I am too thin," the boy acknowledged. The stone did not reply.

They traveled; and no one, not even Beeetheeeor, could say when the queen would appear to judge him, or where. The spring floods brought low meat and easy, together with drowned cattle (which they disdained though the boy did not) and swine, which Nee-neeeaih claimed to relish.

Summer was the best time. Water from farms where all the living had died, they poured into healthful wells and even holy springs, although the latter was unlucky and rarely effective. So bold were they at times in summer that they were seen by moonlight, dancing as they feasted in clothing furnished by their meat: the dead wife's particolored kirtle (fouled now by groundwater and the ichors of decay) beneath her husband's rotted coat.

Autumn found them foolish and fond of jests, hiding in new-dug graves and violated mausoleums, and careless of the fading sun. It had been in autumn that they had found the boy, as Eeesheeea confided, feeding him as a prank, chortling when he vomited and leading him to waters that they hoped might hold the fever still. "When I'm bigger," he had boasted, "I'll be like you," but she had shaken her head.

Winter was the worst season, when the earth of even the freshest graves froze, and month-old meat wore flesh too hard to chew. The boy had snared a hare, skinned it with his teeth, and was sucking the largest bone from a hind leg preparatory to cracking it. "Come with us," Beeetheeeor told him; and he did, flattered, walking alone (as it appeared) through the freezing winter night.

Beside the dark and half-ruinous church, the caretaker's cottage glowed with firelight; and candles stood guard at every window, save the shuttered window of the loft. "They sing," Eeesheeea hissed.

Her ears were sharper even than the boy's. "Send back their song to them."

"I must hear it first," he told her, and cupped both ears.

> *The oracles are dumb,*
> *No voice or hideous hum*
> *Runs through the arched roof in words deceiving*
> *Apollo from his shrine*
> *Can no more divine*
> *With hollow shriek the steep of Delphos leaving*
> *No trace or breathed spell*
> *Inspires the pale-eyed priest from the prophetic cell*

The boy grinned, and as the final note faded, replied.

> *The singers all are dumb,*
> *They voice their hideous hum*
> *Right through the windows wide themselves relieving,*
> *These puppies' worthless whine*
> *Can fright no folk of mine,*
> *When o'er the haunted downs we come a-thieving.*
> *Our night-long dance and sprightly call*
> *Shall tire the pop-eyed beast from out the stall*

Silence fell upon the cottage. Eeesheeea said, "That was better even than last time." And he, creeping closer to the caretaker's cottage, gloried in her praise.

At length a man's quavering voice ventured, "It's the Gray Neighbors in search of a steed."

A woman, "Isn't the White Lady curse enough?"

A boy, "Will they steal Maria?"

The queen had been visiting them," Beeetheeeor explained. "That is why they have opened a grave for us."

Soon out came the caretaker, his wife, and their son, beating pans and calling out: *"No horse, no cow, no byre, no barn But warn ye fair, "twill soon be morn!"* Three times they marched sunwise around the cottage repeating this, their freezing breath a ghostly herald in the moonlight. Then the wife put a bowl of milk upon the step, with bread on one side and salt on the other. *"Bread for life and salt forever. These the bonds between us sever. Milk for mercy, milk for friend. Drink, and let thy mischief end!"*

The boy drank the milk greedily and ate the bread, too; but spit out the salt, angrily scattering it across the step. Then he climbed onto the roof, put his head down the chimney and howled like a wolf. When this evoked only a terrified silence, he peered over the edge of the roof, upside down into the loft through a chink in the shutter, where he saw a yellow-haired girl, much wasted, whose wide frightened eyes stared at nothing; his forefinger soon teased out the wooden bar, and he opened the shutter and swung inside to crouch next to her bed.

Slowly, she turned her head to look at him.

"Tell them iron will keep us out," he whispered, knowing it was what Beeetheeeor would want him to say. "Call to them."

The yellow-haired girl called, but her voice was without strength. When nobody came, the boy plucked an onion from a string of them hanging from the rafters and threw it down the ladder-hole into the fire, scattering sparks and embers over half the room, and hid under a heap of husks.

Soon the caretaker's wife mounted the ladder. "Maria," she inquired, "were the fairies up here?"

"One," the girl said. Her voice was less than the sigh of a leafless tree.

The wife returned to the ladder-hole and called, "Johann, there was one up here troubling the child."

The caretaker, a spare man with a long sad face, climbed into the loft as well, with a tattered old black-letter Bible in one hand. "An ouph, Maria? With a red cap?"

The sick girl rolled her head across the pillow.

"With cobweb wings? An oak-man?"

She said nothing and stared at nothing, as before.

"Describe it."

"Here," the wife said, "I'll help her sit up."

"She'll be dead before the moon," muttered the boy to himself, peeping through the husks and noting how her bones poked the threadbare nightgown she wore. "And little enough for Eeesheeea."

"How looked it, child?" the caretaker asked. "Tell us."

"He. Thin. Dirty."

"Young, Maria? Was he young? Shivering?"

The sick girl nodded.

"A cauld lad." The caretaker shivered himself. "They start fires, they say. That must have been what he was trying to do. You have to leave them a warm coat to be rid of them."

"We've none to give," his wife protested.

"Iron," the sick girl whispered. "Iron will make him go."

Her father rubbed his chin. "It might. Iron charms them hence at childbirth, they say. Scissors open underneath the cradle."

When they had gone, the boy stood up. "That was kindly done," he told the sick girl. "We'll trouble you no more, I think," In the cottage below, he heard the clank of pick-head against the blade of a spade. "I'll do you a favor, if I can."

"Go away," she told him.

"Sometimes I can grant three wishes," he said, and at the moment he almost believed it.

Her head rolled from side to side, as before. "The White Lady will come tonight, and I will die."

"Bar the window after I've left," he told her; but there was no indication that she had heard.

Outside, Reeezthorreee had taken the spade from the back door; Beeetheeeor was already at the reclosed grave, swinging the pick. "They dug this meat up again," Eeesheeea explained, "and broke the frost, though the ground is hard again at the top. They believed it was Her Highness."

Before long Beeetheeeor and Reeezthorreee cast aside the tools and dug with their claws as they always did, making the clods fly.

There was no coffin, the boy saw when he peered into the grave, but a stake had been put through the meat to hold it.

"She comes," Eeesheeea whispered.

Until he heard the horses' hooves, the boy thought she meant only that Beeetheeeor was lifting the meat, as he was.

The clouds parted to show a black carriage racing across the plain, dropping from sight into a declivity, reappearing at the crest of the hill on the opposite side, and rattling across the Roman bridge over the frozen brook. "Her Highness will approve you this night," Eeesheeea assured him, her tone less confident than her words.

"Is that one of our carriages?" he inquired. She did not reply, and he ran to the road for a closer look.

When it drew up in front of the cottage, he saw that the coachman was one of the living, though he had never seen one with a face so savage or eyes so cruel. A groom scuttled off crablike to catch the boy by one arm. "Want him, ma'am? I got him for you!" Eeesheeea stood, and the groom hid behind his wild-eyed horses. A soft laugh came from the carriage.

"I'm all right," the boy told Eeesheeea. "I could've got away. You better eat before they finish it." Neeneeeaih had emerged from a moon-shadow to join the feast.

"Her Highness has seen you," Eeesheeea told him. "I am here to speak for you."

The voice from the carriage murmured, "Come, my child. Let me look more closely." He went to the window and peeped through it, but there was no one inside.

Eeesheeea said, "For seven summers he has been ours, Your Highness. We found and we claim him. If it please you, three more?"

Bright with lions, swords, and crested helms, the door of the carriage pushed the boy back.

In the moonlit silence that followed, he heard a shutter creak. The sick girl appeared at the window of the loft. A moment more, and she was crouching on the sill, then scrambling down the wall.

Save that her eyes were open and staring, her expression was that of one who dreams, and would awaken if she could.

A slender figure in white stood beside the boy, without having come from anywhere. His first impression was of hair; it was black, and he had never seen a woman with so much, a somber aureole about her lined and bloodless face that stirred as if in a wind, though no wind blew.

Beeetheeeor, Reeezthorreee, and Neeneeeaih were ranged behind Eeesheeea now. All knelt; seeing them, the boy knelt too. Eeesheeea raised her face and her hands, her eyes black with tears. "My head in surety for all he does. Have mercy on your slave, Your Highness! Just one summer more?"

The sick girl stood at his shoulder, swaying and trembling in her nightgown. Still on his knees, he put his arm about her waist and felt her febrile heat.

Coldly, the White Lady told Eeesheeea, "This is a child of the living, and already of age. It is time that he return to his own. I shall arrange it," Before she finished, the ghouls vanished as though they had never existed.

"Come with me freely," she said to the boy, "and I will show you wonders, man-child."

He looked about him. "Where's Eeesheeea?"

"Where she has always been."

He got to his feet. This girl's ailing. I'd like to take her back inside."

"Their doors are barred," the White Lady told him, and her coachman laughed.

"Her mother and father will let her in if I knock."

"They sleep," The White Lady's face was as expressionless as a naked skull; the boy found himself wishing she would smile or frown—be impatient, prideful, or even angry.

"I'll pound on the door," he said. "I'll wake them up."

"Do."

He led the sick girl back to the cottage, asking whether she was all right, suggesting she might be cold, and at last pleading, "Won't you say something?"

Picking up the bowl that had held his milk, he rapped the door with it, and at once heard the rattle of the bar. "See," he told the sick girl, "they hadn't gone to sleep yet. You go back to bed and stay there."

The door opened, and the White Lady held the bar. She motioned to the sick girl, who went in and climbed the ladder to the loft.

"You're making her ill, aren't you?" the boy asked.

"I am breaking her bonds, one by one."

"Do you still want me to come with you? Promise you'll let her alone, and I will."

"For one year."

"Forever!" It seemed to the boy that they must surely wake the caretaker and his wife, but no one stirred.

"How long did you live among the ghouls?"

"We call them the People." He was sick with fear, but fought it with boyish stubbornness.

"How long?"

"I don't know. You heard what Eeesheeea said."

"How long? The truth."

"Nine years, I think."

The White Lady nodded slowly. "Go back to my coach. Get in."

The walk from the carriage to the cottage had been short; the walk from the cottage to the carriage seemed long indeed. The boy wanted to run, to hide among gravestones as he had so often, in so many such churchyards He was free, he knew, and could do so if he chose, he knew, also, what the White Lady would do if he did.

The carriage door stood open, the coachman and the little, twisted groom watched him, grinning, as he put his bare foot on the iron step, stepped up, then stepped up again and into the coach.

It rocked ever so slightly on its leather springs, and the door swung shut and latched itself. Through the open window, he noted the earth Beeetheeeor and Reeezthorreee had scattered, black in the moonlight; the pick, the spade, and the stake that they had cast aside, and a few bones. From the meat, he told himself—but something in him turned it to from the dead woman. He was one of the living now, as she had been.

The coachman's whip cracked. The coach creaked and jolted into motion. He had never ridden in a coach before and, boylike, delighted in it, exhilarated by the novelty of effortless speed. There was a rug on the backward-facing seat opposite him; he unfolded it and covered himself with it as he sometimes had with stolen altar cloths, tucking it about him and telling himself that he must accustom himself to such comforts now, as befitted the living. He would wash when the ice broke, get a house of his own by whatever means houses were obtained.

As the carriage rattled across the Roman bridge, he grew conscious of something cold pressing against his right side. His fingers found nothing there, but the pressure continued, and even increased. Feeling again, he discovered that his ragged trousers had parted from waistband to knee.

"I am here," the White Lady said.

"I can't see you," he told her. Only silence answered. He tried to push her fingers away, but there were no fingers. "Don't do that," he said.

"Don't do that," she mocked him.

The rug slid from his lap to the floor.

"Freely," she said, "freely." And then, "You will never know another like me."

"I don't want to," he told her; and yet, he did.

"Kiss me," Hair and chill flesh molded themselves upon his face. He kissed her, and from somewhere near the dark and swaying ceiling she laughed.

"You're cold."

"You are not. Lie down on the seat. I want to show you something."

Reluctantly he did so, and she loved and bit as though her teeth were within her loins.

"You see? You are a man."

"No." He shook his head. "No." He sat up again, and for a long while sat with his face in his hands. He was naked, though he could not remember how he had come to be, or what had become of his clothes.

After a time he covered his shame with the rug, and after a time still longer, began to enjoy the ride again. It seemed their horses could never tire, but galloped on forever through a night no sun would end. Looking out of the windows, he saw a dark castle upon a darker crag and pretended that he was its owner, a great lord—with a white charger—with medals on his chest—with a sword and a fur cloak. His wife would ride in a carriage like this, and he, swifter than the wind, would gallop before her to see that every lamp and cresset blazed, and that the servants had begun their dinner.

"Have you recovered?" the White Lady inquired. "You are young and should recover quickly."

When he looked at the window on her side of the coach, he could see her in the corner very faintly, as a traveler among mountains sees, and then does not see, a face in the profile of a cliff, or a silent traveler like himself in a standing stone. When he tried to look at her directly, she vanished, becoming a glimmer of moonlight on the leather seat. "Please don't," he said. "I don't want to. I want to go back to Eeesheeea."

She laughed—or perhaps it was only the tinkling of a bell on the neck of one of the sheep on the lull below the crag. "You shall. Eventually."

He would have opened the carriage door and thrown himself out, but the door would not open. He dived through the window instead.

And found himself in a deep, soft bed, with sheets and blankets and a puffy comforter over him. Each bedpost was a black candle, and all four candles were lit, sending up smoky flames as long as his forearm, about which the bats clinging to the arched vault above stirred and chittered in complaint. Something cold lay beside him, and for hours he dared not look.

"You were fatigued. I let you rest. Let us see if you are well rested."

He felt her fingers and smiled despite himself, trembling.

"Perhaps you would like food? I would."

"No," he said; and she kissed him on the lips, covering his eyes with her hand.

"Am I so cold? Do I seem a dead thing?" She warmed him between her thighs.

"No," he said again.

She laughed with delight, her laughter like church bells far away. "Nor am I. Do you recall what I taught you in the carriage? Here I lie. It is your turn."

He pressed himself to the face he could scarcely see, and she licked, and tore him with her teeth until her pillow was wet everywhere with his blood. It frightened and sickened him, and yet there was something beyond them both that shone like a gem, turning and beckoning to him—something he seemed about to grasp at each moment.

"These are the pleasures of hell, you see, man-child. In hell they are not punished by pain alone, because pain alone can never be punishment enough. Now do as I taught, and show me that you still live, and I as well." Her hands upon his hips directed his motions, and with each she grew more real, a living woman whose naked body rose from the blood-soaked sheet, bright as morning and white as alabaster. "For the blood is the life," she said.

He slept, and woke alone.

For days, it seemed, he lay dreaming. That he was in the castle on the crag, he knew. There were windows in every wall of the great domed bedchamber—a tower room, then, high above all the rest. So would he have chosen, he decided, could he choose. Black velvet drapes streaked with cobwebs closed each window; and though at times those drapes were drawn back so that he looked down upon the cottages of their peasants or out upon the sea, or up into that endless night through which the queen's carriage, somewhere, still thundered past stars white with anger or red with guilt, always he woke at last and found himself still in the great bed, with candles burning silently at its corners and never burning down, and the soft, stirring tester of bats overhead, bats who sometimes left their places to flutter aimlessly about the room or dart behind the drapes, never to be seen again.

By him, at least.

The White Lady returned, carrying a child of three, a girl with terrified eyes whose tears and struggles the long road had exhausted. The White Lady's countenance was smooth and glowed with health; her red lips smiled as a cat smiles, displaying sharply pointed white teeth. "Do you like me better thus, man-child? Have I not become beautiful for you?"

He nodded, unable to speak or to tear his eyes from her.

"You are not afraid?" She dropped the little girl on a chair, like a parcel.

"Please. Please hurry." He sat up, not bothering to conceal his nakedness.

"You will die. You have rested less than you imagine." Her hands were behind her, loosing her dress. "You have one more in you, possibly. Then death." The dress fell at her feet.

It seemed to the boy that his pounding heart would break his ribs.

"Look upon me, man-child." For a few seconds that seemed eternity to him, her camisole wrapped her marvelous, living hair like a turban. Raising her arms, she pirouetted before him. "I was old when first you met me, but I am young as you, now. Younger, with your youth."

Her body was above perfection, filling him with a hunger that consumed him until it could consume her. He sprang from the bed and rushed upon her.

Like mist she vanished. With her, the captured girl, the great bed with its flickering candles, and the vast bedchamber itself. Briefly he knew snow, and daylight beneath a low gray sky.

When he woke again, it was in a hard, narrow bed with one side against a rough plastered wall. He moaned and closed his eyes and sought to dream again, because it had been of her.

"You can't stay here," Johann the caretaker said when he was able to sit up and drink broth. "Don't you remember your own name"

"I'm called 'the boy,'" the boy said. It was the name Eeesheeea had given him.

"I call him Jon," said fat Anna the caretaker's wife. It had been the name of their first child, born when she and the caretaker had been married less than a year.

"When will I get my bed back?" Robert the caretaker's son demanded.

"Tonight. He can sleep in front of the fire tonight, and tomorrow he'll have to go."

"Where?" the boy asked.

"Anywhere you want, as long as it isn't here." Johann the caretaker was silent a moment, rubbing his chin. "Go into the village. You must've come from there, and dozens of people are sure to know you."

The boy said, "I did?" though he wanted to say I did not.

"Certainly. You must've walked out here last night, the good God knows why, and fallen among the body snatchers. They hit you on the head and knocked the sense out of it, and stole your clothes."

Faintly—very faintly in the distance—the boy heard the jingle of harness, and the rattle of the coach. "It snowed, didn't it?" he said. He was scarcely conscious that he spoke aloud. "That's why I can't hear the horses' hooves."

Anna the caretaker's wife went to the window. "Johann! It's the carriage from the schloss."

Her husband went out into the snow with his hat in his hand.

Sitting at the scarred but sturdy old table, propped on his elbows drinking soup, the boy heard a rough, sneering voice from beyond the front door of the cottage, and knew it for the coachman's, though he had never heard the coachman speak. The carriage, he promised himself, had come with a fur robe for him and a basket of hot food, pheasants and partridges (birds that he had snared for himself when he could) tucked beneath a clean white cloth. The carriage would carry him to the castle, where she would be waiting. They would kiss, tenderly at first.

The coachman's whip cracked, the harness creaked, and the wheels squeaked as the carriage lumbered away. Johann the caretaker opened the door again, stamped snow from his boots, and stepped inside.

"What is it?" his wife wanted to know.

"They—he . . ."

"Is it bad news?"

There came the softest of creakings from the loft; and the boy knew that Maria, the sick girl, had come to the ladder-hole to listen.

"I don't know." Johann the caretaker sat down, his hat still in his hand. "Perhaps it is. Perhaps not."

"Tell us!"

"He asked if we had anyone staying with us. I said only—only—"

"Jon."

"Only a lost boy I found in the snow."

No more broth could be got from the bowl with the spoon, and the boy did not like spoons anyway; he lifted the bowl to his lips and drank the last drops.

"And he—the coachman. There was no one in the coach."

"What did he say, Johann?"

"He said we were to keep him. Keep Jon."

Robert the caretaker's son asked, "Until summer?"

"Not until anything," his father told him. "Until he is a man, or until we are told something else to do with him."

He turned to the boy. "You will call me Master Caretaker, Jon. Is that understood? Otherwise there will be trouble."

Putting down the empty bowl, the boy nodded. "Yes, Master Caretaker. That is understood. There will be no trouble."

"And you will call my wife Madame Caretaker. Our son is Robert. Our daughter is Maria."

So it was settled. The boy called the caretaker's wife "Madame Caretaker" in the presence of her husband and children, and "Mama" when they were alone. The wounds he had suffered (from wild animals during the night, Mama said when she treated them) healed at last, although each left a black scar.

Spring came, and people talked of flooding on the river; the brook under the Roman bridge rose until it flowed across the roadway. With axe and pole, Johann the caretaker and the boy cleared the brush and uprooted trees that sought to dam it there, finding among them the corpse of a girl for whom they dug a shallow grave in the worst corner of the churchyard that kept filling with water.

Summer followed, decked with apple blossoms and loud with bees. Maria grew so strong that she left the loft to play in the sunlight, smiling at the boy with blue eyes that said, I know. He smiled back, and his eyes said, I know you do. But now and again, when the sun was setting and bats set out from the ruined mausoleum in the middle of the churchyard, the boy heard his own voice saying: "Nine years, I think"

And the White Lady, Her Highness the Queen of the Night: *"Go back to my coach. Get in."*

She'll come for Maria, he told himself, and I'll be here waiting for her. Or, she'll come for Maria, and I'll run—help with a barge on the river, join the crew of a ship when the river reaches the sea, and go to Amerika.

Once he dreamed that he rose from his pallet by the hearth, and opening the shutter saw Eeesheeea, Beeetheeeor, and others dancing in the churchyard. Eeesheeea saw him at the window and waved to him; and though he could not quite make out her face, he knew that she smiled. Waking, he wept. But in time he came to understand that not all that is seen waking is real, nor is all that is seen in sleep false. Although he tried over and over to summon that dream again, it never recurred.

One afternoon at the end of summer, when the apples were ripe and the sheep on the downs were knitting themselves new coats, Johann the caretaker sat sighing on the doorstep, with the boy (who had helped him dig three graves that day, for the fever had waked) beside him.

"Jon," said Johann, "you're rich. You think you're poor, I suppose. It's very likely. You'd say you've got nothing. But you've got youth, which is the second greatest treasure in the world. And you've innocence. For a few years more you'll have that, and it's the greatest of all. A poor man can get rich. A rich man who's lost his money may get rich again, that happens, too. But when childhood's past, life's greatest treasure is gone forever. Nothing can replace it, Jon, or even reconcile you to its loss. There's no return to innocence, and beyond youth nothing but sorrow."

"Yes, Master Caretaker," Jon said. "I know. I know."

p. d. cacek

Yrena

She looked like a piece of trash someone had tossed to the side of the road. Tiny she was and pale . . . so, so pale that her skin seemed to glow in the darkness.

At first Konstantin Misurov thought she might not even be real, just some starving sculptor's joke crafted from the late winter snow and draped with rags. Not that it would have surprised him. Since the Great Revolution, Misurov had seen many sculptors starving in the streets of the newly renamed Leningrad. It was only by the greatest luck that he had not joined them; that, and the fact that even a society of equals needed signs to be painted. His talent, once renowned in the Imperial courts, was at least not going to waste.

Ah, she moved . . . slowly as if the cold had already worked its bony fingers into her, and Misurov blinked away the snowflakes building on his lashes. He'd almost forgotten the child was there and *that* worried him. It was not like him to indulge in his own misery such that he would let so tender a morsel get away.

Even if he could not paint, life still had its compensations.

The child moved again, drawing her stockinged legs closer to her chest as Misurov closed the distance between them. Her eyes, dark as the rags she wore and betraying the taint of gypsy blood in her veins, raised to the level of his face and stayed there. Even in the shadows

Misurov could see that they held no fear—mistrust, yes . . . and something else, but not fear.

"Hello, little bird, have you fallen from your nest?"

The child nodded and a ragged seam slipped from her shoulder. Her flesh tone was a subtle mix of cerulean and ash. A less subtle heat filled Misurov's groin an instant before the wind snatched it away.

"You should not be out all alone," he said softly, his breath steaming in the cold. "Aren't you afraid?"

As he crouched on the hard-packed snow in front of her, Misurov was aware of the others who shared the night with them. They were huddled forms . . . vague, faceless shadows . . . background images filling in an unfinished landscape. But one never knew in times like these what a mere shadow might remember, or a background image report to the wolfish authorities.

A lifetime ago, before the revolution, Misurov had relied upon his position in the old regime to make his "indiscretions" invisible. Now they would make him just another target for re-education.

"Where is your mother, little bird?" he asked gently, in a voice as soft as velvet.

Something glistened in the corner of her eye, just for a moment and then it was gone. A *tear*? Misurov wondered.

"Ah," he said, leaning forward over the woollen patches on the knees of his trousers, "you are alone."

She nodded again and an ebony lock slipped from beneath the shawl she wore over her head. Slowly, as if he were trying to pet a feral cat, Misurov reached out a gloved hand. He could feel the coldness of her cheek even through the layer of greased wool. Poor frozen little thing.

"I am Konstantin Ilyich Misurov," he said through the swirling steam of his breath, "I was once a great artist with many friends, but now I too am alone in this world."

She seemed unimpressed. Misurov sighed and watched his breath encircle the child's head like a holy aura. Almost immediately an image appeared on the empty canvas he kept behind his eyelids: a gypsy Madonna huddling before the Angel of the Lord.

A dirty, half-starved gypsy Madonna.

Misurov felt the ice in his beard crack as he smiled. *What a typical bourgeois thought,* he reminded himself. *But what a painting it would have made. Ah, well.*

"What is your name, child?"

The dark eyes left his face, glancing quickly to the left and right, a slight frown creasing the smoothness of her brow. Was his little Madonna looking for help or simply making sure that whatever proposition he was about to offer met no opposition? Bourgeois or not, Misurov prayed it was the latter. It would make things so much simpler if she knew the ways of the world and men. The innocent tended to scream and claw when he dragged them away.

"My name is Yrena."

Her voice was as brittle as the cold and just as numbing. No trace of her breath moved through the darkness. *She must be all but frozen.*

"My mother's name was Yrena," Misurov lied. Again. He had given his mother so many names throughout the years that he no longer remembered what it really was. Part of him hoped it had been Yrena.

"Are you hungry, Yrena?"

Yes! He could see it in her eyes, in the way her body tensed. Of course she was hungry, most of Russia . . . no, most of the Union of Soviet Socialist Republics was hungry.

Nodding, Misurov dropped his hand to her bare shoulder and squeezed gently. Her flesh was as hard and unyielding as polished marble.

"Come then," he said, pulling the child to her feet as he stood, "I don live far."

They walked slowly, the loose rags covering the child's feet leaving serpentine tracks in the snow behind them, only Misurov's breath steaming the air.

Yrena was so quiet that he kept looking down the long, black line of his greatcoat sleeve to make sure she was still there. She was—a silent shadow at his side . . . his own tiny piece of night to caress and bury himself in.

The thought kept Misurov warm.

She had wrapped the scarf across her face so that only her dark eyes showed, twin holes punched into the white canvas of her flesh. And she never blinked, his little Yrena Vojvoda . . . his little girl who named herself for a village that might not even exist anymore. His little child of the night—never looking up at him, never questioning him about their destination. Silent and servile. The way he preferred them.

When another night traveler suddenly appeared in front of them, its gender and purpose disguised by the layers of snow and clothing it wore, Misurov tightened his grip on the child's shoulder. But only *he* trembled.

Yrena continued walking at his side, as indifferent to his touch as she was to the cold and darkness.

Two long blocks down and one across, and Misurov pointed to a narrow garret set above an empty stable. He was lucky to have found the place, with so many going without. The walls were thick and sturdy, the floors solid enough, and the one window faced north. Even the rats, poor thin things, were a source of comfort. They made him feel not so alone.

Misurov paused for a moment and studied the weathered lines of his current home, nodding. Whatever it had been before, it made a passable artist's studio.

Or at least it would have if he were still an artist.

The ice tugged at the hairs in Misurov's beard as he threw back his head and laughed, his breath a white plume billowing into the night sky. It was such a good joke, such a terrible good joke to play on a man who had once lived only to create worlds with pigment and brush. *Ah, God.*

A gentle tug on the hem of his sleeve brought Misurov back.

Looking down, he met Yrena's eyes and nodded.

"I am not as much a madman as I appear, little bird," he said, releasing his grip on her shoulder to take her hand. "Don't be afraid."

"I'm not," came the muffled reply.

Thanking whatever angel or saint it was that had managed to escape detection by the new government in order to place such a child in his hands, Misurov pulled her close and began walking them toward the narrow wooden staircase that led to the garret.

One of the other misplaced denizens of the area was singing, accompanied by a bandura—a sad song, probably gypsy or Ukrainian . . . definitely antirevolutionary. The rich baritone rolled through the frozen darkness, bringing with it memories of palace life—of golden children with satin skin and virgin canvases to fill with the finest Parisian tinctures, and where the light of a thousand candles was captured and reflected by snowflakes created by Fabergé instead of by God.

Misurov shook the frozen tears away from his eyes. *Foolish man,* he chided himself, *those things are gone forever. Dead.*

"Let's hurry and get inside," he whispered, half-tugging, half-carrying the child up the stair. "It's cold and you are hungry."

"Yes," she said, "starving."

Her voice was so pitiful it almost melted Misurov's heart. Almost. But not quite.

The brass hasp screeched as he opened the door, inciting a rolling tide of squeals from the rats as Misurov stepped inside. His palatial estate occupied a space no bigger than a pony stall in the Czar's stables and was as frigid as a grave. Another chorus of angry squeals met his blind fumblings for the wall shelf next to the door where he kept a tallow candle and matches. A thump followed by a high-pitched grunt let him know that the rats had again found a way up to the shelf.

Misurov felt a thumb-size strip gnawed out of the middle of the candle when he picked it up; the empty paint pot he kept the dozen or so matches in had been upended, the precious contents scattered or eaten. It took him another three pats along the shelf before the sodden fingers of his glove found a single match.

"Damn vermin," he growled, igniting the sulfur along the under-side of the shelf. Shadows danced along the empty walls as he fought chills to light the candle. "If this new government of ours really wanted to do something, they would classify rats along with other political dissidents and send them all to Siberia. Bah . . . but enough of things we cannot change, isn't that so, Yrena?"

Silence and darkness answered him.

Misurov tottered slightly as he turned, the narrow, rat-chewed candle quivering. Shadows fled across the walls, solidifying finally into the tiny figure still standing in the open doorway. Perhaps fear had found her last.

"Yrena."

She didn't move—*How many times had he told his models not to move?*—didn't lower her dark eyes from his, the pinprick of light they reflected the only things moving.

"What is it, Yrena?" Misurov asked softly, his voice a lullaby. "I won't hurt you. Come in, there is nothing of which to be afraid."

Her body started moving forward at the word *come.* And by the time the last echo of the last word died Misurov found himself being grasped around the waist in a surprisingly strong bear-hug.

Misurov's laughter clouded the air as he swung her up to his chest and slammed the door with a kick. She didn't seem to notice when he released his hold just long enough to slide the iron inner bolt shut. His quiet little bird didn't even seem to notice when he carried her to the tiny stone fireplace four paces away and set her before it.

A half-dozen thrusts with the fireiron into the bed of coals and a ruddy glow filled the room, exposing piles of dust-covered canvases propped up against the walls. In recent years they had proven to be a better source of fuel than a lasting monument to his genius.

To prove that, Misurov grabbed a painting from the stack near-est the hearth and set it on the embers. The portrait, showing one of the Czar's brood mares, sizzled into flames almost instantly, the heat from it sending shivers down Misurov's back.

"There now," he said, laying the poker aside to rub his hands vigorously in the warmth, "isn't that better?"

Than what? Yrena's dark eyes asked silently.

Another shiver raced through him. Sighing, Misurov pulled one of the only two chairs he owned over to the fire and let the wet coat slip from his shoulders. Wisps of steam that smelled like wet dogs curled up from the material.

"Come, then," he said, gently pulling the shawl away from her face and fingering one of the ebony locks it exposed, "off with those wet things before you catch your death."

Misurov felt his hands tremble, but not from the cold.

"We'll get you warm and dry first," he said, putting a promise into his voice, "and then food."

With that one word, Misurov saw more emotion in the child's face than he had since meeting her. Her need tore at his heart, but it didn't stop him from undressing her. If he could no longer paint, then life owed him *some* sort of compensation.

Without her shawl, dress, and stockings, Yrena was little more than blued flesh and knobby bones; barely a mouthful.

But beggars cannot be choosers, Konstantin, he reminded himself as he reached down to slip the child's gray undershift from her shoulders. *And you most certainly have become a beggar in this—*

Misurov was still chiding fate when Yrena lunged forward and sank her teeth into his wrist. The pain made him react without thinking, backhanding her to the floor, her shift coming away in his hand.

Blood dripped from the jagged wound at his wrist.

She lay naked at his feet, but for the first time in his life Misurov didn't care.

"You little bitch," he screamed, his right boot already cocked and waiting to spring, "why the hell did . . . you . . . do . . . ?"

Misurov's anger and shock transformed, scattered like ash borne before the winds as he gazed into Yrena's dark eyes. The hunger that lurked there was a living creature that reached out to him the way he had once reached out for the tender flesh of children. He felt it close around his soul. Pulling him. Luring him into its depths.

Without any effort on his part, Misurov kneeled before her and held out his bloodied arm. The dark eyes shifted to the wound, a sardonic grin slowly parting her lips. The light from the burning portrait reflecting off strong white fangs.

"Papa," she whispered, reaching up to take Misurov's hand. "Papa."

As Yrena's teeth pierced his flesh a second time an ecstasy Misurov had never found even in the arms of children exploded in his soul, creating images in his mind so real, so sublime that he began painting them on the invisible canvas of air around him.

Yrena . . . his little bird . . . his little gypsy Madonna encircled by the ruby-red light of Heaven as she—

The sound of retching shattered the illusion and Misurov collapsed, tumbling hard to the rough wooden floor.

"What the—?"

Yrena was curled into a ball, hunched over on her heels, the ridges of her backbone writhing snakelike beneath the thin layer of skin as she vomited. It took Misurov a moment to realize what she was throwing up was blood. *His* blood.

"God protect me," he prayed, forgetting that God had been declared dead as he scrambled away from her, stopping only when his own spine collided with the paintings lying against the wall behind him. "What *are* you?"

She looked up, his little bird, tears the color of garnets leaving tracks against her snow-colored cheeks—her fangs, like ivory scimitars, stained with his blood.

"You're not my Papa," she whimpered, "and I'm so hungry."

His little bird. His little Madonna.

A verdalak!

Misurov crossed himself quickly, forgetting again as he pressed his knuckles against the front of his teeth in place of the ceremonial kiss and watched the child slowly lower her head back to the blood-spattered floor.

No wonder she was alone. And starving. If the legends his Baba told him as a child were true, the verdalak was that form of vampire which could feed only on members of its own family.

"My God," he whispered, louder . . . and louder, pounding his fist against the floor. "My God. My God."

And God answered.

It was at that instant the frame within the fire cracked and spat out a smoldering piece of itself next to his hand. lie could still see the intricate carving that had once decorated the wood, reduced now to charcoal . . . nothing . . . useless . . . a shadow of what it had been.

Like Yrena. Like his little bird.

Like himself . . . nothing . . . useless . . .

A painting appeared in his mind: Yrena lying there, cowering, night shadow and firelight playing over the contours of her naked body.

Yrena.

Misurov's fingers stung from the heat of the charcoal sliver as he sketched the outline. The floor was too rough for fine detail, too worn for the delicate features that soon appeared.

"Yrena. Lift your head and look at me . . . no, too much. Lower your chin. To the left, move your chin to the left, you're throwing a shadow across your arm. Yes . . . that's it. That's it."

A moment later two Yrenas stared questioningly back at him—one, the reanimated corpse, hunger filling its empty eyes; the other, a perfect Madonna surrounded by light.

Yes.

Nodding, Misurov stood and grabbed another canvas from the pile behind him. The painting was of a stately young woman in a flowing white gown—a lady of the court or perhaps even one of the Grand Duchesses themselves—walking along a spring path, golden sun dappling her amber hair, pink cherry blossoms cascading about her.

It was soulless. Dead. As imaginative as the signs he now painted.

A thin cloud of dust trailed across the room as he carried it to the long abandoned easel sitting beneath the room's window. The remains of a silken shirt, dust-stained and torn and yellowed with age, hung from the point of the skeletal frame like a decaying corpse. Misurov had placed it there in hopes of hiding one piece of the past with another. *Fool,* he chided himself as he tossed it over his shoulder, fitting the painted canvas into the frame.

A tube of gesso that had been in the tray for God knew how long fell when he moved the easel closer to the fire and shattered. Misurov crushed the hardened plaster flakes beneath his boots. It didn't matter. He could still paint her even without preparing the canvas. He could still *paint.*

Misurov looked at the monster-child over the edge of the canvas and felt something stir in his belly . . . his own buried dead rising from their coffins to feast on his life's blood.

Like Yrena.

The charcoal swept across the painting; obliterating one image as it created another. And Yrena watched, as complacent and silent as stone, only her dark eyes breaking the illusion as they darted left and right, following the blood on his wrist.

"Here," he said, bringing the wound to his face so her eyes would follow. "Look at me *here.*"

"I'm hungry."

Misurov nodded and quickly sketched in the eyes before they broke contact.

"Of that I have no doubt, verdalak," he said, softening the shadows caressing the charcoal face with the side of his hand. "How long did it take you to kill your family? A month? Two? Not even wolves eat their own kind."

A garnet tear blossomed in the corner of one eye. Misurov copied it in charcoal, mentally keeping a list of the colors he'd have to buy to finish the painting.

"But I couldn't help it," she whined—a little girl being chastised for some minor misdoing. "My brother Oleg . . ."

"Ah, your brother," Misurov said, deepening the look of anguish in the thin lips. "Is he here in the city with you?"

"No."

Bold strokes—three, four, five—and ebony curls encircled her unpainted face.

"There is no one left then?"

The garnet tear fell. "No."

"So you decided to come to the big city, huh? Walked all the way from Vojvoda to see if there was some long-forgotten family member . . . like a wolf cub tracking lambs. But it wasn't that easy, was it, little bird?"

Misurov let the charcoal drop from his fingers as he took a step back to look at the sketch. Yrena, like the child Madonna, stared calmly back at him. Where there had been only need and hunger, there was now acceptance. Where there had been only shadow, there was now light.

"You came all that way and you found nothing." Misurov reached out and brushed his fingers lightly over the charcoaled shoulders. "Well, you are in good company . . . even the living have found nothing here."

"But I'm so hungry," the creature moaned, the points of her fangs digging into her colorless bottom lip.

Misurov nodded, understanding. "As I was."

Absently rubbing the charcoal into his beard, he walked back to her and kneeled—slowly pulled the blood-soaked cuff away from his wrist and held it out. Yrena yelped like a booted hound, covering her face with bloodied fingers.

"Go away," she whimpered, "leave me alone."

How many other children had told him that? Fifty? One hundred? And how many times had he heeded that plea? Not once.

Then or now.

"Shush, little bird," Misurov said as softly as he had every other time, "I'm not going to hurt you. Look, see what I have for you." Dark eyes lifted just enough to gaze at the wound. "Come, my Yrena, eat."

Caution, like black ice forming across the surface of a pond, momentarily replaced the hunger in her eyes. In the flickering light, Misurov watched the muscles in her narrow thighs and calves quiver.

"Why are you doing this?" she hissed. "Why aren't you afraid of me? *Why? Why wasn't he?*

The joints in his knees popped as he kneeled next to her. *Why?* Turning his head, Misurov studied the sketch he'd just done. It had been so long since anything had stirred him enough to go back to his easel . . . so very long since he'd felt truly alive.

"Because," Misurov said, on his knees now, moving his bloodied wrist closer even as she backed away, "I need you to model for me."

"But I *can't,*" she whimpered, "I can only feed on . . . I can only . . ."

Her sobs sounded human enough.

"I know, I know," Misurov said, taking both her cold hands in his. "But listen to me, little bird, there is a way. I can adopt you. Do you understand? I *do* adopt you. That makes *me* your Papa now. Understand?"

The skin around Yrena's mouth tightened. She understood.

"My Papa."

"Yes."

"My *Papa.*"

Misurov felt his body jerk as she darted forward, her fangs golden in the firelight and glistening with drool. It was all he could do to keep her at bay, the wound at his wrist held just out of reach.

"Yes, but listen to me, verdalak," he commanded, "I will be your Papa but you will not feed off of me. I have many cousins in this city, many more than any family needs, and each night I will tell you where to find one. You may drain that one to the dregs, I don't care, but then you will come back to me. Only to me, do you understand *that?*"

Yrena nodded, less child and more monster as she nuzzled the wound and whined.

"All right then, you may take just a little . . . to seal our bargain, so to speak. *Ah, God!*"

Light and fire coursed through Misurov when she reopened the wound and began to lap, her slug-white tongue making kitten sounds in the stillness Closing his eyes, Misurov shuddered and saw colors swirl into a hundred paintings . . . masterpieces that had yet to be created. Hundreds? No . . . thousands, and all of Yrena. All of them of his little bird.

Misurov arched his back, groaning at the strength of the spasm that rocked through him.

God, it was good to be painting again.

*   *

He loved her.

Not the way he had once feigned love with living children, using their bodies to fill an emptiness he'd never even known existed until Yrena came into his life.

Because she had given him *back* his life and filled it the way her painted image filled the walls of his room. His little bird, gazing back at him regardless of where he looked—but always in shadows, features highlighted only by candlelight, the colors muted . . . dark.

She required so little of the spectrum: black, mulberry, lapis and cerulean, alabaster and ivory for her flesh, a touch of mustard and primrose for the candle's wan glow, and vermillion for her lips and cheeks.

It was sad in a way, Misurov mused as he swirled a drop of red into black, now that he had money enough to buy every hue ever imagined.

One of the benefits of Yrena's nightly "family visits" was the presents she brought home to her loving Papa. Sometimes rubles and sometimes things that could be more discreetly bartered for the supplies he needed. His lovely little bird.

Misurov felt no remorse. His morally superior family had kept their disapproval of him a secret as long as he was their link to court; but almost at the same moment the Czar and his family were falling beneath a summer rain of bullets, Misurovs were denouncing him to anyone who would listen as a pervert and Menshevik.

Bastards.

Rolling his shoulders against the cramp that had worked its way into them, Misurov stuck the sable-tipped brush between his teeth and took a step back . . . nodding at the Yrena who stared back at him from the finished canvas.

She was standing half hidden by the open door, looking back into the room over her right shoulder . . . the faintest hint of a smile playing at the corners of her mouth.

It was that smile which had driven Misurov back to the easel, the first *real* smile he had ever seen from her. The first, he prayed, of many more to come.

*   *   *

Misurov heard her light step on the stairs only a moment before she opened the door.

"I'm home, Papa," she said, closing the door and walking quickly to his side, her woollen cape fluttering behind her like angel wings.

Smiling around the brush, Misurov leaned forward to receive her offered kiss. And felt a shiver nettle his spine. Her lips were icicles against his flesh, her breath the wind from a slaughterhouse.

His little love.

"Did you remember to do as I told you, Yrena?" He asked as he took the brush from between his teeth, then tossed both it and the palette to the floor. He had asked that same question for twenty-six nights in a row.

"Yes, Papa."

"And there was no trouble?"

"No, Papa."

She was such a good child.

"Come then and tell your Papa all about it."

Misurov flexed the stiffness from his fingers as he walked to the hearth. The roaring fire he had started before beginning to paint had reduced itself to a fist-sized mound of rolling coals. *Where did the time go?* Picking up the wrought-iron poker he stabbed the embers and watched a million sparks fly to heaven.

When he turned around she was standing at his side, the knife blade laid out across both palms. Even though he didn't think the taint of the verdalak would extend to Yrena's adoptive family, Misurov didn't believe in taking chances. Instead of using her fangs, he had instructed his beloved child to slit throats or wrists to feed.

What news there'd been on the streets had been full of the ghastly murders. *The work of a madman,* it was thought, *or a Loyalist out to avenge the Empire.*

Fools, Misurov thought as he curled his fingers around the knife handle and brought it into the light. As usual it had been licked clean. Misurov nodded.

"Well, then," he said, listening to the rustle of her clothing whisper through the gloom behind him, "what have you brought your Papa tonight?"

There was no answer.

Misurov turned to find her staring at her newest portrait. There wasn't a trace of the earlier smile on her florid lips.

"Do you like it?" he asked.

"No, Papa."

"But why not, my little love?"

Her eyes traced the lines of the panting. "Because it's like a mirror," she said. "They all are. Do you hate me that much, Papa?"

"Hate you?" The knife slipped from Misurov's hand, clattering hollowly against the hearthstone as he stood. "How can you say such a thing? Just look around you, Yrena . . . these paintings . . ."

Misurov took a step toward her and spread his arms to the room. Smiled at each image he had made of her.

"These paintings tell how much I *love* you. Look here. And here, look." Misurov spun on the heels of his boots, stopping when he faced the first portrait he'd ever done of her, the night she had come into his life—lying naked before the fire, the soulless eyes glaring back at him. "You are my reason to live, Yrena, my reason to paint. How could I not love you? My God, how could you say such a thing?"

She shrugged. It was so human, so childlike an action that Misurov chuckled.

Until she turned and stared at him.

"What?" he asked. "What is it, my little bird?"

"That was the last one, wasn't it, Papa?"

Misurov made it all the way to his chair by the hearth before his legs gave out from under him.

Something scraped beneath the heel of his boot. Looking down he saw the knife blade gleam like blood in the embers' glow. Like blood. A grinding ache shot through Misurov's back and shoulders as he leaned forward to pick it up.

"I don't know what you mean, little bi—"

"You don't have any more family left. Do you, Papa?"

Misurov stared at his elongated features—*blood red*—in the blade.

"No. How did you know?"

"This one was so old and thin, not even much juice left, like the last apple in a barrel, Papa."

Misurov nodded, watched his reflection shimmer.

"Do you hate me, Yrena?"

"No," she answered from across the room. "Papa."

"Do you love me?"

"No, Papa."

"Are you going to leave me?"

"Yes, Papa."

Letting his eyes gaze at the portraits surrounding him, Misurov lifted the knife and pressed the point of the blade into the throbbing vein at the side of his neck. There was less pain than he had hoped for.

"Well, then," he said, "show your Papa what you have brought before you go."

Misurov heard the rustle of her cape and the *tap, tap, tap* of her boots crossing the room toward him. But already she sounded so very far away.

"Here, Papa."

The goblet was exquisite, turned smoky quartz crystal with a reeded gold base, just the sort of thing his late spinster cousin would keep. A ghost from the past.

Like his paintings.

Like Yrena.

"How fitting," he said, holding the goblet up to catch the blood oozing from his throat.

She took the first brimming goblet full and drained it dry.

He filled it a second time. A third. It was getting harder to talk, to think.

"Will you love me when I'm dead, Yrena?"

"No," she said, licking her lips, "Papa."

Misurov heard glass break as Yrena climbed onto his lap and began kissing his neck. Closing his eyes, Misurov watched the colors fade from dull gray to black to . . . blood red.

jane yolen

Sister Death

You have to understand, it is not the blood. It was never the blood. I swear that on my own child's heart, though I came at last to bear the taste of it, sweetly salted, as warm as milk from the breast.

The first blood I had was from a young man named Abel, but I did not kill him. His own brother had already done that, striking him down in the middle of a quarrel over sheep and me. The brother preferred the sheep. How like a man.

Then the brother called me a whore. His vocabulary was remarkably basic, though it might have been the shock of his own brutality. The name itself did not offend me. It was my profession, after all. He threw me down on my face in the bloody dirt and treated me like one of his beloved ewes. I thought it was the dirt I was eating.

It was blood.

Then he beat me on the head and back with the same stick he had used on his brother, till I knew only night. *Belilah.* Like my name.

How long I lay there, unmoving, I was never to know. But when I came to, the bastard was standing over me with the authorities, descrying my crime, and I was taken as a murderess. The only witnesses to my innocence—though how can one call a whore innocent—were a murderer and a flock of sheep. Was it any wonder I was condemned to die?

Oh how I ranted in that prison. I cursed the name of G-d, saying: "Let the day be darkness wherein I was born and let G-d not inquire about it for little does He care. A woman is nothing in His sight and a man is all, be he a murderer or a thief." Then I vowed not to die at all but to live to destroy the man who would destroy me. I cried and I vowed and then I called on the demonkin to save me. I remembered the taste of blood in my mouth and offered that up to any who would have me.

One must be careful of such prayers.

The night before I was to be executed, Lord Beelzebub himself entered my prison. How did I know him? He insinuated himself through the keyhole as mist, reforming at the foot of my pallet. There were two stubby black horns on his forehead. His feet were like pigs' trotters. He carried around a tail as sinuous as a serpent. His tongue, like an adder's, was black and forked.

"You do not want a man, Lillake," he said, using the pretty pet name my mother called me. "A demon can satisfy you in ways even you cannot imagine."

"I am done with lovemaking," I answered, wondering that he could think me desirable. After a month in the prison I was covered with sores. "Except for giving one a moment's pleasure, it brings nothing but grief."

The mist shaped itself grandly. "This," he said pointing, "is more than a moment's worth. You will be well repaid."

"You can put that," I gestured back, "into another keyhole. Mine is locked forever."

One does not lightly ignore a great lord's proposal, nor make light of his offerings. It was one of the first things I had learned. But I was already expecting to die in the morning. And horribly. So, where would I spend his coin?

"Lillake, hear me," Lord Beelzebub said, his voice no longer cozening but black as a burnt cauldron. *Shema* was the word he used. I had not known that demons could speak the Lord G-d's holy tongue.

I looked up, then, amazed, and saw through the disguise. This was no demon at all but the Lord G-d Himself testing me, though why He should desire a woman—and a whore at that—I could not guess.

"I know you, *Adonai*," I said. "But God or demon, my answer is the same. Women and children are nothing in your sight. You are a bringer of death, a maker of carrion."

His black aspect melted then, the trotters disappeared, the horns became tendrils of white hair. He looked chastened and sad and held out His hand.

I disdained it, turning over on my straw bed and putting my face to the wall.

"It is no easy thing being at the Beginning and at the End," He said. "And so you shall see, my daughter. I shall let you live, and forever. You will see the man, Cain, die. Not once but often. It will bring you no pleasure. You will be Death's sister, chaste till the finish of all time, your mouth filled with the blood of the living."

So saying, He was gone, fading like the last star of night fading into dawn.

Of course I was still in prison. So much for the promises of G-d.

*   *

At length I rose from the mattress. I could not sleep. Believing I had but hours before dying, I did not wish to waste a moment of the time left, though each moment was painful. I walked to the single window where only a sliver of moon was visible. I put my hands between the bars and clutched at the air as though I could hold it in my hands. And then, as if the air itself had fallen in love with me, it gathered me up through the bars, lifted me through the prison wall, and deposited me onto the bosom of the dawn and I was somehow, inexplicably, free.

Free.

As I have been these five thousands years.

*   *

Oh, the years have been kind to me. I have not aged. I have neither gained nor lost weight nor grayed nor felt the pain of advancing years. The blood has been kind to me, the blood I nightly take from the dying children, the true innocents, the Lord G-d's own. Yet for all the children I have sucked rather than suckled, there has been only one I have taken for mine.

I go to them all, you understand. There is no distinction. I take the ones who breathe haltingly, the ones who are misused, the ones whose bodies are ill shaped in the womb, the ones whom fire or famine or war cut down. I take them and suck them dry and send them, dessicated little souls, to the Lord G-d's realm. But as clear-eyed as I had been when I cast out *Adonai* in my prison, so clear-eyed would a child need to be to accept me as I am and thus become my own. So for these five thousand years there has been no one for me in my lonely occupation but my mute companion, the Angel of Death.

If I could still love, he is the one I would desire. His wings are the color of sun and air as mine are fog and fire. Each of the vanes in those wings are hymnals of ivory. He carries the keys to Heaven in his pocket of light. Yet he is neither man nor woman, neither demon nor god. I call the Angel "he" for as I am Sister Death, he is surely my brother.

We travel far on our daily hunt.

We are not always kind.

*   *
*

But the child, my child, I will tell you of her now. It is not a pretty tale.

As always we travel, the Angel and I, wingtips apart over a landscape of doom. War is our backyard, famine our feast. Most fear the wind of our wings and even, in their hurt, pray for life. Only a few, a very few, truly pray for death. But we answer all their prayers with the same coin.

This particular time we were tracking across the landscape of the Pale, where grass grew green and strong right up to the iron railings that bore the boxcars along. In the fields along the way, the peasants swung their silver scythes in rhythm to the trains. They did not hear the counterpoint of cries from the cars or, if they did, they showed their contempt by stopping and waving gaily as the death trains rolled past.

They did not see my brother Death and me riding the screams but inches overhead. But they would see us in their own time.

In the cars below, jammed together like cattle, the people vomited and pissed on themselves, on their neighbors, and prayed. Their prayers were like vomit, too, being raw and stinking and unstoppable.

My companion looked at me, tears in his eyes. I loved him for his pity. Still crying, he plucked the dead to him like faded flowers, looking like a bridegroom waiting at the feast.

And I, no bride, flew through the slats, to suck dry a child held overhead for air. He needed none. A girl crushed by the door, I took her as well. A teenager, his head split open by a soldier's gun, died unnoticed against a wall. He was on the cusp of change but would never now be a man. His blood was bitter in my mouth but I drank it all.

What are Jews that nations swat them like flies? That the Angel of Death picks their faded blooms? That I drink the blood now bitter, now sweet, of their children?

❋   ❋
❋

The train came at last to a railway yard that was ringed about with barbs. BIRKENAU, read the station sign. It creaked back and forth in the wind. BIRKENAU.

When the train slowed, then stopped, and the doors pushed open from the outside, the living got out. The dead were already gathered up to their G-d.

My companion followed the men and boys, but I—I flew right, above the weeping women and their weeping children, as I have done all these years.

There was another Angel of Death that day, standing in the midst of the madness. He hardly moved, only his finger seemed alive, an organism in itself, choosing the dead, choosing the living.

"Please, Herr General," a boy cried out. "I am strong enough to work."

But the finger moved, and having writ, moved on. To the right, boy. To the arms of Lilith, Belilah, Lillake.

"Will we get out?" a child whispered to its mother.

"We will get out," she whispered back.

But I had been here many times before. "You will only get out of here through the chimney," I said.

Neither mother nor child nor General himself heard.

* *

There were warning signs at the camp. BEWARE, they said. TENSION WIRE, they said.

There were other signs, too. Pits filled with charred bones. Prisoners whose faces were imprinted with the bony mask of death.

JEDEM DAS SEINE. Each one gets what he deserves.

* *

In the showers, the naked mothers held their naked children to them. They were too tired to scream, too tired to cry. They had no tears left.

Only one child, a seven-year-old, stood alone. Her face was angry. She was not resigned. She raised her fist and looked at the heavens and then, a little lower, at me.

Surprised, I looked back.

The showers began their rain of poison. Coughing, praying, calling on G-d to save them, the women died with their children in their arms.

The child alone did not cough, did not pray, did not call on G-d. She held out her two little hands to me. *To me.*

"Imma," she said. "Mother."

I trembled, flew down, and took her in my arms. Then we flew through the walls as if they were air.

*   .   *
    *

So I beg you, as you love life, as you master Death, let my brother be the sole harvester. I have served my five thousand years; not once did I complain. But give me a mother's span with my child, and I will serve you again till the end of time. This child alone chose me in all those years. You could not be so cruel a god as to part us now.

susan
shwartz

The Carpetbagger

Legs askew, the dead woman lay in a doorway off Bourbon Street. Her head rested on a battered kilim bag and her eyes stared up like a camera set for time-lapse photography. Gradually the images trapped in the glazed lenses faded—the krewes passing, gaudy and raucous, Rex on his horse, Isis with her crown; men flaunting evening gowns and women wearing almost nothing at all below bobbing breasts; the flight and flash of plastic necklaces; and the avid pale face of her last cavalier.

Constrained by her New England upbringing, she had found it hard to scream, but after the sun plunged like a counterfeit doubloon into the brown water, her eyes had met the eyes of a man in weathered gray. He wore a hat with rifles crossed upon it, a saber, and a fringed gold sash, a Mardi Gras clone of Ashley Wilkes.

Not at all like Ashley then, but like the sailor in the *Life* photo at the end of World War II, he grabbed her, spun her around, and bent her back until she fell splayed upon her spine: and that too was nothing all that abnormal for Mardi Gras.

"How's this for a taste of your own medicine you bloodsuckin' Yankee?" Cold lips against her throat reeked gunpowder and bad blood.

Oh Jesus, just my luck if he's got AIDS, she thought. People danced on by, still screaming Mister, throw me something, letting the good times roll as she tried to roll him off her.

His face changed. She saw the gunshot-ruined mouth, bone and fangs protruding. His teeth sucked scream and blood and breath out of her throat.

She had time before her sight faded to wonder what she had done to deserve . . .

Silence, despite the jazz drifting from the bars.

Stars and streetlights shone down into her eyes. The transvestites picked their ways past her, cruising the Quarter, and the Mississippi rolled on: silent times for one more victim. That's what happened.

Hoofbeats down Bourbon Street: helmeted police with hard bellies, Tabasco tempers, and faith in law, order, and LSU football clattered in a dead march side by side.

Midnight. Mardi Gras is over. To your scattered bodies go.

A water truck whirred behind them, crunching discarded go cups, sprinkling the dead along with the rest of the trash lying in the way: water over the damned.

Easter isn't for weeks yet. What we have here is premature resurrection.

Tears of wretchedness cleaned her face. The dead woman turned her cheek where it rested on her bag and vomited a puddle of reddish brown.

Jesus, the crazy hadn't even bothered to steal her bag. The contempt of that plucked at her nerves. She would have screamed if she had had the strength and no sense left. She fumbled in her bag: wallet intact, cash intact, plastic intact.

Was she?

Fucked over in New Orleans. God. This sort of thing would have been bad enough at home with swabs and doctors, bright lights, the stink of stale coffee and her own unshowered flesh, questions from female cops, as invasive as a second rape, if rape it was. Among the bubbas—didn't the cops beat up on people down here?—it would probably be worse. You could scare hell out of yourself down here, if they didn't get you first.

"Did you know the man, miss?" She could just hear the litany now.

She shut her eyes. That face before it changed and shattered . . . the night before, she'd gone with friends to The Dungeon, just a few doors down.

"You don't want to go to Pat O'Briens; it's for the tourists. And the line for Preservation Hall is just too long. This is neat, you'll like it."

They ventured in at the narrow door, paid up, then headed down a sloping passageway lined with f'rgodssake cobblestones, and over a bridge across an artificial stream. Seriously weird, but not as weird as the picture of the horned and hooved patron on the wall. She was honestly tempted to throw the bounder a cake to let them pass.

Smoke and rock and roll assaulted them. So did The Dungeon's vibes. Very simply, they were the worst she'd ever felt.

"The hell with our three bucks. Let's go!" she nudged her friends.

But her companions were already shrieking at the choice of house drinks: Witch's Brew or Dragon's Blood. The man behind the dark, cramped bar wouldn't say what was in them. They should have gone back to O'Brien's or Preservation Hall. Wasn't as if tourists weren't here, too. You could tell them in their grown-up toddler clothes. You could tell the regulars, who wore dark shirts and pants, almost like New Yorkers. The few women among them had big hair, dyed, fried, and pushed to the side.

She wanted to leave now.

One man wearing gray and an Aussie hat swung down from where he sat near the dance floor, held out a hand.

"Go on!" one friend whispered and gave her a sly push. She saw herself in the mirror, out of place, dancing alone, her eyes enormous.

"You from up North, little lady?" His voice was honey over acid.

"Near Boston."

He danced tense and fast. Under the hat, he was pale, trim beard over a weak mouth, held angry-taut. Well, she could always retreat to the Ladies' Room; Board of Health rules meant they'd have one, wouldn't they?

"After 2:00 A.M., women drink free. You'll like that, won't you?"

What she didn't like was his hostility, only half disguised by the questions.

"I can buy my own drinks."

"Little Miss Independence. I just bet you can. All you Yankees, come down here with your own money, actin' like a queen. What you going to do here, anyhow? Kick up your heels in those Sunday school teacher clothes, then go back home and be a virgin?"

Jesus, why did she have to be the lucky one again? It wasn't an Aussie hat the man was wearing after all: she spotted some kind of Southern thing on the crown. A Confederate die-hard, wouldn't you just know? That war'd been over for a hundred years; but you couldn't tell down here. They were still fighting it, them and their sacred Cause, aided and abetted by book publishers. No wonder the place was such a mess. They were still fighting a guerrilla war against the Reconstruction.

She turned and left the dance floor. "I'm out of here," she told her friends.

This long after midnight, she knew to find a cab back to the Quality Inn. The driver, hunched over the wheel, had a slow islanders accent. "Lady like you shouldn't be walkin' around here alone. Shouldn't be alone. They's all kind of lowlife."

He drove off, made some turns, and she was lost. Down the road, past a darkness in which she saw blurs in which long structures with pointed roofs emerged.

"Now, doan' you go in there—" It was St. Louis Cemetery Number 3, where Creoles, carpetbaggers, Cajuns, and voodoo queens lay above ground, their bodies protected from the seep of Lake Pontchartrain and the Mississippi for the short years till they decomposed. Whitewash, plastered over brick, coffins stacked within, tomb upon tomb, the dead yielded place to more recent dead and to the predators who hid among the green, shadowed lanes.

Her driver's eyes glazed sideways and his hand went to touch something round his neck. "They hide behind the tombs. You starin' at some angel and they' jump out at you!"

She tightened her grip on her bag, an expensive new one made out of a Turkish rug, and promised not to go there or go anywhere alone. She tipped him, and he waited till she readied the lobby before he drove away.

Yes, she had seen a pale face, twisted with anger beneath the shadow of a hat. And knew it before it changed. She wondered if any cop would buy that.

What did you suppose a Louisiana mental hospital would be like? Probably a snakepit. Like the bayou.

Sit up, why don't you? She struggled up, then rubbed her hands over her face to smear away the tears. Her fingers looked dark, as if she had worn mascara; and she knew she hadn't. Dark tears? She must be a worse mess than she thought.

She leaned out beneath the streetlight. The yowls of karaoke and rum-sodden drunks overpowered the blue notes of a jazz trombone, wailing like a train in the night. How pale her hand looked in the dark. She knew she'd caught some sun up on the levee by the Aquarium the other day, drinking Hurricanes and watching the dirty umber Mississippi flow by. Weird river, with its centuries of freight; weird city, like the shards of mirror in a burnt-out funhouse. By the waters of Babylon. Buy the waters of Babylon—and anything else they could try to sell her.

Again, she rubbed her eyes. Her tears were tainted almost red. Jesus.

She pulled a mirror from her bag to see the damages. And she saw precisely nothing at all. Oh, she saw the street, the pools of filth dissolving in the water from the truck. She saw the shopfronts. Saw a drunk embrace a post. But of herself, her reddened hands, her ruined clothes—not a trace of a reflection.

She could put a name for the type of creature that died, then rose and couldn't see its face in its mirror.

God.

That wasn't the name.

So, saying "God" wouldn't choke her. Maybe she wouldn't react to holy water, crosses, or garlic either. Amazing.

She rubbed her throat, at the rawness there from the bite. Her mouth tasted of salt and worse. Gagging, she made herself look down. She had retched, bringing up a tiny pool of blood. Dregs.

Apparently, draining her the rest of the way hadn't been worth the trouble.

Come to New Orleans! her friends had urged. We can eat our way cross town. Let the good times roll—they make an industry of it!

That wasn't all New Orleans had turned into a cottage industry. She had taken the quaint old streetcar up St. Charles to the Garden District.

"Can we see Anne Rice's house?" some idiot had called, to suppressed snickers. The writer lived here, behind a gate, amid lattices of painted iron and green trees and sunlight, glaring on the banquettes.

Sunlight. She would never see the sun again.

She forced herself to her feet, her eyes darting to the sky. When was dawn? Thank God, she had her watch. What if she went out calling to the Garden District now? Excuse me, ma'am, but I've had this accident, you know; and I was wondering—do you have a spare coffin?

Right!

If she had to be a monster, why'd it have to be a vampire? They were such a Goddammed cliché.

There. She had said the word.

What time was it? Her eyes darted frantically from her watch to the night sky. Hours left till dawn. That wasn't a real long life-span, was it?

But she was dead already. Or undead. And she would die again unless she could think of something.

For God's sake, think of something.

I don't want to be a vampire. Want to go home! She doubted that North American Van Lines carried coffins. After giggling that she'd probably run off with a man in romantic New Orlean's, her girl-friends would have reported that she'd vanished: they'd track her down, when she used her plastic to pay for something like that. And what would she do, even if she could get home? Would an emergency ward test her for porphyria or give her standing appointments for transfusions? Did shrinks have office hours at night? For certain, she would have to hit up the weirdo shrinks at Cambridge Hospital for this. Well, John Mack had switched from shrinking Lawrence of Arabia to saucer people. He'd be sure to get another book contract out of her.

When they gave up on her, would they at least sterilize the stake they brought into the operating room?

You can't sit here all night, panicking under the streetlights.

Think it through.

She needed a place to rest. She needed a place to clean up, assuming running water didn't send her into screaming fits. The dregs of her own blood and the spoor of the one who changed her assaulted her nose. So that much was true: her senses were more keen. Maybe she could track him, could ask him why. I'll kill him. So help me God, I'll kill him.

Did she really think that was safe?

Safe? Was anything? She laughed. Several blocks over, dogs began to howl.

Well, did she have a better idea?

Food, perhaps. She was desperately hungry. There was nothing left in her to throw up. You can eat your way across town, they'd told her. Cajun cooking. Creole cooking. Dinner at Antoine's, yeah, sure; and she'd love to hear what Frances Parkinson Keyes sweet wimps said about vampires, too: probably faint on the spot. Beignets with a veritable blizzard of powdered sugar at Cafe du Monde. Sometimes you get the beignet: sometimes the beignet gets you. It had gotten her for sure this time.

It's much too rich! the well-fed types would cry at food down here, lifting hands in mock horror. Lettuce-eaters, all of them, examining each leaf as if a slug lay beneath it, maybe poking it with a fork just in case. Center-parted hair, sallow, muscles gone to ropey lines down arms and calves—but damn, they ate healthy. Bloodless.

Something, not her stomach, lurched hungrily.

If she could not eat, she would have to feed. And find some answers.

She started off down Bourbon Street, passing drunks and hookers like a wisp of dark cloud. Well, she had always had a talent for invisibility. It might help her now. A black man, rolling like a sailor too long from land, stopped. He shrank into himself, trying for invisibility. The salt of his flesh and blood lured her. His pulse thudded in her ears: alive, afraid, terrifyingly magnetic. The woman with him drew herself up and placed her own powerful frame between them. Go away.

She went.

Listen to that. The morning of Ash Wednesday, but The Dungeon's inmates still partied hearty. Perhaps she could put thumbscrews—no, she thought with a chuckle that appalled her too—perhaps she could put the bite on it for information. No one tried to collect $3.00. The bouncer actually stepped back. His belly under its ripped T-shirt twitched visibly.

Her feet felt every roughness in the cobblestones as she crossed the bridge. Another myth: running water didn't hurt. If the Ladies' Room wasn't empty when she entered, it cleared out fast as she washed. The sight of wall and towel dispenser and the rest of the room where her reflection should have been turned her slightly queasy. Maybe that was hunger, too.

When she was as clean as she could get (her clothes were beyond redemption), she walked into the bar. She half expected to see, beneath his slouch hat, the face of her attacker the vampire. The other vampire.

"He changed you. Why did he change you?"

The voice was breathless, magnolia over scraped slate, and it came from a woman crammed into a black leather—no, vinyl—dress. She was powdered pale, if sweaty, and she wore a ribbon around her neck. Black ribbon, not yellow.

Oh God, this vampire even had wannabes. She knew the type: the professional neurasthenic who read romance and popular history and quoted it like Gospel when she wasn't fluffing back her hair, or who combed genealogies to make herself look good. Eager to party, but the most stalwart virgin in the sorority house.

Tonight, though, the chittering spite—"he changed you?"—annoyed her. And it was even possible that "he" had left a message with this creature, who knew enough to recognize what she was.

"What do you know about him?"

"He say's he'll make me like he is, when I am stronger. I am so sensitive, so delicate, he say's. And then we'll be together forever." Exaggerated rapture. Not so much a wannabe as a groupie.

The woman laid one bruised hand on an ample breast, hiked up beneath her dress. Under the creaking heated vinyl, her heartbeat thudded.

The groupie stared at her with that look such women got when they eyed what they considered their physical inferiors, rendering them invisible with a flick of their eyeliner.

"Why did he pick a wicked little nothing like you? And a Yankee to boot! You just don't think you'll do as he say's. But you won't have a choice! You'll want to. And it will serve you right!"

She hadn't time for this. With a scream of rage that sent shards of mirror cascading down the walls, she pounced upon the woman. Her teeth closed on the ribboned neck, near the wound the vampire had left: she smelled him as well as stale perfume.

Don't drain her.

If she drained this woman, she would never learn the message she sensed driven like a stake into her clouded mind. A shop on Royal Street? That was all?

In disappointment, she released the woman, who sagged against the bar, her eyes appealing for rescue. Not even the bartender moved.

"You're not worth draining. You haven't got the guts to rise again. That's not protection you're bragging about, that's contempt."

The woman pushed away from the bar with surprising angry strength. She shoved her back easily.

"Look at you! You despise your own life. I want mine."

Not "wanted": I *want* mine. How had she survived her own transformation? Maybe the very force of that desire had pushed her back beyond the edge.

She glanced about the room. No one screamed. No one even moved. But their eyes glittered, not with fear or loathing, but with desire. She could feel the heightened pulses, the quickened heartbeats. They repelled her even as they drew her closer. Even the small amount of stolen blood had made her glow like a candle to these pathetic, sodden moths. One drink, one drunk. She didn't want to want them. But, God, she was starving.

She made herself laugh and hit a scornful high note that would have turned Mozart's Queen of the Night bloodless with envy. Gathering her new strength about her, she stalked out as if a cape indeed trailed from her shoulders. The bouncer held his arms out before the crowd, trying to protect it.

The first time in her life she made an exit, and it had to be Final Exit time. Damn.

She could not have drained that female rabbit. But the paltry sip of blood she had taken would not sustain her for long. Disgusting: there might be some glamour to being the Bride of Dracula, but none at all to being a vampire groupie.

She headed toward Royal Street and prowled until she saw a shop that matched the image she had seized. An antique shop, selling not Creole memorabilia, but guns, bullets, pictures, papers, swords: costly relics of the Civil War.

In the window lay a yellowed newspaper with crumbled corners, its print uneven and broken the way type was back in the 1860s and 1870s. Although the shadow of a tattered Stars and Bars half hid it, her changed eyes made it easy for her to make out a restrained headline. Beneath it was an engraving of a body lying across a floor, a blanket thrown across it to conceal—what? A shattered head?

Beneath the picture ran the story, which could have happened today: a man broken by the war, fighting in disguise in the West, but returning at last to his home and his old identity to take his life.

He had failed even at suicide. Suicides sometimes rose; and his anger had no doubt pushed him beyond the peace of death. No doubt, too, his people, those rational, blond people who never let anyone forget how reasonable they were, had despised what they would call mumbo-jumbo, worthy only of slaves or immigrants. They had not taken precautions; and so he had risen.

Gave new meaning to "the South shall rise again," didn't it just?

Why had he chosen her? She was a Yankee, therefore, as he saw it, his enemy. Maybe he thought to play the old hatreds out beyond the grave. She was strong enough to make the change, and there would be, even beyond the grave, some satisfaction in binding an enemy to his will. It probably even helped that she was female.

You still want to die, Mister? You tell me how I can find you and drive a stake through your heart. Assuming you've got one.

Could you just imagine? If every suicide rose—think of Faulkner's Quentin Compson as a vampire. I don't hate the South I don't I don't. She wondered how they'd have worked it out in Cambridge when Quentin threw himself off the Andersen Bridge into the Charles amid the odor of the honeysuckle, not the beer, sweat, rum, and tainted magnolias of this city, precarious beneath the level of the water. The Compson blood had thinned out; at least this way, he'd restore it after a fashion.

She'd always wondered if he and Shreve were lovers. Buried in one coffin, roommates again, to rise and let straight-arrow Shreve live for the first time. Right.

Wasn't as if you didn't find that theme in the South, either; just look at Blanche's husband in *Streetcar* here in New Orleans. Another suicide. She should write this, publish it; but she never had—never had the nerve, and never would now; oh, but it was funny.

God, she was losing it . . . Soon it would be dawn, and she had no leads at all, no place to stay. What was she going to do? Wait out till dawn and then fry? It wasn't as if she outlived centuries so she could just fall away to ash. Maybe she was a wicked little nothing, and maybe it wasn't much of a life that she'd had; but she'd wanted it, never more than now. And she was damned if she was going to lose what she had left because someone had been too cowardly to stay alive and let an old grudge die.

What would become of her?

The panic she had suppressed flooded in on her the way some hurricane in years to come would make Lake Pontchartrain burst its levees and inundate this gumbo Atlantis.

"Oh help me, God!"

Dogs howled descant to her howl of anguish. The glass front of the store next to the gun shop shattered. A burglar alarm began to shriek. The white of old lace and muslin billowed from the darkness, to be restrained by iron grating.

Clean, fragrant cloth—yes! She tried the grates. The lock yielded to her new strength. She seized the gown that had caught her eye. Police would surely come soon. She peeled out of her soiled clothes (Sunday school teacher clothes, he had called them) and pulled the dress over her head, eased its genteel folds down over her waist, then squandered a moment smoothing her hair. The dress would have cost more than a month's salary.

She wished she could see herself—pale, glowing skin, dark hair, Giselle rising from the grave, not to save life, but to seek it. Her friends would giggle: just think, she'd met someone and stayed out all night! Tomorrow, maybe, they'd get round to panicking. They wouldn't miss her long; she was a spare. Next of kin would get her insurance. No, no home for her.

Where to? She would need a place to stay, some place safely dark. What about that rusty, torpedo-shaped thing in Jackson Square by the Cabildo? A submarine, it looked like. It would be dark inside. Yes; and she'd bet money she didn't have that it was sealed, so people could not climb inside and screw, just to say they had.

As she wandered down Royal, she thought she almost fit in here now, here, in this dancing dress that might have belonged once to some Creole *jeune fille bien elevee* who would not have been let out this late at night. It made sense. New Orleans spent more than half its time steeped in the past. Living and dead slept close together, and time here was twisty. It flowed sideways like a cat, to rub against the living or jump them, out of the shadows, and sink in claws and fangs.

She could go to the cemetery the driver'd warned her to avoid. Surely, no mugger could harm her now, or even meet her eyes. Perhaps there might even be some familiar name there, some scalawag or Yankee trooper whom a fever had borne off, and she could find houseroom. She would rather not lie among strangers. She shut her eyes, seeking the thread of awareness that she'd heard (when she bothered to think of it) must draw a vampire to her creator. She found nothing. It hardly seemed fair just to leave her on her own, but it didn't seem as if chivalry worked for vampires. This was his turf. He knew how to hunt and track and stalk. He might even enjoy it. Besides, she was . . . oh God, she was so hungry.

She would have to feed. She was afraid.

"Excuse me, Mademoiselle. Miss, are you all right?" At a respectful distance, addressing her with respect: heartbeats, blood, sweat, life. Inclining forward in a half-bow, careful not to spook a woman all in white who should not be out alone before Ash Wednesday's dawn.

Go away.

He was coming at her: dark, reserved, more European than Southern. One of the Creoles, then, who mostly kept to themselves unlike the more boisterous Cajuns. Why did he have to be out, strolling back, no doubt, to some discreetly inherited flat in the Pontalba Buildings or to an even more discreet house whose iron grilles barred it from the riffraff of the city? Confident, or why would he investigate an alarm all by himself?

Hunger made her dizzier than she thought she could be, yet still keep her feet. She sensed the cleanness in his blood along with some subtle cologne and the starch in his shirt. He wore a wedding ring. Even worse, a family man. She shrank away.

"Were you hurt? Did the thieves touch you?"

What a reward for his kindness, to drain him till he died.

She shrank back. It was the wrong thing to do, she saw that in a flash; now he thought she had been raped and he'd want to help her.

Carefully, he stepped toward her. Slowly. He could not know how that tantalized her. He held out his hand. "Let me help you."

She shook her head, mute.

Dear little one, rest easy.

She never could. Her back touched the wall. His outstretched hand touched hers.

God help her; she could not help herself. She pounced.

Grabbing him with that strength she had not gotten used to, she bent back his head for the unnatural kiss. She would take no more, she promised herself, than would fill a go-cup.

His blood had all the savor of the food here: bell pepper and red wine and rice and meat. Oh God, make that a big go-cup. The blood tide flowed over her, bright memories frothing in its wake like bubbles in sparkling wine. A dark-eyed son, a shy daughter. Generations passing serenely despite upheavals beyond the iron grilles, years and years in which the dead and the living danced together, Spanish and French—*Vive l'Empereur.* Casting a cold, punctilious eye on the blond invaders, withdrawing further into the land itself, a land of camellias, of sun upon the river flowing past white homes, tumbling down in these latter years; a land of shadows in the bayou, of *feu follet* and *loup-garou.*

Breast against her breast, his heartbeat making her even more drunk, he knew her, knew what she was, knew how she had come there. Anger at the lanky enemies fired the blood she drank. They fought at our side, but they are still strangers.

J'ai peur, maman. Mother, I'm scared . . .

His eyes rolled up, and he knew she could not restrain herself. Hail Mary Mother God and Into Thy hands rang in his fainting mind. His pulse beat like angel wings.

In that moment, understanding blossomed in his mind, and a terrible compassion. Poor little one. Just tonight? *Fais dodo, chere.* It was Cajun; it was rowdy; and it stopped her dead.

She wrenched her head away, holding him lest he fall.

"Dear God," victim and vampire said at once, in different languages.

She released him. He took a step or two, testing his ability to walk, then returned. Of course: she might leave him if she chose; but he must wait to be dismissed.

"Hey! Excuse me, you two. Did either of you see anything?" She whirled, but the man with her pressed her back and turned more slowly to face a large policeman, brother to the cavalry on Bourbon Street. His partner waited silent by his side. Could she take them both?

"Good evening," said her victim. He drew himself up, the perfect gentleman. "I very much regret, sir, but no. I was walking this lady home when we heard a noise. I am distressed I brought her down this street. What if the thieves had seen us?"

She followed his clue and took his arm, edging behind him. Don't overact.

The police straightened, touched hatbrims.

"But of course I should be glad to give you my card if you have further questions. Perhaps tomorrow, since today is a Holy Day?"

He moved his hand. Aristocrat or not, the policeman raised a hand: stop right there.

"Your name and address will do."

He gave it. Prosperous, well-connected, judging by the policeman's response.

"We may send a man around tomorrow, sir. But: if you say you saw nothin' . . . "

"Neither I nor this lady. Now, if you will excuse us . . ."

He turned and escorted her away.

"Thank you," she whispered.

He touched his throat. "Of course I shall assist you," he said, his voice husky.

"I am sorry," she whispered.

"This is very terrible," her victim said. "You were a guest here."

"I am sorry," she said again. She had spent her life apologizing for inconsequential things; here, beyond the end of it, she saw how foolish those earlier regrets had been.

"So am I." Her victim reached out to her. He shimmered in the sudden flood of tears in her eyes. Then victim, knowing her need, comforted vampire, and she forbore to weep blood tears upon his shirt.

At length, she stood aside. She shivered. Though she had fed, the air was turning grey. He nodded.

"Those upstarts. *Canaille* with this money and their guns, their boots and their loud voices. And we had to listen to their bitterness when the war ended—a double bitterness, a double theft when the other thieves came from the North. And you, a guest, are treated thus . . ."

Another feud, then, passed down the generations, not against the Yankees or modern tourists, but against the strangers who had barged in and actually bought this entire area without their consent, trampled all over it with the barbarian they hailed as Old Hickory, and turned a sultry, almost European city into something more vulgar, if just as sinister.

"I thought . . ."

"Because he was born here, and you were not? What is the likes of him but a Scalawag to us?"

They were allied now by blood: she had an image of centuries of dark-haired men and women, profoundly loyal to family, silent in the face of outsiders, but quick to seize advantage. "Remember how long we have lived here. Do you think you are the first? You are not the first."

It happens in the very best of families. She almost laughed.

An older tradition by far, for which the Code Napoleon was still the law whenever the code duello was not. And this was what she, sensing his cleanliness and his strength, had made her servant.

For how long? Until his fear of her outweighed his fear of death? Or longer? He had said he was bound by honor as well as blood, that she was not the first.

Perhaps his people had a way of handling this, handing down the knowledge—and the bond in the blood—from son to son (the spare, not the precious heir, perhaps) out of love for the man who first brought home the pledge. Maybe they had a family tradition: the special friend, with children as they grew up permitted to stay awake past bedtime to be presented to their night-time *Tante*. Down the generations: tending the vampire's coffin alongside the quiet graves.

It might just work. All those vampire stories had to come from somewhere.

He eyed her shrewdly. "You are wondering if your life, even as you are, is worth the price. I should remind you: our Church teaches us that life is to be preserved. Even as . . . " A gesture with one hand, so graceful that she almost saw ghostly lace swirl from his cuff. Life even for such as she. Apostle to the Undead. He smiled. She had not made a witless servant.

What did she want? Revenge? A stake through her maker's heart? He had left her one clue: the newspaper. And in it, the vampire's name, his history, his death.

"If he controls me . . ." A wind brushed the folds of her gown, her hair where it flowed over her shoulders. Almost dawn. Swiftly, she told him about her maker, his suicide, his rise from the grave.

"He had his life in the sun, and he despised it. And he hates this other existence too. So he chose you—someone he could treat as an enemy, someone he could take out his anger on; but someone strong enough to make him lose again. Because he wants to lose."

Like her maker, she would sleep during the day. But this man, so ready to serve her, so sure that her enemy was his, and had been his family's enemy for centuries: he could check court records. He could search the graveyards, probably did, at any rate. And he could enter a tomb by day, open the coffin, bring out stake and hammer . . .

He eyed her shrewdly.

"Do you want to give him what he wants?"

She flinched.

"I do not wish to kill," she said. "It strikes me as a paltry sort of vengeance.

He nodded respect and waited.

"He wants to die? Let us not oblige him. When we find his grave . . . " She knew her eyes glowed like coals, because the living man stepped back. "Do not stab him or burn him. But wrap his coffin in chains." A memory of old stories came to her. "With silver locks. And trap him till doomsday."

He smiled and kissed her hand. In the shadows and damp of before dawn, the gesture did not seem absurd.

She heard stirrings as New Orleans woke from a drunken sleep and returned to life. Ships' horns boomed over the river. Why should she not survive, dancing down the generations with this ally and his family? This seemed to be a useful city for casual violence and ancestral feuds. Why not, for vampires—even for the likes of her?

There would be an investigation when people missed her. Highly placed as this man's family was, she could evade it. They would protect her, would help her contrive financial means of her own. She could survive. She could.

"I must hide before dawn," she said. If worst came to worst, surely some of the tombs had been forced open. Or she could force her own way in. Bodies didn't last long in the city's heat and humidity: she would have her choice.

He touched his breast pocket. "My family has such a place, locked and tended. I will drive you there." Room in the inn, after all.

"I've heard the graveyards aren't safe," she objected. "No one will attack me, or if they do, I think they will run the instant they see me. But once I am . . . Safe . . . You . . ."

His laughter startled her.

"After surviving tonight, how shall I succumb to what you call a mugger? Come with me. Hurry."

The victim held out his arm. The vampire took it.

His discreet black car whirred over the road. The necropolis rose out of the waning night, whitewashed tombs, some crumbling into their original brick, a morbid slum four coffins high. She opened the window, trying to discern the live-in-death from the mere dead and living. She smelled only mud and wet vegetation. The dead were stored above the level of the water.

Some day, she knew, a hurricane would drive Lake Pontchartrain down upon this place, living and the dead together. Coffins would stir upon the face of the waters, the living clinging to the dead. Then, they would find her.

Perhaps. First, survive the day.

They hurried, a guide and his anemic Juliet searching for her tomb, through the shadowed lanes of the cemetery, past a tumbled angel, a whitened Gothic arch, a low-branched tree. The setting moon glinted on a plastic necklace, a glinting fake doubloon, tawdry images of the sun. She must preserve her memories of the sun as best she could. She would not, she thought, forgive that in a hurry. Anger made her shiver.

"Not far now," whispered her guide.

If thieves or killers lurked beneath the bulk of the chapel to the left (she heard their breathing), they sensed her rage and forbore to strike.

She would not let the Creole carry her carpetbag. It seemed hardly fitting.

Drawing a tiny key from his breast pocket, he opened the door and bowed her inside a tiny chapel. He crossed himself. A veritable Creole Chartres, she thought.

The approach of dawn was making her dizzy.

Visibly, he wavered. She suppressed a laugh. What should a gentleman do? Hold open the coffin lid of *grandmère* for this stranger guest?

"I must learn to do for myself," she said. She held out her hand again for his salute. He shut the door behind him and locked it. She would want an inside lock. That first of all.

Yes. She would learn to speak the husky softened French of her protector. And she would make herself at home here in the heart of this city of the dead. Perhaps her enemy would find her, or perhaps priests or police. Though she had not wanted life like this, she wouldn't let them take it from her. At least, not yet. By God, she'd lead them a chase and have herself a dance or two or five. Perhaps, she would dance one night outside that writer's home, and maybe be invited inside for tea or I-never-drink-wine. Or just talk. She would have many years for talk.

That was settled, at least for now.

She chose a coffin at random and opened it. Empty, or all but. The bones did not disturb her, but perhaps she should have one all her own. She whispered thanks and made herself lie down.

So much could go wrong. The tomb, the coffin, her servant, her enemy, her vengeance—she could not shut the lid upon herself, could she?

She must.

Darkness reached out to draw her down. *J'ai peur!* She cried out to it, a frightened child. A memory from the night floated back into her mind. *Fais dodo, chere.*

There, my dearest. There.

Now rest.

Whimpering at first, the vampire sang herself a lullaby. As the deadly sun came up, she learned to sleep.

tanya
huff

This Town
Ain't Big Enough

"Ow! Vicki, be careful!"

"Sorry. Sometimes I forget how sharp they are."

"Terrific." He wove his fingers through her hair and pulled just hard enough to make his point. "Don't."

"Don't what?" She grinned up at him, teeth gleaming ivory in the moonlight spilling across the bed. "Don't forget or don't . . ."

The sudden demand of the telephone for attention buried the last of her question.

Detective-Sergeant Michael Celluci sighed. "Hold that thought," he said, rolled over, and reached for the phone. "Celluci."

"Fifty-two division just called. They've found a body down at Richmond and Peter they think we might want to have a look at."

"Dave, it's . . ." He squinted at the clock. ". . . one twenty-nine in the A.M. and I'm off duty."

On the other end of the line, his partner, theoretically off duty as well, refused to take the hint. "Ask me who the stiff is?"

Celluci sighed again "Who's the stiff?"

"Mac Eisler."

"Shit."

"Funny, that's exactly what I said." Nothing in Dave Graham's voice indicated he appreciated the joke. "I'll be there in ten."

212

"Make it fifteen."

"You in the middle of something?"

Celluci watched as Vicki sat up and glared at him. "I was."

"Welcome to the wonderful world of law enforcement."

Vicki's hand shot out and caught Celluci's wrist before he could heave the phone across the room. "Who's Mac Eisler?" she asked as, scowling, he dropped the receiver back in its cradle and swung his legs off the bed.

"You heard that?"

"I can hear the beating of your heart, the movement of your blood, the song of your life." She scratched the back of her leg with one bare foot. "I should think I can overhear a lousy phone conversation."

"Eisler's a pimp." Celluci reached for the light switch, changed his mind, and began pulling on his clothes. Given the full moon riding just outside the window, it wasn't exactly dark and given Vicki's sensitivity to bright light, not to mention her temper, he figured it was safer to cope. "We're pretty sure he offed one of his girls a couple of weeks ago."

Vicki scooped her shirt up off the floor. "Irene MacDonald?"

"What? You overheard that, too?"

"I get around. How sure's pretty sure?"

"Personally positive. But we had nothing solid to hold him on."

"And now he's dead." Skimming her jeans up over her hips, she dipped her brows in a parody of deep thought. "Golly, I wonder if there's a connection."

"Golly yourself," Celluci snarled. "You're not coming with me."

"Did I ask?"

"I recognized the tone of voice. I know you, Vicki. I knew you when you were a cop, I knew you when you were a P.I. and I don't care how much you've changed physically, I know you now you're a . . . a . . ."

"Vampire." Her pale eyes seemed more silver than gray. "You can say it, Mike. It won't hurt my feelings. Bloodsucker. Nightwalker. Creature of Darkness."

"Pain in the butt." Carefully avoiding her gaze, he shrugged into his shoulder holster and slipped a jacket on over it. "This is police business, Vicki, stay out of it. Please." He didn't wait for a response but crossed the shadows to the bedroom door. Then he paused, one foot over the threshold. "I doubt I'll be back by dawn. Don't wait up."

Vicki Nelson, ex of the Metropolitan Toronto Police Force, ex private investigator, recent vampire, decided to let him go. If he could joke about the change, he accepted it. And besides, it was always more fun to make him pay for smart-ass remarks when he least expected it.

She watched from the darkness as Celluci climbed into Dave Graham's car. Then, with the taillights disappearing in the distance, she dug out his spare set of car keys and proceeded to leave tangled entrails of Highway Traffic Act strewn from Downsview to the heart of Toronto.

*   *   *

It took no supernatural ability to find the scene of the crime. What with the police, the press, and the morbidly curious, the area seethed with people. Vicki slipped past the constable stationed at the far end of the alley and followed the paths of shadow until she stood just outside the circle of police around the body.

Mac Eisler had been a somewhat attractive, not very tall, white male Caucasian. Eschewing the traditional clothing excesses of his profession, he was dressed simply in designer jeans and an olive-green raw silk jacket. At the moment, he wasn't looking his best. A pair of rusty nails had been shoved through each manicured hand, securing his body upright across the back entrance of a trendy restaurant. Although the pointed toes of his tooled leather cowboy boots indented the wood of the door, Eisler's head had been turned completely around so that he stared, in apparent astonishment, out into the alley.

The smell of death fought with the stink of urine and garbage.

Vicki frowned. There was another scent, a pungent predator scent that raised the hair on the back of her neck and drew her lips up off her teeth. Surprised by the strength of her reaction, she stepped silently into a deeper patch of night lest she give herself away.

"Why the hell would I have a comment?"

Preoccupied with an inexplicable rage, she hadn't heard Celluci arrive until he greeted the press. Shifting position slightly, she watched as he and his partner moved in off the street and got their first look at the body.

"Jesus H. Christ."

"On crutches," agreed the younger of the two detectives already on the scene.

"Who found him?"

"Dishwasher, coming out with the trash. He was obviously meant to be found; they nailed the bastard right across the door."

"The kitchen's on the other side and no one heard hammering?"

"I'll go you one better than that. Look at the rust on the head of those nails—they haven't *been* hammered."

"What? Someone just pushed the nails through Eisler's hands and into solid wood?"

"Looks like."

Celluci snorted. "You trying to tell me that Superman's gone bad?"

Under the cover of their laughter, Vicki bent and picked up a piece of planking. There were four holes in the unbroken end and two remaining three-inch spikes. She pulled a spike out of the wood and pressed it into the wall of the building by her side. A smut of rust marked the ball of her thumb, but the nail looked no different.

She remembered the scent.

Vampire.

*   *
*

". . . unable to come to the phone. Please leave a message after the long beep."

"Henry? It's Vicki. If you're there, pick up." She stared across the dark kitchen, twisting the phone cord between her fingers. "Come on, Fitzroy, I don't care what you're doing, this is important." Why wasn't he home writing? Or chewing on Tony. Or something. "Look, Henry, I need some information. There's another one of, of us, hunting my territory and I don't know what I should do. I know what I want to do . . ." The rage remained, interlaced with the knowledge of *another*. ". . . but I'm new at this bloodsucking undead stuff, maybe I'm overreacting. Call me. I'm still at Mike's."

She hung up and sighed. Vampires didn't share territory. Which was why Henry had stayed in Vancouver and she'd come back to Toronto.

Well, all right, it's not the only reason I came back. She tossed Celluci's spare car keys into the drawer in the phone table and wondered if she should write him a note to explain the mysterious emptying of his gas tank. "Nah. He's a detective, let him figure it out."

Sunrise was at five twelve. Vicki didn't need a clock to tell her that it was almost time. She could feel the sun stroking the edges of her awareness.

"It's like that final instant, just before someone hits you from behind, when you know it's going to happen, but you can't do a damn thing about it." She crossed her arms on Celluci's chest and pillowed her head on them, adding, *"Only it lasts longer."*

"And this happens every morning?"

"Just before dawn."

"And you're going to live forever?"

"That's what they tell me."

Celluci snorted. "You can have it."

Although Celluci had offered to light-proof one of the two unused bedrooms, Vicki had been uneasy about the concept. At four and a half centuries, maybe Henry Fitzroy could afford to be blase about immolation, but Vicki still found the whole idea terrifying and had no intention of being both helpless and exposed. Anyone could walk into a bedroom.

No one would accidentally walk into an enclosed plywood box, covered in a blackout curtain, at the far end of a five-foot-high crawl space—but just to be on the safe side, Vicki dropped two by fours into iron brackets over the entrance. Folded nearly in half, she hurried to her sanctuary, feeling the sun drawing closer, closer. Somehow she resisted the urge to turn.

"There's nothing behind me," she muttered, awkwardly stripping off her clothes. Her heart slamming against her ribs, she crawled under the front flap of the box, latched it behind her, and squirmed into her sleeping bag, stretched out ready for dawn.

"Jesus H. Christ, Vicki," Celluci had said squatting at one end while she'd wrestled the twin bed mattress inside. *"At least a coffin would have a bit of historical dignity."*

"You know where I can get one?"

"I'm not having a coffin in my basement."

"Then quit flapping your mouth."

She wondered, as she lay there waiting for oblivion, where the *other* was. Did they feel the same near panic knowing that they had no control over the hours from dawn to dusk? Or had they, like Henry, come to accept the daily death that governed an immortal life? There should, she supposed, be a sense of kinship between them, but all she could feel was a possessive fury. No one hunted in *her* territory.

"Pleasant dreams," she said as the sun teetered on the edge of the horizon. "And when I find you, you're toast."

Celluci had been and gone by the time the darkness returned. The note he'd left about the car was profane and to the point. Vicki added a couple of words he'd missed and stuck it under a refrigerator magnet in case he got home before she did.

She'd pick up the scent and follow it, the hunter becoming the hunted and, by dawn, the streets would be hers again.

The yellow police tape still stretched across the mouth of the alley. Vicki ignored it. Wrapping the night around her like a cloak, she stood outside the restaurant door and sifted the air.

Apparently, a pimp crucified over the fire exit hadn't been enough to close the place and Tex Mex had nearly obliterated the scent of a death not yet twenty-four hours old. Instead of the predator, all she could smell was fajitas.

"Goddamn it," she muttered, stepping closer and sniffing the wood. "How the hell am I supposed to find . . . ?"

She sensed his life the moment before he spoke.

"What are you doing?"

Vicki sighed and turned. "I'm sniffing the door frame. What's it look like I'm doing?"

"Let me be more specific," Celluci snarled. "What are you doing *here?*"

"I'm looking for the person who offed Mac Eisler," Vicki began. She wasn't sure how much more explanation she was willing to offer.

"No, you're not. You are not a cop. You aren't even a P.I. anymore. And how the hell am I going to explain you if Dave sees you?"

Her eyes narrowed. "You don't have to explain me, Mike."

"Yeah? He thinks you're in Vancouver."

"Tell him I came back."

"And do I tell him that you spend your days in a box in my basement? And that you combust in sunlight? And what do I tell him about your eyes?"

Vicki's hand rose to push at the bridge of her glasses but her fingers touched only air. The retinitis pigmentosa that had forced her from the Metro Police and denied her the night had been reversed when Henry'd changed her. The darkness held no secrets from her now. "Tell him they got better."

"RP doesn't get better."

"Mine did."

"Vicki, I know what you're doing." He dragged both hands up through his hair. "You've done it before. You had to quit the force. You were half-blind. So what? Your life may have changed, but you were still going to prove that you were "Victory" Nelson. And it wasn't enough to be a private investigator. You threw yourself into stupidly dangerous situations just to prove you were still who you wanted to be. And now your life has changed again and you're playing the same game."

She could hear his heart pounding, see a vein pulsing framed in the white vee of his open collar, feel the blood surging just below the surface in reach of her teeth. The Hunger rose and she had to use every bit of control Henry had taught her to force it back down. This wasn't about that.

Since she'd returned to Toronto, she'd been drifting; feeding, hunting, relearning the night, relearning her relationship with Michael Celluci. The early morning phone call had crystallized a subconscious discontent and, as Celluci pointed out, there was really only one thing she knew how to do.

Part of his diatribe was based on concern. After all their years together playing cops and lovers, she knew how he thought; if something as basic as sunlight could kill her, what else waited to strike her down. It was only human nature for him to want to protect the people he loved—for him to want to protect her.

But that was only the basis for *part* of the diatribe.

"You can't have been happy with me lazing around your house. I can't cook and I don't do windows." She stepped toward him. "I should think you'd be thrilled that I'm finding my feet again."

"Vicki."

"I wonder," she mused, holding tight to the Hunger, "how you'd feel about me being involved in this if it wasn't your case. I am, after all, better equipped to hunt the night than, oh, detective-sergeants."

"Vicki . . ." Her name had become a nearly inarticulate growl.

She leaned forward until her lips brushed his ear. "Bet you I solve this one first." Then she was gone, moving into shadow too quickly for mortal eyes to track.

"Who you talking to, Mike?" Dave Graham glanced around the empty alley. "I thought I heard . . ." Then he caught sight of the expression on his partner's face. "Never mind."

＊　　＊
＊

Vicki couldn't remember the last time she felt so alive. *Which, as I'm now a card-carrying member of the bloodsucking undead, makes for an interesting feeling.* She strode down Queen Street West, almost intoxicated by the lives surrounding her, fully aware of crowds parting to let her through and the admiring glances that traced her path. A connection had been made between her old life and her new one.

"You must surrender the day," Henry had told her, *"but you need not surrender anything else."*

"So what you're trying to tell me," she'd snarled, *"is that we're just normal people who drink blood?"*

Henry had smiled. *"How many* normal *people do you know?"*

She hated it when he answered a question with a question, but now she recognized his point. Honesty forced her to admit that Celluci had a point as well. She did need to prove to herself that she was still herself. She always had. The more things changed, the more they stayed the same.

"Well, now we've got that settled—" She looked around for a place to sit and think. In her old life, that would have meant a donut shop or the window seat in a cheap restaurant and as many cups of coffee as it took. In this new life, being enclosed with humanity did not encourage contemplation. Besides, coffee, a major component of the old equation, made her violently ill, a fact she deeply resented.

A few years back, CITY TV, a local Toronto station, had renovated a deco building on the corner of Queen and John. They'd done a beautiful job and the six-story, white building with its ornately molded modern windows, had become a focal point of the neighborhood. Vicki slid into the narrow walkway that separated it from its more down-at-the-heels neighbor and swarmed up what effectively amounted to a staircase for one of her kind.

When she reached the roof a few seconds later, she perched on one crenelated corner and looked out over the downtown core. These were her streets; not Celluci's and not some out-of-town bloodsucker's. It was time she took them back. She grinned and fought the urge to strike a dramatic pose.

All things considered, it wasn't likely that the Metropolitan Toronto Police Department—in the person of Detective-Sergeant Michael Celluci—would be willing to share information. Briefly, she regretted issuing the challenge, then she shrugged it off. As Henry said, the night was too long for regrets.

She sat and watched the crowds jostling about on the sidewalks below, clumps of color indicating tourists among the Queen Street regulars. On a Friday night in August, this was the place to be as the Toronto artistic community rubbed elbows with wanna-bes and never-woulds.

Vicki frowned. Mac Eisler had been killed before midnight on a Thursday night in an area that never completely slept. Someone had to have seen or heard something. Something they probably didn't believe and were busy denying. Murder was one thing, creatures of the night were something else again.

"Now then," she murmured, "where would a person like that—and considering the time of day we're assuming a regular not a tourist—where would that person be tonight?"

*   *   *

She found him in the third bar she checked, tucked back in a corner, trying desperately to get drunk, and failing. His eyes darted from side to side, both hands were locked around his glass, and his body language screamed *I'm dealing with some bad shit here, leave me alone.*

Vicki sat down beside him and for an instant let the Hunter show. His reaction was everything she could have hoped for.

He stared at her, frozen in terror, his mouth working but no sound coming out.

"Breathe," she suggested.

The ragged intake of air did little to calm him, but it did break the paralysis. He shoved his chair back from the table and started to stand.

Vicki closed her fingers around his wrist. "Stay."

He swallowed and sat down again.

His skin was so hot it nearly burned and she could feel his pulse beating against it like a small wild creature struggling to be free. The Hunger clawed at her and her own breathing became a little ragged. "What's your name?"

"Ph . . . Phil."

She caught his gaze with hers and held it. "You saw something last night."

"Yes." Stretched almost to the breaking point he began to tremble.

"Do you live around here?"

"Yes."

Vicki stood and pulled him to his feet, her tone half command-half caress. "Take me there. We have to talk."

Phil stared at her. "Talk?"

She could barely hear the question over the call of his blood. "Well, talk first."

*　　*

"It was a woman. Dressed all in black. Hair like a thousand strands of shadow, skin like snow, eyes like black ice. She chuckled, deep in her throat, when she saw me and licked her lips. They were painfully red. Then she vanished, so quickly that she left an image on the night."

"Did you see what she was doing?"

"No. But then, she didn't have be doing anything to be terrifying. I've spent the last twenty-four hours feeling like I met my death."

Phil had turned out to be a bit of a poet. *And* a bit of an athlete. All in all, Vicki considered their time together well spent. Working carefully after he fell asleep, she took away his memory of her and muted the meeting in the alley. It was the least she could do for him.

Description sounds like someone escaped from a Hammer film; The Bride of Dracula Kills a Pimp.

She paused, key in the lock, and cocked her head. Celluci was home, she could feel his life and if she listened very hard, she could hear the regular rhythm of breathing that told her he was asleep. Hardly surprising as it was only three hours to dawn.

There was no reason to wake him as she had no intention of sharing what she'd discovered and no need to feed, but after a long, hot shower, she found herself standing at the door of his room. And then at the side of his bed.

Mike Celluci was thirty-seven. There were strands of gray in his hair and although sleep had smoothed out many of the lines, the deeper creases around his eyes remained. He would grow older. In time, he would die. What would she do then?

She lifted the sheet and tucked herself up close to his side. He sighed and without completely waking scooped her closer still.

"Hair's wet," he muttered.

Vicki twisted, reached up, and brushed the long curl back off his forehead. "I had a shower."

"Where'd you leave the towel?"

"In a sopping pile on the floor."

Celluci grunted inarticulately and surrendered to sleep again.

Vicki smiled and kissed his eyelids. "I love you, too."

She stayed beside him until the threat of sunrise drove her away.

*   *

"Irene MacDonald."

Vicki lay in the darkness and stared unseeing up at the plywood. The sun was down and she was free to leave her sanctuary, but she remained a moment longer, turning over the name that had been on her tongue when she woke. She remembered facetiously wondering if the deaths of Irene MacDonald and her pimp were connected.

Irene had been found beaten nearly to death m the bathroom of her apartment. She'd died two hours later in the hospital.

Celluci said that he was personally certain Mac Eisler was responsible. That was good enough for Vicki.

Eisler could've been unlucky enough to run into a vampire who fed on terror as well as blood—Vicki had tasted terror once or twice during her first year when the Hunger occasionally slipped from her control and she knew how addictive it could be—or he could've been killed in revenge for Irene.

Vicki could think of one sure way to find out.

*   *

"Brandon? It's Vicki Nelson."

"Victoria?" Surprise lifted most of the Oxford accent off Dr. Brandon Singh's voice. "I thought you'd relocated to British Columbia."

"Yeah, well, I came back."

"I suppose that might account for the improvement over the last month or so in a certain detective we both know."

She couldn't resist asking. "Was he really bad while I was gone?"

Brandon laughed. "He was unbearable and, as you know, I am able to bear a great deal. So, are you still in the same line of work?"

"Yes, I am." Yes, she was. God, it felt good. "Are you still the Assistant Coroner?"

"Yes, I am. As I think I can safely assume you didn't call me, at home, long after office hours, just to inform me that you're back on the job, what do you want?"

Vicki winced. "I was wondering if you'd had a look at Mac Eisler."

"Yes, Victoria, I have. And I'm wondering why you can't call me during regular business hours. You must know how much I enjoy discussing autopsies in front of my children."

"Oh, God, I'm sorry, Brandon, but it's important."

"Yes. It always is." His tone was so dry it crumbled. "But since you've already interrupted my evening, try to keep my part of the conversation to a simple yes or no."

"Did you do a blood volume check on Eisler?"

"Yes."

"Was there any missing?"

"No. Fortunately, in spite of the trauma to the neck, the integrity of the blood vessels had not been breached."

So much for yes or no; she knew he couldn't keep to it. "You've been a big help, Brandon, thanks."

"I'd say *any time*, but you'd likely hold me to it." He hung up abruptly.

Vicki replaced the receiver and frowned. She—the *other*—hadn't fed. The odds moved in favor of Eisler killed because he murdered Irene.

*   *

"Well, if it isn't Andrew P." Vicki leaned back against the black Trans Am and adjusted the pair of nonprescription glasses she'd picked up just after sunset. With her hair brushed off her face and the window-glass lenses in front of her eyes, she didn't look much different than she had a year ago. Until she smiled.

The pimp slopped dead in his tracks, bluster fading before he could get the first obscenity out. He swallowed, audibly. "Nelson. I heard you were gone."

Listening to his heart race, Vicki's smile broadened. "I came back. I need some information. I need the name of one of Eisler's other girls."

"I don't know." Unable to look away, he started to shake. "I didn't have anything to do with him. I don't remember."

Vicki straightened and took a slow step toward him. "Try, Andrew."

There was a sudden smell of urine and a darkening stain down the front of the pimp's cotton drawstring pants. "Uh, D . . . D . . . Debbie Ho. That's all I can remember. Really."

"And she works?"

"Middle of the track." His tongue tripped over the words in the rush to spit them at her. "Jarvis and Carlton."

"Thank you." Sweeping a hand toward his car, Vicki stepped aside.

He dove past her and into the driver's seat, jabbing the key into the ignition. The powerful engine roared to life and with one last panicked look into the shadows, he screamed out of the driveway, ground his way through three gear changes, and hit eighty before he reached the corner.

The two cops, quietly sitting in the parking lot of the donut shop on that same corner, hit their siren and took off after him.

Vicki slipped the glasses into the inner pocket of the tweed jacket she'd borrowed from Celluci's closet and grinned. "To paraphrase a certain adolescent crime-fighting amphibian, I *love* being a vampire."

*   *
*

"I need to talk to you Debbie."

The young woman started and whirled around, glaring suspiciously at Vicki. "You a cop?"

Vicki sighed. "Not any more." Apparently, it was easier to hide the vampire than the detective. "I'm a private investigator and I want to ask you some questions about Irene MacDonald."

"If you're looking for the shithead who killed her, you're too late. Someone already found him."

"And that's who I'm looking for."

"Why?" Debbie shifted her weight to one hip.

"Maybe I want to give him a medal."

The hooker's laugh held little humor. "You got that right. Mac got everything he deserved."

"Did Irene ever do women?"

Debbie snorted. "Not for free," she said pointedly.

Vicki handed her a twenty.

"Yeah, sometimes. It's safer, medically, you know?"

Editing out Phil's more ornate phrases, Vicki repeated his description of the woman in the alley.

Debbie snorted again. "Who the hell looks at their faces?"

"You'd remember this one if you saw her. She's . . ." Vicki weighed and discarded several possibilities and finally settled on, ". . . powerful."

"Powerful." Debbie hesitated, frowned, and continued in a rush. "There was this person Irene was seeing a lot but she wasn't charging. That's one of the things that set Mac off, not that the shithead needed much encouragement. We knew it was gonna happen, I mean we've all felt Mac's temper, but Irene wouldn't stop. She said that just being with this person was a high better than drugs. I guess it could've been a woman. And since she was sort of the reason Irene died, well, I know they used to meet in this bar on Queen West. Why are you hissing?"

"Hissing?" Vicki quickly yanked a mask of composure down over her rage. The other hadn't come into her territory only to kill Eisler—she was definitely hunting it. "I'm not hissing. I'm just having a little trouble breathing."

"Yeah, tell me about it." Debbie waved a hand ending in three-inch scarlet nails at the traffic on Jarvis. "You should try standing here sucking carbon monoxide all night."

In another mood, Vicki might have reapplied the verb to a different object, but she was still too angry. "Do you know which bar?"

"What, now I'm her social director? No, I don't know which bar." Apparently they'd come to the end of the information twenty dollars could buy as Debbie turned her attention to a prospective client in a gray sedan. The interview was clearly over.

Vicki sucked the humid air past her teeth. There weren't that many bars on Queen West. Last night she'd found Phil in one. Tonight; who knew.

* * *

Now that she knew enough to search for it, minute traces of the other predator hung in the air—diffused and scattered by the paths of prey. With so many lives masking the trail, it would be impossible to track her. Vicki snarled. A pair of teenagers, noses pierced, heads shaved, and Doc Martens laced to the knee, decided against asking for change and hastily crossed the street.

It was Saturday night, minutes to Sunday. The bars would be closing soon. If the *other* was hunting, she would have already chosen her prey.

I wish Henry had called back. Maybe over the centuries they've— we've—evolved ways to deal with this. Maybe we're supposed to talk first. Maybe it's considered bad manners to rip her face off and feed it to her if she doesn't agree to leave.

Standing in the shadow of a recessed storefront, just beyond the edge of the artificial safety the streetlight offered to the children of the sun, she extended her senses the way she'd been taught and touched death within the maelstrom of life.

She found Phil, moments later, lying in yet another of the alleys that serviced the business of the day and provided a safe haven for the darker business of the night. His body was still warm, but his heart had stopped beating and his blood no longer sang. Vicki touched the tiny, nearly closed wound she'd made in his wrist the night before and then the fresh wound in the bend of his elbow. She didn't know how he had died, but she knew who had done it. He stank of the *other*.

Vicki no longer cared what was traditionally "done" in these instances. There would be no talking. No negotiating. It had gone one life beyond that.

"I rather thought that if I killed him you'd come and save me the trouble of tracking you down. And here you are, charging in without taking the slightest of precautions." Her voice was low, not so much threatening as in itself a threat. "You're hunting in my territory, child."

Still kneeling by Phil's side, Vicki lifted her head. Ten feet away, only her face and hands clearly visible, the other vampire stood. Without thinking—unable to think clearly through the red rage that shrieked for release—Vicki launched herself at the snow-white column of throat, finger hooked to talons, teeth bared.

The Beast Henry had spent a year teaching her to control, was loose. She felt herself lost in its raw power and she reveled in it.

The *other* made no move until the last possible second then she lithely twisted and slammed Vicki to one side.

Pain eventually brought reason back. Vicki lay panting in the fetid damp at the base of a dumpster, one eye swollen shut, a gash across her forehead still sluggishly bleeding. Her right arm was broken.

"You're strong," the other told her, a contemptuous gaze pinning her to the ground. "In another hundred years you might have stood a chance. But you're an infant. A child. You haven't the experience to control what you are. This will be your only warning. Get out of my territory. If we meet again, I *will* kill you."

*   *   *

Vicki sagged against the inside of the door and tried to lift her arm. During the two and a half hours it had taken her to get back to Celluci's house, the bone had begun to set. By tomorrow night, provided she fed in the hours remaining until dawn, she should be able to use it.

"Vicki?"

She started. Although she'd known he was home, she'd assumed—without checking—that because of the hour he'd be asleep. She squinted as the hall light came on and wondered, listening to him pad down the stairs in bare feet, whether she had the energy to make it into the basement bathroom before he saw her.

He came into the kitchen, tying his bathrobe belt around him, and flicked on the overhead light. "We need to talk," he said grimly as the shadows that might have hidden her fled. "Jesus H. Christ. What the hell happened to you?"

"Nothing much." Eyes squinted nearly shut, Vicki gingerly probed the swelling on her forehead. "You should see the other guy."

Without speaking, Celluci reached over and hit the play button on the telephone answering machine.

"Vicki? Henry. If someone's hunting your territory, whatever you do, don't challenge. Do you hear me? *Don't* challenge. You can't win. They're going to be older, able to overcome the instinctive rage and remain in full command of their power. If you won't surrender the territory . . ." The sigh the tape played back gave a clear opinion of how likely he thought that was to occur. ". . . you're going to have to negotiate. If you can agree on boundaries, there's no reason why you can't share the city." His voice suddenly belonged again to the lover she'd lost with the change. "Call me, please, before you do anything."

It was the only message on the tape.

"Why," Celluci asked as it rewound, his gaze taking in the cuts and the bruising and the filth, "do I get the impression that it's "the other guy" Fitzroy's talking about?"

Vicki tried to shrug. Her shoulders refused to cooperate. "It's my city, Mike. It always has been. I'm going to take it back."

He stared at her for a long moment then he shook his head. "You heard what Henry said. You can't win. You haven't been . . . what you are, long enough. It's only been fourteen months."

"I know." The rich scent of his life prodded the Hunger and she moved to put a little distance between them.

He closed it up again. "Come on." Laying his hand in the center of her back, he steered her toward the stairs. *Put it aside for now,* his tone told her. *We'll argue about it later.* "You need a bath."

"I need . . ."

"I know. But you need a bath first. I just changed the sheets."

*   *   *

The darkness wakes us all in different ways, Henry had told her. *We were all human once and we carried our differences through the change.*

For Vicki, it was like the flicking of a switch; one moment she wasn't, the next she was. This time, when she returned from the little death of the day, an idea returned with her.

Four-hundred-and-fifty-odd years a vampire, Henry had been seventeen when he changed. The *other* had walked the night for perhaps as long—her gaze had carried the weight of several lifetimes—but her physical appearance suggested that her mortal life had lasted even less time than Henry's had. Vicki allowed that it made sense. Disaster may have precipitated *her* change, but passion was the usual cause.

And no one does that kind of never-say-die passion like a teenager.

It would be difficult for either Henry or the other to imagine a response that came out of a mortal rather than a vampiric experience. They'd both had centuries of the latter and not enough of the former to count.

Vicki had been only fourteen months a vampire, but she'd been human thirty-two years when Henry'd saved her by drawing her to his blood to feed. During those thirty-two years, she'd been nine years a cop—two accelerated promotions, three citations, and the best arrest record on the force.

There was no chance of negotiation.

She couldn't win if she fought.

She'd be damned if she'd flee.

"Besides . . ." For all she realized where her strength had to be, Vicki's expression held no humanity. ". . . she owes me for Phil."

* * *

Celluci had left her a note on the fridge.

Does this have anything to do with Mac Eisler?

Vicki stared at it for a moment then scribbled her answer underneath.

Not anymore.

It took three weeks to find where the *other* spent her days. Vicki used old contacts where she could and made new ones where she had to. Any modern Van Helsing could have done the same.

For the next three weeks, Vicki hired someone to watch the *other* come and go, giving reinforced instructions to stay in the car with the windows closed and the air-conditioning running. Life had an infinite number of variations, but one piece of machinery smelled pretty much like any other. It irritated her that she couldn't sit stakeout herself, but the information she needed would've kept her out after sunrise.

* * *

"How the hell did you burn your hand?"

Vicki continued to smear ointment over the blister. Unlike the injuries she'd taken in the alley, this would heal slowly and painfully. "Accident in a tanning salon."

"That's not funny."

She picked up the roll of gauze from the counter. "You're losing your sense of humor, Mike."

Celluci snorted and handed her the scissors. "I never had one."

"Mike, I wanted to warn you, I won't be back by sunrise."

Celluci turned slowly, the TV dinner he'd just taken from the microwave held in both hands. "What do you mean?"

She read the fear in his voice and lifted the edge of the tray so that the gravy didn't pour out and over his shoes. "I mean I'll be spending the day somewhere else."

"Where?"

"I can't tell you."

"Why? Never mind." He raised a hand as her eyes narrowed. "Don't tell me. I don't want to know. You're going after that other vampire aren't you? The one Fitzroy told you to leave alone."

"I thought you didn't want to know."

"I already know," he grunted. "I can read you like a book. With large type. And pictures."

Vicki pulled the tray from his grip and set it on the counter. "She's killed two people. Eisler was a scumbag who may have deserved it, but the other . . ."

"Other?" Celluci exploded. "Jesus H. Christ, Vicki, in case you've forgotten, murder's against the law! Who the hell painted a big vee on your long Johns and made you the vampire vigilante?"

"Don't you remember?" Vicki snapped. "You were there. I didn't make this decision, Mike. You and Henry made it for me. You'd just better learn to live with it." She fought her way back to calm. "Look, you can't stop her, but I can. I know that galls, but that's the way it is."

They glared at each other, toe to toe. Finally Celluci looked away.

"I can't stop you, can I?" he asked bitterly. "I'm only human after all."

"Don't sell yourself short," Vicki snarled. "You're quintessentially human. If you want to stop me, you face me and ask me not to go and *then* you remember it every time *you* go into a situation that could get your ass shot off."

After a long moment, he swallowed, lifted his head, and met her eyes. "Don't die. I thought I lost you once and I'm not strong enough to go through that again."

"Are you asking me not to go?"

He snorted. "I'm asking you to be careful. Not that you ever listen."

She took a step forward and rested her head against his shoulder, wrapping herself in the beating of his heart. "This time, I'm listening."

＊　　＊
＊

The studios in the converted warehouse on King Street were not supposed to be live-in. A good seventy-five percent of the tenants ignored that. The studio Vicki wanted was at the back on the third floor. The heavy steel door—an obvious upgrade by the occupant—had been secured by the best lock money could buy.

New senses and old skills got through it in record time.

Vicki pushed open the door with her foot and began carrying boxes inside. She had a lot to do before dawn.

"She goes out every night between ten and eleven, then she comes home every morning between four and five. You could set your watch by her."

Vicki handed him an envelope.

He looked inside, thumbed through the money, then grinned up at her. "Pleasure doing business for you. Any time you need my services, you know where to call."

"Forget it," she told him.

And he did.

＊　　＊
＊

Because she expected her, Vicki knew the moment the *other* entered the building. The Beast stirred and she tightened her grip on it. To lose control now would be disaster.

She heard the elevator, then footsteps in the hall.

"You know I'm in here," she said silently, *"and you know you can take me. Be overconfident, believe I'm a fool, and walk right in."*

"I thought you were smarter than this." The *other* stepped into the apartment, then casually turned to lock the door. "I told you when I saw you again I'd kill you."

Vicki shrugged, the motion masking her fight to remain calm. "Don't you even want to know why I'm here?"

"I assume you've come to negotiate." She raised ivory hands and released thick, black hair from its bindings. "We went past that when you attacked me." Crossing the room, she preened before a large ornate mirror that dominated one wall of the studio.

"I attacked you because you murdered Phil."

"Was that his name?" The other laughed. The sound had razored edges. "I didn't bother to ask it."

"Before you murdered him."

"Murdered? You *are* a child. They are prey, we are predators—their deaths are ours if we desire them. You'd have learned that in time." She turned, the patina of civilization stripped away. "Too bad you haven't any time left."

Vicki snarled but somehow managed to stop herself from attacking. Years of training whispered, *Not yet.* She had to stay exactly where she was.

"Oh, yes." The sibilants flayed the air between them. "I almost forgot. You wanted me to ask you why you came. Very well Why?"

Given the address and the reason, Celluci could've come to the studio during the day and slammed a stake through the *other's* heart. The vampire's strongest protection, would be of no use against him. Mike Celluci believed in vampires.

"I came," Vicki told her, "because some things you have to do yourself."

The wire ran up the wall, tucked beside the surface-mounted cable of a cheap renovation, and disappeared into the shadows that clung to a ceiling sixteen feet from the floor. The switch had been stapled down beside her foot. A tiny motion, too small to evoke attack, flipped it.

Vicki had realized from the beginning that there were a number of problems with her plan. The first involved placement. Every living space included an area where the occupant felt secure—a favorite chair, a window . . . a mirror. The second problem was how to mask what she'd done. While the *other* would not be able to sense the various bits of wiring and equipment, she'd lie fully aware of Vicki's scent *on* the wiring and equipment. Only if Vicki remained in the studio, could that smaller trace be lost in the larger.

The third problem was directly connected with the second. Given that Vicki had to remain, how was she to survive?

Attached to the ceiling by sheer brute strength, positioned so that they shone directly down into the space in front of the mirror, were a double bank of lights cannibalized from a tanning bed. The sun held a double menace for the vampire—its return to the sky brought complete vulnerability and its rays burned.

Henry had a round scar on the back of one hand from too close an encounter with the sun. When her burn healed, Vicki would have a matching one from a deliberate encounter with an imitation.

The *other* screamed as the lights came on, the sound pure rage and so inhuman that those who heard it would have to deny it for sanity's sake.

Vicki dove forward, ripped the heavy brocade off the back of the couch, and burrowed frantically into its depths. Even that instant of light had bathed her skin in flame and she moaned as, for a moment, the searing pain became all she was. After a time, when it grew no worse, she managed to open her eyes.

The light couldn't reach her, but neither could she reach the switch to turn it off. She could see it, three feet away, just beyond the shadow of the couch. She shifted her weight and a line of blister rose across one leg. Biting back a shriek, she curled into a fetal position, realizing her refuge was not entirely secure.

Okay, genius, now what?

Moving very, very carefully, Vicki wrapped her hand around the one by two that braced the lower edge of the couch. From the tension running along it, she suspected that breaking it off would result in at least a partial collapse of the piece of furniture.

And if it goes, I very well may go with it.

And then she heard the sound of something dragging itself across the floor.

Oh, shit! She's not dead!

The wood broke, the couch began to fall in on itself, and Vicki, realizing that luck would have a large part to play in her survival, smacked the switch and rolled clear in the same motion.

The room plunged into darkness.

Vicki froze as her eyes slowly readjusted to the night. Which was when she finally became conscious of the smell. It had been there all along, but her senses had refused to acknowledge it until they had to.

Sunlight burned.

Vicki gagged.

The dragging sound continued.

The hell with this! She didn't have time to wait for her eyes to repair the damage they'd obviously taken. She needed to see *now*. Fortunately, although it hadn't seemed fortunate at the time, she'd learned to maneuver without sight.

She threw herself across the room.

The light switch was where they always were, to the right of the door.

The thing on the floor pushed itself up on fingerless hands and glared at her out of the blackened ruin of a face. Laboriously it turned, hate radiating off it in palpable waves and began to pull itself toward her again.

Vicki stepped forward to meet it.

While the part of her that remembered being human writhed in revulsion, she wrapped her hands around its skull and twisted it in a full circle. The spine snapped. Another full twist and what was left of the head came off in her hands.

She'd been human for thirty-two years, but she'd been fourteen months a vampire.

"No one hunts in *my* territory," she snarled as the *other* crumbled to dust.

She limped over to the wall and pulled the plug supplying power to the lights. Later, she'd remove them completely—the whole concept of sunlamps gave her the creeps.

When she turned, she was facing the mirror.

The woman who stared out at her through bloodshot eyes, exposed skin blistered and red, was a hunter. Always had been really. The question became, who was she to hunt?

Vicki smiled. Before the sun drove her to use her inherited sanctuary, she had a few quick phone calls to make. The first to Celluci; she owed him the knowledge that she'd survived the night. The second to Henry for much the same reason.

The third call would be to the eight hundred line that covered the classifieds of Toronto's largest alternative newspaper. This ad was going to be a little different than the one she'd placed upon leaving the force. Back then, she'd been incredibly depressed about leaving a job she loved for a life she saw as only marginally useful. This time, she had no regrets.

Victory Nelson, Investigator: Otherworldly Crimes a Specialty.

esther m.
friesner

Claim-Jumpin' Woman,
You Got a Stake
in My Heart

Honestly, Binks, old man, we'd just love coming over for cocktails. You've simply got the wrong impression. Everyone in our—I mean my—old set does. Awfully white of you to overlook what people are saying. People will say anything for effect; they'll do anything for love, but that's another story. Mine, in fact.

Go on? Of course I'll go on. The whole sordid tale, if you like; it's your quarter. In spite of this *ghastly* hour, I'm still awake enough to know the real reason you've tendered us this invitation. You want the dirt. *Quelle* cowinkydink, Binks. You're dying to know how it happened, aren't you? They all are, but let's keep this just between old frat buddies, *n'est-ce pas?* It's hardly cocktail party chat. For Gawd, for country, and for pity's sake, don't tell the alumni office. No knowing how Mother Yale will react to the news, even if I do keep giving the old girl a shitload of *dinero* every year. I always did think *alma mater* meant one mean mother.

Well, all right, you can tell whatever you like to the little woman, but only because Whitney and I go *way* back. I was sleeping with her first. In fact, you owe me one, Binks. Without me, there never would have been a Whitney to glide down the aisle to your eagerly waiting arms. And on the flip side, I wouldn't be in this—situation—if not for your wifey.

She broke my heart, did Whitney M. Webster—yes, I know she's Whitney M. Webster-Winston now. Binks, but this was two years ago. We were in our senior year at Yale, it was Christmas break, absolutely *no way* on earth for us to know whether we'd gotten into Harvard Law, and the obligatory holiday pop-in on Mums and Dads about as tempting a prospect as a drug-free vasectomy. You remember how it was. I simply did not need my woman calling me up on *Navidad* morning to say, "I'm just *frightfully* sorry, Tripsy, but our engagement is off. I've found someone new." And not a word more; she rang off.

Christmas Day, Binks! When any *sane* woman knows a man is firmly lodged in the bosom of his family, and suicide looks like a damned pleasing prospect: To say nothing of the hangover from Dad's special Yuletide-recipe Bloody Marys. The Bloody's red, and you turn green; so festive. I was not prepared. She should have known I'd do something stupid.

Which I did. I made some excuse to the near-and-dear and *flung* myself into the Beemer. Drove *all* the way from Chestnut Hill to Webster's Mills, Georgia, in two days flat, just to—

What's that, Binks? . . . Yes, I said Webster's Mills. You won't have heard of it. Whitney never went back after *that* Christmas—not that I blame her—but the year of which I speak, she was spending the holidays there, at the ancestral *pied-à-terre* with her Daddy. Not that Bentley Webster ever stayed sober long enough to realize that his little girl wasn't another D.T. spawned by an overdose of Chivas and the swimsuit issue of L. L. Bean. Surely by now you know that it's a tradition for Bentley to get as high as a Macy's parade balloon every Thanksgiving, and stay right up there until the big apple comes down in Times Square on New Year's Eve. Of course, having *seen* Webster's Mills, I must say there are worse ways to view it than completely blotto.

It's an utterly hideous little pimple of a Georgia mill town, no bigger than a polo pony's poo-poo, but it was good enough for Whitney's great gumpa to start up the textile plant that kicked off the family fortune . . . . Oh, thought they were Old Money, did you? That's not the only secret your little wifey's got to tell. Ask her about her darling Mumsy some time—the one you've never met because she's always . . . doing a little charity work in Bermuda, isn't it? Or else ask Whitney M. Webster-Winston what the M. stands for. You'll be surprised. So will I, if she tells you the truth.

All that's beside the point. I certainly don't bear the girl any grudges. Now. Two years ago, it was another kettle of *coq au vin*. Lord, Binks, I wanted to kill her! Then marry her. I didn't see any problem with that, because when love walks in the door, logic flies out your gonads, particularly when the object of your tender feelings has such a superb set of hooters. Passion blinds a man. You know what I mean; I've seen you at The Game when the Bulldogs bite it. Once you even got ketchup on your ecru Versaces; don't deny it. Well, I was so peeved about Whitney that I didn't even bother to put the mud screen up when I pulled the Beemer into the center of Webster's Mills.

Which center is, *in toto*—I kid you not—the Bop 'n' Burger Drive-In. People actually *eat* there, though I don't think it's food. It was nighttime when I arrived. A pink-and-yellow neon hamburger twirled lazily round and round at the top of a twenty-foot-high puke-green pole high above that symposium of sorghum fanciers. Below, what wasn't cinder block and asphalt was plastic and chrome. The sound of a jukebox wailed clear across the parking lot. There was nowhere to hide from the strains of "Take Me Closer to Jesus, Elvis." My Gawd, do they *still* manufacture that many denim-blue Ford pickups? I swear, Binks, somewhere someone is making a fucking *fortune* stonewashing trucks. How else could they all have that same air of prefab shabbiness? Between those venerable vehicles and the dented red two-door Chevies cluttering up the Bop 'n' Burger, the old Beemer stuck out like a virgin at Vassar.

Now, mark me, old man, ordinarily I wouldn't be caught dead in such a place. Kitsch went o-u-t simply *ages* ago. But I needed directions. A man can't very well lay his torn and bleeding heart at the feet of *La belle dame sans* timing if he doesn't know where said feet currently are. Whitney's mailing address over break was just The Aspens, Webster's Mills, Georgia, so I did have to do the odd spot of inquiry.

I leaned against the hood of the Beemer while contemplating which of the locals would understand a question phrased in grammatical English. The atmosphere was not conducive to clear-headed thought. The smell of paleolithic grease emanating from the Bop 'n' Burger kitchen was appalling. The whole parking lot reeked of it. And then, cutting through the miasma of deep-fried possum and sludgeburgers, there came a flying wedge of Tabu cologne that nailed me right between the eyes.

"Take your order, honey?" she said. You may have heard of Georgia peaches, Binks. Well, they're nothing compared to the Georgia honeydews this lady was attempting to conceal under her red cotton blouse; badly. You know I'm a gentleman. I didn't intend to ogle the Edams, but I couldn't help it; they were on eye level. I wondered whether Webster's Mills made a habit of spawning the Fifty-Foot Woman, until I realized that my hayseed Hebe was mounted on a pair of roller skates.

"Actually, I'm just trying to get some information," I told her, to which she replied: "This ain't Ma Bell, sugar. You just order you a Cocola, I'll be real happy to point you any which way you want to go."

Coca Cola; yes, Binks, I know. But for better or worse, that was how I met Miss Rubilene Nash. My mind was on other matters than correcting her quaint pronunciation. She was a vision of delight, old man, either in approach or retreat. Is your Whitney still the ruthlessly articulate girls'-rights advocate I once knew? . . . *Quelle dommage.* Well, then you know she would never have approved of Miss Rubilene's carhop outfit. Why do they call them carhops, anyway? One good hop in *that* rig-out, and more than Atlanta would burn.

I managed to hold on to some of the old Apollonian calm when she came skating back with my beverage. After all, I told myself, I was the jilted swain come to pound Sweet Reason back into dear Whitney's skull. It lacks a certain note of moral superiority if one's mouth is full of love's most persuasive rhetoric for one girl while one's loins are full of school spirit for another.

"The Aspens?" she repeated once I posed my question. "You don't mean Bojo Webster's place?"

"The Aspens, dear girl, is the residence of Mr. *Bentley* Webster," I informed her. "And his daughter Whitney," I thought it prudent to add.

"Oh, Whitney," she said. "You must be him." Her lips pursed out in a manner that would have been too delicious but for the fact that she was looking at me as if I were an especially cute and furry road kill.

"Him—I mean *he*—who?" I asked. Perhaps she had me confused with a different squashed cat of Whitney's acquaintance.

No such luck. "You're that Yale fella Whitney dumped," she informed me. Her golden brows knotted with the effort of recalling my name. "Gordon Franford III?"

I nodded. Despair made me heedless—my Gawd, if the working classes in this guanoburg knew the details of my recent *contretemps d'amour*, what did I have left to lose? I told her to call me Trip.

Never did I see such sympathy in female eyes, Binks; not that I felt like being the object of rural pity. "You poor thing," she said. "Driving all this way for nothing. Honey, unless there's two Whitney Maybelle Websters in this world, you have lost her, and you have lost her for good and all."

Yes, Binks, I've let your little helpmate's secret go whoopsy: *Maybelle*. Perhaps Whitney never saw fit to tell you the too-romantic tale of how her parents met. Mumsy was a waitress at one of the finer resorts on Hilton Head, when Daddy showed up at the bar a teensy bit borneo. When he took out his money clip to pay the tab, the lady saw what she liked, and married it before Bentley sobered up. You *do* know Whitney's words to live by? Either she gets things her way, or somebody dies. Got *that* single-minded spunk from her Mumsy. Also her charming middle name.

But to return: I was not raised to take defeat lightly; not with that much mileage on the Beemer. I drew myself up, adopted an air of dogged determination, and said, "I'll be the judge of that, young lady."

Whereat the toothsome Miss Rubilene burst into giggles. "'Young lady'?" she repeated. "Oh, sugar, if you only knew!"

I didn't. I assumed her mirth stemmed from my perchance inappropriate pomposity coupled with the obvious fact that she looked only a year or so younger than I. Still, *la coeura sais raisons que la raison ne connait point,* so I continued to make an ass of myself.

"If you don't know the way to The Aspens, then I'll thank you to say so," I informed her. "I haven't all the time in the world."

She looked chastened at that; sad, at any rate. "Honey," she said, "I could send you off on a wild-goose chase to The Aspens right now, but that wouldn't do you a lick of good. You want to see Miss Whitney, and Miss Whitney's not there. She's right here in this town, not a coon's spit from where we're standing. But if you know what's good for you, you'll leave her be, hustle those cute little buns into your fancy car, and hightail it back up North while you still can." And before I could register any pleasure at her evaluation of my *derriere* (it's all that time I spent on the Yale crew; tightens up the old glutens whatzits so well), Miss Rubilene went on to say: "She's Randy Russell's woman now."

The hell she was, I said, which only evoked another of those *poor, ignorant boy* looks from her. Before she could explain, the anthropoid ape who owned the Bop 'n' Burger came out of Hell's kitchen to yell at my winsome informant to quit fraternizing with the damyankees and take orders from the Phil Donahue Fan Club currently cluttering up the parking lot and leaning on their klaxons for service.

Before she whirred away, she managed to whisper to me, "I get off work 'long to'ad midnight. You wait for me, and I'll do what I can to help you. Don't try scooting off on your own after that girl of yours, or you'll be real sorry. My truck's over there. Meet me by it." A scrape of skate wheels, and she was gone.

I strolled over to check out said chariot. It was a sky-blue pickup with a Confederate flag sticker on the windshield and a stuffed Garfield hanging upside down from suction-cup paws in the rear window. There was an "If You're Rich I'm Single" bumper sticker over the tail pipe, and one saying, "This Is My Other Car," for aesthetic and philosophical balance. Thank Gawd it had no gun rack, or I'd never have been able to pick it out of the crowd. I glanced into the back and noted that the lady was obviously a gardening enthusiast. Either that, or the Webster's Mills locals take it literally when they say they're going to dish the dirt.

It lacked but three hours of midnight. It wouldn't have been any skin off my tan to wait for Rubilene. I should have scouted out a local roach motel and checked in for a few hours' bidey-bye in the meanwhile. However, when have you ever known me to do the sage thing, Binks? I was the one who signed up for Organic Chem in freshman year when anyone with half a brain took Gut Psych to fulfill the science requirement. I confess, the undertone of doom in her voice when she spoke of Whitney and this Russell person intrigued me. It was like some divine Wagnerian motif to remind the audience that the gods were going to fall in the Rhine any hour now; so why bother. I should have waited to hear more.

Not I. Now I knew that my rival had a name; Randy Russell. How too, too goober. From the way Rubilene spoke with such assurance of the hopelessness of my cause, I gathered that this Russell was a known quantity in those there parts. What is named and known can be hunted down, like a wild skeet. I didn't wait. I drove to the nearest gas station and asked the pump jockey whether he knew the whereabouts of one Randy Russell.

Binks, if you could have seen the fond, lobotomized grin that o'erspread those zitful features, you'd have thought I was offering the lad the chance to evolve into one of the higher primates. "Cowboy Randy Russell," he breathed. "I got just about all his albums. Wish I had me enough money to buy a ticket to his concert tonight, though." He said no more, but gazed at me meaningfully. The implication was clear: aphasia *can* he cured for about twenty dollars in most civilized societies. Isn't science wonderful?

Quasimodo Jukes recked without that fine old Yale tradition that requires all her students, even unto the least of us, to learn how to do research. Usually I'm hard put to deduce breakfast, but love is a great smartener-upper. A concert, was it? And nearby, I should venture to guess, else why would this walking testimony to inbreeding seem so sanguine about obtaining the bribe from me and being able to attend said musical that very evening? Too, hadn't Rubilene just said that Whitney was—how did she phrase it?—less than a coon's spit away? Though I didn't know how far said beast could hawk a lugie, I still had clues aplenty.

I feigned stiff joints, got out of the Beemer, and strolled over to the front window of the filling station while Gasoline Alley Oop continued to blither on about how he had a bad memory for times and places, but might be subject to the electroshock of ready green. I let him natter away. Where there are concerts, my dear Binks, there are also adverts for the same posted in plain sight at most local businesses. Sure enough, there among the cans of thirty-weight reposed a placard advertising Cowboy Randy Russell's Homecoming Tour, with a gig at the East Webster's Mills Melodrome in—good Lord, it had begun at nine o'clock! And no doubt Whitney would be there, eyes ashine with socially misplaced *tendresse.* If I wanted to find her and dissuade her from what *had* to be the world's biggest *mesalliance* since Leda and the Swanson TV Dinner, I knew I'd best make tracks. I thanked my informant and absolutely *floored* the Beemer. Pity, really. Now I shall never know his full critical opinion of my Mums's morals.

Oh, I had no trouble finding the Melodrome, despite the fact that East Webster's Mills lies north of its patronymic town. It looked like a converted bowling alley. Either that, or all the best odea shall soon sport a giant phosphorescent duckpin atop their CURRENT ATTRACTION signs.

Parking was at a premium. Whoever this Cowboy Randy Russell was, I reasoned he must be pulling down a tender dollar. Perhaps Whitney hadn't lost quite so much of her sanity as I suspected, but still . . . a Country-Western singer? Even for New Money, Whitney should have had some pride.

I bought an SRO ticket from a very bored young box-office bimbette and entered the gates of Orphic Hell. The Melodrome was

one of these theater-in-the-round bits, where, if the audience did-
n't like an act, there was no possible escape for the luckless per-
former as they swarmed the stage from all sides to pick his bones.
Cowboy Randy Russell did not seem in any such immediate peril.
He sat atop a backless wooden barstool in a puddle of klieg light
and grinned at the applauding mob over the hump of his white
guitar.

You know, Binks, we men have it all sewn up. When a woman
gets as many wrinkles as Russell showed, it's time to look up the
number of a good, expensive, discreet plastic surgeon. He was, I
believe the term is, *craggy*. Rugged. Weathered and browned as an
old saddle, or a cruise director. He had blue eyes of a piercing brightness found only in Louis L'Amour books. The obligatory Stetson
atop nigh metallic golden curls, and his smile caused snow blindness
in the first four rows. Truly *primo* teeth. He must have been the most
popular boy in the bunkhouse until he learned to fight. You could
smell the horse sweat clear back to the cheap seats.

"Thank you, folks, thank you very much," he said. "Now, I'd like
to dedicate this next number to a very special little lady who couldn't
be here tonight." My heart plunged into my Reeboks. Had I come so
far—paid cash money—to hear *this*? *That* Whitney wasn't there? But
then he went on to say; "Now, I don't mean for you to get the wrong
idea. The lady in question's just a good friend, and we go way back
together, but there's only one woman in my heart. A man can't ride
two horses with one set of chaps—ain't that so, Miss Whitney?"

I heard a familiar giggle from the front row as he lavished a fond
gaze upon my—I mean *your*—beloved. Yes, there she sat. I could
catch only a glimpse of the back of her head, but I knew it was she.
It was the only head of hair present untouched by mousse or Miss
Clairol, and sporting a darling little navy grosgrain bow.

Cowboy Randy Russell shifted the white guitar and thumbed his
hat farther back on his head. "So this here song's for my old pal and
good drinkin' buddy, Miss Rubilene Nash, wherever she may be
tonight; 'If Jesus Drove a Semi.'"

If Jesus drove a semi, he'd steer it straight and well.
He'd pick up lonesome hitchhikers bound for the road to Hell.
At each and every truck stop, an angel gets aboard.
It's eighteen-wheel salvation on the semi of the L—

What's that, Binks? . . . Yes, it *was* necessary to sing. I shall never forget that song so long as I—Anyway, my voice isn't *that* bad. The notes of the second verse were still echoing in my ears as I walked out of the Melodrome like one entranced.

Outside, a breath of cool air washed away the last dregs of Cowboy Randy Russell going on about paying the tolls to Heaven and splitting gas costs with his Savior. I was able to think clearly again, and the first thought that crossed my mind was to snoop about and see whether I couldn't be waiting for the happy couple backstage when the concert was over.

There was no problem about it. The twenty I'd saved on useless information from the grease monkey now went to slick the palm of the bubba guarding the stage door. He pointed me at Cowboy Randy Russell's dressing room as soon as he was able to get his hand out of his pocket. I believe I told him that I was the Singer's cousin, though I'd wager that, for another ten, he'd have let me through had I claimed to be the Angel of Death making a house call.

I moved quickly, not wanting to run into any other backstage personnel who might require additional *baksheesh*. The door to Cowboy Randy Russell's dressing room had a chintzy star on it, silvered plastic, but no lock. I slipped inside and turned on the lights.

There she sat, perched on the edge of the sleekest, blackest, most tasteful and elegant coffin I'd ever seen. Rubilene Nash uncrossed her excellent legs, slid to the floor, and said, "Didn't I tell you to wait for me?"

I'm afraid I was still gaping at the body box. You will recall the stories about the great Sarah Bernhardt catching forty winks in a casket, but a Country-Western singer? Astonishment froze me, though I swiftly defrosted under a *numero uno* case of the creepy-crawlies.

"You *can't* mean—" was all I managed to utter.

Rubilene nodded.

"But that's—*kinky!*" I said, my mind still limited to commonplace speculations. "He and Whitney do it in *there?*" I extended a trembling finger at the blue satin interior.

"Of course not!" Rubilene exclaimed. She gave me a look of revulsion. "You Yankees just have the filthiest minds. Do it in a *coffin?* Lord! Cowboy Randy Russell may be a no-account, two timing, womanizing, undead sumbitch, but by God, he ain't no *pervert.*"

Undead, the lady said. Just so. You'll understand why I laughed in her face then, won't you, Binks?

She was even prettier when she was angry. She also had a good right cross, quite staggering even when all it delivered was an open-handed slap. I stopped laughing. "You don't believe me," she said. "Fine. I don't care do you believe or not, just so long as you get the bell out of this room before he comes back. If you don't, you're dead."

I recouped some poise and pulled up the only chair in the room. Slinging one leg athwart the other, I gave her rather a cool reply, viz: "I am a Yale man. *We* don't do vampires."

Rubilene rolled her lovely eyes. "I swear, you won't be worth the rope to hang you, boy. You want proof? All right, I'll see can I find some; only, you better be a speed reader is all, because if you're not out of here before the concert's over . . ." She made the sign of someone cutting off more than my allowance, then flung herself into the large steamer trunk at the foot of the coffin.

I confess to a mounting *malaise.* Consider: This woman had doubtless abandoned her paying job to follow me here and warn me off. Either there was a real vampiric threat to my welfare—in which case I had better do my damndest to recall how they disposed of Langella in the Broadway production of *Dracula* and I don't think it was bad reviews—else Miss Rubilene Nash was several pearls short of a strand, in which case I was in questionable circumstances of personal safety by being alone with her that way. I was debating flight, when she heaved a thick album out of the trunk and pitched it into my lap.

It was a scrapbook. Some of the reviews dated back over thirty years. There were many photographs among the newspaper clippings. In each and every one, Cowboy Randy Russell was clearly identifiable, surrounded by gaggles of sweet young things. He was also just as clearly the same age, whether snapped in 1950 or 1980. "I thought vampires didn't register on film," I remarked, trying to keep a choirboy tremor out of my voice.

Rubilene snorted. "Cowboy Randy, he's *show* bidness," she said. "You don't just give up being photogenic over a little thing like unnatural life." She spoke with an expert's conviction. I had to believe.

Thirty years, Binks; almost forty, and he hadn't aged. There is just so much that Minoxidil and Retin-A can account for. I stood up, still holding onto the album. "How has he managed to get away with it? Surely someone else must have noticed—? Those closest to him: his agent, his manager, his—toadies? I mean, roadies."

She sighed. "And cut their own throats? Sugar, Cowboy Randy Russell's box office. Long as a man keeps on a-hauling in the green, ain't no one going to ask, like, *uncomfortable* questions 'bout his books. By the time *do* they think to get suspicious, he maybe fires them and gets new folks on too stupid to find their ass with both hands and a road map. And his fans wouldn't give a gold-plated shit even was he dead and buried, long as he keeps singing."

I considered the phenomenon of Elvis Everlasting and had to concur.

"But you're on to him" I said.

She nodded. "I told him I'd caught wise," she said. "I guess that's what broke us up, him being dead and all. He just laughed."

I was stunned. "He knows you know," I said, "and he lets you live?" From what I gathered during an all-night Halloween film festival at Yale, vampires were notoriously tidy when it came to tucking away those who discovered their secret. Permanently.

"You heard him out there," she said. Her lips curved into an embittered smile. "Called me his *pal*. Used to be I was more. I guess you know how when you swear to your *pal* as how you'll keep all his secrets, it's binding."

Uh-oh, I told myself. A woman scorned, that which Hell hath no Fury like. I pictured the Stetson-sporting beast pulling up to the Bop 'n' Burger and ordering a patty, *ever* so rare, then sweeping poor Rubilene off her wheelies. A celebrity, after all; a Country-Western singer. Poor child, stars in eyes one minute, fangs in her throat the next. And then *el dumpo supremo*. Between the pain of a broken heart and the fear of a broken neck if she squealed, no wonder Rubilene kept silent.

Besides, who in this civic chancre would ever believe her tale of vampires, even if they saw the fatal scrapbook? The *Enquirer* hadn't covered the story yet, nor had *Reader's Digest* touted "My Most Unforgettable Ghoul."

"I'm sorry," I told her. I meant it.

A single tear trickled down her cheek. I lifted it with a fingertip and battled manfully the urge to kiss her. However, doesn't Whitney go on about how *real* men aren't afraid to give in to their emotions now and then? Let no one dare brand me an MCP. I took the lady into my arms and helped my yang side happen.

She pushed me away, but not immediately, and she didn't smack me again. In a deliciously breathless way, she said, "Why, aren't you the sweetest thing." There was a momentary look of cool cunning in her eyes—that special female fluoroscopic vision that can count the contents of your wallet through four layers of clothing—but she doused it quickly. She was a wise woman, my dear Rubilene, and subtle as good wine.

"No need for you to feel sorry for me, sugar," she said. "Though I do appreciate the attention. I'm glad I got shut of Randy before it was too late. I'm just afraid your Whitney isn't going to be so lucky."

Too late indeed. You *do* know the drill when it comes to the hemophagocytic hoi polloi, don't you, Binks? A nip or two does no more harm than mild anemia, but chugalug over the limit, and the victim turns vampire, too. Now I ask you, could you see poor Whitney flittering around the night sky, sucking total strangers? People who were just Not Her Kind? *Princeton men?* Besides, she looks such a bowwow in black, and Bloomie's is so seldom open after dark. Hello, eternal life; ta-ta, charge cards. *Not* a good trade.

I asked Rubilene whether she was certain in her apprehensions. She nodded vigorously and said, "He's going to make her his bride. That means he'll have to take her all the way, make her like he is. He sealed that when he gave her a ring on Christmas Day." And she gave me one, too, but it wasn't quite the same. Rubilene shivered. "He's been taking the change nice and slow, kinda savoring it, like, but it can't go any farther 'thout she crosses over. Tonight's the night."

Whitney, the bride of a C&W vampire. My own girl, trapped with that man—that monster—that *music*—for all eternity. The mind boggled. "I must save her," I told Rubilene. "Quickly, where can I get a stake?" She suggested the Grill Room of the Dew Drop Inn on S.R. 47-A, until I explained my strictly vegetarian intentions.

"Through the *heart?*" she exclaimed, making the same face Whitney does when something strikes her as euw, gross.

"It's the only way," I maintained, having flashed on the final scene from *Dracula* in this, my hour of need. I cast about the dressing room, but found nothing remotely stake-ish. Determined, though stupid, I instructed Rubilene to run out and fetch me something apropos while I hid behind the curtains, ready to spring out and prevent the villain from sealing his unholy purpose in Whitney's blood.

Yes, Binks, I *did* talk like that. I was upset.

Rubilene protested, but I stood firm. There were a pair of gingham drapes dangling from the wall behind the coffin—a nice, homey touch, considering that they framed no accompanying window, just a poster of Hank Williams. I shimmied past the long box and yanked them shut before me. It was quite the tight squeeze. I've seen tax men with hearts more capacious than that miserable boxcar of a room, though I grant you perhaps the coffin did contribute to the general claustrophobia. The only way it would fit was wedged between one wall and a dingy, iron-stained sink. I knocked two big, ratty towels off the attached chrome drying rack as I wormed by.

No doubt my voice came somewhat muffled as I instructed Rubilene to replace the towels and get a move on. She crammed them back in place angrily and tried one last time to make me see reason. I remained adamant behind the draperies, refusing even to look at her. I assumed I had convinced her of my determination. I didn't hear her retreating footsteps, but I did hear the dressing room door slam, then silence.

One turns rather philosophical when all one has to stare at is a pattern of itsy-bitsy red-and-white checks. The wall felt cold against my back. It was pure cinder block, covered over with that yucky rubberized paint, except where Hank made it crinkly. I dared to part the curtains by a fingertip, just to have something *different* to stare at mindlessly. Thank Gawd we Branfords have always had the aristocrat's slender fingertips, because *that* moment and no other was when Cowboy Randy Russell and Whitney came in.

I froze in place rather than try to jerk back the offending digit. No sense in catching mine enemy's eye with an inopportune flutter of the draperies, *à la* Polonius. We both know what became of *him*. Binks, you would have been proud of me, standing there like one of your Dad's best bird dogs on point. I was entirely rigid.

I wasn't the only one. Impressive. There was no mistaking it, either; not in those jeans. My Gawd, they never do cover that aspect of being a vampire in *Dracula,* though I confess to having an inkling. No woman I ever knew was willing to settle for a hickey. When Cowboy Randy Russell initially rose from the grave, I know which portion of his anatomy surfaced first, the swine. *Definitely* the undead.

Oh, the pain, Binks! To have to stand there, helpless, and watch my—I mean, *your*—Whitney's clothes drop faster than the Dow Jones. Cowboy Randy Russell was quite the quick-draw man himself. There was a brief vertical scrimmage, and then—I remember being idiotically smug about this and wishing Rubilene could see her words proved wrong—he *did* carry her to the coffin.

I don't know, Binks; does she ever get vocal when you and she—? Well, she never did with *me,* and I was asking out of strictly scientific curiosity. You know she's nothing to me now. Perhaps it was the fact that Cowboy Randy Russell was a singer. He even left that tacky white guitar of his propped up at the foot of the casket. The dear girl must have felt obliged to provide backup group accompaniment so he'd feel at home. Just one *ooooh-wah* after another.

My view of the proceedings was unimpeachably perfect. Lord, do we all look that ludicrous *in flagrante?* You won't catch *me* putting any mirrors on the bedroom ceiling. My palms grew slick with sweat as I gazed down upon them from behind the draperies. I felt like a guest at a funeral giving the dear departed one final goggle and discovering they'd laid out Uncle Randolph in a Chanel tea gown. You wouldn't believe where some people have dimples.

And then, just when I thought someone ought to adjust dear Whitney's treble, Cowboy Randy Russell raised himself on his elbows, opened his month—Yes, of *course* he had fangs, Binks; what did you think he was going to use on her? A Swiss Army knife corkscrew? Don't interrupt; you're *ruining* the climax—and said, "Now, sugarlips, you're gonna ride with me till God and Satan slap leather at high noon on a dirt street in Eternity."

Well, *that* tore it. I grabbed one of the towels, twisted it into the great grandfather of all locker-room rattails, and flicked it hard across the foul fiend's Country and Western buttocks.

Gallant? Noble? Heroic? No. I'd call it moronic, if anything. Anyone who saw that creature's blazing red eyes jerk up and fix themselves on me would agree. Homicide would be the least of it. Whitney tried to cast her arms around his neck and get his mind back on business, but *cui bono?* He shook her off like raindrops from a Burberry. He was enraged, and I was dogmeat.

His face contorted into a hellish grimace that I only peripherally recognized as a smile. "Now, why'd you want to go and do a fool thing like that for, son?,' he drawled, clambering out of the coffin with disturbing agility.

"It's your own fault," I temporized, still clutching the towel. "Whitney and I have—had—an understanding. Besides, we're Yale, and I cannot in good conscience allow her to form an alliance with one so uncultured as yourself. Did you actually *say*, 'till God and Satan slap leather'? What *have* you been reading?"

From the coffin, Whitney peeped, "He's *Cowboy* Randy Russell, Tripsy. Cowboys are *always* saying cute things like that."

"A cowboy from *Georgia?*" I countered. "Gawd, Whitney, it's bad enough you dumped me for a vampire, but a *poseur?* And you made such a fuss when Buffy got pinned by that Community College yahoo."

Whitney's immaculately French-manicured nails gripped the edge of the coffin. "You won't *tell* Buffs about this, will you, Tripsy? Even after I'm undead? That bitch would put just the wrong light on this. Randy and I wouldn't be able to go *anywhere* that mattered."

"I'll think about it," I said coolly. Such a treat to watch her beg.

It didn't last long. I heard a growl in the key of G, and felt a hand heavy with gold rings fall on my shoulder. "Son," said Cowboy Randy Russell, "onliest thing you're gonna have to think about is where we ship the body."

Which was approximately when the white guitar came smashing down atop his head. He and I both turned simultaneously to see Miss Rubilene Nash standing there holding the splintered neck of the instrument and screaming some pret-ty strong epithets at the vampire. I was too shocked by her Parris Island vocabulary to ask myself where she'd dropped from. I hadn't *heard* the door open, but I'd been a tad distracted, true.

Russell reeled, though more from her guttersnipe words than the blow. You know vampires: bullets won't stop them, so why should a whack upside the skull with a Fender? Now understand, the man was stark raving naked. We're none of us at our most self-possessed in that state. He *cringed*, poor soul, then snatched the towel from my hands and wrapped it around his middle.

"Young lady," he said, wagging a finger at her. "Young lady, this ain't none of your bidness."

"I'll say it is!" Rubilene countered. She cast a positively scoriac eye at Whitney's fair young bod in the coffin. How your darling wifey shrank beneath that glare! "Jesus, Randy," said Rubilene, "bad enough you're trying to murder this poor boy here, but social climbing, too? Think you can take up with Miss Hot Shit On Toast, and that'll make you any better than the backwoods trash you always been?" She shook her head. "Fine time you pick for sucking up to a Webster. I thought higher of you, boy."

Cowboy Randy Russell's avuncular air dropped by the wayside. He was miffed. His eyes went from bright scarlet to Harvard crimson—never a good sign. I tried to sidle away, but there was no space to permit free-lance sidling. Without bothering to look around, he grabbed me by the collar of my best Land's End polo.

I believe I remarked, "Ackh."

He was more voluble. "Time I need your goodwill's long past, Rubilene," he said. "Seems as you've taken a fancy to this candy-ass Yankee. Try telling *me* you're not just as hot to haul yourself up a rung now you got the chance!"

Rubilene lowered her eyes. It was then, for the first time, she murmured those three little words every man so longs to hear: "I love him." These to be swiftly followed by three more, viz: "Drop him, dickhead."

Cowboy Randy Russell only twisted my polo collar a few additional points to starboard. "I'll drop him, honey, soon's he stops breathing."

Through blurring vision I caught the glimmer of his bared fangs. Rubilene hung back, still clutching the neckpiece of the broken guitar. Could you blame her? She owed her life to this monster's previous forbearance. She was his . . . *pal*. There had to be limits to how far one could push the privileges of such a social connection. I assumed she didn't wish to discover them just yet.

All of which spoke well for Rubilene's prudence, but wasn't doing jack shit to save my neck. Binks, you know I abhor violence, but when your own life's on the line, kicking ass seems like a *darned* good idea. No matter that I knew that a vampire possesses superhuman strength, I would not go gentle into that good night. I hauled back and gave him a right to the jaw.

I don't know which of us was the more shocked: he when that wild punch landed, or I when he shrieked in pain and dropped me. A nasty gash opened up on his cheek, deep and bloodless, but no less impressive. He staggered back, stumbling against the coffin. Whitney uttered a maternal whinny of distress and flung her arms about him, pleading to kiss the boo-boo and make it all better. It was the only favor that woman ever did me, and all unwitting. Her effusions kept him tied up just long enough for me to slip between him and the sink and make for freedom.

Well, almost freedom. He gave a roar and shrugged her aside, shouting, "You goddam sushi-suckin' sumbitch!" Before I could escape the room, he clamped onto my shoulders. I made a fruitless grab for Rubilene's hand, but the vampire spun me around to face him.

"I'm here for you, Trip," I heard her say softly. Her breath stirred the short hairs on my neck. Russell ignored her as unworthy of attention, all his rage focused on me.

"What in hell did you hit me with?" he demanded.

"A—my—the—," I stammered, my hands clenching and unclenching like onanistic starfish. Then I felt it, the thick metal band encircling the third finger of my right hand. You know how some things are always there, so you never really think about them. Like the family trust fund? Briarcliff girls? One's Yale ring? One's *sterling silver* Yale ring? I stared at the monster, and instantly every bit of B-movie lore about silver and its perfectly charming effect on creatures of darkness came flooding through the old brainpan. The scar on his cheek was smoldering. Surprise, surprise, all that silver-bullet bushwa was true.

"Well, *what?* he repeated. He was a most persistent fiend, and his breath—? *Mega* yuckorama.

"This," I retorted, and, raising the fist in question, I let him have another paste across the chops. He hit the floor on that one. Now I did seize Rubilene's free hand and yelped something thoroughly original, like: "Let's get out of here!"

She was yanked from my grasp so hard that she dropped the guitar neck. I watched in horror as Cowboy Randy Russell dragged her back toward the coffin. "Traitor," he growled. "We got ways of dealing with your kind." I might well have gotten away then, for all of him. Turning his back on me, he bent her over the crook of one arm, his fangs bared, heedless of Whitney's clamorous objections that he'd sworn to quit sipping around on her. "Now it's *really* all over," he said.

Which it was, but not for her. Never turn your back on a Yale man. I picked up the splintered guitar neck and thrust it home. Easier than I hoped, really. No trouble at all from little details like intervening ribs and spine. Either there's truth to what they say about the strength of desperation, or else that sorry creature had the worst case of osteoporosis you'd ever see. When it comes to a reliable source of calcium, Brie beats blood every time. His bones snapped like melba toast, and I skewered the heart on the first try. But it was messy. No free lunches, Binks. Whitney fainted.

We left her there. Her late paramour conveniently dwindled to a towel-wrapped pile of primal dust that looked like someone had been dipping snuff a whisker too enthusiastically. No *corpus*, no *habeas*. Whitney would have no trouble from the authorities over the singer's vanishment. The evanescent nature and gypsy habits of *show bidness* people are legendary. Anyway, Webster's Mills was hardly going to make a stereo stink about anything concerning the heir to the town's main industry. I could throw Whitney to the wolves with a clear conscience based on the tacit understanding that cannibalism is *not* a lupine trait. She'd survive. She did, didn't she?

As for Rubilene and myself we judged it wise to get while the getting was good. We eluded all backstage personnel and slipped unnoted onto the parking lot—empty by now. I followed her truck with the Beemer, assuming that we were heading back to town. I just wanted to put as much distance between my ass and Cowboy Randy Russell's earthly remains as possible.

It was well after midnight, most of the Melodrome lights were out, and the asphalt dribble of a state road was illumined only by our headlights. I was too undone by my recent ordeal to do my own nav-igation. I supposed that soon we would be back in the center of town, and then I could barf my guts up at leisure.

I was taken aback when she pulled the truck off into a roadside picnic grove halfway to Hades, turned off the headlights, and got out. I followed suit, thoroughly disoriented and confused. More so when she sat down at one of the wobbly tables, cradled her head in her arms, and began to cry.

I admit she had reason to. She had just aided and abetted the extinction of that rarest of endangered species, a vampire who knew all the lyrics to "If Jesus Drove a Semi." Too, she must have had some fond memories of the fiend, back in the days when she, and not Whit-ney, was his—I blush to say it—drinking buddy. My heart went out to her. To think she had done so much, risked everything, for me!

I sat beside her, patted her on the back, stroked her hair, threw a purely companionable arm around her shoulders, lifted her chin and kissed her a bit to cheer her up, loosened any constricting clothing to prevent a faint. She looked a fright, dark circles under her eyes, and they all red; from crying I concluded. At the time I was so preoccu-pied with cheering her up that I failed to wonder why I could *see* the color of her eyes when we were sitting in total, pitchy dark.

The occasional sob shook her as we kissed. One devolved into a modest burp. Poor child, she was *terribly* embarrassed. She told me that she'd been so caught up in saving my life that she'd missed her dinner entirely. How guilelessly her eyes shone when she said that; how incandescently they crimsoned.

I told her she'd feel better with something in the old tum. Seeing as how much we'd recently meant to one another, and always the sport, I offered to treat her to a bite.

No need. She helped herself.

You know, I *thought* one of those sweet young things in the 1950s photos of Cowboy Randy Russell looked familiar. Ditto in the six-ties. And of course *everyone* looked alike in the seventies, even rhine-stone carhops, but still . . . . Drinking buddy indeed. Back there in the dressing room, it was almost as if she'd plopped down from some perch among the rafters. *Traitor,* he'd called her. When someone calls you a traitor, it means you both must have played on the same team before. Suddenly all the pieces came together.

Which would have been just fine if Revelation had struck about ten minutes earlier. Fat lot of good it did me then, with Rubilene's fangs more firmly embedded in my throat than my dear Mums is foxholed into the D.A.R. My brilliant deductions were swept away in the tide of life-memories passing before my eyes. I lost consciousness just as I was weeing in the baptismal font at St. George's Episcopal.

I woke up the next night covered over with a layer of that good ol' Georgia red clay Rubilene hauled around in back of her pickup for emergencies. I was thirsty; not, I assure you, for another *Cocola*. It was dark, but I was having no problem with night vision. Somewhere in the old mental file cabinet was the spanking new idea that Frequent Flyer had just taken on a whole fresh meaning. Then I saw her anxious face hovering above me.

"You're not mad at me, are you, sugar?" she asked demurely.

What could a gentleman say?

Binks, I married her. Didn't have much choice, did I? And she does love me. It's the crew buns that get 'em, every time, stroke, stroke, stroke. Most of my old crowd developed ingrown previous engagements when the wedding rolled around. They thought I was marrying beneath me, like your wifey's Daddy. Darling Buffy was the first to cut us dead. Ah, if she only knew. There's no saying how much I appreciated you and Whitney attending the ceremony, but I really thought it was in execrable taste for her to pick out that set of *silver* fish-forks as a wedding present. Meow, meow. It's not as if she doesn't know.

Now you do, too.

No, no, no, I won't *hear* of you putting off our date. Rubilene would be utterly crushed. She doesn't handle disappointment at all well. No more do I.

You'll be expecting us seven-ish, then? Good. Mix Bloodies. We'll be there. *A bientôt,* Binks. Hugs to the little woman.

roxanne
longstreet

Faith Like Wine

She was young yet, but I knew what she would become—it was obvious from the first sight of her. One does not forget that sort of face, those extraordinary eyes.

Her name was Aimee Semple McPherson, and she was said to be a prophet.

The tent I stood beneath, waiting for her to speak, had taken laborers half a day to put up—a new tent, astonishingly enough, and these days with the whole world at war there were no new tents of any size.

Tents were not the only scarcity. I stood quite near the front of a large and still-growing crowd, but as I looked around I saw only old men, women, and children. I blended with them, as I meant to—an older woman, to all appearances, gray-haired, not yet out of my prime. Well-dressed, I liked to think, though not ostentatious. Age and womanhood had granted me an automatic aristocracy in such a crowd, and no one tried to push past me for a better view.

I had never been particularly well-mannered, but I certainly knew how to take advantage of it in others.

It had been a tiring walk all the way to the Philadelphia countryside on the strength of rumors, nothing more. Sister Aimee spoke with the voice of God, people said. She healed with His hands. I, doubting, had come expecting an evening of lukewarm platitudes. Such was the state of Christianity—it had been raw, intoxicating wine when I was young, but now it was milk, suitable for children at their mothers' knees. I had walked with martyrs in the shadow of crosses, and I had never learned to love milk.

The buzz of conversation went on around me. A farmer to my left was worried for his daughter, taken ill with a fever—not the dreaded and still-raging influenza, he hastened to add. He received medicinal advice from a young plump woman and her stick-thin husband. If anyone looked for me to join the conversation, they were kind enough not to demand it; I watched the dais and waited. Sister Aimee sat passive, eyes closed now, while her assistants whispered around her, measuring the crowd with piercing looks, checking the time against a battered pocket watch.

They could not wait much longer, not with safety. The crowd stretched to the limits of the tent, a swelling, murmuring beast with thousands of heads. So many years since the first such crowd I'd been part of. I'd been far to the back, then, and the words had come faint but clear in the silence. Five thousand people, that day, crowded together, and I the least of them. Sometimes I could still hear the sound of his voice, smell the goaty stink of too many people crowded together. Nothing in my life had ever been the same again.

Sister Aimee rose and stepped forward, arms upraised, eyes still tightly shut. The crowd rippled into silence, responding to some electric presence gathering like lightning. I could feel its fire from where I stood. No fraud, this one. No false prophet.

She stood, arms upraised, quivering with tension as if held on an invisible rack, the torture of the Lord's favor. Quiet washed over the crowd. Were they afraid? I began to think I was. My life had become comfortable and routine, and here she was, fire in her eyes, to rip it apart again. It was what I craved, what I feared. A spark of light in a long, familiar darkness.

She wore a plain white dress, severely cut, well-used. Her hair was dark and worn in a conservative bun; she wore no jewelry except for a wedding band. A plain woman, except for her face, that radiant face.

It was blinding, now, as she gave herself to the ecstasy of God.

The effect of her still, silent prayer caused the crowd-beast to whisper prayers of its own. Next to me, an old woman carrying a photograph of her son wept into a ragged handkerchief. She'd come for a blessing on him.

An hour before I would have told her, kindly, that it would be useless. But—

But.

Sister Aimee lowered her arms; her eyes opened and they were the eyes of a savage saint, so full of love they were fatal.

And she began to speak.

I cannot remember what she said, it was not the words, the words have been said before and to little effect. It was the naked terrible beauty of her belief. Her voice was a sword, piercing every person in the tent, sending some to their knees in pain, driving most to tears. She burned so bright, the sun in my eyes, the pulse of her heart like a drum in my ears. As she spoke, she ran with sweat and her white dress clung like a lover's hand, skin pink beneath. She paced the platform like an animal, screaming out her pain, God's pain, her love, God's love.

Likely the trouble had been going on for some time before the ripples of it reached me so far in the front, shaking me from my trance; Sister Aimee had stopped speaking and waited, staring toward the back. The world tasted flat and dusty after the glory I'd seen, the sound of screams and shouts harsh. A wedge of young men—a shock to see so many together—came driving through the crowd, heading for the stage.

Mrs. Dowd, the greengrocer's wife, had warned me of Catholic protesters at the revival meetings, but these young men looked more serious than that. They had the righteous look of men steeling themselves to violence. And they were heading directly toward me. I looked for an exit, but escape seemed very far away; I would force a way through, if I must, anything to avoid being caught in the riot that must surely erupt any moment. The boys were taking their lives in their hands. They had no idea how certain Sister Aimee's control was of her people, or what those people might do to protect her.

A dark-haired, pink-cheeked boy leading them raised his hand and pointed at Sister Aimee, and shouted, "Whore!" The other boys took it up like a battle cry and began to lay about them with makeshift weapons—knobby clubs, homemade blackjacks, boots, fists. The crowd surged back from them, pushing me into the arms of a thin old man with the pinched face of a banker.

Sister Aimee stood like a porcelain statue, illuminated with sweat and the halo of her passion, and watched the violence with unnerving eyes. Few of her audience scattered for the exits: there was a curious sense of *waiting*. Frustrated with their lack of success, one of the boys slammed his club into the ribs of the farmer near me who'd come to pray for his daughter; the old man went down, weeping. I stayed where I was, unwilling to flee but certain that I was watching the destruction of the glory I'd glimpsed. Prophets were fragile things, made and broken in a day.

And then Sister Aimee said, in a cold clear voice that carried to every ear, "Kneel and pray, brothers and sisters. Kneel and pray for our burdens to be lifted."

I remained standing, waiting, watching her face. Next to me, the weeping mother clutched the picture of her son and sank to the hard-packed earth. Behind me I heard rustles of cloth, creaks of protesting joints.

In ripples of obedience, the crowd knelt. I lowered myself as the last few touched earth, and folded my hands in a position of piety. I turned my head so that I could watch the reaction of the ruffians from the corner of my eye.

They were the only ones left standing, and it clearly unnerved them. They spun in circles, looking for a fight. With a scream of rage, a boy farther off to my right brought his club down on the head of a middle-aged woman. She toppled against an elderly man in expensively cut clothes. The boy smashed him in the face and kicked him, turned on the woman, then on a young girl. No one rose to fight. He screamed his rage, over and over, *cowards, cowards, cowards,* and stopped, panting, in the destruction he'd done.

Sister Aimee closed her eyes and began to dance. I turned to watch her, riveted by surprise. Her hips swayed slowly, her shoulders followed the curve, her arms lifted and carried the motion above into the air. It was breathtakingly, frighteningly sensual, as if her body had given itself over to another power. She began to turn, slowly, deliberately, to the beat of her unheard song.

Her tormentors came to a standstill, staring, weapons forgotten in their hands. We were all her creatures, trapped in the sway of her body, the jut of her hip, the slow circle of her feet. I closed my eyes and still saw her, heard her, felt her as she moved.

For the first time in a hundred years or more, I took a breath. She had touched something within me that was fearfully strong, love and death and desire and pain all bound together, the dark wine of the faith I'd known in my youth when we were slaughtered by the thousands and kissed the knives that killed us.

She had discovered the secret of ecstasy. I had not been so close to the light in so long, felt its heat, heard the echo of his voice inside it. It was painful and glorious and horrifying. I had kept control of myself for so long, and now she offered—no, *demanded*—my surrender.

Someone cried out, and I heard myself crying, too, lost in the bright vision, the knife-edged fear of falling. She was near the piano now, and, still dancing, reached out and struck a thunderous chord, chaotic and intense, a thunderstorm of music like the cries and prayers around me. And she continued beating the piano, punishing it, and we were all dancing now, swaying to the strange wonderful beat of her song. Someone touched my arm, feather-light, and the breath I'd taken in burst out in a rush. I was trembling, near to falling. Close, so close . . .

Sister Aimee turned from the piano and stepped down from the stage to dance with us, a silent striving of bodies toward God. Her eyes were dark as wells, promising salvation, promising a reunion with all that I'd lost so long ago, and before I could stop myself I reached out to her.

Our hands met, shock of her hot flesh on my cool. The clamor of her pulse was deafening.

"Dance with me," Sister Aimee whispered. "Oh, sister, dance with God."

My feet moved without me, drifting to the beat of her heart, and the tent spun in a glory of light and shadow, faces and eyes. I felt nothing but her skin pressed against mine and frantic hunger inside me, driving me on.

She had turned me to face the crowd, and as she stepped forward and I back, I felt the smooth cool wood of the podium behind me. She stepped forward again, close, so close, God staring out of her eyes. I had forgotten so much, oh Lord, so much.

She placed her hands palm to palm with mine and pressed my arms back and up, toward the crossbars of an invisible cross. When she released them, they stayed, I could not have moved them if I'd wished. She was too bright to be so close to me, and her heart raced like a deer, mad with ecstasy.

She drew back her right hand and brought it in a wide swinging circle up, fingers clasped around an invisible hammer, and her left hand held an invisible nail to my palm.

I opened my mouth to scream as she brought the hammer down, the pain was blinding and horrifying and ecstatic but there was no pain, only knowledge, only God. The doors had been thrown open, and the light, the light . . . I felt her fingers holding another invisible nail to my left palm, and as she drove it home, she transfixed me in the agony of the lamb.

When I was able to scream, I fell forward into her strong, warm arms. She held me while she fought for breath, while her heart raced and then quieted and, passion fading, she eased me to the cold ground. I lay helpless while she folded my hands, one over the other, on my breast.

She turned toward the crowd, but not before I saw the fevered bliss in her eyes.

"Thy busy feet that have walked the world must be nailed to the cross," she said. In the utter silence, one of the Catholic boys fled, then another. The rest followed. Watching their retreat, she said, "Thy heart that has beat for this world must be pierced for me."

I closed my eyes and wept silently, tears streaming away through my gray hair to drip on the hungry ground. Her warmth swept in again, and her fingers touched my tears.

"What's your name, sister?" she asked kindly. I gasped and gasped and finally, like some secret treasure from the depths of a well, brought out my true name.

"Joanna," I whispered. "Joanna, wife of Chuza, servant of Herod."

*   *
*

They kept her long into the night, but finally even the most ardent of her converts slipped away, toward home and bed. I sat outside on the cool grass, lit by the moon, and waited. Lanterns dimmed inside the tent. Her assistants and rough dressed tent-pullers started back for town.

One light glowed inside the tent, a spot of emerald on black shadows. It moved toward the huge main opening and became the yellow halo of a lantern. She carried it casually, dangling from her right hand, and it cast a long golden path in front of her.

She turned and looked toward where I sat, though I was a shadow in shadow.

"Sister?" She tried to keep her tone quiet and reassuring, but I heard a tremor buried deep. "I hadn't thought you would wait so long."

"Not so long," I said, rose to my feet and brushed grass from my skirt. "By my standards."

She took a tentative step toward me and raised the lantern. The light flowed over the cool, serene lines of her face, made secrets of her dark eyes. Her lips parted as I stepped into the circle of light.

"I would not harm you," I said. "I would never do that. I only wanted—wondered—"

She was weary. The lamplight had given her a false color, but her arm trembled with the weight of the lantern and her shoulders sagged. Of course she was weary. *He* had been weary in the press of a crowd. So many hungering, needing, demanding.

And here I was, hungering, too.

"If I could heal you," she finished for me. "Take away your thirst and give you peace."

She could not have known, not just looking at me. I was hearing the voice of God.

"No, sister, I'm not the one." Her arm was trembling so much she was forced to lower the lantern and set it beside her feet. "I'm so sorry, Sister Joanna."

I looked down at the light, glowing between us. "I had no hope, really. But I thank you for showing me my faith again."

I turned to walk off into the darkness that was my home. Before I could enter it completely, she called after me, and I turned and met her eyes.

"Joanna, wife of Chuza, servant of Herod." Sister Aimee's voice broke as she repeated my name. "You knew Him, didn't you?"

I closed my eyes against the radiance of the light.

"Yes," I said. A surge of wind blew the grass in billowing waves, a lapping silver lake in the moonlight. The tent sighed and groaned. "I knew them all."

※   ※
　　　※

I had come with the lepers, wrapped in layers of rags and castoffs. The crowd was still great, even at so late an hour, but no man held his place before lepers; we moved through solitude even here, in this sweating throng. Some of the faces knew me, another reason to veil myself. They would know me for a follower of Simon Magus, and stone me.

I saw him for a brief second as the crowd shifted, and his eyes

were wonderful and terrible and knowing. The veils, the conceal-
ment, all that was useless. He recognized me for what I was.

I fell back, hoping to drift off quietly, but a hand closed around
my arm. I turned, shocked that anyone would dare to touch a leper,
and saw a stocky, bearded man with a kind face and smile.

"Quiet," he advised me. "I have been sent to bring you."

His name, I learned, was Judas Iscariot, one of the twelve who
served. He took me to a small, ill-repaired house with blankets and
packs spread out on the rough floor, and told me to sit. He offered
food, not knowing how useless it was, and then wine and water. I
took a little of the water to allay his suspicion.

"You should not drink after me," I said as he took the bowl back
and raised it to his lips. He had an impudent grin.

"You are no leper," he said, and drank the rest.

At the doorway, a shadow, a confusion of movement. The
shadow turned and spoke, and the protesting murmurs melted into
silence. He ducked through the door and came to sit opposite me as
Judas put an oil lamp between us.

For all the strength of his eyes, he was only a man, no taller than
most, no more beautiful. He had the smell of the road on him, and
the sweat of a hard day's work. No longer young, but not old. Not
yet. He had lines of weariness in his face that had not been there
when last I'd seen him, when last I'd believed his lovely words.

"Lord," I murmured, and bowed my head to the floor. When I
looked up, he was watching with a small, amused smile.

"Humility should come from the heart," he said. Judas came forward to clear a place for him to sit, and he lowered himself into it
with a sigh of relief.

"Master, this is the one—" Judas began, but his master lifted a
hand to stop him.

"Joanna," he said. "Chuza's wife. I remember you well."

I sat upright, more afraid of him than ever. I had not unveiled, I was
as anonymous as a thousand women outside his door. He had seen me
before only once, and I'd been different then. So very different.

"I heard that Chuza died," he continued. "I am sorry. He was a good man."

"How—"

"Did I know you would come here? Because I know." The amusement was closer to the surface now, but not cruel—a child's gentle amusement, full of wonder. "Your road has been hard."

"I have not traveled far."

"I did not say you had." His smile faded. "You may take away the disguise now. I am not afraid."

I unwound the scarves to show him my unnatural pallor, my too-red lips, my too-green eyes. I smiled to show him my sharp teeth.

"A long road," he said, unmoved. "It will be longer still, Joanna. Have you the strength?"

"I—" I swallowed; begging did not come to me as easily as even mock humility. "Can you help me, master?"

"Did not Simon Magus promise to heal you?" I bowed my head, but he continued, kind and merciless. "My rival took you in when you were dying and promised you ever-lasting life. Are you happy with your bargain?"

"No." I felt tears welling up, but they were mortal tears, and my body no longer knew them. "No, master, please, help me. I went to Simon Magus because I needed—Master, I asked you for healing, and you said my time was done."

"It was."

"He said he could—give me—"

He took the plate of figs that I had refused and chewed on one while I sat in silence, ashamed. He sipped from a bowl of wine Judas handed him.

"I only want to die," I said at last. Judas, wide-eyed, sank back on his haunches and shook his head. "I killed a man, master, because I was so thirsty. I can't bear it anymore. Please, give me rest."

His eyes were full of sorrow and pain, knifing through me and leaving ice in their path. I reached out to him and touched his hand. He did not draw it away.

"It is not my place to take your life," he said. "But I can give you rest, of a kind."

He reached into a pack leaning against a cracked wall and found a sturdy sharp knife. He held it out toward our joined hands and, before I knew what he would do, drew it across his own wrist. I cried out, and Judas lunged forward and grabbed for the knife. The master hissed a little with pain and held our joined hands over the empty bowl that had held his wine.

His blood dripped like jewels into the plain clay, fast at first, then slowing. When he turned his wounded wrist upward to show me, there was no cut at all.

"Drink," he said, and let go of my hand. I looked down at the bowl.

He'd only bled a little, but the bowl shimmered with blood, full to the brim. I raised it and sipped, the raw fire of it burning down my throat and into my veins. It tasted of honey and flowers and tears, and I drank until the bowl was empty.

"You will not need to kill," he said. I clutched the bowl to my breast and bowed, no mock humility this time, wishing I could weep for joy. Here was the water of life, in my body, and in my heart I felt the pulse of God. "When you hunger, the bowl will fill again."

"Master, what do you ask of me?" I whispered. Simon Magus had asked, everyone had always asked. There were no gifts, only exchanges. His hand touched my graying hair, gentle as the wind.

"Walk your road," he said. "Walk to the end, where you will find your healing."

*   *   *

I waited at the train platform in the beating fury of the sun, protected by a hat and heavy clothes and a parasol topped with faded satin flowers. It was early morning, the sunrise an orange cream confection behind the unlovely black hissing box of the train. Passengers scuttled around me, bound here and there, clutching hats against the white steam and cool breeze.

I held a single suitcase in my left hand. The burden was too precious to set down, even for a minute.

Sister Aimee's party emerged from the station, a threadbare gaggle of white dresses and severely dressed, sober-faced men—her roughnecks had passed through earlier, loading baggage and tents. Near the center of the crowd I saw the porcelain curve of her face, a lovely smile. She had her hand on the shoulder of a young girl who walked with her.

I did nothing, said nothing, as the party passed me on the way to the train. Pride had always been my downfall, but I could not beg, not now, not ever. I watched them board, one by one, and no one so much as glanced in my direction.

Then Sister Aimee turned, one foot on the iron steps, and looked directly at me with a smile warmer than the furious sun.

"Sister Joanna," she said, and the sound of her voice silenced those around her. It woke tingles in my back; I fought them off with a straightening of my shoulders. "Come to see us off?"

No begging. Not now, not ever. I met her eyes.

"I come to join you," I said. Her smile faded. Perhaps she was thinking of what I was, what the presence of so much shadow might do in the midst of her light.

"Do you?" she asked. My hand tightened around the grip of my suitcase and I willed it to relax. Her assistants were frankly staring, whispering among themselves. There was doubt in Sister Aimee's eyes, moving like clouds over a clear sky. I was something old and unknown, something dark. I had a second's grave disquiet and thought, *I should not have come. It's too late to go home.*

She held out her hand to me. I moved forward, skirts brushing aside those who stood in my way, and realised as I arrived that I had no free hands to take hers. I must put down the suitcase, or put away the parasol.

I folded the parasol. The sun pressed on me with cruel, unforgiving hands, burning even through the layers of clothes, through the straw hat that shaded my face. I pressed the parasol into the crook of my arm and reached out to take Sister Aimee's hand. Her fingers folded warm around mine.

Only a moment of agony, and then the cool shadow of the train was around me, and Sister Aimee's fingers touched my face. I couldn't see her; even so small an exposure to the sun had turned my vision to grays and blacks. It would be minutes or even hours before I could see clearly again.

"Brave," she commented, a smile in her voice. "Come aboard, Joanna. We have a long way to go."

*　　*　　*

He had a huge, expansive house outside Jerusalem's walls, surrounded always by knots of people seeking blessings or miracles or just a good look. He also had disciples, rough men, ready with fists and knives. Two of them were on duty outside the door when I arrived in my leper's disguise; one reached down to find a rock to throw. I pulled the veil away and showed my face. The one with the rock grinned and shrugged and tossed the stone over his shoulder. The other just spat near my feet and settled back against the wall more comfortably.

No pauper's hut would have done for Simon Magus. Inside, soft lamplight glimmered on fine cedar tables, delicate pottery, gold lamps and jars. The floor was covered with soft carpets and furs. A doorway at the oilier end of the room was covered by a black drape that glittered with sewn gold coins; they chimed in the cool evening breeze. The air simmered with costly incense, gifts from rich benefactors.

"Simon?" I called. The coins chimed. Outside, the guards laughed coarsely.

"You used to call me 'master,'" he observed. I whirled to find him standing quite near me in the shadows. As he came into the light, I saw that he wore a new robe, no doubt another gift. The umber and gold of it put spark in his large dark eyes, made his skin seem gilded. Beautiful Simon. Never a man born so beautiful. "I missed you, Joanna."

His voice sounded sad and fond, and it shamed me. I found

myself looking away and knew that weakness would destroy me unless I was careful.

"I went to him," I said. He reached out to touch my cheek and it was like being touched by fire, beautiful and agonizing at once. Before I could recover, he was gone past me to settle himself on a thick tasseled pillow—master greeting servant.

"And how did you find the carpenter?" Simon made the word sound faintly scandalous. "Still working miracles, is he?"

I had the bowl hidden inside my robes. My hand brushed it before I could stop myself, like a woman betraying a disgraceful, ill-gotten child. He saw it, of course; I saw the delight flare in his eyes.

"What miracle did he work for you, my love?" he asked voice low like a cat's purr. "Did he offer you forgiveness for your sins? Did he heal you? Oh, no, my apologies, I see he did not. Too bad, really. That would have been a miracle."

I stood silent, watching him, his beauty like a whip against my skin. Simon made a graceful gesture with his hands and produced from thin air a gilded bowl of wine from which he drank slow, measured mouthfuls.

"Thirsty?" he asked. I shook my head. "Liar. Joanna, I will forgive these indiscretions of yours with my rival if you will sit and drink with me. Will you do that?"

I had lain there on those same soft pillows, fever burning me to ash, and he'd lifted my head and held a bowl to my lips and said, *Drink, woman, drink and live,* and I had taken bitter mouthfuls, feeling the stain of it in my soul even a I swallowed. If I had been strong, I would have spit it out. Would have refused a second mouthful.

But I had drained the bowl, and now I had to pay the price for that selfishness.

"I believe in him. I am going to join him," I said quietly "I came to tell you."

Silence. The curtain of coins tinkled like dreams breaking. Simon held his bowl in both hands, mouth curled into a smile, and watched me.

"Then do that," he said, and shrugged. "What do I care? You are nothing, less than nothing. You served Herod, and betrayed him by skipping off to follow your carpenter when he crooked a finger; you turned your back on the carpenter when you sickened, and came to me for miracles. Now that you are well, you betray me. You are a whore of the spirit, Joanna."

It seemed impossible that he could still hurt me so deeply, but the casual chill in his voice, the sharp edges of the words, made me feel sick with grief. I looked down at my clenched hands. When I looked up again, Simon was gone. There was a hollow in the pillows where he'd sat. Outside, the guards laughed. Where had he—?

His hand closed around my throat from behind me, dragged me into the heat of his embrace. He had strong hands, clever hands, and before I could fight he reached beneath my robes and pulled out the bowl.

"This?" He let me go, and I whirled to face him, terrified by the sight of my salvation in his casual grasp. He turned the bowl this way and that, looking at the poor quality of the clay, running his fingers across the uneven surface. "A miracle? Perhaps a miracle that the potter managed to give it away. Here."

He tossed it to me. I clutched it gently, like a newborn. Simon's smile was no longer beautiful, only wide.

"Or is it this one?" He snapped his fingers and another bowl appeared, identical to the one I held. He tossed it toward me; I caught it, fumbling, panicked. "Perhaps this one?"

He produced another bowl, and another. The fourth I could not catch; it fell against the corner of a cedarwood table and smashed. I went to my knees and scraped blindly at the mess.

When I looked up from gathering the fragments, distraught, I saw him looking down on me with rage in his eyes. Perhaps he knew then how completely he'd lost me.

"Put them down," he ordered. "Put them all down."

I tried to keep the bowls, tried desperately, but they writhed out of my fingers and thumped to the carpet, one after another.

"Simon—" I could not beg, not even now. He raised his foot and brought it down on the first bowl. It shattered into a thousand dusty pieces.

"Come back," he invited, and put his sandaled foot over the second bowl I shook my head, not knowing whether I was denying him or denying the moment's pain. "Come back to me and I'll forget all this foolishness."

Another bowl smashed into clay dust and shards. One left. I stared at it with fevered eyes.

"You don't belong with him, Joanna. You know that." He raised his foot. In his dark eyes, my reflection flickered and stretched into shadows. "I am doing you a favor, you know."

There was a film of red at the bottom of the last bowl. As I watched, it bubbled up, a magic spring of life. His foot came down toward it.

I leaped forward and knocked him away. He fell against a table and overset a lamp and jug; wine spilled over his robes and the carpets in a purple tide. I scooped up my bowl and drained it in two quick, guilty gulps and backed away, toward the doorway, as Simon turned on me.

He did not scream, he did not curse. He only stared. It was enough.

I lunged out into the darkness, between the two startled guards, and ran, leaving strips of leper's gauze flying on the wind as I ran toward the moonlit walls of Jerusalem.

Someone waited at the side of the road. The moonlight touched his face and his kindly smile.

"He said you'd come this way," Judas said. "It's not safe to walk alone."

I cast a look back at Simon's house. He was standing in the doorway, arms folded, watching me go.

*   *

It was a queer change, silting behind Sister Aimee as she exploded into the fury of her belief; she directed it out, at all those hungry faces, those empty eyes. In the backwash, where I sat, there was only a tingle of power, nothing like the tide I'd been swept away on before. I was grateful, in a way. One should not know God so closely on a daily basis.

I learned quickly that every revival looked the same—another empty field, sometimes dry, sometimes muddy, another town on the horizon. Sometimes the crowd was older, sometimes younger. The routine was grinding. Sister Aimee preached and prayed far into the night, rose with the sun and participated in the camp chores like anyone else. I did one-handed tasks, like fetching water or scrubbing cluthes, everywhere I went in the sunlight, I carried my parasol. One acute young lady said that I must have a skin disorder, perhaps leprosy, that made my skin so white. They all thought it was highly appropriate that Sister Aimee should count a leper among her followers, though privately they must have wondered why I hadn't been healed.

I realized, as I knelt beside a lake in Idaho and scrubbed spots of mud from the hem of Sister Yancy's dress, that I had done such work before. I had only misplaced the memories, never forgotten. They loomed so close now that I could smell the dust of Jerusalem, feel the harsh fabric on my skin, see the heat shimmer from the stones of the courtyard where I had gone daily to fetch water. I had been shunned there, too, and had gone at odd hours to avoid the curses and thrown stones of the other women.

I pushed the painful, precious memory aside and scrubbed industriously. A cooling shadow fell over me, and I squinted up to see Sister Aimee dropping down next to me, a load of washing in her arms.

"I thought I might find you here," she said. She had not spoken to me—to anyone—for days now, lost in the routine of preaching, healing, sleeping, working. She was visibly worn, and had a tremble in her hands that had not been present before. "How are you, Joanna?"

"I am well," I said. "You're tired."

She gave a little laugh and lowered her head toward her work, soaking the clothes, wringing them, scrubbing them with soap. The water was very, very cold. Her fingers took on a more pronounced shiver and a bluish tint.

"Perhaps I am," she admitted. "Perhaps that's all it is."

I stopped working and watched her. I had been traveling with her for almost a year, though the time hadn't seemed so long. A year was nothing to me, but for her, burning so bright, a year was an eternity.

"Did you notice, last night?" she continued more slowly. "Something felt wrong. I felt—lost. I called, but he didn't come, it was only me. Only me."

I *had* noticed, and not only last night. Some nights Sister Aimee seemed to be searching for that fire I'd always seen so clearly before, nurturing a spark, not a conflagration. Sometimes she'd fallen into a routine, like a salesman's patter. Perhaps that was to be expected, as weariness gutted her spirit. Even *he* had needed rest.

"I'm afraid," Sister Aimee said. She was staring down at the petticoat she was wringing, and there were tears coursing down her cheeks. "Oh, sister, what if he never comes back? They come looking for miracles, you know. For faith. What if I have nothing to give them?"

I took the petticoat from her and put it aside, dried her chilled hands in the folds of my skirt. She put her head on my shoulder and I rocked her gently, stroking her hair. My poor prophet, burning so bright.

What happens when the candle burns out?

I should have known better than to come here and destroy her faith.

* * *

He stepped out of the shadows like fog swirling, a simple trick he often used to impress his followers. I was carrying a jar of water across the courtyard, hurrying to get out o the burning sun, but I came to a breathless stop when I saw him. The sun pressed on me like the hands of a giant and my arms tightened around the heavy jar. I was going blind, but he stood out like a brilliant stain on the dark.

"Fetching water?" Simon Magus asked, and leaned hi shoulders negligently against the rough stone wall. He looked the part of a savior—beautiful, wide eyes as gentle as an angel's. "Sweet Joanna, surely our misunderstanding didn't lead you to slavery to a Galileean carpenter? What will people say?"

"Go," I said, not loudly because I did not want the men inside to hear. "Go, please. You have no right to be here."

"I have every right." Simon Magus stood straight and tugged his robes into place. "Come into the shadows, my dear, before you burn yourself beyond repair. Such as you don't belong in the light."

The pain of the sun was intolerable; my arms shook violently, spilling water over the front of my robe. My eyes were fading, but I saw him hold out his hand to me. Beckoning. Commanding.

"No!" The jar slipped from my arms and shattered on the stones with a crash. "Simon, I left you! You have no right!"

"He's left you lost between light and dark," Simon continued. "Come back where you belong, where you are loved. Don't run any longer, Joanna."

I sank to my knees, gray hair a veil over my sweating face, and tried to find my faith. In Simon's presence it curdled and vanished.

And then Judas said, "You, what do you want here?"

I looked up but he was only a vague shape in the sun-blindness. He knew Simon Magus, of course, they all did. I thought he would call for help, but he stepped out into the sunlight. Alone.

"My property," Simon purred; I heard the gloating smile in his voice. "Little man, run and tell your master that I've come to worship at his royal feet."

"He will not come."

"No? Then I'll take what is mine and go." He held his hand out to me again and snapped his fingers. "Up, Joanna."

A man's arms went around me, holding me close. Judas. He was trembling, though not enough that Simon would see; afraid, after all. But willing to risk everything in spite of that fear.

"In the name of God, go!" he shouted. His words brought a stir of movement from the house; I heard sandals scrape on the courtyard stones and knew others were joining us, ready to fight. Which? Peter, perhaps, good-hearted as ever. John, with his chilly, determined eyes, always ready for conflict.

"She must say it," Simon Magus said. His voice was as warm and sad as I remembered, and traitorous. I had believed once, so strongly, and been so vastly betrayed. "Joanna, my dear? Won't you come home?"

Home, I thought with a piercing grief. There was no home now, only Simon's fraudulent smiles or the harsher, more honest love of the Twelve and the One. I could never be one of them, even if I stepped out of shadow entirely.

But I could never go to Simon Magus. Never again.

"Go," I said. It did not sound as strong as I wished. "Leave me."

Judas' arms went around me as my knees buckled; as he picked me up to carry me inside, I sensed that the shadows were empty. Simon was gone, vanished like a nightmare.

My sight was entirely gone now; I knew that he carried me inside only because of the sudden relief on my skin and the babble of voices around us. Peter shouted for order and began telling of Simon Magus; the words drifted into distance as Judas carried me away into the room set aside for stores and my pallet. Someone followed us; I heard the scrape of his footsteps behind us. Judas lowered me to my blankets and smoothed sweaty hair back from my face.

"She is ill," he said over his shoulder toward whoever watched. "Get the master."

"No," I protested, and caught at his hand. "No, give me time, I am well. It's only the sun."

The other man made a disgusted sound deep in his throat, and I did not have to see him to know him; John would be staring with those chilled eyes that saw so much, so far away.

"Leave her," John said. "We must report what she did."

Judas' hand left my forehead as he turned. "What did she do, John, but renounce a false messiah? Don't bring this out again, it's an old argument. Joanna, would you like some water?"

I had spilled the water outside on the cobbles, but he'd forgotten it. I summoned up a smile and shook my head. After the dreadful punishment of the sun, I felt languid and lost.

"Just rest, please," I said. He squeezed my hand gently and stood. "Judas, I—I didn't bring him here. I would never want him to come here."

"I know," he said kindly. "Rest now."

I turned my face to the wall and listened to them go.

Hours passed, filled with the muted buzz of heated conversation outside. My vision lightened from black to gray. Colors returned dusty and bleached. I would be days recovering, but I could see well enough to move around, to straighten up the meager supplies kept in the room with me. While I ordered sealed jars of oil, someone slapped the stone outside my door, asking entrance. I rose to pull the curtain aside and found James standing there, head down, avoiding my eyes. He was a small man, wiry and strong, quick to laugh. I had always liked him, had always believed he liked me, as well as a man could like a widow whose eyes had the taint of poisonous hunger.

"You are wanted," he said, and turned away. I watched him walk quickly away, shoulders hunched, and knew with a sinking heart that my welcome was ended.

It was not a very long walk, of course, only one short hallway, but the silence that greeted my approach made it seem longer. The twelve of them were present, seated in a rough circle. Judas had left a place open beside him and I took it, kneeling decorously on the hard-packed floor.

"Brothers," I said, and bowed my head. It was only the twelve, no sign of the master. I had seen little of him, lately, and when I did, his eyes seemed unfathomably far away. Perhaps he was gone again. I could hardly imagine the Twelve meeting like this without him, but surely he would have come if he could. Surely.

"She is humble," Peter said, and he meant it as praise. "She knows her place. What harm can she do?"

I put my hands flat on my thighs and looked down at them. No pride, not now, Joanna. Pride is your enemy.

"She is causing rifts in our brotherhood," John said. Ah, John, I had known it was you, I had known. But it was not simple jealousy, or even simple fear. John was the protector, and he fought higher battles than that. "You all know what's being said. How can we teach truth when our enemies have such fertile ground for sowing lies? Surely it is true that we keep women in our house—she and Mary Magdalene, women of uncertain virtue at best! How can we stop the lies if we do not eliminate the cause of them?"

"It would be different if she were a wife, or even a sister," Simon Peter offered. He was a big man, scarred from the years he'd spent working the sea, but his voice was strangely smooth and calm. He was not a man I cared to have arguing against me. "But a woman alone, even a widow, can hardly be above suspicion. We must be seen to be righteous. Sometimes truth alone is not enough."

"Are we speaking of Joanna or all women?" James asked, frowning. "Should we forbid the master's mother entrance? Should we turn away believers? He has never said so."

"Joanna is different." John's voice stopped James cold, stopped even the breeze traveling through the room. "We all know that. It is that difference that is at issue. She is not a creature of God. She cannot bear the light of day."

"Many of the sick cannot," Peter said.

"And many are possessed! But we should not lie down with devils, brother! Let us heal them, and send them on their way." I felt John's eyes rake over me and suppressed a shiver. "I think her true master came for her today. Will she say differently?"

The silence that fell was deadly. Surely they were all looking to me. I kept my eyes down, kept my voice even as I said, "Simon Magus made me what I am. Do you think I am grateful for that? He is no master of mine. Not ever again."

"So you say now. What if you sicken? What if—"

"Enough, John!" Judas stirred next to me; I looked up to see him staring across at John's rigid face. "You've accused enough. Joanna is not causing a rift here, you are. If the master wants her to leave, he will tell her. He will tell us all. Until he does—"

I felt the surge of a presence suddenly, like a strike of lightning behind me. He had not been there before, I knew, and others knew it, too. I saw John's face go feverishly brilliant with worship. The master burned hotter as the days went by, a force of power and love that warmed us even in passing.

And he said, "You are right to be concerned. Joanna must leave us tomorrow."

I cried out, turned, and threw myself full length on the floor at his feet. Such hardened, well-traveled feet, in dusty patched sandals, so different from Simon Magus' pampered, well-cared-for flesh. I laid my cheek on them and wished I could weep, wished I could wash his feet with my tears, wipe them clean with my hair. Instead I could only pray, silently, for mercy.

"'It is my wish that you leave us," he said quietly. He sounded so sad, so final. I looked up into his face and saw bottomless sorrow m his eyes, a pain that had no human definition.

"Then I must go," I whispered, and kissed his feet and remained lying there until he reached down to lift me up. I had never been so close to him face-to-face, near enough to feel God beneath his skin and see heaven in his eyes. Words burst out of me like blood. "Master, I would never betray you!"

It was as if the rest of them had vanished for us, as if he saw only me. I was no longer looking at a man, I knew. I was no longer speaking to a mortal. The light in his eyes reached deep inside me and woke something vast and fragile. Something more than love, more than devotion. Faith. Absolute faith.

"I know," he said, and smiled sadly. "That is why you must go, my faithful Joanna, before it is too late."

*   *

I shared a tent with Sister Tabitha, a sweet young girl with a voice like a songbird; she led the hymns before and after Sister Aimee's service. Lately, Sister Tabitha had voiced her doubts to me about Sister Aimee. They were no longer doubts for me, but certainties.

In the two years in Sister Aimee's service I had watched the flame burn lower and lower, and now there were only fading sparks. Sister Aimee no longer paced the stage like a lion, she strode like an actor remembering marks. Her frenzies were carefully crafted, discussed at length with one or two of her close companions; Sister Aimee rarely spoke to me now, except during the service. She had asked me to dance with her once, in Indianapolis, but there had been nothing of God in her eyes, only a desperate hunger like lust. She had wanted me to give back her faith. I had become something to touch in place of God.

I had stepped away from her, grieving, and seen the trust die. I had been wrong to come, so wrong. There was no healing with Sister Aimee, and now I was watching my beloved prophet die, inch by inch, and I was helpless to prevent it.

I had come to a decision; I would leave when we reached the next stop. The decision soothed my grief, if not my conscience. A night's sleep, and then I would be gone. Simple enough.

I woke in agonizing hunger. Not the gentle hunger I was used to, but a painful, ripping hunger, a need for flesh and blood, a need to rend and tear and scream. It took me that way, sometimes—not often, perhaps once in five or ten years. But when it came, it was like dying, mortally terrifying. I lay in my narrow bed and pressed trembling hands to my convulsing stomach and stared up at the tree-shadows waving on the roof of the tent. God, God, Sister Tabitha lay no more than two steps away, sweet young face upturned to the dim moonglow. Her heartbeat ached in my ears, a torment I would give all to stop.

Kill her, a whisper from the shadows said, but it was not Simon Magus, not after all these years. It was only my own darkness, subtle and powerful. I *had* to drink, *must* drink, before the tide of madness sucked me down.

I rose in the dark and found my bag, clawed aside layers of clothing and precious, ancient memories—a Greek Bible, bare scraps of words after all these centuries—a newer Tyndale version, one of the few saved from burning in those dark days in England—a single piece of silver. The tarnished coin rolled unevenly across the dirt floor and tilted to a stop.

I could not stop, not even for the coin, not even for that most precious memory. I found the smooth clay of the bowl and hugged it to my chest, careful, careful. There was some magic in it that had kept it unbroken all these ages, but still, I did not dare trust it too far.

The hunger rose like a living creature inside me, clawing, destroying. I gasped and heard Sister Tabitha move behind me, sitting up perhaps. The rustle of the sheet was as loud as a gunshot. Her heartbeat speeded faster.

"Sister Joanna?" she whispered. "Is everything all right?"

Oh, no, child, no, not all right. I could not do it here, not with her awake. The need to flee took me out of the tent, out into cold dewy grass, the chilly tingle of moonlight. I was wearing only my nightdress but I dared not stop for anything more; Tabitha was rising, calling after me. I forced myself to pause and turn back toward her.

"It's nothing, child," I whispered. So hard to speak, with the beast so close. "A call of nature."

She murmured something doubtful, but I turned and strode away, through the cool chilling grass, scattering dew like diamonds where I stepped. Up the hill, then, toward the moon, toward safe solitude. Tabitha had not followed. I clutched the bowl close and panted as I climbed, not for the air but to hold off the attack of the beast.

I gained the top of the hill and turned a quick circle—the camp glimmered below me, one huge waving ocean of revival tent, the smaller ponds of camp tents where Aimee's faithful slept. The grass waved silver-green as the wind stroked it.

I went to my knees and took my bowl in both hands. Hunger beat at me with clenched, bruising fists and I waited for the red to collect at the bottom of the bowl, to bubble up like Moses' desert spring. It was slow, this time, or perhaps that was only my own desperation.

He would not betray me now. Could not.

I closed my eyes and whispered a prayer, first in Hebrew, then in Greek, then in every language I could call to mind.

Warmth cascaded over my fingers. I gasped and opened my eyes to see the bowl brimming with life, with light, with salvation. I could almost see his face, sad and worn, his hands welling with open wounds.

"Joanna?"

No, oh, no. It could not be, not now.

Sister Aimee came around to face me, face wild and white, hair loose. The wind teased it out into a veil of shadow. She was dressed, like me, only in a flickering white gown, feet bare and pale as marble. Tears tracked silver down her cheeks.

"Go," I whispered. "Go away."

My arms trembled with the strain of holding the beast back, the shadows were not whispering now, they screamed, *kill her, kill her, kill her,* and I was close, so very close. Sister Aimee knelt down opposite me, the bowl trembling between us, bat she was not watching the bowl, only my face. Such desperation there. Such hunger.

"I have lost him," she said. More tears, spilling diamond bright. "Oh, sister, help me. Only you can help me find what I've lost. I can't go on, I can't, so many hungry, feeding on me, I have nothing left, nothing, you understand, *I can't feel Him anywhere now.*"

I understood, had spent lonely years tending my few precious sparks of faith but none of that was important now only the beast was important, only the shadows, the bowl that was my person, precious salvation.

Her eyes flared wide with dark grief, and before I could stop her, she struck the bowl out of my hands. It spun away, spilling a precious red ribbon over the grass, and disappeared into the shadows.

*   *

I woke from a nightmare to cry out, and found a man's hand across my lips, sealing in the noise. His skin felt fever-hot. I twisted away to sit up against the wall, blanket drawn over me, shivering.

"Shhh," Judas touched a trembling finger to his lips. I understood well enough; if he were discovered here the penalty would be grave. For me, it would be fatal. "You must go."

He turned away to start gathering my pitiful things, wrapping them together with trembling hands. I clasped his wrist to stop him.

"I have until tomorrow. The master said."

"Tonight. You must go tonight." Judas breathed in suddenly, a tormented gasp as though a knife had been driven into his side, and tears sheeted over his eyes. "If he asked you—"

"Judas?"

"If he asked you for your life, would you give it?" he whispered. His voice seemed to echo off the stone, loud as a shout. *"Would you?"*

"Yes."

The tears spilled over, coursing down his face, catching in his beard like stars.

"He asked for my soul."

"Judas—" I reached out for him, but he scrambled up and bolted away. I hurried after, but the outer room was empty, only the flut- tering door curtain witness to his passage. I turned to go back to my pallet, my weary confusion.

The master stood in my way. I had never seen him look so weary, so worn.

"I have asked him for the greatest of gifts," he said, though I did not have the courage to ask. Had I thought Judas suffered? There was all the grief of the world in these eyes. "Of all of them, only he has the strength, the faith, and the love. The others could only do it out of hate."

"Master, please don't send me away," I whispered. Around us lay the sleeping forms of his disciples, but somehow I knew they would not wake, not until he wished it.

"You must go. All roads branch from here. You cannot follow where I am going, none of them can. You have the longest road, and you must be sure of your course. I will not always be with you."

The dazzle of his love broke, through, glowed like the sun on my skin, and I knew he was not turning me away, only lighting me to another path. Even so, I tasted ashes at the thought of walking away from him, from all of them.

"You will always be with me," I said, and touched my fingers over my heart. "Here."

He leaned close and kissed me on the forehead, a brief brush of light and love against my cool skin.

I thought about the horror in Judas' eyes, the desolation. Had he also received this kiss of peace?

"I'll go tomorrow," I said. He shook his head, frowning. "Tomorrow. I'll stay for Judas."

He looked at me for a moment, then smiled through the sorrow and said, "Yes. He will need you."

＊　　　＊
＊

The pain of loss was so extreme that for a moment the world went gray, lifeless, and hunger was shocked into silence. I could only stare at the darkness, where the bowl had fallen.

Sister Aimee grabbed my shoulders and shook me, crying out. I wrapped my hands around her wrists and pressed. When I turned my eyes to her, she saw the beast staring, and fell silent. Her face went the color of cold ash.

"Never do that again," I said, as calmly as I could. "It's not for you to touch. Ever. It is *mine*."

Her wrists pulsed with life under my crushing fingers—red, warm, easy to find. How long had it been since I tasted mortal flesh? Long enough that it had been in that expensive, long-lost house outside the Jerusalem wall among the cedarwood tables and gold lamps.

Simon Magus had stood watching while I'd fed, his smile gentle and protective. He'd loved the beast well. The memory of his beautiful smile sickened me, and I let Sister Aimee go and crawled slowly, painfully, into the shadow where the bowl had fallen.

It had struck a stone, but there was only a small chip on the rim, a raw, rough gouge in the ancient finish. I lifted it in both hands and closed my eyes, heard my beloved master's voice, felt his touch around me.

I lifted the bowl and drank until the beast was drowned in honey and flowers. I drank so much that it spilled red over my lips and down my chin to patter dark on the grass and even then I could not stop taking it in. So close to him, so close.

This is my blood, which is shed for you. Only for me, this blood. None other.

I was senseless with the ecstasy and hardly felt the brush of Sister Aimee's hands against mine. When I blinked and the world came back in dusty blacks and shadows, she was holding the bowl and backing away from me. Her eyes had a dangerous shine. I tried to reach out, to tell her, but she stepped back and I was too weak to follow. As she cradled the bowl, her face came alight with understanding.

"*His,*" she breathed. "Communion. This is My blood, He said. And it is. It *is.*"

She did not understand. Miracles were personal. They could not be traded, like unused tokens at the county fair. That way lay defeat, and madness. That way lay Simon Magus, and the false glitter of easy faith. Her face took on the fever of passion, the hunger of lust, and behind her Simon Magus stepped out of the shadows, as if I'd somehow conjured him, shimmering with beauty and treachery, that sad smile, those angelic eyes.

"Drink," Simon whispered. His voice was the shadows, the wind, the leaves. "Drink, woman, and live. Live forever."

Impossible. It was not Simon's dark, poisoned bowl, it was holy, it was sacred. Surely she could take no harm from it.

But damnation, like miracles, was a personal thing, and I was not sure.

*   *   *

The house was cold, the fires all burned to ashes. I sat in the gray dawn and listened to the chaos outside on the street. Running feet, now, and screams in the distance. The house was deadly, deathly silent.

I heard his footsteps outside in the courtyard before he entered—slow, clumsy, stumbling. He pushed aside the curtain to my room, gripping the fabric in one white-knuckled hand as he stared.

"I betrayed him," Judas said hoarsely. "They took him at the garden. I betrayed him."

He sank to his knees there in the doorway, all strength bled away. I took him in my arms and rocked him gently, back and forth. His skin was cold and gray, and he shivered. I put my blanket around him and held him in silence while the noise continued on the street. The followers of Simon Magus would be rejoicing. There might be rioting before the day was out. I could not guess where the rest of the Twelve had gone—fled, most likely, before the devastating betrayal.

"I warned you to go," he said, and he sounded so tired. I rested my cheek against his and felt his tears run hot on my skin. "They will come here. They will kill you if they find you."

"He asked you for this."

"They'll show you no mercy."

"He asked you to betray him," I said again. Against my cold silent flesh, his heartbeat continued, a strong, desperate beat like fists on a wall. "You bear no shame."

"I love him," he answered, and turned his face against my neck and wept like a sick and grieving child. "I have never loved anyone so much."

I kissed his forehead, gentle, as the master had kissed me. I had no tears, only a great hole in my heart where tears would have been. *All roads branch from here,* he had said. But he had not said the roads would be so short, or so bitter.

In the distance, a cock crowed.

"Time," Judas whispered. "Time to go."

I walked with him into the courtyard. He stripped off his robe in silence, folded it carefully, and put it aside. Over his shoulder the sun rose, as glorious as the eye of God.

I knelt there on the hard stones while the sun burned me, and watched as he hanged himself from the tree, with the silver coins scattered at his feet like a gleaming fallen halo. He never spoke, not even a prayer.

I had no prayers left in the ashes of my heart, only a vast, aching silence. I took one of the coins, only one, to remember him.

Oh, Judas, my love.

*   *   *

"She is already doomed," Simon said to me. Was he really there, or only my own doubt and fear given form? Did she see him? Sister Aimee only had eyes for the bowl, the ecstasy she had so loved and lost that glimmered dark in its depths. He only offered what we most wanted, of course. What we most had to have. "If you save her now, there will only be another time, and another. She is no carpenter from Galilee, Joanna. And people cannot bear so much arrogance without smearing mud on it. Eventually, she will fall."

"She is stronger than you know," I whispered. The beast had sapped every ounce of strength and left only the grief, only the pain. "Stronger than I was."

"You only wanted your life," he smiled, and walked a half-circle around her. His sandaled feet left no mark in the dewy grass. "Her pride is much greater. She thinks she can drag the whole world to heaven."

Strange, but I had missed him, missed the casual cruelty of his smile, the graceful contempt in the way he looked at me. One needs enemies, I found, in order to feel alive. And he was my enemy, my last and truest one, closer than any lover, any friend.

Simon's smile turned deadly.

"You choose bad companions," he said. "Men of dishonor and treachery. Men so faithless their names become curses. Tell me, has the world forgiven him yet, your Judas?"

Trust him to strike at my weakest point, at my most precious, most hidden memory. It had not mattered, really, whether the world cursed Judas, or even whether the master had. It was Judas who had been unable to forgive himself.

Sister Aimee raised the bowl toward her lips, and I remembered a thousand things about her, good things, bad things, moments of pridefulness and arrogance, moments of love and kindness. She was strong, but he was subtle. It might destroy her.

All of us, trapped by our own greatest sins. Judas, unable to forgive. Aimee, too proud to admit her faith was incomplete. Me—

Me, too selfish to die. What had the master said, that evening when I'd sat so close to him? *It is not my place to take your life.* No.

I had *stolen* my life. Only I could give it back.

All these years I had looked for healing, believing that I deserved another chance at mortal life. All these years, and I had not learned from my errors.

Now my pride dragged her down. I knew where our healing lay, if only I had the courage.

He knew I did not.

I knew I did not.

"Mine," Simon sighed in satisfaction, as the bowl touched Sister Aimee's lips.

I stumbled to my feet and grabbed the bowl away. She stared at me dull-eyed, mouth dripping red, and I had no time for thought.

I found the rock that had chipped the edge of the bowl, my salvation, my precious miracle.

And I brought the bowl down on it.

The sound of it breaking was lost in Sister Aimee's cry, in my own gasp. Three sharp pieces. The edges slashed my fingers like steel. I smashed them again and again, mixing my own blood with the red clay.

When I was done, there was nothing but rubble left of my dream.

In the silence, Sister Aimee whimpered and dropped to her knees. Behind me, Simon Magus said, "I never thought you would have the courage. Welcome to the end of your road, Joanna."

The world was empty and quiet. Dawn blushed the horizon. I felt an easing in my chest, as if some long-tightened spring had begun to unwind.

"You have not saved her, you know," Simon continued. He sounded very far away, one of the fading shadows. "She cannot last."

"I know," I said. So quiet, the world. My cut hands ran ruby now, a thick continuous stream. My stolen life escaped. "None of us can last, Simon. That is the lesson."

When I looked back, he was gone. As my strength bled away, I curled on my side, where the grass was soft. The dew touched my cheek like teardrops.

For the first nine, the sun warmed me without burning.

A hand stroked my cheek, and I opened drowsy eyes to see Judas' face, his kind, sweet smile.

"Time to go home," he said. I sat up and looked at Sister Aimee, lying asleep near by. "She will be safe. Time to go home."

There was another man standing over me, holding out his hand. Luminous eyes, smiling now, no longer sad.

"Master," I said, and felt his fingers closed over mine. "It's good to be home."

Author's Note:

Aimee Semple McPherson began as a preacher in the early 1900s and quickly progressed to a nationwide phenomenon as she led startling, charismatic tent revivals in cities all across the country. Her mission led to the founding of the Foursquare Baptist Church, which exists to this day.

In 1926, Sister Aimee disappeared for a month and was later found wandering alone. She insisted that she had been kidnapped and held for ransom, and managed to escape her abductors. Rumors claimed that she had run away with a lover, but though several inquiries were staged, nothing was ever proved. However, she was convicted in the court of public opinion, and that was enough.

Though she continued to preach until her death, Sister Aimee never lived down the scandal of that event.

Joanna, wife of Chuza, servant of Herod, is one of the women mentioned in Luke 8:3. Really. Any other heresies are entirely my own.

norman
partridge

Do Not Hasten
to Bid Me Adieu

i

He was done up all mysterious-like—black bandanna covering half his face, black duster, black boots and hat. Traveling incognito, just like that coachman who picked up Harker at the Borgo Pass.

Yeah. As a red man might figure it, that was many moons ago . . . at the beginning of the story. Stoker's story, anyway. But that tale of mannered woe and stiff-upper-lip bravado was as crazy as the lies Texans told about Crockett and his Alamo bunch. Harker didn't exist. Leastways, the man in black had never met him.

Nobody argued sweet-told lies, though. Nobody in England, anyhow. Especially with Stoker tying things up so neat and proper, and the count gone to dust and dirt and all.

A grin wrinkled the masked man's face as he remembered the vampire crumbling to nothing finger-snap quick, like the remnants of a cow-flop campfire worried by an unbridled prairie wind. Son of a bitch must have been mucho old. Count Dracula had departed this vale of tears, gone off to suckle the devil's own tit . . . though the man in black doubted that Dracula's scientific turn of mind would allow him to believe in Old Scratch.

You could slice it fine or thick—ultimately, the fate of Count Dracula didn't make no nevermind. The man in black was one hell of a long way from Whitby, and his dealings with the count seemed about as unreal as Stoker's scribblings. Leastways, that business was behind him. This was to be his story. And he was just about to slap the ribbons to it.

Slap the ribbons he did, and the horses picked up the pace. The wagon bucked over ruts, creaking like an arthritic dinosaur. Big black box jostling in the back. Tired horses sweating steam up front. West Texas sky a quilt for the night, patched blood red and bruise purple and shot through with blue-pink streaks, same color as the meat that lines a woman's heart.

And black. Thick black squares in that quilt, too. More coming every second. Awful soon, there'd be nothing but those black squares and a round white moon.

Not yet, though. The man could still see the faint outline of a town on the horizon. There was Morrisville, up ahead, waiting in the red and purple and blue-pink shadows.

He wondered what she'd make of Morrisville. It was about as far from the stone manors of Whitby as one could possibly get. No vine-covered mysteries here. No cool salt breezes whispering from the green sea, blanketing emerald lawns, traveling lush garden paths. Not much of anything green at all. No crumbling Carfax estate, either. And no swirling fog to mask the night—everything right out in the open, just as plain as the nose on your face. A West Texas shit-splat. Cattle business, mostly. A matchstick kind of town. Wooden buildings—wind-dried, sun-bleached—that weren't much more than tinder dreading the match.

The people who lived there were the same way.

But it wasn't the town that made this place. He'd told her that. It was that big blanket of a sky, an eternal wave threatening to break over the dead dry husk of the prairie, fading darker with each turn of the wagon wheels—cresting, cresting—ready to smother the earth like a hungry thing.

Not a bigger, blacker night anywhere on the planet. When that nightwave broke, as it did all too rarely—wide and mean and full-up with mad lightning and thunder—it was something to see.

He'd promised her that. He'd promised to show her the heart

of a wild Texas night, the way she'd shown him the shadows of Whitby.

Not that he always kept his promises. But this one was a promise to himself as much as it was a promise to her.

He'd hidden from it for a while. Sure. In the wake of all that horror, he'd run. But finally he'd returned to Whitby, and to her. He'd returned to keep his promise.

And now he was coming home.

*   *   *

"Not another place like it anywhere, Miss Lucy. Damn sure not on this side of the pond, anyhow."

She didn't fake a blush or get all offended by his language, like so many of the English missies did, and he liked that. She played right with him, like she knew the game. Not just knew it, but thrived on it. "No," she said. "Nothing here could possibly resemble your Texas, Quincey P. Morris. Because no one here resembles you."

She took him by the lapels and kissed him like she was so hungry for it, like she couldn't wait another moment, and then he had her in his arms and they were moving together, off the terrace, away from the house and the party and the dry rattle of polite conversation. He was pulling her and she was pushing him and together they were going back, back into the shadows of Whitby, deep into the garden where fog settled like velvet and the air carried what for him would always be the green scent of England.

And then they were alone. The party sounds were a world away. But those sounds were nothing worth hearing—they were dead sounds compared to the music secret lovers could make. Matched with the rustle of her skirts, and the whisper of his fingers on her tender thighs, and the sweet duet of hungry lips, the sounds locked up in the big stone house were as sad and empty as the cries of the damned souls in Dr Seward's loony bin, and he drew her away from them, and she pushed him away from them, and together they entered another world where strange shadows met, cloaking them like fringed buckskin, like gathered satin.

Buckskin and satin. It wasn't what you'd call a likely match. They'd been dancing around it for months. But now the dancing was over.

"God, I want you," he said.

She didn't say anything. There was really nothing more to say. She gave. She took. And he did the same.

＊   ＊   ＊

He reined in the horses just short of town. Everything was black but that one circle of white hanging high in the sky.

He stepped down from the driver's box and stretched. He drew the night air deep into his lungs. The air was dry and dusty, and there wasn't anything in it that was pleasant.

He was tired. He lay down on top of the big black box in the back of the wagon and thought of her. His fingers traveled wood warped in the leaky cargo hold of a British ship. Splinters fought his callused hands, lost the battle. But he lost the war, because the dissonant rasp of rough fingers on warped wood was nothing like the music the same rough fingers could make when exploring a young woman's thighs.

He didn't give up easy, though. He searched for the memory of the green scent of England, and the music he'd made there, and shadows of satin and buckskin. He searched for the perfume of her hair, and her skin. The ready, eager perfume of her sex.

His hands traveled the wood. Scurrying like scorpions. Damn things just wouldn't give up, and he couldn't help laughing.

Raindrops beaded on the box. The nightwave was breaking.

No. Not raindrops at all. Only his tears.

The sky was empty. No clouds No rain.

No lightning.

But there was lightning in his eyes.

ii

The morning sunlight couldn't penetrate the filthy jailhouse window. That didn't bother the man in black. He had grown to appreciate the darkness.

Sheriff Josh Muller scratched his head. "This is the damnednest thing, Quincey. You got to admit that that Stoker fella made it pretty plain in his book."

Quincey smiled. "You believe the lies that Buntline wrote about Buffalo Bill, too?"

"Shit no. Quince. But hell, that Stoker is an Englishman. I thought they was different and all—"

"I used to think that. Until I got to know a few of the bastards, that is."

"Well," the sheriff said, "that may be . . . but the way it was, was . . . we all thought that you had been killed by them Transylvanian gypsies, like you was in the book."

"I've been some places, before and since. But we never got to Transylvania. Not one of us. And I ain't even feelin' poorly."

"But in the book—"

"Just how stupid are you. Josh? You believe in vampires, too? Your bowels get loose thinkin' about Count Dracula?"

"Hell, no, of course not, but—"

"Shit, Josh, I didn't mean that like a question you were supposed to answer."

"Huh?"

Quincey sighed. "Let's toss this on the fire and watch it sizzle. It's real simple—I *ain't* dead. I'm *back*. Things are gonna be just like they used to be. We can start with this here window."

Quincey Monis shot a thumb over his shoulder The sheriff looked up and saw how dirty the window was. He grabbed a rag from his desk. "I'll take care of it, Quince."

"You don't get it," the man in black said.

"Huh?"

Again, Quincey sighed. "I *ain't* dead. I'm *back*. Things are gonna be just like they used to be. And this *is* Morrisville, right?"

The sheriff squinted at the words painted on the window. He wasn't a particularly fast reader—he'd been four months reading the Stoker book, and that was with his son doing most of the reading out loud. On top of that, he had to read this backwards. He started in, reading right to left—O-W-E-N-S-V-I-L-L . . .

That was as far as he got. Quincey Morris picked up a chair and sent it flying through the glass, and then the word wasn't there anymore.

Morris stepped through the opening and started toward his wagon. He stopped in the street, which was like a river of sunlight, turned, and squinted at the sheriff "Get that window fixed," he said. "Before I come back."

"Where are you headed?" The words were out of Josh Muller's mouth before he could stop himself, and he flinched at the grin Morris gave him in return.

"I'm goin' home," was all he said.

*   •   *

There in the shadows, none of it mattered, because it was only the two of them. Two creatures from different worlds, but with hearts that were the same.

He'd come one hell of a long way to find this. Searched the world over. He'd known that he'd find it, once he went looking, same as he'd known that it was something he had to go out and find if he wanted to keep on living His gut told him, *Find it, or put a bullet in your brainpan.* But he hadn't known it would feel like this. It never had before. But this time, with this person . . . she filled him up like no one else. And he figured it was the same with her.

"I want you."

"I think you just had me, Mr. Morris."

Her laughter tickled his neck, warm breath washing a cool patch traced by her tongue, drawn by her lips. Just a bruise, but as sure and real as a brand. He belonged to her. He knew that. But he didn't know—

The words slipped out before he could think them through. "I want you, forever."

That about said it, all right.

He felt her shiver, and then her lips found his.

"Forever is a long time," she said.

They laughed about that, embracing in the shadows.

They actually laughed.

*　　*　　*

She came running out of the big house as soon as he turned in from the road. Seeing her, he didn't feel a thing. That made him happy, because in England, in the midst of everything else, he'd thought about her a lot. He'd wondered just what kind of fuel made her belly burn, and why she wasn't more honest about it, in the way of the count. He wondered why she'd never gone ahead and torn open his jugular, the way a vampire would, because she sure as hell had torn open his heart.

Leonora ran through the blowing dust, her hair a blond tangle, and she was up on the driver's box sitting next to him before he could slow the horses—her arms around him, her lips on his cheek, her little flute of a voice all happy. "Quince! Oh, Quince! It is you! We thought you were dead!"

He shook his head. His eyes were on the big house. It hadn't changed. Not in the looks department, anyway. The occupants . . . now that was a different story.

"Miss me?" he asked, and his tone of voice was not a pleasant thing.

I'm sorry." She said it like she'd done something silly, like maybe she'd spilled some salt at the supper table or something. "I'm glad you came back." She hugged him. "It'll be different now We've both had a chance to grow up."

He chuckled at that one, and she got it crossed up. "Oh, Quince, we'll work it out . . . you'll see. We both made mistakes. But it's not too late to straighten them out." She leaned over and kissed his neck, her tongue working between her lips.

Quincey flushed with anger and embarrassment. The bitch. And with the box right there, behind them, in plain view. With him dressed head to toe in black. God, Leonora had the perceptive abilities of a blind armadillo.

He shoved her, hard. She tumbled off the driver's box. Her skirts caught on the seat, tearing as she fell. She landed in the dirt, petticoats bunched up around her waist

She cussed him real good. But he didn't hear her at all, because suddenly he could see everything so clearly. The golden wedding band on her finger didn't mean much. Not to her it didn't, so it didn't mean anything to him. But the fist-sized bruises on her legs did.

He'd seen enough. He'd drawn a couple conclusions. Hal Owens hadn't changed. Looking at those bruises, that was for damn sure. And it was misery that filled up Leonora's belly—that had to be the answer which had eluded him for so long—and at present it seemed that she was having to make do with her own. Knowing Leonora as he did, he figured that she was probably about ready for a change of menu, and he wanted to make it real clear that he wasn't going to be the next course.

"You bastard," she yelled "You're finished around here. You can't just come walkin' back into town, big as you please! This ain't Morrisville, anymore, Quincey! It's Owensville! And Hal's gonna kill you! I'm his wife, dammit! And when I tell him what you did to me, he's gonna flat-out kill you!" She scooped up fistfuls of dirt, threw them at him. "You don't belong here anymore, you bastard!"

She was right about that. He didn't belong here anymore This wasn't his world. His world was contained in a big black box. That was the only place for him anymore. Anywhere else there was only trouble.

Didn't matter where he went these days, folks were always threatening him.

Threats seemed to be his lot in life.

✳   ✳
✳

Take Arthur Holmwood, for instance. He was a big one for threats. The morning after the Westenras' party, he'd visited Quincey's lodgings, bringing with him Dr Seward and a varnished box with brass hinges.

"I demand satisfaction," he'd said, opening the box and setting it on the table.

Quincey stared down at the pistols. Flintlocks. Real pioneer stuff. "Hell, Art," he said, snatching his Peacemaker from beneath his breakfast napkin (Texas habits died hard, after all), "let's you and me get real satisfied, then."

The doctor went ahead and pissed in the pot. "Look here, Morris. You're in England now. A man does things in a certain way here. A gentleman, I should say."

Quincey was sufficiently cowed to table his Peacemaker. "Maybe I am a fish out of water, like you say, Doc." He examined one of the dueling pistols. "But ain't these a little old-fashioned, even for England? I thought this kind of thing went out with powdered wigs and such."

"A concession to you," Holmwood sneered. "We understand that in your Texas, men duel in the streets quite regularly."

Quincey grinned. "That's kind of an exaggeration."

"The fact remains that you compromised Miss Lucy's honor."

"Who says?"

Seward straightened. "I myself observed the way you thrust yourself upon her last night, on the terrace. And I saw Miss Lucy leave the party in your charge."

"You get a real good look, Doc?" Quincey's eyes narrowed "You get a right proper fly-on-a-dung-pile-close-up view, or are you just telling tales out of school?"

Holmwood's hand darled out. Fisted, but he did his business with a pair of kid gloves knotted in his grip. The gloves slapped the Texan's left cheek and came back for his right, at which time Quincey Morris exploded from his chair and kneed Arthur Holmwood in the balls.

Holmwood was a tall man. He seemed to go down in sections. Dr. Seward trembled as Quincey retrieved his Peacemaker, and he didn't calm down at all when the Texan holstered the weapon.

Quincey didn't see any point to stretching things out, not when there was serious fence-mending to do at the Westenras' house. "I hope you boys will think on this real seriously," he said as he stepped over Holmwood and made for the door.

There was a Mexican kid pretending to do some work behind the big house. Quincey gave him a nickel and took him around front.

The kid wasn't happy to see the box. He crossed himself several times. Then he spit on his palms and took one end, delighted to find that the box wasn't as heavy as it looked.

They set it in the parlor. Quincey had to take a chair and catch his breath. After all that time on the ship, and then more time sitting on his butt slapping reins to a pair of swaybacks, he wasn't much good. Of course, this wasn't as tough as when he'd had to haul the box from the Westenra family tomb, all by his lonesome, but it was bad enough. By the time he remembered to thank the kid, the kid had already gone.

Nothing for it, then.

Nothing, but to do it.

The words came back to him, echoing in his head. And it wasn't the voice of some European doctor, like in Stoker's book. It was Seward's voice. *"One moment's courage, and it is done."*

He shook those words away. He was alone here. The parlor hadn't changed much since the day he'd left to tour the world. The curtains were heavy and dark, and the deep shadows seemed to brush his cheek, one moment buckskin-rough, next moment satin-smooth.

Like the shadows in the Westenras' garden. The shadows where he'd held Lucy to him. Held her so close.

No. He wouldn't think of that. Not now. He had work to do. He couldn't start thinking about how it had been, because then he'd certainly start thinking about how it might be, again . . .

One moment's courage, and it is done.

God, how he wanted to laugh, but he kept it inside. His big bowie knife was in his hand. He didn't know quite how it had gotten there.

He went to work on the lid of the box, first removing brass screws, then removing the hinges.

One moment's courage . . .

The lid crashed heavily to the floor, but he never heard it. His horror was too great for that. After all this time, the stink of garlic burned his nostrils, scorched his lungs. But that wasn't the hell of it.

The hell of it was that she had moved.

Oh, *she* hadn't moved. He knew that. He could see the stake spearing her poor breast, the breast that he had teased between his own lips. She couldn't move. Not with the stake there.

But the churning Atlantic had rocked a sailing ship, and that had moved her. And a bucking wagon had jostled over the rutted roads of Texas, and that had moved her. And now her poor head, her poor severed head with all that dark and beautiful hair, was trapped between her own sweet legs, nestled between her own tender thighs, just as his head had been.

Once. A long time ago.

Maybe, once again . . .

No. He wouldn't start thinking like that. He stared at her head, knowing he'd have to touch it. There was no sign of decay, no stink of corruption. But he could see the buds of garlic jammed into the open hole of her throat, the ragged gashes and severed muscles, the dangling ropes of flesh.

In his mind's eye, he saw Seward standing stiff and straight with a scalpel in his bloodstained grip.

And that bastard called himself a doctor.

*   *   *

There were shadows, of course, in their secret place in the Westenra garden. And he held her, as he had before. But now she never stopped shaking.

"You shouldn't have done it," she said. "Arthur is behaving like one of Seward's lunatics. You must be careful."

"You're the one has to be careful, Lucy," he said.

"No." She laughed. "Mother has disregarded the entire episode. Well, nearly so. She's convinced that I behaved quite recklessly—and this judging from one kiss on the terrace. I had to assure her that we did nothing more than tour the garden in search of a better view of the moon. I said that was the custom in Texas. I'm not certain that she accepted my story, but . . ." She kissed him, very quickly. "I've feigned illness for her benefit, and she believes that I am in the grip of a rare and exotic fever. Seward has convinced her of this, I think. Once I'm pronounced fit, I'm certain that she will forgive your imagined indiscretion."

"Now, Miss Lucy, I don't think that was my *imagination*," he joked.

She laughed, trembling laughter there in his arms. "Seward has consulted a specialist. A European fellow. He's said to be an expert in fevers of the blood. I'm to see him tomorrow. That ought to put an end to the charade."

He wanted to say it. More than anything, he wanted to say, *Forget tomorrow. Let's leave here, tonight*. But he didn't say it, because she was trembling so.

"You English," he said, "You do love your charades."

Moonlight washed the shadows. He caught the wild look in her eye. A twin to the fearful look a colt gels just before it's broken.

He kept his silence. He was imagining things He held her

It was the last time he would hold her, alive.

⁂

Quincey pushed through the double doors of the saloon and was surprised to find it deserted except for a sleepy-eyed man who was polishing the piano.

"You the piano player?" Quincey asked.

"Sure," the fellow said.

Quincey brought out the Peacemaker. "Can you play 'Red River Valley'?"

"S-sure," The man sat down, rolled up his sleeves.

"Not here," Quincey said.

"H-huh?"

"I got a big house on the edge of town."

The man swallowed hard. "You mean Mr. Owens's place?"

"No. I mean my place."

"H-huh?"

"Anyway, you go on up there, and you wait for me."

The man rose from the piano stool, both eyes on the Peacemaker, and started toward the double doors.

"Wait a minute," Quincey said. "You're forgetting something."

"W-what?"

"Well, I don't have a piano up at the house."

"Y-you don't?"

"Nope."

"Well . . . Hell, mister, what do you want me to do?"

Quincey cocked the Peacemaker. "I guess you'd better start pushing."

"You mean . . . you want me to take the piano with me?"

Quincey nodded. "Now, I'll be home in a couple hours or so. You put the piano in the parlor, then you help yourself to a glass of whiskey. But don't linger in the parlor, hear?"

The man nodded. He seemed to catch on pretty quick. Had to be that he was a stranger in these parts.

Quincey moved on. He stopped off at Murphy's laundry, asked a few questions about garlic, received a few expansive answers detailing the amazing restorative power of Mrs. Murphy's soap, after which he set a gunnysack on the counter. He set it down real gentle-like, and the rough material settled over something kind of round, and, seeing this, Mr. Murphy excused himself and made a beeline for the saloon.

Next Quincey stopped off at the church with a bottle of whiskey for the preacher. They chatted a bit, and Quincey had a snort before moving on, just to be sociable.

He had just stepped into the home of Mrs. Danvers, the best seamstress in town, when he glanced through the window and spotted Hal Owens coming his way, two men in tow, one of them being the sheriff.

*   *

*

Things were never quite so plain in England. Oh, they were just as dangerous, that was for sure. But, with the exception of lunatics like Arthur Holmwood, the upper crust of Whitby cloaked their confrontational behavior in a veil of politeness.

Three nights running, Quincey stood alone in the garden, just waiting. Finally, he went to Lucy's mother in the light of day, hat literally in hand. He inquired as to Lucy's health. Mrs. Westenra said that Lucy was convalescing. Three similar visits, and his testiness began to show through.

So did Mrs Westenra's. She blamed Quincey for her daughter's poor health. He wanted to tell her that the whole thing was melodrama, and for her benefit, too, but he held off.

And that was when the old woman slipped up. Or maybe she didn't, because her voice was as sharp as his bowie, and it was plain that she intended to do damage with it. "Lucy's condition is quite serious," she said. "Her behavior of late, which Dr Seward has described in no small detail . . . Well, I mean to tell you that Lucy has shown little consideration for her family or her station, and there is no doubt that she is quite ill. We have placed her in hospital, under the care of Dr Seward and his associates."

Mrs. Westenra had torn away the veil. He would not keep silent now. He made it as plain as plain could be. "You want to break her. You want to pocket her, heart and soul."

She seemed to consider her answer very carefully. Finally, she said, "We only do what we must."

*   *

*

"Nobody wants you here," Owens said.

Quincey grinned. Funny that Owens should say that. Those were the same words that had spilled from Seward's lips when Quincey confronted him at the asylum.

Of course, that had happened an ocean away, and Dr Seward hadn't had a gun. But he'd had a needle, and that had done the job for him right proper.

Quincey stared down at Mrs. Danvers's sewing table. There were needles here, too. Sharp ones, little slivers of metal. But these needles weren't attached to syringes. They weren't like Dr Seward's needles at all.

Something pressed against Quincey's stomach. He blinked several times, but he couldn't decide who was standing in front of him. Owens, or Seward, or . . .

Someone said, "Get out of town, or I'll make you wish you was dead." There was a sharp click. The pressure on Quincey's belly increased, and a heavy hand dropped onto his shoulder.

The hand of Count Dracula. A European nobleman and scientist. Stoker had split him into two characters—a kindly doctor and a hellborn monster. But Quincey knew that the truth was somewhere in between.

"Start movin', Quince. Otherwise, I'll spill your innards all over the floor."

The count had only held him. He didn't make idle threats. He didn't use his teeth. He didn't spill a single drop of Quincey's blood. He let Seward do all the work, jabbing Quincey's arm with the needle, day after day, week after week.

That wasn't how the count handled Lucy, though. He had a special way with Dr. Seward's most combative patient, a method that brought real results. He emptied her bit by bit, draining her blood, and with it the strength that so disturbed Lucy's mother and the independent spirit that so troubled unsuccessful suitors such as Seward and Holmwood. The blind fools had been so happy at first, until they realized that they'd been suckered by another outsider, a Transylvanian bastard with good manners who was much worse than anything that had ever come out of Texas.

They'd come to him, of course. The stranger with the wild gleam in his eyes. Told him the whole awful tale. Cut him out of the straitjacket with his own bowie, placed the Peacemaker in one hand. A silver crucifix and an iron stake jammed in a cricketing bag filled the other.

"You make your play, Quince," Owens said. "I'm not goin' to give you forever."

"Forever is a long time."

"You ain't listenin' to me, Quince."

"One moment's courage, and it is done."

Count Dracula, waiting for him in the ruins of the chapel at Carfax. His fangs gleaming in the dark . . . fangs that could take everything . . .

The pistol bucked against Quincey's belly. The slug ripped straight through him, shattered the window behind. Blood spilled out of him, running down his leg. Lucy's blood on the count's lips, spilling from her neck as he took and took and took some more. Quincey could see it from the depths of Seward's hell, he could see the garden and the shadows and their love flowing in Lucy's blood. Her strength, her dreams, her spirit . . .

"This is my town," Owens said, his hand still heavy on Quincey's shoulder. "I took it, and I mean to keep it."

Quincey opened his mouth. A gout of blood bubbled over his lips. He couldn't find words. Only blood, rushing away, running down his leg, spilling over his lips. It seemed his blood was everywhere, rushing wild, like once-still waters escaping the rubble of a collapsed dam.

He sagged against Owens. The big man laughed.

And then the big man screamed.

Quincey's teeth were at Owens's neck. He ripped through flesh, tore muscle and artery. Blood filled his mouth, and the Peacemaker thundered again and again in his hand, and then Owens was nothing but a leaking mess there in his arms, a husk of a man puddling red, washing away to nothing so fast, spurting red rich blood one second, then stagnant-pool dead the next.

Quincey's gun was empty. He fumbled for his bowie, arming himself against Owens's compadres.

There was no need.

Mrs Danvers stood over them, a smoking shotgun in her hands. Quincey released Owens's corpse. Watched it drop to the floor.

"Let me get a look at you," Mrs Danvers said.

"There ain't no time for that," he said.

*   *   *

Dracula chuckled. "I can't believe it is you they sent. The American cowboy. The romantic."

Quincey studied the count's amused grin. Unnatural canines gleamed in the moonlight. In the ruined wasteland of Carfax, Dracula seemed strangely alive.

"Make your play," Quincey offered.

Icy laughter rode the shadows. "There is no need for such melodrama, Mr. Morris. I only wanted the blood. Nothing else. And I have taken that."

"That ain't what Seward says," Quincey squinted, his eyes adjusting to the darkness. "He claims you're after Miss Lucy's soul."

Again, the laughter. "I am a man of science, Mr Morris. I accept my condition, and my biological need. Disease, and the transmission of disease, make for interesting study. I am more skeptical concerning the mythology of my kind. Fairy stories bore me. Certainly, powers exist which I cannot explain. But I cannot explain the moon and the stars, yet I know that these things exist because I see them in the night sky. It is the same with my special abilities—they exist, I use them, hence I believe in them. As for the human soul, I cannot see any evidence of such a thing. What I cannot see, I refuse to believe."

But Quincey could see. He could see Dracula, clearer every second. The narrow outline of his jaw. The eyes burning beneath his heavy brow. The long, thin line of his lips hiding jaws that could gape so wide.

"You don't want her," Quincey said. "That's what you're saying."

"I only want a full belly, Mr. Morris. That is the way of it." He stepped forward, his eyes like coals. "I only take the blood. Your kind is different. You want everything. The flesh, the heart, the . . . soul, which of course has a certain tangibility fueled by your belief. You take it all. In comparison, I demand very little—"

"We take. But we give, too."

"That is what your kind would have me believe. I have seen little evidence that this is the truth." Red eyes swam in the darkness. "Think about it, Mr. Morris. They have sent you here to kill me. They have told you how evil I am. But who are they—these men who brought me to your Miss Lucy? What do they want?" He did not blink; he only advanced. "Think on it, Mr. Morris. Examine the needs of these men, Seward and Holmwood. Look into your own heart. Examine your needs."

And now Quincey smiled. "Maybe I ain't as smart as you, Count," He stepped forward. "Maybe you could take a look for me . . . let me know just what you see '

Their eyes met.

The vampire stumbled backward. He had looked into Quincey Morris's eyes. Seen a pair of empty green wells. Bottomless green pits. Something was alive there, undying, something that had known pain and hurt, and, very briefly, ecstasy.

Very suddenly, the vampire realized that he had never known real hunger at all.

The vampire tried to steady himself, but his voice trembled. "What I can see . . . I believe."

Quincey Morris did not blink.

He took the stake from Seward's bag.

"I want you to know that this ain't something I take lightly," he said.

iv

He'd drawn a sash around his belly, but it hadn't done much good. His jeans were stiff with blood, and his left boot seemed to be swimming with the stuff. That was his guess, anyway—there wasn't much more than a tingle of feeling in his left foot, and he wasn't going to stoop low and investigate.

Seeing himself in the mirror was bad enough. His face was so white. Almost like the count's.

Almost like her face, in death.

Mrs. Danvers stepped away from the coffin, tucking a pair of scissors into a carpetbag. "I did the best I could," she said.

"I'm much obliged, ma'am." Quincey leaned against the lip of the box, numb fingers brushing the yellow ribbon that circled Lucy's neck.

"You can't see them stitches at all," the whiskey-breathed preacher said, and the seamstress cut him off with a glance.

"You did a fine job, Mrs. Danvers," Quincey tried to smile. "You can go on home now."

"If you don't mind, I think I'd like to stay."

"That'll be fine," Quincey said.

He turned to the preacher, but he didn't look at him. Instead, he stared through the parlor window. Outside, the sky was going to blood red and bruise purple.

He reached into the box. His fingers were cold, clumsy. Lucy's delicate hand almost seemed warm by comparison.

Quincey nodded at the preacher. "Let's get on with it."

The preacher started in. Quincey had heard the words many times. He'd seen people stand up to them, and he'd seen people totter under their weight, and he'd seen plenty who didn't care a damn for them at all.

But this time it was him hearing those words. Him answering them. And when the preacher got to the part about taking . . . *do you take this woman* . . . Quincey said, "Right now I just want to give."

That's what the count couldn't understand, him with all the emotion of a tick. Seward and Holmwood, even Lucy's mother, they weren't much better. But Quincey understood. Now more than ever. He held tight to Lucy's hand.

"If you've a mind to, you can go ahead and kiss her now," the preacher said.

Quincey bent low. His lips brushed hers, ever so gently. He caught a faint whiff of Mrs. Murphy's soap, no trace of garlic at all.

With some effort, he straightened. It seemed some time had passed, because the preacher was gone, and the evening sky was veined with blue-pink streaks.

The piano player just sat there, his eyes closed tight, his hands fisted in his lap. "You can play it now," Quincey said, and the man got right to it, fingers light and shaky on the keys, voice no more than a whisper:

> *Come sit by my side if you love me,*
> *Do not hasten to bid me adieu,*
> *But remember the Red River Valley,*
> *And the cowboy who loved you so true.*

Quincey listened to the words, holding Lucy's hand, watching the night. The sky was going black now, blacker every second. There was no blood left in it at all.

Just like you, you damn fool, he thought.

He pulled his bowie from its sheath. Seward's words rang in his ears: *"A moment's courage, and it is done."*

But Seward hadn't been talking to Quincey when he'd said those words. Those words were for Holmwood. And Quincey had heard them, but he'd been about ten steps short of doing something about them. If he hadn't taken the time to discuss philosophy with Count Dracula, that might have been different. As it was, Holmwood had had plenty of time to use the stake, while Seward had done his business with a scalpel.

For too many moments, Quincey had watched them, too stunned to move. But when he did move, there was no stopping him.

He used the bowie, and he left Whitby that night.

He ran out. He wasn't proud of that. And all the time he was running, he'd thought. *So much blood, all spilled for no good reason. Dracula, with the needs of a tick. Holmwood and Seward, who wanted to be masters or nothing at all.*

He ran out. Sure. But he came back. Because he knew that there was more to the blood, more than just the taking.

One moment's courage . . .

Quincey stared down at the stake jammed through his beloved's heart, the cold shaft spearing the blue-pink muscle that had thundered at the touch of his fingers. The bowie shook in his hand. The piano man sang:

There could never be such a longing,
In the heart of a poor cowboy's breast,
As dwells in this heart you are breaking,
While I wait in my home in the West.

Outside, the sky was black. Every square in the quilt. No moon tonight.

Thunder rumbled, rattling the windows.

Quincey put the bowie to his neck. Lightning flashed, and white spiderwebs of brightness danced on Lucy's flesh. The shadows receded for the briefest moment, then flooded the parlor once more, and Quincey was lost in them. Lost in shadows he'd brought home from Whitby.

One moment's courage . . .

He sliced his neck, praying that there was some red left in him. A thin line of blood welled from the wound, overflowing the spot where Lucy had branded him with eager kisses.

He sagged against the box. Pressed his neck to her lips.

He dropped the bowie. His hand closed around the stake.

One moment's courage . . .

He tore the wooden shaft from her heart, and waited.

Minutes passed. He closed his eyes. Buried his face in her dark hair. His hands were scorpions, scurrying every where dancing to the music of her tender thighs.

Her breast did not rise, did not fall She did not breathe.

She would never breathe again.

But her lips parted. Her fangs gleamed. And she drank.

Together, they welcomed the night.

Acknowledgments

Introduction copyright © 2007 by John Helfers

"One for the Road," by Stephen King. Copyright © 1977 by Maine Magazine Co., Inc. from *Night Shift* by Stephen King. Reprinted by permission of Doubleday, a division of Random House, Inc.

"Snow, Glass, Apples," by Neil Gaiman. Copyright © by 1994 by Neil Gaiman. Reprinted by permission of the author.

"In Darkness, Angels," by Eric Van Lustbader. Copyright © 1983 by Eric Van Lustbader. Reprinted by permission of the author and the author's agent, Henry Morrison, Inc.

"The Cookie Lady," by Philip K. Dick. Copyright © 1953 by Philip K. Dick. Reprinted by permission of the author's agent, Russell Galen of the Scovil Chichak Galen Agency, Inc.

"Food Chain," by Nina Kiriki Hoffman. Copyright © 1995 by Nina Kiriki Hoffman. Reprinted by permission of the author.

"Victims," by Kristine Kathryn Rusch. Copyright © 1995 by Kristine Kathryn Rusch. Reprinted by permission of the author.

"Cafe Endless: Spring Rain," by Nancy Holder. Copyright © 1994 by Nancy Holder. Reprinted by permission of the author.

"Bite-Me-Not, or Fleur de Fur," by Tanith Lee. Copyright © 1984 by Tanith Lee. Reprinted by permission of the author.

"Queen of the Night," by Gene Wolfe. Copyright © 1994 by Gene Wolfe. Reprinted by permission of the author and his agents, the Virginia Kidd Literary Agency, Inc.

"Yrena," by P.D. Cacek. Copyright © 1995 by P. D. Cacek. Reprinted by permission of the author.

"The Carpetbagger" by Susan Shwartz. Copyright © 1994 by Susan Shwartz. Reprinted by permission of the author.

"Sister Death," by Jane Yolen. Copyright © 1995 by Jane Yolen. Reprinted by permission of the author and her agent, Curtis Brown, Ltd.

"This Town Ain't Big Enough," by Tanya Huff. Copyright © 1995 by Tanya Huff. Reprinted by permission of the author.

"Claim-Jumpin' Woman, You Got a Stake in My Heart," by Esther M. Friesner. Copyright © 1991 by Esther M. Friesner. Reprinted by permission of the author.

"Faith Like Wine," By Roxanne Longstreet. Copyright © 1996 by Roxanne Longstreet Conrad. Reprinted by permission of the author.

"Do Not Hasten to Bid Me Adieu," by Norman Partridge, copyright © 1994 by Norman Partridge. Reprinted by permission of the author.